KU-656-444

HUNGRY
JANE
BARRY

BANTAM PRESS

LONDON · NEW YORK · TORONTO · SYDNEY · AUCKLAND

TRANSWORLD PUBLISHERS LTD
61–63 Uxbridge Road, London W5 5SA

TRANSWORLD PUBLISHERS (AUSTRALIA) PTY LTD
15–23 Helles Avenue, Moorebank, NSW 2170

TRANSWORLD PUBLISHERS (NZ) LTD
3 Pickering Drive, Albany, Auckland

Published 1993 by Bantam Press
a division of Transworld Publishers Ltd
Copyright © Jane Barry 1993

The right of Jane Barry to be identified
as the author of this work has been asserted in accordance
with sections 77 and 78 of the Copyright Designs and Patents
Act 1988.

All of the characters in this book
are fictitious, and any resemblance
to actual persons, living or dead,
is purely coincidental.

A catalogue for this book is available from
the British Library

ISBN 0593 020383

This book is sold subject to the Conditions of
Sale of Net Books and may not be resold in the UK
below the net price fixed by the publishers for the book.

All rights reserved. No part of this publication may be
reproduced, stored in a retrieval system, or transmitted
in any form or by any means, electronic, mechanical,
photocopying, recording, or otherwise, without the
prior permission of the publishers.

Typeset in 11.5/12.8 pt Bembo by Photoprint, Torquay, S. Devon.

This book proof printed by Antony Rowe Ltd., Chippenham

Dedication
———

HUNGRY

PART ONE

'In 1985, while the American administration sent $500 million to help save the lives of the wasted skeletons of Ethiopia, Americans themselves spent $5,000 million trying to lose weight.'

Reay Tannahill: *Food in History*

Telephone conversation, April, between Mr Art Khan, Managing Director, Granny Garfunkel Gourmet Gateaux (UK) Inc., and Ms Fizz St Clair, Senior Account Director, BBW&S Advertising.

ST CLAIR: Hi, Art! Great meeting yesterday with your guys on Project Pandora. We all agree this new concept just screams aspirational, while zapping it home to the consumer that slimming the Granny Garfunkel way can be *fun*—

KHAN: Diddleysquat.

ST CLAIR: I beg your pardon, Art?

KHAN: I said, it sucks.

ST CLAIR: But, Art – don't you feel the cartoon calorie is a great property, a visual mnemonic that could build a unique character for the brand?

KHAN: The cartoon sucks.

ST CLAIR: Well, Art, we could play down the animation and up the emphasis on the production values in the tropical beach scenes—

KHAN: The cartoon sucks, the beach scene sucks. It sucks a big one, read me?

ST CLAIR: I think so, Art.

KHAN: Listen, little lady, you wanna piss or you wanna get off the pot?

ST CLAIR: Yes, Art – I mean, no, Art.

KHAN: Then hear me and hear me good. This is the future we're talking, the future of Granny Garfunkel Inc., the future of a multi-million-dollar multi-national corporation that outsells and outsmarts the competition from Peru to Poughkeepsie.

11

	That's my future we're talking. And yours, little lady.

ST CLAIR: I hear you, Art.

KHAN: So we're talking our futures, right? And what do we see?

ST CLAIR: We see a small decline in the sales of Granny Garfunkel's Devils Delight.

KHAN: We see our worldwide brand leader haemor-rhaging shipment and share like a stab wound on the sidewalk. And why's that, kid?

ST CLAIR: Research indicates a continuing trend towards fitness and health, towards a more self-aware, body-conscious consumer—

KHAN: Towards fat broads trying to get thin. Right?

ST CLAIR: Right, Art.

KHAN: And what do we offer them? We offer them chocolate and fudge and whipped cream and nuts and Maraschino cherries. We offer them calories, right? Three thousand goddam calories per goddam gateau!

ST CLAIR: Research shows loyal nucleus of comfort eaters who are still highly motivated by Devils Delight.

KHAN: A loyal nucleus is a can of worms, okay?

ST CLAIR: Okay, Art.

KHAN: Okay, OKAY! So what do we do in the teeth of this negative situation? Do we serve ourselves up as ritual sacrifices for the goddam competition's goddam breakfast?

ST CLAIR: We're proactive, Art.

KHAN: Right! Granny Garfunkel is a proactive company. We hire brains, right. We hire the best chemists and scientific geniuses that megabucks can buy. And they come up with the breakthrough – no, not just a breakthrough, something that smashes the whole goddam mould, something so cosmic it's like Christopher Columbus discovering the US of A or Albert Einstein splitting the atom—

12

ST CLAIR:	The agency certainly feels very positive about Slimmers Supreme—
KHAN:	Jesus! How often must I tell you guys?
ST CLAIR:	Sorry, Art. Project Pandora.
KHAN:	Je-sus! Sure, we've got the jump on the competition by at least two years. But we've got to have more security on this one than the goddam Oval Office. No martini-mouths in bars or burger joints. Every office gets locked, every ounce of paper gets shredded—
ST CLAIR:	We're shredding all before us, Art. Even our sandwich wrappers.
KHAN:	Jesus goddam fucking Christ!
ST CLAIR:	I'm sorry, Art, just a slip of the brain. Project Pandora.
KHAN:	Right! RIGHT! Project Pandora. Open the box and things fly out. And what beautiful things come out of the Pandora gateau box, little lady?
ST CLAIR:	The same tantalizing temptation to the taste buds as Devils Delight . . .
KHAN:	It looks like chocolate, fudge, whipped cream, nuts and Maraschino cherries.
ST CLAIR:	The same organoleptic and olfactory satisfactions . . .
KHAN:	It even tastes like chocolate, fudge, whipped cream, nuts and Maraschino cherries. But what's the key difference, the cosmic breakthrough?
ST CLAIR:	The key difference is, Art—
KHAN:	C'mon! Give it to me, give it to me, little lady!
ST CLAIR:	The key difference is that Project Pandora has only an amazing ten calories per unit.
KHAN:	Ten calories per gateau. One microscopic calorie per portion. A compulsive eater could gorge ten Pandoras a day and still take in fewer calories than a carton of cottage cheese. She could wolf a hundred Pandoras a week and still be no worse off than if she would've eaten one mushroom pizza. Project Pandora, kid, is slimming without

13

sacrifice, bingeing without responsibility, greed without guilt. It's bigger than Marie Antoinette feeding gateau to the peasants, bigger than Eve serving up the apple. It's not just cosmic, it's stratospheric, it's intergalactic—

ST CLAIR: It's certainly a step forward in the cake and confectionery market, Art.

KHAN: *Pause* You think so, kid?

ST CLAIR: I definitely do, Art.

KHAN: *Pause* Then I want you to tell me something?

ST CLAIR: What's that, Art?

KHAN: *Pause* I want you to tell me, little lady, why – when your agency is offered the challenge of this account – when your agency, Brooks, Bellini, Waldo and Stretch, is given the once-in-a-lifetime opportunity to testlaunch this miracle product right here in the UK – when your agency is currently drooling over a TV budget Saatchi and Saatchi or J. Walter Thompson would shoot their grandmothers for – why is it that every single goddam idea you've shown me in the last six weeks sucks harder than a hooker in a Harlem whorehouse?

ST CLAIR: I'm on my way to the Creative Department now, Art. We'll be back to you like – yesterday.

KHAN: You bet you will, kid. And when you speak to those long-haired dead-beats you just tell them one word.

ST CLAIR: What's that, Art?

KHAN: Testimony.

ST CLAIR: I beg your pardon, Art.

KHAN: Housewife testimony. Get some ordinary obese broad, put her in front of the camera, have her tell it like it is.

ST CLAIR: But, Art—

KHAN: Show her before and after, have her say she lost a hundred pounds and got young and beautiful, all through Granny Garfunkel.

14

ST CLAIR:	But, Art—
KHAN:	And show a big goddam picture of her eating the goddam product and goddam enjoying it!
ST CLAIR:	But, Art, with respect, isn't that a bit old-fashioned? I mean, Slim – Project Pandora – is an innovatory product with a young up-beat image which—
KHAN:	Listen, little lady. I don't want no goddam beach parties at kinky camera angles, I don't want no so-called creatives taking a Caribbean vacation on my bucks. Testimony worked in Venezuela for Pecan Paradise, it worked in Belgium for Sponge Splendide, it's worked world-wide for Granny Garfunkel Inc. for the last forty years. So it'll work here and now, in little old London, England. It'll work real good – since it's our futures we're talking here. Right?
ST CLAIR:	Right, Art.
KHAN:	*Right*. So take the bull by the horns and run with it, little lady.
ST CLAIR:	Right, Art.
KHAN:	R-I-G-H-T. You find me a turkey and turn her into a goddam swan.

15

I

For the last four years Maggie had been plagued by a recurrent dream. In the dream her teeth fell out, first her front teeth and then, when she put up her hand to the gap, all the others, falling faster the harder she tried to stop them, dropping between her fingers, pale and dead like sliced mushrooms.

Even when she woke, running her tongue quickly over familiar planes and ridges and the punctuating jaggedness of fillings, she was not reassured but, opening her eyes cautiously, was almost surprised to see the gleam of the dressing table mirror, the huddled shadow of the little boudoir chair, the hump of the duvet on the other side of the bed.

Edging upright by inches so as not to disturb him, she leant over to examine her husband, as if she half expected the head on the pillow to belong to a stranger. But no, Keith's face, turned in towards her, left cheek partly hidden, still wore the look it had worn every morning for twenty-two years, his Teddy Bear look she called it, the features fuzzy with sleep, the mouth gentle, the cheeks smoothed and rounded to a youthful chubbiness, even the little knot in his chin where the razor never reached softened, blurred, unravelled into a boyish dimple. She remembered how it had moved her, that look, in their early days when Brian's teething had left them ragged, when they were still struggling for accommodations over soggy bathroom flannels and sugar spoons used for tea-stirring. She listened to the steady whine and churr of his snoring, smelt the sweet fug of his body and was comforted.

The red digits of the Teasmade glowed 6.00. Running her tongue over her teeth again, just to be certain, she climbed out of bed and tiptoed to the window, twitching back first the curtain, then the net. Here too in Spellthorne Avenue everything seemed normal. Beneath a faltering April sky the

17

neat file of odd numbers cast blank early-morning eyes on Maggie, staring back from their mirror-image evens. Half-timbered houses, semi-detached, white-painted or Sandtexed, each with its front bay and frosted bathroom window over the porch, yet each sporting its badge of individuality, here a stained-wood Georgian fanlight door, there carriage lamps or picture double-glazing. Well-tended houses, bedded down solidly in nourishing loam like the pampas and evergreens in their front gardens, untainted by the blights of London, the muggings, the drug addicts, the terrorist bombs, miraculously protected by the twenty-minute train distance from Waterloo. 'Thirties' ribbon development' the estate agent had said fifteen years ago when they'd moved from the flat. Now the same office in the High Street advertised Deco Town Houses, 2 recep. 3 bed. g.c.h. all mod cons. But it was only words; beyond the occasional blue and white continental number replacing a 'Fir Trees' or 'Kenorma', nothing much had altered. Simonized cars toed the kerb in well-spaced formation, their own green Sierra, the Datsun from number twenty-one, the red Golf belonging to the Salts, the Pearsons' white Granada. The paper boy went on his round, gently clicking the latches of sun-ray gates. In number seventeen's magnolia a thrush was singing. Maggie stood for a moment listening to the birdsong, the distant rumble of a milk float, her husband's snoring, all the sounds of an average morning. She let the curtain fall and pulled on her housecoat.

Yet downstairs, in the kitchen, she froze. She'd always loved this half hour of solitary peace before the clamour for the bathroom, the cries for missing socks and football kit. Even now, when Brian was married and Neil away at college and there was only Nicola to bully out from under the duvet, she loved it still. Yet here, in the silence, came the panic again, the falling, the blackness.

The cat, perhaps? Hadn't she formed the habit recently of checking the kitchen chair in case its motheaten burden had failed to survive the night? But the flick of a battle-scarred ear indicated that Fluffy was merely sleeping, dreaming of rumbles with tomcats and the pilfered chicken legs of her youth.

Then, catching sight of the glossy brochure, Maggie remembered. Keith and she had decided. Last night, talking carefully, or so she felt, choosing words that avoided expanding the conversation, they had nevertheless agreed that it needed doing, could be afforded, couldn't be put off a year longer – what with the unit doors hanging off their hinges and the laminate on the plinths curling and that burn on the worktop where the kettle had boiled dry. A designer fitted kitchen, just like Ivy's next door, with hand-made units, leaded glass display cabinets, built-in dishwasher, split-level and microwave, waste disposal, quarry tiles, the works. Keith would tear out the old, Craft Kitchens DeLuxe would install the new. And wasn't it what she wanted, wasn't a new fitted kitchen supposed to be every woman's dream?

But now, suddenly, as she looked around her, she saw Keith's claw-hammer tearing at the plaster, saw the walls crack, the vinyl beneath her feet split and open into a chasm, saw the doors tumbling from the units, falling, falling, crashing all about her, flat and greyish-white like dead incisors.

It was ridiculous really, this dread of changing things, a phobia, like people screaming at spiders. Four years. Time was a healer, didn't they say? How could a new fitted kitchen be an ill omen?

Presently, taking a deep breath, she began to lay out the breakfast things, boiling the kettle and loading the toaster with two fresh slices of crusty bread. The everyday chores soothed her, the aroma of toast drifted in upon her senses like a gentle anaesthetic. Through the kitchen window she could glimpse the cascading yellow of forsythia, the purple spears of grape hyacinths bordering neatly-dug beds. Soon, when she had made more toast for Keith and nagged Nicki into a bowl of cereal, she would begin chopping carrots and onions, preparing the brisket for the slow cooker. She would cut sandwiches and pack them in Tupperware containers, with a fruit yoghurt and a Kit-Kat, or a slice of her own banana bread, one for Nicki to take to school, one for her own lunch break, her gossip with Jackie amongst the computer terminals.

She thought of the brisket simmering gently, dissolving

into tenderness, instilling the gravy with its rich juices. She thought of the crumbly density of banana bread, the smoothness of chocolate, the sharp crunch of wafer biscuit. She took the toast, still hot, juggling it with her fingers, and spread butter liberally, then honey, watching the melting gold overflow in negligent pools upon the plate.

There was a comfort in this too, like the solidity of the houses in the street. Breakfast, lunch, tea, a necessary, unvarying pattern, marking out the day, restraining its vagaries, giving it shape and order. She lifted the toast and gingerly inserted one corner between her teeth. But her front caps held, her lower incisors rose decisively to meet them, her canines tore efficiently through the crust.

She sighed, licked her fingers, wiped butter and honey from her chin. The dream faded. She was Maggie Hapgood (Mrs), a few months past the Big Four O, but not bad for her age, considering. She had a nice home perhaps not *House and Gardens* like Ivy Pearson's, but welcoming, lived-in. She had a husband who was a wonderful father, who came home regularly from the office and stayed home, not slouching out after he'd fed his face for a pint or twelve like her Dad always used to. She had three children she'd willingly die for, even if Nicola was going through a phase at the moment. The sun was struggling to shine and her horoscope read: 'Your planetary conjunctions look favourably aspected.'

With any luck today would not turn out to be one of those days.

It was one of those days when Fizz was particularly glad to be Fizz.

Of course the night before's being a Dean night had helped. Waking, stretching, she let her eye follow the sunlight where it filtered through the louvred blinds and concertinaed across the expanse of dove-grey carpet, past the attenuated black tulip of the Italian lamp, past the single stark leather chair, strategically placed, to the base of the futon and the deco rug with its pearly scattering of lace and silk, sole evidence now of last night's indulgences. It never failed to satisfy her, this leisurely contemplation of her own art direction, as if through the viewfinder of the World of Interiors camera – 'Fizz St Clair transforms Parson's Green Edwardiana into Modish Minimalism'. She was aware that this studied perfection could disconcert lesser mortals, witness poor Dean looking round uneasily for somewhere to deposit his champagne glass. But then – what was style, except the courage to go to extremes? She had created the ideal setting for her accomplishments; and Dean, of course, was the ideal accessory – Dean with his art-nouveau-bronze torso tapering to tight, pubescent buttocks, Dean awed, out of his depth, adoring her. Shifting her legs, she felt a raw stickiness, proof of his adoration. She extended one arm, pillowing her cheek against it to observe how slim and youthful it was, fancying she could still smell his sweat on her skin. Dear Dean. Pity about the tattoos, poor darling – although didn't they, on second thoughts, merely add piquancy to the dish?

Her satisfaction stayed with her as she guided her white Porsche Carrera Targa through the slalom of rush-hour traffic, as she climbed out into the gritty sunlight of Garrick Street, answering with appropriate hauteur the chorus of whistles from the adjacent scaffolding that greeted her elegant display of leg. Pausing before the plate glass frontage of Brooks Bellini, she saw herself mirrored briefly; beige Rive Gauche belted pigskin jacket with brown leather skirt, swaying auburn bob, discreet Cartier glint at ears and wrists. Sailing through the swing doors, tossing her car keys nonchalantly to uniformed Fred, where he lurked behind the is-it-or-isn't-it foliage of the fabric imitation yuccas and weeping figs, she swept on in a drift of Arpege towards the elevators. Ms Fizz St Clair, company director, with a fashionable town house and a twenty-three-year-old toyboy and a reserved parking space in Central London. Oh yes, it was good to be Fizz.

II

Up on the third floor of Brooks, Bellini, Waldo and Stretch, Fizz negotiated the builders' debris that bordered her domain. For as long as she had worked there, the agency had been in the process of redecoration. This constant refurbishment had little to do with wear and tear or the desire of the management to bestow upon their staff the benefits of an ideal working environment; rather, it symbolized the cannibalistic tendencies of the founding partners. Bellini had been eaten years ago: when Fizz had joined they were already tearing down his Lichtenstein Wendy house of primary colours and replacing it with Waldo's folksy rush matting and pine. Then Brooks and Stretch consumed Waldo, occasioning the slow transformation to smoked glass and grey hessian with ubiquitous scarlet trim. Of course, even before the last missing keys were found to fit the last delivery of scarlet filing cabinets, Brooks and Stretch were measuring each other for the pot. But Stretch was clever; while Brooks had been holding out for a three-course meal, Stretch had been quietly snacking – an arm here, a leg there – until, consigning Brooks's remains to cold storage in the Chairman's office, he was at last free to gobble up the Chief Executive's title as sauce to his Managing Director's portion. The consequent redecoration reflected the eating pattern – the smoked glass was being rehashed, but fresh ingredients were being added with the post-modern friezes and columns, and the seasoning had been adjusted to cool blue.

Personally, Fizz viewed the disruption with equanimity. She had always inclined towards Stretch. Brooks was a chalk-stripe public school fossil, with all the usual sexual inhibitions, whereas Stretch was a barrow boy, nervous of classy, Oxbridge-educated women, yet nevertheless susceptible to the negligently buttoned blouse, those extra few inches of thigh. And besides, there were advantages to be gained from constant upheaval. Indeed, picking her way through the tangled cables and half-constructed block-board partitions that would soon constitute the fiefdom of her fellow director, Dick Saunders Blair, Fizz spotted one now. There, in the no-man's-land of corridor that separated his empire from hers, stood two five-foot blue storage cabinets, brand-new and empty, obviously abandoned by a perplexed workman summoned to another job. Fizz scrutinized the cabinets for a moment. Then she swept across the border into her own territory.

In the suite of offices that housed the Granny Garfunkel group there was a muted but purposeful hum, the satisfying adrenalin buzz of nervous subordinates, who, anxious to acquire brownie points, were already two hours into their working day. In the central play pen, the open-plan space devoted to below-the-line people (juniors, secretaries and the like), printers clattered industriously, VDU screens flickered. Flashing a cool glance in acknowledgement of this diligence and ignoring an unmannerly screech at her rear, Fizz reached the haven of her own office.

Here, as at Parson's Green, she had stamped her own inimitable mark, despite the blue and the post-modern frills. Here was the same economical conjunction of expensive objects, the Memphis sofa, the Pentagon steel and rubber shelving, the Studio 80 halogen lamp. Here was the sleek enamel vase filled with white irises, understated echo of a Hockney etching; here the opalescent plate-glass table, barren of paper or other testament to endeavour, of course, bearing only the flask of fresh coffee, clean white cups and doilied plate of biscuits which were her perquisite, every morning, as a member of the board. She surveyed it all with a glow of satisfaction; (a judicious champagne cocktail with the architect had ensured that her personal office space exceeded that of Dick Saunders Blair, Adrian Melrose and even poor half-eaten Brooks by thirty square feet).

Jettisoning her briefcase and Louis Vuitton bag, observing in her passage that one or two of the understated irises were browning at the edges, evidence that yet again her secretary had slipped up on the job, Fizz was reaching for the coffee flask – ah, that first caffeine hit of the day – when a penetrating screech alerted her to the presence of this very minion in her doorway.

'Actually, Fizz, I wish you'd warn me when you're going to come in late.'

Fizz poured the coffee carefully before looking up. Most of the secretaries at Brooks Bellini were no more than lapwarmers, ready to desert their desks at the first hint of an open wine bottle, happy only when jiggling flirtatiously on some graduate trainee's knee. And her own secretary, the Hon. Sonia Beckwith, was the biggest lapwarmer of them all. Oh, she might have a family estate in Gloucestershire and an engagement photograph imminent in *Country Life*, but Fizz had seen her, when she should have been manning the phones or rendering Fizz's memos into the obscure Serbo-Croat dialect she passed off as typing – she'd seen her thrusting out her assets beneath the lambswool sweater, and pushing back her Alice band, and nibbling her pearls. Added to which, there was a bumptiousness in The Lapwarmer's manner, stemming no doubt from her youth and class, that definitely grated. Fizz had complained several times to the Human Resources Director – after all, someone of her status deserved efficiency and dedication – but she'd been told that for the money on offer the creature was the best they could recruit. As the man said, when you paid peanuts . . . Still, where would the Hon. Son be when she was Fizz's age? What would she have when that creamy-sweet complexion started to curdle and that overstuffed lambswool bolster began to sag? She wouldn't have a 34-22-34 figure, would she? And she wouldn't have spent the night cavorting with a twenty-three-year-old toyboy, that was for sure.

'Sorry, lovey,' Fizz said, smiling sweetly. 'Didn't see you there. Got held up at the pool, had to fight for a shower.' While sleeping late, in these days of the protestant work ethic, was a cardinal sin, lateness occasioned by manic exercise was a token of virtue, particularly when authenticated by a convincingly soggy costume and towel. 'Be a dear' – she indicated the Louis Vuitton holdall – 'and find somewhere for those to dry.'

'Actually, Fizz—'

'And while I think of it, shouldn't my Azzedine Alaia be back from the cleaners? And what's happened to my supply of chilled Perrier? And why am I sitting in an office full of dead flowers?'

'Actually, Fizz—'

'And how come no messages? You're saying it's gone ten and nobody's phoned?'

'Actually, Fizz, I was trying to tell you—'

'The fact that I'm a weeny bit late doesn't give you all a charter to skive. This is the Granny Garfunkel group, lovey. And what are we in the Granny Garfunkel group?'

The Lapwarmer stared down at her ladylike colourless nail polish, seeming suitably chastened. 'We're proactive,' she muttered.

'Right. So let's get up a head of steam, as our revered client would say.'

The Lapwarmer took a deep breath before gabbling in a toneless voice, 'Art Khan phoned twice, Vic Stretch phoned, the Creative Director phoned, Barbara Donkin needs to see you ASAP, and Vic Stretch's secretary asked me to give you this.'

Taking the white envelope she proffered, Fizz sipped her coffee. 'Tell everyone I'm in a meeting.'

'Actually, that's what I told them, Fizz. Actually, that's what I always tell them.'

'Good girl. We'll make a top class PA of you yet.'

She was still inspecting her nails. 'But—'

'But what, lovey?'

'What shall I do about Barbara? She said it was very urgent.'

Barbara, The Workhouse Donkey. Fizz would need at least three more coffees before she could cope with The Donkey's earnest braying. Then she remembered her trip through Dick Saunders Blair's nascent empire and a thought struck her. 'OK, give me five, then send her in. Then fix the cozzie, fix the cleaning, fix the flowers. Oh and, lovey—'

The Lapwarmer had hefted the Louis Vuitton halfway to the door.

'Smile,' Fizz said, suiting her lips to the word. 'Remember, positive thoughts bring a positive day.'

Left to herself Fizz poured more coffee and opened the envelope, which proved to contain an FYI on an all-staff memo to be issued later in the morning. Adrian Melrose, after seven years invaluable service on Country Fayre Margarines and Hinoki Computers, had resigned in order to set up his own consultancy. His contribution as a team player and loyal agency member etc., etc. would be sorely missed.

Poor old Adrian. His fellow board directors, of course, had seen it coming for months. He was always far too well in with the Country Fayre client – all those pally rounds of golf and weekends in the Cotswolds. Nothing like the suspicion of a non-aligned power base to start Stretch sharpening his teeth. Dick Saunders Blair had better watch out, too, not flaunt his hold on Tancred Toiletries, make sure to tell Stretch when he so much as blew his nose. And what about Fizz's own position, vis-à-vis Granny Garfunkel? She smiled to herself. At least she was safe there. She had Mr Art (Genghis) Khan for her insurance. Dear old Art, he'd driven two of her predecessors to the headhunters, given Jeff Thurlow a coronary, and then there was that business with poor Humphrey Slater – found starkers and gibbering under his desk one morning, claiming to be the reincarnation of Oliver Cromwell. Even Stretch got antsy after ten minutes with Genghis. But, for some reason, Fizz seemed to be able to handle him. Of course, she was a touch cleverer than Jeff Thurlow or Humphrey Slater – never show blood, it was like a dinner invitation to a piranha – and she flattered herself that being a woman helped. You just batted your eyelids and crossed your legs ostentatiously when the killer jaws opened, and it left him quite goggle-eyed, the poor old piranha, snapping at air and flapping his gills. True, Art was as ugly, arrogant, treacherous, foul-mouthed, pig-ignorant a psychopath as you were ever likely to meet. But he was hers, all hers.

And as long as he was at the helm of Granny Garfunkel Gourmet Gateaux (UK) Inc., her prospects look rosy.

Alas, poor Adrian. Fizz hoped her letting slip to Stretch that she'd seen him lunching *à deux* with Brooks in Boulestin's hadn't hastened his demise. But all the same. . . she wondered if she might not benefit from the reading of the will. Hinoki Computers would prove a useful little legacy, establish a buffer zone between herself and Saunders Blair.

That reminded her of The Workhouse Donkey. After she'd made her customary visit to the executive ladies to retouch her Dior pout, Fizz buzzed The Lapwarmer to wheel her round.

Barbara Donkin. Granted, she was reliable with statistics and flow-charts in her plodding, red-brick university way. And she certainly kept the babies, the bag-carriers and taxi-hailers, out from under Fizz's feet. But as for style . . . For a start Fizz would have changed her name (well, she had, hadn't she?). And she'd have taken a strong dose of elocution for that dreary ecky-thump accent – 'bewk' for book, 'lust' for last (although that was scarcely what The Donkey inspired). Perhaps she couldn't be expected to do much about her milk-bottle legs, but she could try a rinse on her hair and take the tweezers to her eyebrows once in a while. And as for that navy chain-store suit – sometimes it positively shamed Fizz to introduce her to clients as her second-in-command. Of course, Fizz had endeavoured to explain that an encyclopaedic grasp of indices and Nielsen figures, while all very well in its way, simply wasn't where it was at; she'd tried, as with The Lapwarmer, to bring The Donkey on, imbue her with a little of her own special flair. But in vain. The Donkey would never achieve a company parking space. Even now, as she whinnied in the doorway, Fizz could observe a zit burgeoning on her unmade-up chin.

'Fizz, I need a few minutes on Project Pandora. I've spoken to Ed Monks down at Croydon and he says they're right behind the cartoon calorie, but he'd like a production quote and some idea of the beach location—'

Fizz sat back, sipping her coffee with a smile. 'Relax, Barbara. Relax.'

'I have some sympathy with Ed, Fizz. He feels the quote will help when he shows the concept to Art.'

'I said, relax, lovey. The cartoon calorie is dead.'

The Donkey almost dropped the efficient ring binder she carried like an extension of her arm. 'I thought – last night—'

'Last night was last night.'

'But I spoke to Ed at six thirty.'

'And I spoke to Art at eight. After you'd swanned home early for – what is it you do on Mondays? – your Scottish Dancing class?'

'I was on a store check, Fizz. Dulwich and Peckham.'

'Well, you weren't at your desk, were you, lovey? It seems Art sneaked a look in Ed's office and wasn't impressed by what he saw.'

The single eyebrow that partitioned The Donkey's face in woeful ignorance of the golden section twitched for a moment, before settling in a smear across the bridge of her nose. 'I see. Well, we'll need to rebrief the creative department. I'll get on to the Creative Director.'

'Don't worry, lovey, it's all in hand.'

Again the eyebrow squirmed, like a centipede in contact with insecticide. 'If I'm to talk to Ed, Fizz, perhaps you should fill me in. Is there a new strategy? What's the deadline? Who's working on the project?'

Fizz gestured airily. 'I'll give you an up-date when I have a moment. Right now, I need you to concentrate on something far more important.'

The centipede writhed.

'Storage cabinets,' Fizz said.

'Pardon?'

'If you traverse the corridor between the Tancred Toiletries offices and ours you will observe two virgin storage cabinets. Get some taxi-hailers to fill them with Granny Garfunkel filing – old memos, out-dated research, anything will do. Then find a couple of workmen to move them to the Tancred Toiletries end of the corridor, right next to the fire doors, as far as you can go. Treat the project as a matter of urgency. I want to see those cabinets in their new location when I return from lunch.'

Clicking the locks on her briefcase, Fizz began to take out her paperwork. (Never leave important documents lying round your office where anyone may read them. Survival Rule Number One: secrecy is power.) But although she had so clearly been dismissed, The Donkey was still pawing the threshold.

'Is there a problem?' Fizz said.

'No, Fizz. Except that – I mean, we've a lot on our plates with Pandora. I don't really see . . .'

'Why the urgency with the storage cabinets? Because, lovey, whoever left them there may come back and collect them. Or worse still, Dick Saunders Blair may take it into his head to nick them. That's why we've got to act now.'

'But, I mean – why move them at all?'

Fizz sighed. Really, the poor Donkey would never attain the company Amex card, let alone the parking space. 'Because once we have filled them with our paperwork and moved them into position we have established the corridor as Granny Garfunkel territory.'

The Donkey was gaping as if it were Fizz and not she whose brain power was in question. 'R-right, Fizz.'

'Right. And that's why I'm entrusting you with the task, Barbara lovey, instead of someone more junior. Because it's A1 top priority.'

'Right, Fizz. I'll see to it now.'

'Right. Let's push the peanut forward, as the esteemed Art would say. Oh and, Barbara—'

'Yes, Fizz.'

'You really should do something about your complexion. Ask your secretary to pop to the chemist for a medicated face wash. Remember, it's not the content that counts, lovey, but the style.'

For a moment her mouth was once more agape. But then it closed in what seemed at last an expression of grateful under-standing. 'Thank you for telling me, Fizz. I'll make it A1 top priority, shall I? Second top after the filing cabinets?'

29

Poor Donkey, thought Fizz. Perhaps she was finally getting through to her. She permitted herself a small sigh of satisfaction. Then she buzzed The Lapwarmer on her squawk-box. 'Get me Spike Bentley, will you, lovey. Tell him I'll buy him lunch, any restaurant, his choice.'

Remorselessly true to its name, L'Eglise had the two of them sitting bolt upright on oak pews and blinking at each other through a hallowed twilight, into which dank reminders of the afternoon sun oozed, seeping across the tablecloth in stained-glass puddles. At their backs a decrepit pipe organ loomed, to their left the coat-check girl lurked behind a canopied chest tomb complete with effigy, and above Fizz's head a monstrance and bishop's crozier were bracketed (securely, she prayed) to the rendered wall. A Gregorian chant droned through concealed speakers; the menu, in the form of a leatherette psalter, proffered by a surpliced acolyte with carefully gelled hair, promised medieval cuisine, venison with frumenty, suckling pig with 'wortes, garlyke and onyons', lampreys, pottage – 'Our chef reproduces in authentic detail recipes first created in the thirteenth and fourteenth centuries for the refectory of the Benedictine Abbey of Cluny'. Fizz stifled a cough as an acolyte zealously swished a thurible between the pews.

'Only opened two days ago,' murmured Spike Bentley. 'Huge advance PR.'

'Spike, why are we whispering?'

'Interesting ambience, though, don't you think?'

'I'll certainly bear it in mind when I host my next exorcism.'

'Theme restaurants are the thing, Fizz. I'm covering them for this month's *L'Entrée* magazine.'

Spike Bentley was a hack. He was also the agency stud. Surprisingly enough, these two attributes were not unrelated. Oh, once upon a time, in the days when all copywriters had Eng. Lit. 2.2s from Cambridge and an unfinished Booker prize winner in their desk drawer, Spike had been a rising star, crafting witty slogans for sports cars and vodka and married to a nice, ordinary girl from Guildford. But that was before he fell victim to his own carefully-constructed persona; that was before his creative angst, his absent-mindedness, his incompetence, so irresistible to lapwarmers with typewriters and other mechanical objects, caused him to impale himself on his own charm. Now, three ex-wives, four children at fee-paying schools and one messy palimony suit later, Spike's career had descended from wit and sophistication to the murky but highly-rewarded depths of lavatory cleaners and acne lotions. He took in freelance as impoverished crones once took in washing. As well as his restaurant columns, he wrote obituary notices for a national newspaper. If you visited his office you'd find some silent, Doc Martened art director drawing S-bends in one corner; but Spike himself (when not in anguished phone consultation with his solicitor or accountant) would be clattering away, two-fingered, at his 1960s' manual Olympia, trying to beat some deadline – a thousand words here on Andalusian cuisine, five hundred there on some African statesman or Scandinavian Nobel prize winner. Indeed, it was Fizz's opinion that he must get muddled occasionally, praising the contribution of paté de foie gras to Third World famine relief and bestowing Michelin rosettes on obscure biochemists.

Sometimes, after the first bottle of claret, he talked about making a fresh start – giving up women, paying off his various mortgages and resurrecting the novel. But then the second bottle would take hold and there he would be, the old recidivist, offering Dick Saunders Blair's minion a lift home, or slinking off to Art Stores with the lurex-sheathed temp at the Christmas party.

Not that you'd have suspected it of him at first glance. He admitted to forty and it was Fizz's view that he looked not a day younger, with those blood hound eyes, that face like an unmade bed. He'd kept his hair, of course, that was a point in his favour. But all the same, you'd scarcely describe him as macho (not like dear Dean – oh, the recollection of those quadriceps, those exquisitely-moulded pectorals). He seemed insubstantial, ramshackle, modishly designed but ergonomically deficient. Despite his eating constantly to pacify his ulcer, his bony shoulders and long, skinny legs conveyed an impression of deprivation, of insatiable hunger.

Of course, it was the hunger that got to them, the tortured brow, the sad eyes belying the vivacious smile, the romantic-novel intimations of some nobly endured secret sorrow (although in Spike's case that was likely to be a chopped-up credit card or a back-dated demand from the tax man). Still, he drove almost the right car (a Lancia), wined them and dined them in the right places (sometimes), and chose the right designer labels (no matter that he wore his Issey Miyake jacket like an old parka, or that his Gaultier tortoiseshells were held together with a paper clip above the left eye). Certainly you couldn't quarrel with his success rate – in fact Fizz must be the only woman in Brooks Bellini not to have sampled his wares. Of course, it wasn't that he didn't fancy her – she'd felt him eyeing her legs in the corridor, pressing that little bit too close in the lift. But, well . . . she *worked* with him, for God's sake. That sort of thing could do immense damage to a woman's career, she was grateful she had escaped from her last place before any whisper came out of those after-hours sessions in the boardroom with Spunky Dunkie, the Mad Molester. Besides, dear old Spike's star wasn't exactly rising in the Brooks Bellini firmament – imagine, Fizz St Clair sleeping her way to the bottom? And now there was Dean, wasn't there? No, it was best the way things were, Spike ogling Fizz, she batting her eyelids and taking evasive action, a refreshing sorbet between indigestible slabs of office fare. And after all it was not his priapic prowess that had occasioned her taking Spike to L'Eglise this lunchtime; it was his willingness to write anything for money.

They perused the menu, Spike cautious of his ulcer while Fizz, of course, had her dairy allergy to bear in mind (it wasn't that dairy products gave her any very specific symptoms, more that she felt better without them; but then, most sensitive people had some food allergy these days). She managed to ascertain that capon with mandrake root was butter-free and Spike, having opted rashly for the lampreys, gave his attention to the wine list, selecting a Puligny-Montrachet

32

–comforted, no doubt, by the knowledge that it would be Fizz's credit card which bore the strain.

'You'll appreciate it, Fizz,' he said, with an optimistic smile of self-justification.

She gestured at her Perrier, which had arrived in what appeared to be a communion chalice.

'Oh gosh, yes. I forgot you don't drink.'

'Only champagne. And never at lunchtime.'

'Very professional.' There was an edge to his voice which Fizz assumed was honed by guilt.

Nevertheless, he looked on with enthusiasm as the Puligny-Montrachet was uncorked and poured reverently for his approval. She watched him perform the rituals of sniffing and sipping and swilling and observed that the hovering acolytes were suitably impressed. Only when they had gone did he take a great gulp, like a man quaffing at an oasis. 'Aaaah!' he said. And then 'Mmmm.' Then he considered the crystal goblet thoughtfully before taking a second huge swig. 'Aaaaaah,' he said again, closing his eyes.

'Is there some problem?'

'Just waiting for the strychnine to take effect.'

Fizz raised her eyebrows.

'Come on, Lucrezia Borgia, I assume the chalice is poisoned. You'd scarcely be buying me lunch, would you, if all you had in mind was my welfare?'

'How deplorably cynical, Spike darling.'

'Its just whenever I see you, Lucrezia, I glimpse an incubus at your elbow, I perceive the monstrous bulk of Genghis Khan pulling your strings.'

'Poor Art. He's a much misunderstood guy. This is an opportunity I'm offering you.'

'God save me from insurmountable opportunities.'

'A challenge, then.'

Spike took out a tube of antacid pills. 'I'm a tired man, Lucrezia. I can't be doing with any more challenges. Your last one – Pecan Paradise, was it? – playing havoc with my ulcer. And I think the one before gave me the damned thing.'

Their hors d'oeuvres appeared, pottage for Fizz, mortrews

33

for Spike, served with a reverence that suggested they might be expected to say grace. Fizz delved in her bag for her silver Tiffany box of vitamin capsules, while Spike devoured more chalk pills. Then they stirred and prodded L'Eglise's offerings gingerly.

'Why don't you talk to Brad?'

'Who?' she said.

'No-ads Brad, our esteemed Creative Director.'

They'd been through so many Creative Directors since Waldo got eaten that Fizz had long since given up trying to remember their names. 'I'm not in the business of supervising spotty boy geniuses in the art of joined-up writing. I need proven track record here.'

'You mean, a hack.'

'I mean a true professional, Spike.'

'You mean someone devoid of all aesthetic scruples, who'll do anything for money.'

'Spike, you're so insecure and negative about yourself. You're a fine writer, a genuine craftsman. You're the one person at Brooks Bellini who can make a contribution to Project Pandora at this crucial stage.'

'Crucial, may I ask, to whom?'

'To the agency, Spike.'

'To your acquisition of an answering machine for your car phone or a company country estate?'

'To the agency and to Granny Garfunkel. Art is getting a lot of pressure from the Heavy Breathers in Chicago.'

'May they press till he squeals.'

'Poor Art is human like the rest of us – well, almost. He never wanted to come to the UK, he was sent here for offending one of the Breathers. But he has every hope, if he can jack up enough brownie points, they'll welcome him back to Chicago.'

'And will they?'

'Not a chance.'

'No, I suppose if you'd had the good fortune to get rid of Art Khan, you'd want to keep it that way.'

'As a matter of fact, what with the sales decline in Devils

34

Delight, Art could be in deep shit if he doesn't come up covered in glory over Project Pandora. Never mind Chicago, Siberia could beckon, or, to be more precise, Malaysia or Puerto Rico. So he's having a bad time at the moment. And when Art has a bad time, I have a bad time.'

Leaning his elbows on the table, Spike favoured her with the lopsided smile that lapwarmers found so compelling. 'Lucrezia, my heart bleeds.'

She felt it judicious to counter the smile by lowering her eyelashes and running her tongue over her lip. 'Seriously, Spike. You're the only person who can help me. The only one who's up to it. I've spoken to Stretch. I think you'll find – apart from the obvious honour and glory within the agency – it would make a significant difference to your end-of-year bonus.'

'Ah. The usual twenty pieces of silver.'

'Don't be pompous, Spike darling.'

The pottage could have passed for farmhouse vegetable and the mortrews for meat balls; and now, from what she could see of Spike's lampreys, fish pie might have been a more appropriate description. Her capon looked equally unimpressive. No matter – there was a fine distinction between lunching and eating lunch which anyone anxious to retain a number ten dress size would be foolish to ignore. With practised technique she dissected her chicken, distributing it around the wooden paten so as to leave a convincing emptiness in the quarter nearest her. Then, neatly replacing her knife and fork, she began to fill Spike in on Pandora.

He listened in silence, the tortured expression in his bloodhound eyes seeming to intensify, though whether in response to her briefing or to the lampreys she was unsure. When she had finished he paused, dabbed his lips with his napkin.

'Yes?' she said.

'You know, this Puligny-Montrachet's pretty jolly decent. D'you think we should go for the second bottle?'

'Jesus, Spike.'

'Oh, fear not, Lucrezia. I get your general drift. Ten calories, cosmic breakthrough . . . cement overcoat if I

35

breathe a word. Unfortunate code name though. Fudge, chocolate, whipped cream, nuts, Maraschino cherries and all the sorrows of the world. Or is our learned client unaware of the true contents of Pandora's box?'

'You know Genghis. He thinks *Pride and Prejudice* is the book of the movie. Besides, Pandora is his wife's name.'

'Very appropriate. Gosh, it's a shame you're missing this wine, Lucrezia. Still, what I don't understand is how they do it?'

Fizz waited for the acolyte to conclude his genuflections over the wine bottle before reminding him she had ordered more Perrier. 'Do what?' she said.

'Fudge and chocolate and stuff? All for ten calories? Or is the technology so secret you get shredded if you tell?'

'Oh, it's just a simple combination of pectins, alginates, cellulose and methylethylcellulose, chemically modified by sodium carbonate, calcium and tetrasodium pyrophosphate, and synthetically coloured, flavoured and textured.'

'Ah, yes, of course. Silly of me to ask.'

'It's non-food. Its molecular structure is such that the body cannot metabolize it, so it just passes straight through with nil contribution to nutrition.'

'Even the Maraschino cherries?'

'Particularly the Maraschino cherries. By a unique combination of sodium alginate and calcium chloride, insoluble calcium alginate is created, which—'

Spike fumbled for his chalk pills. 'Please, Lucrezia—'

'Oh, Pandora is perfectly harmless, when consumed as part of a calorie controlled diet. It's been tested to eliminate deleterious side effects to the digestive tract, liver and kidney. The beauty is, since it's totally non-nutritious, it has no calorific value.'

'Then what about these ten calories?'

'It seems the research shows that consumers found the idea of non-food hard to come to terms with, even a little disturbing—'

'You amaze me.'

36

'So Granny Garfunkel's chemists experimented with sprinkling two grams of real chocolate vermicelli on the top.'

'Gosh.'

'Those ten little calories give Pandora complete consumer credibility.'

'Golly gosh.' Spike paused to stare ruminatively at the tip of his Gauloise. 'What the hell does it taste like? Soggy cardboard?'

'Research placements affirm it tastes exactly like fudge, chocolate, whipped cream, etc., etc.'

'Of course, you've sampled it yourself.'

'I have The Donkey to do that sort of thing.'

'Well, what did she think?'

'She thought it was pleasant, but perhaps a trifle bland.'

'No kidding.'

'The majority of consumers find blandness a positive attribute. But if you'd care to pass your own verdict, Spike darling, as our resident gourmet, I'll send you down a case of Pandora as soon as we get back to the office.'

He laughed. 'No, no, Lucrezia. I don't want to get too subjective about the product – it might impair my creative judgement. That's if I agree to take your blood money, of course. You did mention blood money, didn't you?'

'You'll agree.'

'I'm very busy with the ballcocks and the buboles. And I've started a fifth draft of my novel.'

She laughed. He favoured her with the lopsided smile in return and, though perhaps it was her imagination, she thought his knee nudged hers under the table. She was contemplating the advisability of nudging back, in the interests, of course, of winning her case, when an acolyte appeared to clear their plates, tut-tutting over their leavings.

'What does he expect?' Fizz asked, flapping her napkin at fresh billows of incense. 'How can one eat when even the cruet looks like equipment for performing the last rites? Personally, I'd be surprised if this place survives two weeks.'

Spike, who had been downing chalk pills and scribbling in his filofax, nodded gloomily. 'You never know. Just so long as it's still going by my publication data. And anyway, as you're so fond of saying, Lucrezia, people don't go to restaurants to eat.'

'True. They go to see and be seen.'

'They go to screw their colleagues or their secretaries. They go to pick up a hangover or the waiters. They go to boast to their friends they forked out a hundred quid a head. Food? What the hell has that to do with it? We live in a world of soya and quorn, Lucrezia. And now, at last, courtesy of Genghis Khan, the ultimate – non-food. Soon we'll have non-cuisine, no doubt. Soon we'll sit at restaurant tables consuming our quenelles and our boeuf en croute and our petits pots au chocolat, safe in the knowledge that, with no side effects to the liver and kidneys and nil nutritional contribution, it's all passing straight through. Honestly, Lucrezia, doesn't it sometimes bother you . . . ?' He tore savagely at his packet of chalk pills. 'No, I don't suppose it does.'

This seemed to be the moment for reciprocal knee-nudging. Yet when she thrust her leg forward she found his had moved and she was obliged to cover herself by a pretence of searching for her handbag, in the course of which she tore her tights on the edge of the pew, picking up two vicious splinters in the underside of her thigh for good measure.

'Oh, for God's sake, Spike,' she said. 'This isn't a difficult job. After all, Genghis has virtually written the script.'

'Housewives,' he said gloomily.

'You'll need a celebrity interviewer for added interest. And a snappy campaign theme. And there you are. Piece of cake.'

'Ha, bloody ha!'

Fizz inspected the predictably absurd bill which had arrived with the coffee and Spike's armagnac. Her thigh hurt; the wound was unlikely to have healed before her next session with Dean. 'I can see you and The Donkey were right. I shall have to throw myself on the mercy of No-ads Brad.'

He glanced up from his armagnac, visibly peeved, she was delighted to observe.

'I thought you wanted a professional?'

38

'I simply hadn't realized how busy you were.'

'Look, maybe I could juggle a few deadlines.'

'Of course, I'll have to tell Stretch. He'll be disappointed. It's unusual to turn down a personal request from the managing director to fire-brigade on key business.'

'Maybe I could find some free time next week.'

'But when I explain your artistic scruples I'm sure he'll understand.'

'OK, this week. Thursday or Friday.'

'We can't use part-timers on Project Pandora. Don't fret about Stretch. I'm sure he's not aware of all the freelance you do in office hours, or the great novel . . .'

She shuffled her deck of credit cards, considering a trump for the preposterous bill. She heard Spike sigh.

'When do you need the script?'

'This afternoon, close of play.'

'Well, since you mentioned the bonus . . .'

'Did I?' She dealt the bill a gold Visa. 'I shouldn't have really, it's in Stretch's gift, not mine. But I'll certainly put in a word for you, don't worry. Meanwhile I'll call The Donkey and have her assemble the briefing documents in your office.'

When she came off her mobile phone he was looking the picture of artistic anguish. 'Smile, darling,' she said, leaning forward to clink her coffee cup with his glass. 'Project Pandora is going to be the most exciting fast-moving packaged goods launch ever seen in the UK. We're talking megabucks here, we're talking stardom. And you, Spike darling, are *the* key player on the team.'

She was aware, as she leaned forward, that he could see below the V-line of her lapels to the cream lace of her bra, could breathe in the heat of her breasts. He drained his armagnac. 'Gosh, Fizz. Golly fucking gosh!' But she could tell he was striving against a grudging admiration.

39

III

At the beginning of May Brian phoned from Solihull to announce that Keith and Maggie would become grandparents in December. That was on Sunday. On Monday it looked as though Fluffy were fading.

Despite her anticipatory checks on the kitchen chair, Maggie could hardly believe it. Poor Fluffy. Though for some time her main contribution to family life had been tiddling on the carpet behind the settee, she'd never really been ill, just shrivelled gradually into dry twigs. Still, since Monday anyway was Maggie's day off, perhaps it was as well for a visit to the V-E-T.

Twenty years. An age – and yesterday. Brian had been two when they'd collected the kitten from the Cats Protection League. (Keith hadn't yet been bitten by the bird watching bug, Maggie remembered.) Brian had chosen the name. Not that she ever had been – Fluffy, that is – but a tiny venomous matted tortoiseshell bundle, runny-eyed and jumping with fleas, who had shot behind the twin-tub the moment the cardboard box was opened and stayed there, hissing and spitting, for a week. Funny to think of that puzzled little boy, dirtying his clean dungarees as he tried to tempt her out with saucers of milk or the cotton reel Maggie had threaded with string. Funny to think of him married to Stephanie and about to become a father. About to make Maggie a grandmother, for goodness sake.

Naturally, she was delighted, but all the same . . . Forty was young these days, wasn't it? True, if you went to the doctor's with so much as a sniffle he'd ask you accusingly if you still had your periods. And yes, there was that look Nicki gave you when you walked in on her whispering with

40

that little madam Kimberly, as if you were some sort of sub-
human species. But forty-year-old women had the world at
their feet nowadays – posing naked in Playboy and discoing
till all hours with rock stars and having babies themselves.
Blue rinses and knitting needles, that was Mum's generation.
Maggie's hormones were fine, thank you very much, and she
wasn't ready for the Zimmer frame, not just at the moment.

Still, twenty years . . . She'd been so certain then, twenty
years old and an experienced married woman, skilled at
winkling commission out of the Clothing Club catalogue
and knocking up gastronomic miracles from best end of neck.
She'd never wanted to be a pop singer or an air hostess or even
the kindergarten teacher Mum had kept telling everybody she
was all set to become. She'd been gone on Keith since the
first time she'd seen him, with his gentleness and his daft
jokes and his blond Scott Walker looks. She'd never regretted
them having their little accident, it had sorted things out very
nicely. Strange to think of herself, twenty years old but such
a grown-up. Sometimes Maggie Hapgood, grandmother-to-
be, didn't seem quite as grown-up by comparison.

Maggie reached into her handbag for a tissue, moving
carefully so as not to disturb the basket on her lap. Fluffy
was lying quietly now, no longer making that rasping sound
with her breathing. Maybe she would rally. She'd survived
two guinea pigs, the rabbit and any number of fish.

Fluffy was gone almost the moment the needle touched her.
Maggie had a bit of a cry, then the vet asked, did she want the
body cremated? Maggie shook her head – Fluffy had earned
the full burial rites in the back garden. Then she remembered
the others in the waiting room, the teenager with the two
kittens, the old dear with the tabby. It didn't seem right to
walk out there with Fluffy's corpse on display. She had a
carrier in her handbag, so the vet and she put Fluffy into it,
and she wiped her eyes and paid her bill and hurried out to
the car with an empty basket and Fluffy's remains shrouded
in green Shop-Kwik plastic.

In the car she had another little cry. She remembered when

41

they'd buried the rabbit, how they'd all moped until Keith had suggested a wake. Fluffy deserved a wake too. It was a long time since they'd sat down for a family meal together, apart from Christmas – Keith liked his meat and two veg, but Nicki usually heated up a pizza and ate it in her room. Boeuf bourguignonne perhaps, or steak in brown ale. And there was that quick cake made from boudoir biscuits dipped in coffee, layered with whipped cream and mocha butter icing and decorated with flaked almonds, chocolate drops and macaroons. Not the kitchen, Maggie thought, but the dining table for a change. She'd clear away the maps of bird sanctuaries, bring out the Irish linen serviettes, polish the crystal glasses, Keith's present for their tenth anniversary, and they'd forget the telly for once, spend the evening together, the three of them, giving poor Fluffy the send-off that was her due.

Struggling over the step with her bags, Maggie tried not to see the catnip mouse in the hall, or the kitchen chair cushion with its cat-shaped furry hollow. She lowered Fluffy's plastic bag gently onto the cushion while she unpacked her shopping – there'd been some reasonably-priced Dublin Bay prawns on the Shop-Kwik fish counter, an extra treat for a starter, and she'd even picked up an inexpensive bottle of Beaujolais while she'd been hunting for brown ale. But first, of course, she had to find a resting place for poor old Fluffy. There was that space in the back bed where Keith had dug up the buddleia and not yet found the Comtesse de Tudor tree peony to replace it. She carried the empty cat basket down to the shed and fetched the spade. She couldn't help remembering the rabbit again – how they'd mustered a full turn-out for his burial. But there it was, Nicola couldn't miss school with her CSEs coming up, and Keith had the auditors in.

Maggie was down a foot and a half when the doorbell rang. Debbie Salt (the other side from Ivy Pearson) stood on the step with her little boy, Justin. Debbie would move on from Potter's Park, you could tell. Her husband worked in a design studio and commuted to London, her lounge sported sanded boards and sag bags, and she disdained maternity clothes, preferring to flaunt her bump in clinging jersey. She was staring at Maggie's blotchy face and looking, Maggie thought, put out.

'Oh,' she said, 'have I called at a bad time?'

'The cat's just passed on,' Maggie said.

'Does that mean you won't be able to have Justin for a couple of hours? Only it's my ante-natal appointment and when I last took him he acted up the whole time and was sick over one of the nurses.'

Maggie could never imagine Justin acting up. He was small for his age, smaller than any of hers at four, and he looked hunched, burdened, like a little old man worrying how to live on his pension.

'That's all right,' Maggie said, and felt Justin's tiny damp hand slide into hers.

'I'll be back around half two. Oh, and Maggie – Maggie, I don't mean to be rude, but—'

'Yes?' Maggie said.

'Last time you gave him some sweets. So bad for growing children, not to mention tooth decay. And the sort you gave him contain artificial colouring. That's really quite dangerous. They could have made him hyperactive.'

Maggie wanted to say that, in her experience, you could no more keep children from sweets than you could stop politicians making speeches. But Debbie was his mother, after all. So instead she squeezed the boy's hand and said, 'No sweets today, then?' and he nodded sadly, following her over the step.

Inside, he ran ahead of her down the hall, into the kitchen, and at once she thought of Fluffy in the Shop-Kwik bag. If it had been any other child he'd have made a bee line straight for it, but as it was Maggie managed to pounce before he reached the chair. Her hasty movement aroused his interest, however.

'Sweeties?' he said, eying the bag.

Maggie would have welcomed Justin's assistance in burying Fluffy. He would have made a sympathetic mourner. But

43

a mother who already suspected her of being a bad influence would be none too pleased to discover she'd been explaining about the happy hunting ground and the mousies in the sky. Better keep him out of the garden, too, in case he spotted the hole in the flower bed. At least he wouldn't try looking for Fluffy – Debbie had instructed him never to go near her, as animals carry germs.

Shutting the bag in the downstairs toilet, Maggie settled Justin with an orange squash, and soon he was scribbling in his colouring book while she made a start on her cake. Foolish to reckon without the squash, however. She reached the toilet before him and grabbed the bag.

The deep freeze was in the lobby at the back opposite the toilet. With the toilet door shut firmly on Justin, a thought occurred to Maggie. She supposed it wasn't very hygienic, but everything in the freezer was wrapped and the weather was warm for early May, with the odd fly buzzing. And, besides, it seemed appropriate somehow. She lifted the lid, moving several packets of frozen peas and folding the top of Fluffy's plastic bag over securely. She was in the act of lowering the bag into place when Justin hobbled out of the toilet with his trousers round his ankles. She must have jumped, or looked as shifty as she felt; he stared at the bag where it nestled amongst the ice and frozen peas.

'Sweeties!' he said accusingly.

She rescued his trousers and ushered him back to the kitchen.

The rest of his stay passed peacefully enough. He helped her decorate the cake, then they tidied the butter icing and whipped cream bowls together, dipping in with their fingers, licking the wooden spoons, 'just helping the washer-upper', as Mum used to say. By the time Debbie reappeared, Maggie had taken good care to mop him clean of all traces of helpfulness.

'Mummy,' she heard him call as he ran after Debbie, and she hoped he wasn't going to snitch. But no. 'Auntie Maggie's got a big bag of sweeties,' he announced excitedly.

'Come along, there's a good boy.'

'She hides them so they're secret.'

'Come along, Justin!'

'She hides them. Then she eats them. When you're not looking.'

And as Maggie was closing the door Debbie's voice drifted back to her. 'Well, let that be a lesson, Jus. You don't want to be a podge, do you, when you grow up?'

Maggie paused on the door mat, immobilized. She might not be the skinniest woman in Potter's Park, in fact she might well carry an extra pound here and there. But even so . . . If Debbie Salt fancied asking any more favours . . .

There were chocolate drops, just a handful, left in the wrapper. Maggie munched them down, almost without thinking. When you were forty and you'd carried three children you couldn't expect to tip the scales like an eighteen-year-old, could you? Still, give Debbie another ten years, she'd find out. Meanwhile, Maggie had better get on with the business of burying poor old Fluffy.

She had just lifted the Shop-Kwik bag out of the freezer when the door bell went again. Ivy Pearson, 'popping', as she called it. Ivy always popped on Monday afternoons, knowing that Maggie wasn't working. Not that Maggie begrudged her. Poor soul, no doubt she was lonely with Alan out and nothing to do all day except that sewing-machine embroidery from her adult education class. Anyway, she was a friend, really – the two of them worked up solidarity swapping notes on their husbands' obsessions, Keith's ticking and twitching and Alan's passion for World War tanks. And if Ivy made her feel scruffy in her T-shirt and jeans, somehow had her noticing the dust on the mantelpiece, Maggie was sure she didn't intend it.

Ivy, indeed, was immaculate, as usual, in a lilac velour track suit with mauve high heels, her hair fresh from the salon. She followed Maggie cautiously into the kitchen, shooting a glance at the patch of fur on the cushion, trying not to appear relieved when Maggie mentioned number sixteen's sad loss.

'Well, she wasn't young any more, was she, love?' She

paused, inhaling the gentle aroma of onions and brown ale that was rising from the oven. She clicked her tongue. 'Dear, oh dear, when will we ever get you out of the Dark Ages, Maggie. Just as well I popped to show you these.'

Ivy always brought an excuse for popping, an advert that might be of interest or some home decor booklet. This time, as Maggie could see from her Shop-Kwik carrier, she was back on her crusade to liberate her neighbour for the greater fulfilment of embroidery collages.

'New recipes, love. They've only just got them in. Pork with Apricots, Duck with Black Cherries, Scampi in Sauce Mornay with Mushrooms.'

For thirty-three years, Ivy had taxed her creativity, dreaming up new ideas for Alan's supper – only to watch him shovel away her creations with no further comment than the occasional grunt. Then Shop-Kwik had brought out their Miracle Menus. Now she just selected a Miracle Menu from the freezer and transferred it to the microwave. The closest she came to slaving over a hot stove was snipping open the packet.

'They've got all kinds of new lines, love. Roasted parsnips. Ready-chopped salad. There's even bacon and egg, if Keith fancies a full English breakfast.'

Maggie watched Ivy displaying her purchases. No point in arguing, better to avoid any mention of Fluffy's wake. To oblige, she picked up a packet and studied the photograph on the front. She'd noticed Miracle Menus, of course, on her trips to Shop-Kwik, you could hardly avoid the cabinets beckoning, whispering, serpent-tongued, that you'd better give in. But all the same . . . it just didn't seem right. Why was it these days a shame-faced admission, that you enjoyed cooking? And anyway, the photographs made Maggie feel uneasy, with their fancy china and origami serviettes. She was a good cook, but plain, scarcely what you'd call Cordon Blue. Supposing Keith developed a taste for gourmet eating . . . ?

'Oh . . . I don't know, Ivy,' she said.

'You've got to get your Keith better trained. I'm no women's libber, but let's face it, we've better things to do, haven't we, in this day and age?'

Ivy gathered up her exhibits, wondering whether to nip home and restore them to the deep freeze. 'Or perhaps, till I pop off, dear, I could put them in yours.'

Maggie stared at the Shop-Kwik carrier. An alarming thought struck her.

'Er, yes, Ivy – yes, of course.'

Out in the back lobby Maggie looked furtively over her shoulder. Quite apart from the fact that Ivy had scarcely been Fluffy's greatest fan, there was little doubt how she would view the present contents of Maggie's freezer, never mind how hygienically wrapped. And then there were the identical carrier bags to consider. Supposing, her pop finished, she took it into her head to retrieve her Miracle Menus while Maggie's back was turned. Working with speed, Maggie dug a space for Alan's rations the furthest end of the cabinet from Fluffy. Then she removed Fluffy's bag, shovelling frozen peas to fill the gap. But where to put her? It took Maggie a moment to gather her wits.

The cupboard by the front door for the gas and electric meters – even Ivy Pearson wouldn't snoop around in there. Putting tea things and a plate of Jaffa cakes on a tray, Maggie settled Ivy in the lounge, then rushed back, seized Fluffy and, scuttling past the lounge door on tiptoe, heaved the bag into the meter cupboard, closing it firmly with a sigh of relief.

'You look frazzled, dear,' said Ivy, on her return to the lounge.

'Just checking the casserole.'

She was rewarded with an I-told-you-so smile.

The Jaffa cakes offered consolation. Ivy, however, waved the plate away. 'Oh, my goodness! Not if I'm going to be seen in my swimsuit, ta very much.'

Maggie's second Jaffa cake turned sour on her tongue. She remembered Debbie Salt's carrying voice. She watched guiltily as Ivy, producing Hermesetas, added one to her tea, whereas Maggie had sweetened hers with her usual two sugars.

'Oh yes, Alan's finally agreed on Florida. Of course he'd really prefer the Bovington Tank Museum—'

Maggie stared at her, hardly listening. Though Ivy was fond of maintaining they were neither of them spring chickens, she was, in truth, further from springtime than Maggie by a good fifteen years. Yet here she was, not giving up, watching the sugar. And yes, Maggie was obliged to admit she looked enviably trim. Maggie felt enormous beside her suddenly, felt the denim of her jeans straining as though her thighs were swelling as she watched.

Ivy was still extolling Florida. Keith and Maggie weren't having a holiday this year, on account of the new kitchen like Ivy's. Not that it would ever look quite like Ivy's, Maggie reflected – those vistas of sterile chrome and surgically-scrubbed formica, with never a stray crumb or a tea-bag stain. It gave you a reverential feeling, Ivy Pearson's kitchen, like a temple. Still, it wouldn't make much mess, would it, opening packets?

Ivy was reaching the end of her pop at last, putting aside her cup. Maggie said quickly that she would fetch Ivy's bag from the freezer. She had just set foot in the hall when the door went again. A balding man stood on the step, holding out an ID card.

'Electric,' he said gloomily. 'Read the meter.'

Her face must have been a picture. But as he wiped his feet she recovered herself and snatched Fluffy's bag from the cupboard. Ivy appeared from the lounge, and Maggie hastily dumped the bag beside the telephone table. They said their goodbyes and Ivy went out, down the front path, as Maggie thanked the electric man. And it was only then Maggie noticed the empty space beside the telephone table.

She sat in the kitchen distractedly eating Jaffa cakes – who cared about Debbie Salt. It had taken three cups of tea to soothe Ivy. Even after her palpitations had subsided she had continued to swat her lilac velour as if it were infested. Maggie dreaded to imagine what the electric man had thought, let alone the two girls on bicycles who had wobbled to a halt at her ear-splitting scream, or the old dear opposite, twitching her nets to get a better view of the drama. By the time she had gone Maggie was well behind, with the vegetables still to prepare and the dining table not touched.

Through rigor mortis or her spell in the deep freeze, Fluffy had stiffened considerably. Maggie lowered her into the grave, plastic bag and all, collecting up her catnip mouse and her bowl and her ping pong ball from the lounge, piling them into the bag too as an afterthought, burying her with her possessions like an ancient Egyptian. Yet even this small ceremony did not console Maggie. She felt ashamed of herself, as if, with the indignity of Fluffy's passing, she'd let them all down – not just the poor dead cat, but Keith and Nicki.

Nicola was late. It was ten to six when Maggie heard her key – no doubt she'd been round at Kimberly's, she seemed to live there these days. She was already thundering up the stairs as Maggie reached the hall.

'Nicki, dear.'

Nicola halted in mid-stride like a football player caught by the pause button on the video. She looked pale, Maggie thought.

'Nicki dear, I'm afraid poor Fluffy's gone.'

'Not now, Mum!' she hissed. Then the video clicked back to 'play' and she pounded on upwards, shaking the landing as she slammed her bedroom door.

There was no point in running after her. Maggie had evolved, from memories of her own childhood, a set of personal rules, one of which banned the use of such phrases as 'Listen to me when I'm talking', and 'I suppose you think this house is a hotel . . .' Anyway, ten more minutes and Keith was due home.

Talking, Maggie reflected, was like smoking or biting your nails. Once you'd decided it was undesirable, you couldn't take it up again for special occasions, you were too conscious of where it might lead. So she shouldn't have been surprised when Keith, arriving as grim-faced as Nicola, made no pause to enquire about Fluffy before rushing off to change. The most she could glean was that Polar Foods was restructuring again – more work, presumably, for all of them in Finance.

She retreated to the kitchen. Nicki remained deaf to the invitation downstairs – perhaps family meals were yet another habit they had put behind them. When Keith reappeared, settling automatically at the kitchen table, unaware of the empty cushion or of anything, it seemed, but the evening paper, she did not explain or redirect him. What was the point? She simply laid up a place around him and thrust the Dublin Bay prawns into it.

Yet, as she set about clearing the dining table, as she slammed plates together, jammed wedding present silver back into its canteen, she began to feel increasingly aggrieved. Well, if he couldn't be bothered to ask about Fluffy, she couldn't be bothered to tell him. Nevertheless, when she returned to empty prawn shells and silence, she could stand it no longer.

'Do you notice anything different?' she said.

He glanced up from the paper. 'We don't usually run to starters on a Monday.'

She lifted out the casserole, hurling the oven door shut with a crash. 'I mean something – *somebody* – missing.'

Glancing round, he spotted the forlorn cushion at last. He had, she would grant it to him, the grace to look ashamed. 'Oh Mags. The all-staff meeting put it clean out of my mind. Still, we mustn't be too upset. She'd come to the end of a long and happy life, hadn't she?'

'Had she?' Maggie said.

'Look on the positive side. We might get a robin now. And we could set up a bird table without worrying.'

She dolloped vegetables onto his plate. 'Fluffy wasn't a danger to birds. Fluffy couldn't have caught a bird if it had dropped dead out of the sky into her jaws.'

But he didn't seem disposed to discuss it. Instead, as he demolished the stew and his portion of cake, he became pre-occupied again, frowning occasionally between mouthfuls. (Whatever was worrying him, it couldn't be said to be putting him off his food.) At last, he scraped back his chair.

'Well up to your usual standard, Mags. I must say, you

50

always do us proud. But – you know, with money the way it is – we might have to be satisfied with egg and chips a bit more often in the future.'

Maggie was standing at the sink with the washing-up cloth in her hand. Orange liver spots darted before her eyes, she felt her arm go up to hurl the cloth, imagined a satisfying splatter of mashed potato and greasy water. But her heart went out of it. She let him take the cloth and replace her at the sink, and soon, while she was stowing left-overs in the fridge, she heard him drift off to the lounge. In five minutes she would find him snoring, Duke Ellington in his earphones, *The Dictionary of Birds in Colour* clutched to his chest.

Maggie switched on the telly. There was a game show, followed by a soap. It had seemed a shame to see so much cake going begging. She cut herself a slice, consuming it without hunger, yet feeling consolation in its sweetness. She cut a second slice, folded herself into her chair, allowed the mingled sounds of snoring and television to recede to a soothing drone. She had reached her fourth slice when it ocurred to her something was wrong with this peaceful domestic scene. That's just what it was, too peaceful. Though Nicki was upstairs, the house did not vibrate with the thump-boom-thud of George Michael or Madonna.

Maggie glanced at the cake guiltily. She'd better save some for Nicki, perhaps she could even tempt her out if she took it to her in her room. Fetching a plate, Maggie tiptoed to the landing. She seemed to hear a faint snuffling. She put her ear to Nicki's door and the snuffling grew louder. Poor Nicola, Maggie should have known she'd be upset really – she was a soft-hearted girl, underneath.

Maggie knocked gently. There was a gurgle, a sniff. Then silence. She knocked again.

'Go away, Mum. I'm busy.'

'Don't be silly, love. Let me come in.'

The door was not locked. Maggie opened it, bracing herself against the sight she would meet. Clothes strewn everywhere, of course, dirty pizza dishes on the dressing table. A sea of

51

shoes, cassettes, exercise books, lipsticks and Diet Coke cans stretching across the floor to the window, covering the carpet so you could scarcely see the nail varnish stains (Maggie supposed that was a mercy). Sellotape scars on the wallpaper where Kylie Minogue and Jason Donovan had given way to Tom Cruise and Bruce Willis. A whiff of hair spray and talcum and something Maggie tried to convince herself wasn't mould. Still, Nicki must see for herself how this pigsty scarcely fitted with her new sophisticated image. Maggie tried not to nag or worry about germs, she just tiptoed in once a week and collected the washing, depositing clean things in a pile on the chair. She thought she could see this week's pile now, where she'd left it, beneath a tangle of T-shirts and tights. Nicki herself was sprawled on the duvet amongst a scatter of soggy tissues. Though she had changed out of her uniform she was, Maggie noticed, wearing a long-sleeved polo-necked jumper, as if, despite the airless room, she were cold.

'Mum, I said leave me *alone!*'

Her Nicola, such a pretty little thing, with that heart-shaped face and fine, shiny, brown hair. It cut Maggie to the quick to see her this way, eyes and lips all bruised and swollen, nose like a three-year-old's needing a good blow.

'Nicki, love, it's ever so sad, but it's not the end of the world.'

'How can you say that, Mum? How can you even know?'

'But I do know, Nick, of course I do. I was there.'

Nicki blinked. 'What are you on about, Mum?'

'It was just like going to sleep. She didn't suffer any pain.'

Nicki grabbed a ball of tissues and hurled it at the wall. 'For pity's sake, Mum! Is that what you barged in here for – to go on and on about Fluffy? Look, she was senile, she stank the place out, she should have been put down years ago.'

Maggie took a step backwards, crunching a coke can with her heel. Remember, Maggie, you were once sixteen too. 'Love, I brought you some cake.'

The sight of the cake seemed to provoke a fresh crisis. Nicki pounded the duvet with her fist.

'Well . . . if it's not Fluffy . . . Nick, love, what's happened? Is it something at school?'

'It's nothing.'

'Is it the exams?'

'Like I said, it's nothing.'

'Or a boy, then?'

'Mum, how many times do I have to tell you the only boys I meet are pimply wallies in smelly trainers whose idea of a cool night out is necking up the shopping precinct with a six-pack of Fosters.'

She flung herself on the duvet. Moving a pile of CDs and a battered Snoopy, Maggie sat down to stroke her hair.

'Anyway,' Nicki sobbed, 'what does it matter? No boy's ever going to look at me.'

'Nick, don't be so silly. You're beautiful.'

'You would say that, wouldn't you? You're my mother. Now just leave it out, go away.'

Maggie sat helplessly listening to her sobs. Amongst the rubbish on the floor, she noticed a heap of clothes that seemed more deliberate than the rest. On the top lay Nicki's favourite party get-up, a silver lurex camisole they'd found in C&A's sale. Or what was left of it – when Maggie picked it up she found her eyes had not deceived her, it had been snipped to rags. She went through the rest of the pile. Everything – the sleeveless white cotton jumper, the T-vests, the little black satin dress from Top Shop that Keith said looked like a slip – all of it had been scissored to shreds.

She gathered up the tatters of lurex. 'Nicki, how could you do this?'

No reply.

'Nicola! Why have you ruined your nice silver top?'

'Because I'm never ever going to wear it again!'

'For goodness sake! Why not?'

'Because I've got fat arms, that's why.'

'Oh Nick, of course you haven't.'

'I have, I have. Horrible and fat and disgusting.'

'Who says?'

'Kimberly says. And she's right.' Tearing at the sleeve of

53

her jersey, rolling it up as far as it would go, she seized the skin on the underside of her arm and pinched it savagely till it made a fold. 'Look, yukky revolting flab. Disgusting inches of it. I can never wear anything sleeveless, ever again.'

'Kimberly's an ignorant little cow. You've got lovely arms. What on earth does precious Kimberly know?'

She had squeezed the fold of skin till her nails made purple marks. 'Kimberly's arms are normal. Kimberly's arms don't do this.'

'If you think it's normal to look like a stick insect . . . Your arms are rounded and feminine. It's the way you're built.'

'Yes, it is, isn't it? The way I'm built. And whose fault, Mum, is that?'

Maggie stared at her.

Nicki yanked down the sleeve of her jersey till it hid her arm to the wrist. 'Kimberly says my heredity's against me. Kimberly says I'm going to have to be really, really careful. Otherwise it won't only be my arms. When I'm twenty, I'll run to fat just like you.'

Maggie sat quietly on the landing, clutching the plate of cake. Nicki didn't mean to be cruel, it was only that she was unhappy. Maggie considered this for a while, and when she noticed the plate again it was empty. She went slowly downstairs.

Back in the lounge, Keith was still snoring, his head-phones askew. On the telly an old horror film had started, vampires by the sound of it. Maggie tried to pay attention, but as Dracula bared his fangs all she could see was his victim: how slim she looked in that diaphanous nightie. She switched channels, but everywhere it was the same; a beanpole actress holding a gun on two gangsters, skinny women in adverts talking about washing powder or banking facilities – even the weather forecast lady was not so much demonstrating troughs and depressions as showing off her thirty-four-inch hips. Maggie groped miserably for more cake, then snatched her hand back. But anyway, she'd eaten most of it, hadn't she?

She switched off the telly and began the usual chore of puffing up the cushions and setting the lounge to rights. The silence woke Keith, as per usual. He sat up, yawning, and asked, as he usually asked, 'Getting late, is it?' And she was going to reply, as she usually did, 'Yes, time for bed.' But somehow the words did not come, somehow what came out was a strangled howl.

'I'm sorry,' she mumbled, as, still clutching the cushion, she sank to her knees.

She heard Keith get up, and she didn't know what she'd expected, but suddenly there he was kneeling beside her, trying to prise the cushion from her grasp, suddenly he was winding his arms around her shoulders. 'Mags. Mags, love. It's Fluffy, isn't it? I'm sorry I was rotten earlier.'

'Oh Keith,' she sobbed, 'am I f-f-fat?'

'I know you'll miss her – I mean, we all will, of course, but it'll be you that misses her most.'

'I'm fat. I'm fat and horrible, aren't I?'

'And I should have realized, about the meal. That you'd splashed out a bit to cheer us up.'

'Stuff the meal! If I didn't like cooking I wouldn't be so fat and repulsive.'

'Don't be daft, love. What's brought this on, eh?'

She knew if she told him about Nicola it would only make him angry. So instead she just sobbed into his shoulder, making his shirt collar damp.

'Come on, Mags, tell us. Tell your Pooh-bear what's up.'

It was as though he were suddenly the old Keith again, which made her cry the harder. Besides, she felt stupid, not knowing what to say. She could no more tell him about Debbie Salt than about Nicola – neighbours had to be neighbours, it would only remind him they'd borrowed his hedge trimmer and never given it back. In the end she related the events of Fluffy's burial. And of course when she got to Ivy Pearson's nasty surprise he couldn't help laughing, and she was hiccuping and laughing too. And suddenly it felt like the old days, and she was pleased they could still remember how to laugh, even though they'd become so out of practice.

'Poor Ivy,' he said, wiping his eyes. 'It's probably the most exciting thing that's happened to the old bat for weeks. I bet you Alan never hears the end of it. He'll have to fork out for another five star holiday just to keep her quiet.'

'Or a lounge extension.'

'Or a sauna and jacuzzi.' He pulled her to him and gave her a squeeze. 'Look, Mags, forget what I said about the bird table. We could always get a kitten if you like. One without personality problems and chronic fleas.'

'You can't replace Fluffy as if she was a washing-machine or a clapped-out lawn mower.'

'Oh well – maybe not. But I don't like to see my girl upsetting herself. Oh – and what's all this about you being fat?'

He was smiling at her, she was smiling back. She didn't want to break the spell. 'Nothing,' she said.

If it were not a spell that had been cast as they knelt together on the lounge shag pile, it was certainly something, a tiny thaw in the general frost. Mind you, it had happened before, only for sub-zero temperatures to set in again shortly after. But all the same, Keith came to bed without his bird book.

'Come on, Mags,' he said, putting out the light and worming his arm around her under the duvet, 'give us a cuddle.'

She moved towards him, stiffly at first, being out of practice at that too. But soon she was wedged in the crook of his arm with her head on his chest, feeling his warmth through the pyjama jacket, hearing his heart beat.

'You're not fat, Mags. Anyway, who fancies skinny women? You're nice and comfortable.'

'Sounds like an old settee.'

'Well, curvaceous, then. Womanly. You're my girl, Mags. You're just the way I like you.'

He gave her a peck on the forehead and she gave his ribs a little squeeze, not knowing quite what to say. She knew what she wanted to do, though, as they lay there in silence. She wanted to tear aside the pyjama jacket and bury her face in his skin, she wanted to tongue it and kiss it and run her hands down the length of his body, touch his thighs, feel the curve of his buttocks and the muscles at the base of his spine, she wanted it to be as if that afternoon had never happened, as if they'd never thrown a barbecue for Mum's seventieth, never been there, missed that day out of their calendar completely. But she couldn't do it all by herself. Not after such a while. He'd have to make the first move. And he wanted to, didn't he? Wasn't he lying there like she was, breathing shallowly in the silence, wasn't he waiting, waiting for the right moment?

She waited too.

Then his voice came. 'Mags?'

'Yes, Keith?'

'Mags, love—'

Despite herself, she stiffened.

'Mags – did you say you buried Fluffy in that plastic bag?'

She rose on one elbow. 'You what?' she said.

'Only they're not biodegradable, plastic bags. They don't decompose.'

'You *what*?'

'It's just that – well, it could cause problems. If I choose the wrong place to dig in a couple of months' time . . .'

She struggled into a sitting position. 'Keith Hapgood, it took me all day to bury that cat. I buried her by myself, in circumstances that were, to put it mildly, difficult. I admit I did this without the benefit of your expert advice. But then, you weren't around, were you? So what are you suggesting now, may I ask? An exhumation? That having spent today burying her I spend tomorrow digging her up—'

'Shush, Mags. Keep your perm on. All I was saying was—'

'Yes?'

'Well, maybe we could put a marker on the spot or something. Anyway, there's no point in upsetting yourself all over again, you did your best. Let's get some sleep.'

He rolled over onto his side of the bed and pretty soon she could hear him snoring. She lay on her back, listening to the tick-click of the Teasmade, wanting to scream.

She thought of Fluffy, lying in the earth on the site of the Comtesse de Tudor tree peony, undead in her plastic bag. Twenty years of family life, of Sunday dinners and shared jokes and cosy evenings, of joyfully planned treats for Christmas and birthdays – a life she thought she'd helped make, her life. But now it was gone, and who even missed it? Brian had Stephanie, Neil spent his holidays on a kibbutz or campaigning for Greenpeace, Nicola preferred Kimberly and as for Keith . . . But who was to blame? You couldn't hold back change, it was like carrying water in a basket. Maggie was the one who wouldn't see, who clung on, refusing to accept that what she treasured was superannuated. Maggie was the one who couldn't even manage to give it a decent burial. She was like poor Fluffy, a thing of the past, last season's line, in need of replacement with a younger model. She was a middle-aged failure. And the proof was – she was fat.

IV

Fat people depressed Fizz. It wasn't just that she agreed with Wallis Simpson that you couldn't be too rich or too thin. It wasn't just the aesthetic affront. It was the sheer weakness of character. Sometimes, sitting through five hour meetings while Genghis' underlings discussed the psychodynamics of adipose tissue, she wanted to throw aside her papers and scream. Why couldn't these women pull themselves together? What price their shame and their endless self-justification? Why couldn't the just stop guzzling chocolate?

After all, no one could force you to eat. Her house-mistress, Miss Truelove, had taught her that. Inaptly named Miss Truelove with her hairy lip and her lisle stockings and the baggy old-maid's bloomers she displayed, legs astraddle in her scratchy Harris tweed. 'Eat your tapioca, Felicity, or you'll be kept in until you do.' 'Eat your tapioca, Felicity, or it'll be served to you instead of supper.' 'Eat your tapioca or you'll go to bed early, lose your sweet ration, forfeit your weekend privileges, be sent to sit in the dark untangling parcel string.'

Fizz could still see that tapioca, glutinous and greyish-white in its thick, grey-white plate. She could smell the sour oil-cloth on the table and the sweaty cabbage reek from the kitchen, hear the other girls giggling in the garden, feel the smooth globes of the frogspawn on her tongue, slithery smooth like tiny detached eyeballs. Breakfast, dinner and supper Miss Truelove had presented her with that tapioca, but she wouldn't eat it. For two days she drank water and battled with her hunger. But she didn't eat. Oh, Caroline Judd might sneer at her parents' second-hand Vauxhall, Ffiona Bingham-Walter might mock the last traces of her South London accent, Araminta Pope might write 'ugh' next to her name in all her books but she had one over them now, a power they lacked, a strength that could not be broken. So what if her body-checking were deficient and her back-hand non-existent? She could wear skinny ribs and hipsters, she could turn the pages of Vogue without flinching.

What had happened to them, she wondered, Caroline, Ffiona, Minty, with their au pairs and their Harrods-account Mummies and their Daddies who rode at point-to-points? 'You want to be careful, Felicity. Mummy says girls with narrow hips have frightful problems having babies.' Where were they now with their child-bearing hips? Blaming their glands and metabolisms, no doubt, wondering why their husbands were always kept late at the office, moaning about lack of fulfilment and empty nests. Anyone could let themselves go, anyone could be a loser. She'd worked hard since that plate of tapioca transforming Felicity Dummer into Fizz St Clair. She hadn't needed a man to authenticate her or squalling children to justify her existence; she'd got where she was by sheer will power, by being clever and tough and looking like a winner. And yes, for win read thin.

Sometimes she dreamed of going back on Old Girls' Day, seeing their faces as she drove up in the Porsche, watching them wilt in their frumpy Jaeger and their support tights as they wondered how she'd done it – how weedy-wet Dummy, whose knickers they'd dangled from the fire escape after lights-out, was the one who had ended up having it all. But then – school reunions were scarcely Fizz's style.

Still, she was obliged to admit she could find Pandora testing – subduing her natural inclination towards the world's beautiful people, sifting through the research reports as she struggled for empathy with the overweight housewife, knowing it was lowest common denominator time yet again. But she was a professional, she wasn't paid to be subjective. They weren't there to judge – Genghis, Stretch, Spike, her-self – they didn't create attitudes, they simply reflected them. If punters wanted to gorge themselves on calorie-crammed Devils Delight they gave it to them; and if a little self-mortification were in order, in the shape of Pandora, well, they provided that too. Fizz couldn't afford Spike's pseudo-intellectual agonizing. If Pandora took off she'd be a hotter contender than Dick Saunders Blair for Deputy Managing Director, should Stretch decide to establish his succession, which inevitably he must.

Fizz's prospects of elevation were looking healthier by the moment, now she had dragooned Spike to the cause. Despite his literary pretensions (or perhaps because of them) he possessed an unerring instinct when it came to banality, an almost uncanny certainty of touch. They had acquired a celebrity interviewer, one Tel Travers (catchphrase: You Can Tell Tel), who had been let go from the TV game show he had hosted and was therefore available on terms even Granny Garfunkel's paymasters would agree. They had acquired a production company, Slik Piks, whose director, Coleby Whiteside, though currently specializing in soap powder commercials, had once, it was rumoured, worked as clapper loader on a John Huston picture. And, despite a debate occasioned by the strict moral code appropriate to Granny Garfunkel as a wholesome family-image company, they had acquired a script and a campaign line: 'With Granny Garfunkel Slimmers Supreme as part of your calorie-controlled diet NOW YOU CAN SIN *AND* SLIM.' (It was eventually agreed after three days of closely-argued conversation that the use of the word 'sin', being figurative rather than theological, was permissible as long as the voice-over artist was directed to pronounce the monosyllable so as to indicate charm and wit rather than a biblical injunction.) A shoot date had been fixed for the beginning of May, a Shop-Kwik supermarket had been persuaded into co-operation, and Genghis' underlings had finally been prevailed upon to sign the production quote.

In fact, adjourning with Spike to the agency's local Tapas bar for a debrief after the preproduction meeting, Fizz was definitely buoyant. As she sipped a Kir Royale, she considered the benefits likely to accrue to a newly appointed Deputy MD. A weekend cottage in Provence, perhaps, not too far from Stretch's. A further donation to the fund she had prudently set aside for the inevitable face lift She would need a bigger office, of course, but that could be achieved with the minimum of disruption by requisitioning The Donkey's workspace and knocking it into her own. Yes, on the whole she should be grateful to the chocaholic housewife, whose failures ensured her success.

Spike, hunched over his third large La Ina, did not seem to share her light-heartedness. 'Gosh,' he kept muttering, clutching his forehead. 'Golly bloody gosh.'

'Come, come, my dear. It was a tour de force.'

He raised his bloodhound eyes dolefully. 'Other copywriters get locations in Venice or Rio de Janeiro. I get the Shop-Kwik supermarket in Potter's Park.'

'Well, don't blame me, Spike darling. You wrote the script.'

This seemed to provoke a further paroxysm.

'Cheer up. At least it's not north of Watford.'

'It's not listed in the Good Food Guide. I've looked.'

'Of course not, Spike. It's in that hinterland around Heathrow airport. Monkey puzzle trees and pampas grass sandwiched between motorways and shopping precincts. Don't get drunk there – you won't be able to tell if you've come to in Staines or Chertsey.'

'I didn't expect a Michelin entry. But it doesn't even feature in the AA Hotel Guide.'

'Spike, it's where the punters live. Real people.'

'I suppose I'd better pack extra chalk pills. And a bottle of Collis Browne.'

'Think positive, Spike darling. Don't forget we're in this together. I promised Genghis I'd personally supervise this shoot. I'll be with you on location, at your side every step of the way.'

Although this prospect must have cheered him, he continued to stare into his empty La Ina schooner Finally, sighing deeply, he consulted his watch.

Suddenly she understood what was troubling him. 'Yes, I will have one more eentsy Kir Royale – since we're celebrating.'

'Well, I—'

Embarrassed, poor lamb. Trying to find a way to ask her to

dinner, but worried about losing face when, as was inevitable, she turned him down. Still, she was enjoying the champagne and she didn't, come to think of it, have anything much on this evening. Maybe just this once, just for fun . . . She manoeuvred herself on her bar stool, adjusting her skirt and crossing her legs to display their tan. She smiled. 'I suppose you're off to review yet another fashionable eaterie tonight?'

'Got to rush home, as it happens.'

Really, the male ego was such a sensitive plant.

'Need to knock out five hundred words on a Mexican.'

'Refried beans?'

'Magical Realism. Due yesterday, as a matter of fact.'

She supposed her being a board director was a little frightening – there was so much more at stake when a woman was high-powered. 'How absolutely fascinating, but ohmigod, I'm late already, I promised I'd be home to take a call from my toy – well, from a friend.'

'Oh, right.'

'So much as I'd like to talk about literature into the small hours, Spike darling, I'm afraid I must decline.'

'Oh. Right.'

Fizz extended her credit card into the awkward silence. Poor Spike. But really, if he wanted to add her notch to his bedpost he'd have to try more finesse.

That Tuesday morning Maggie didn't bother to change out of her housecoat after she'd made Keith and Nicola breakfast. She phoned Mr Gupta at Magipost and told him she had a migraine. Then, going upstairs, bracing herself, she stood before the mirrored doors of the fitted wardrobe, stripped off the housecoat and examined her naked body.

Until now, she'd supposed that a bit of slippage over the years was only natural. It was like pouring glacé icing over a fruit cake – everything tended to slide downwards and settle at the bottom. So when you couldn't squeeze into that outfit you bought for your sister's first wedding, when your jeans seemed to shrink more than usual in the wash and you were forced to admit your bikini days were definitely over – well, you might give up ice cream for a week or two, or cut out potatoes, but in the end it was gravity, wasn't it, no point in fighting it? You bought skirts with elasticated waists and comfy, baggy jerseys and after a while – you'd a busy life to lead, why waste time looking in mirrors? But she was looking now, wasn't she? Oh yes, she was looking now.

Comfortable, Keith had said. Curvaceous, womanly. But men entertained funny ideas about these things. And anyway he'd doubtless stopped looking too, long before she had. It wasn't even as if she ate very much – not like Keith, who was a vacuum cleaner, hoovering up everything on his plate. (Mind you, Keith was a touch chubbier than Scott Walker now, not that it mattered – in this unfair world it wouldn't have mattered, would it, if he'd been the size of a Sumo wrestler, him being a man, of course.) But Maggie – his other half? Curvaceous? Womanly? As she gritted her teeth and studied the mirror what she saw reminded her of strawberry blancmange, tipped out of the mould before it had properly set.

Dressing hastily, she returned to the kitchen. Over forty and fabulous? Had she thought, poring over photos of Jane Fonda and Cher, that she could halt her own disintegration by osmosis? Though, mind you, it was easy for them, with millions in the bank and the plastic surgeon's scalpel at their command. They could order up new breasts or buttocks just as you might go to Curry's for a dishwasher. Maggie sighed, and despair, with a pain like hunger, took shape, forming itself seductively into a chocolate digestive biscuit.

Yet didn't they work for it too, Jane Fonda and the like, sweating in gyms, torturing their bodies into shape? Effort was required, not feeble excuses. Maggie remembered spotting in the rubbish tip that was Nicki's bedroom a small red book, 'Your Pocket Calorie Counter'.

Although only a little book, it made depressing reading. 'Chocolate digestive: 1, 65 calories, Jaffa cake: 1, 50 calories.' Maggie sent the biscuit tin into eternal banishment but the book continued, without pity. 'Chocolate drops: 1 packet, 585 calories, whipped cream: 1oz, 105 calories, butter: 1oz, 220 calories, icing sugar: 110 calories . . .'

Maggie couldn't say why, but the longer it grew, this litany of her misdemeanours, the more insistently hunger pains plagued her. The biscuit vision reappeared, stealthily at first, as if craftily materializing from a different direction, then taking on a sudden intolerable clarity, the perfect circle of the perfect chocolate digestive. She could see every ridge and whorl in the sheen of its chocolate coating, smell it, feel it crumbling on her tongue.

Eight stone eleven, the book claimed, was her ideal weight as a five-foot-five woman. But when had she ever weighed that? She'd always been what Mum called 'well-covered', more Conference pear than Twiglet. Perhaps she should climb on the bathroom scales – but didn't she recall that they'd recently gone missing? She certainly wasn't up to a hunt. The biscuit still danced before her, sometimes flaunting itself, sometimes beckoning from the periphery of her vision. It seemed, like a will o' the wisp, to be luring her, drawing her towards the food cupboard.

To escape, she went out to the garden and, fetching green wire from the shed, made a cross out of bamboo stakes to mark Fluffy's grave. But the biscuit came too, subtly insinuating itself, filling her mind with its essence. The sound of the telephone brought her round with a gasp, as if she had narrowly escaped possession.

'They said at your work you were having a day off.'

'Mum, it's not a day off, I'm—'

'I waited in yesterday for you, Margaret.'

'But, Mum—'

'I thought if my little bit of shopping was too much for you you might at least phone.'

'But, Mum, you said you'd be out. You said that nice Mrs O'Brien was taking you to the shops.'

'Of course I realize nobody has time for the elderly these days. Still, I thought you might have been worried in case I'd had a fall.'

'But you haven't had a fall, have you, Mum? You're all right, aren't you?'

'Of course I'm not all right, Peggy. Why else would

I be bothering you? Would you be all right if you'd had burglars?'

'Burglars? Oh, Mum, I'm sorry. Have you called the police?'

'The police don't want to be bothered with pensioners. That's why I'm calling you, Peg. Even if it doesn't count for much nowadays, there's such a thing as your own flesh and blood.'

'What have you lost? Did they take the TV?'

'No, dear, they didn't.'

'Well, what did they take?'

'My dentures, Peg.'

Maggie sighed. 'Oh, Mum!'

'They took both plates, top and bottom. They were in the beaker in the bathroom—'

'Mum, you've been hiding them again. Have you looked in the airing cupboard?'

'I never touched them, Peg.'

'Or the fridge? Or the cake tin?'

'I never touched them all night. So it stands to reason—'

'Yes, Mum, of course it does. Burglars probably get really sick of pinching the same old tellies and diamond tiaras. They probably crept out in the small hours saying to themselves, stuff this for a lark, let's go round to Rene Cribbens at Flat 43, make a few headlines, hit the big time . . .'

'A heavy silence fell on the other end of the line. 'So that's your attitude, is it, Margaret?'

'Mum, I—'

'In that case, if my own daughter won't show any interest, perhaps I had better ring the police.'

Maggie found the dentures, at last, carefully wrapped in a kitchen towel and crammed into the powder compartment of the washing machine.

'Well, don't ask me,' Mum said. 'Search me how they got there.'

'Must have been the fairies,' Maggie said.

'Or a Leprechaun—' Mum muttered sourly.

The Leprechaun – poor Mrs O'Brien. She was not so much a home help, more a sainted martyr. On the kitchen shelves Maggie found evidence that the Leprechaun had indeed been at work – a new jar of instant, tinned fruit, corned beef, fresh supplies of Ajax and washing-liquid.

'So Mrs O'Brien did take you to the shops yesterday, like she promised?'

'I had to do something when my own daughter had forgotten me. I couldn't just sit here all day, a prisoner to my legs.'

Maggie busied herself straightening the antimacassars and tidying the copies of *Sporting Life*. 'I'm sorry, Mum. We had a bit of a tragedy yesterday, poor Fluffy—'

'Yes, the doctor says they are very puffy.'

Mum's deafness was strategic at the best of times – whisper a juicy piece of gossip, start any conversation from which she felt excluded, and suddenly she was equipped with sonic radar like a bat. Maggie abandoned the subject. After a while, however, it occurred to her that there was an odd feeling to the silence, as if she'd missed something, failed some elementary test.

'Well,' Rene said eventually, 'I suppose I'm lucky to have one daughter who doesn't forget her poor old Mum.'

A preening smile had spread across her soft pink cheeks. So here was the true reason Maggie had been summoned over.

'Joy's written at last, has she?'

This was Mum's cue to produce the air mail envelope from behind the settee cushion. 'All the way from California. She's settled in nicely in her ranch-style bungalow, she says. And she's even sent colour snaps of her and Duane.'

Maggie had long since conceded the Perfect Daughter Contest to her sister Joy. From their teens, while Maggie might rate a 'sweet' or even a grudging 'pretty', Joy had been glamorous, what people called striking. While Maggie had settled for motherhood at eighteen, Joy was an achiever – make-up artist, dancer, air hostess, fashion designer, tour operator, real estate, public relations. While Maggie stayed at home in Potter's Park, Joy had moved all over the world, New Zealand, Australia, Spain, Israel, Canada, America, picking up and discarding three husbands and any number of devoted boyfriends along the way. Joy had only to look at something she wanted and it was hers for the taking. (Oh, yes, Maggie could certainly vouch for that.) But then Joy was climbing elegantly out of Martin Brewer's Lotus Elan when Maggie was just a wallflower in one of her let-out cast-offs. Joy was the Virgin Mary in the school nativity play when Maggie was a sheep. Even when they were tiny babies Mum and Dad must have noticed the difference. When Joy was born they saw what they'd got all right – they must have thumbed their way through the books searching for the name to fit their little miracle. But when they looked at their second daughter, two years later, they'd known it wasn't worth the bother. Mags, Peg, Peggy, Maggie – whatever you did with it, it was hardly a glamorous name, was it? Right from the start, she was bound to be a let-down, a real common-or-garden Margaret.

'Don't you want to know what your sister has to say for herself?'

Beneath the *Sporting Lifes* on the hearth rug lurked a brown stain – Guinness, probably. 'How's her boutique going?' Maggie said, on her way to the kitchenette for a cloth.

'Oh, she gave that up – some trouble with a lease, she says. She's in the costume jewellery business now.'

'That's nice.'

'And she says Duane's adorable, treats her like a princess. She's so glad she's found Mr Wonderful at last.'

'Ah well, fourth time lucky.'

'And the ranch has all mod cons, including – what's this say? – a hot tub? And listen, Peg, wait till you hear this bit!'

Maggie applied herself with vigour to the rug.

Mommy, I'm so sad to hear you are still suffering with your same old trouble and that you must put on a brave face, what with the British Health Service and the waiting lists. Oh Mommy, we have such wonderful medicare out here in LA, I am sure if we would just fly you out here you would be cured in no time. Duane and myself will pay for your treatment of course and your air fares and you could make a real holiday of it, it would be so wonderful to see you. When I have the jewellery franchise up and running and we have fixed up the guest room let's make a date for your visit, let's make it real soon . . .

'That's nice,' Maggie said.
'Don't overdo the enthusiasm, will you.'
'I said, that's nice.'
'Your sister Joy is offering me a trip to California, all expenses paid, and the only thing you can say is, that's nice?'
'I wouldn't be in a hurry to cancel your next out-patients' appointment.'
'And what, may I ask, do you mean by that?'
'Remember when you had your bags packed for Australia? I just don't want you to be disappointed.'
Mum sniffed. 'Your sister has never been a disappointment to me. You're jealous, that's all.'
Chivving the settee cushions, Maggie glimpsed the photos in Mum's lap, the white Spanish-style bungalow, Duane rugged and tanned, and Joy beside him with her blond film-star mane and her sparkling teeth, Joy, in her clinging top and matador pants, brown and lithe and youthful. Joy wouldn't let herself go in middle age, no fear of that.
'Jealous? Oh, don't be so silly, Mum.'
'Of course you are. You always have been, ever since you two were girls. Ever since your Keith was smitten with Joy first and only married you on the rebound.'
Maggie, pummelling a cushion, remembered what she had promised herself earlier. Since she would end up dropping into Shop-Kwik for Mum, she would shop for herself too. She would buy lettuce and cottage cheese and begin her diet at once.
'Honestly, Mum, don't be soppy,' she said.

V

Some places, it seemed to Fizz, were purpose-built for grey English weather. You could no more imagine Mediterranean sun scorching the flat, blank concrete of the Potter's Park Shop-Kwik than you could see the dusty macadam of its car park transfigured by a crisp blanket of snow. Beneath an appropriately overcast sky half-heartedly threatening drizzle, a clump of cankered weeds struggled for life where forecourt wall met tarmac; a scurf of paper bags and sweet wrappers stirred listlessly between the parked Datsuns and Cortinas; here and there wire trolleys stood, splay-wheeled, forlorn, like disillusioned visitors from another planet.

They had been here since six this morning, concealing the camera, making sure the sound system worked, checking that their hung-over celebrity had some recollection of his lines. By eight, when the supermarket doors had opened, the camera crew had been installed behind a wall of cat-food cans directly overlooking the baited gateaux cabinet. There, in the butts, they waited for the early birds to flutter down the aisles, while production assistants with two-way radios, strategically positioned like beaters, stood ready to alert Tel Travers to home in on his prey. Tel's task was in theory simple: wired for outgoing sound via a small mike on his lapel, and with an incoming wire from the director via a prompt mike in his right ear, he had only to advance on any stray pigeon winged by the gateaux cabinet and manoeuvre her towards the taped mark on the floor which put her within shooting range. He would then ask her if she was dieting and, were the answer positive, flourish the Pandora pack. Once shot, the twittering victim would be bagged by a production assistant, who would take her name, address and phone number and attempt to extract an agreement for a follow-up off-camera interview the next week. To ensure four or five successful follow-ups – slimmers who would stick to their diets and agree to be filmed again when they had lost weight – eat least thirty of these celluloid encounters were required. By three o'clock it had already begun to feel like a long, long day.

Fizz and Spike were at least excused from lurking in the supermarket – despite the pretence that it was business as usual, there were already enough conspicuously inconspicuous figures trailing cables or mumbling into walkie-talkies to make Shop-Kwik look as if it had been hit by an MI6 stake-out. An office had been established in the car park, in the charabanc that had transported everyone to the location Fizz and Spike had a walkie-talkie of their own to convey their instructions to Coleby Whiteside; there was a TV monitor, on which they could view the camera action; there was even, as Spike pointed out, (with inappropriate enthusiasm, Fizz thought) a video system, should they wish to distract themselves by watching old movies, as well as an amply stocked bar. They were not, Fizz conceded, uncomfortable; they could assess the punters at ease from reclining seats, making an impartial evaluation of their qualities and taking notes. But, ohmigod, things were *slow*. Even as the fifth or sixth housewife goggled, fish-like, from the monitor, intoning the dreary litany of her diet failures, Fizz began to feel the oppression of her confinement. By lunchtime (catering van meat-and-two-veg, liberally coated with coagulating gravy) she could sense her professionalism, rigorous though it was, might soon start to flag.

On the monitor, in lulls between punters, a static view of supermarket cabinets prevailed, broken occasionally by glimpses of their celebrity, Tel Travers, mopping his brow or hastily consulting his script before galvanizing himself into his studied rendering of a casual shopper. Outside the coach, the faces of real shoppers stared up at them, flashes of curiosity dimming quickly to blank indifference as they scurried off with their trolleys. So many shell suits and trainers – interesting how sports clothes now held an inverse relationship to athletic activity, how the average suburbanite seemed to believe her

71

life of coffee mornings and shopping excursions acquired credibility if she dressed for a ten mile run.

Fizz had herself found clothes problematic this morning – after all, what did one wear for a day in a coach in a super-market car park? – but had decided in the end on her Calvin Klein jeans and a cheap chic patchwork shirt she had found on a stall in Berwick Street. Cheap chic – or was it merely cheap and nasty? One was never quite sure with things that weren't designer. She had rolled up the sleeves and knotted the tails, Carmen-Miranda fashion, at the waist, to give it a touch more style. But when she had asked Spike about it he had simply grunted and continued scribbling on the back of his call-sheet where, in between punters, he was constructing a tribute to a Commonwealth dignitary. Oh, when she'd shifted in her seat, revealing the tanned skin between her jeans and the Carmen-Miranda knot, she'd caught him glancing up from his endeavours, caught him nibbling his pentel distractedly, so she was safe in assuming the shirt was a success. But now he'd finished the Commonwealth dignitary and was engrossed in transforming his paper napkin into a spidery attack on a fruitarian bistro.

Fizz sighed. She had retouched her make-up three times. She had made numerous calls on her mobile phone, hair-dresser's appointment, leg-waxing, instructions to The Don-key back at the office, to her broker, to her cleaning lady, once even (against her principles, this) a call, unanswered, to darling Dean. She'd reapplied her nail polish. She'd dallied with the bottle of Dom Perignon thoughtfully provided for her at lunch and (though she never drank while she was working) had even permitted Spike to open a further half bottle he'd found in the bar. But now it was four o'clock, the monitor had been blank for half an hour, and she felt like screaming.

She sighed again.

Spike looked up, baring his teeth. 'Smile, Lucrezia. Remember, think positive.'

'Ohmigod!'

'Who was it said this was going to be fun?'

'I want some action.'

'Well, let me think . . . How about a nice game of Battleships?'

'Jesus, Spike!'

'Or an old movie. There's *Mary Poppins* AND *The Sound of Music*.'

'I want us to push the peanut forward. Get onto Coleby and ask him what he's playing at.'

'It's a temporary lull in shopping traffic. Things will pick up.'

Maggie always put herself on auto-pilot when she visited e Shop-Kwik. It was like being processed by a machine – a vast, hygienic, echoing machine, funnelling you down the aisles, gearing you up to its system with all its sinister mechanisms tempting you to buy, then disgorging you at the check-out, where you moved slowly down the line until you were rung up and bagged up and pushed out into the world again, a satisfied shopper. She usually just grabbed a trolley and kept her head down, hoping they had everything on her list and hadn't swapped any shelves around.

This Tuesday afternoon, however, she felt dazed before she'd even started. To begin with she had no list, only Nicky's little red book of calories, which she had with forethought slipped into her bag. (Goodness knows what this excursion would do to her housekeeping budget – still, she could always institute an economy drive next week, or ask Mr Gupta for some overtime.) Curious too, Shop-Kwik seemed very busy for a Tuesday, with a coach and two big vans in the car park, and little groups of people standing about chatting.

She gazed at the shelves, not knowing quite where to begin. Fifteen hundred calories a day, the little red book suggested. She'd never considered food like this, never seen these familiar jars and packets as suspicious, crammed, like parcel bombs, with danger for the unwary. After twenty years, she supposed, she'd become sloppy, taken things for granted, assumed all was well as long as the family ate enough to stay healthy. But now she was on the alert, now she remembered being a newly-wed, and how she'd worried – was Keith still longing for his mum's Yorkshire pudding, would Brian grow up stunted if she failed to get anything down him but soft-boiled eggs, would they brand her an unfit mother at the clinic? 'Food is love,' Mum would say when she refused cabbage, or Joy, always a picky eater, pushed her corned beef to the side of her plate. But now food was calories, units of carbohydrate, weakness, failure, humiliation . . .

Maggie stared at the shelves. They seemed fraught and threatening, like the Amazon jungle in a documentary. Brand names screeched at her, packs flashed war-dance plumage, labels blossomed like poisonous flowers. Wheeling her trolley cautiously, her eyes fixed ahead, she shut out the treacherous scent of baps and doughnuts, skirted the ice cream cabinet as though it were a pit of snakes. There were snares everywhere – chocolate mousse lurking in ambush beside the yoghurts, sweetened orange juice waiting to be mistaken for unsweetened, 95-calorie bananas camouflaged by the slimming grapefruits and healthy apples. Closing her ears to the drum-beat of the biscuits, she snatched a packet of crisp-bread and retreated to green vegetables, safe territory.

Considering the distance she'd trekked, circling gondolas, back-tracking down aisles, she seemed to have little to show for her effort. Two plain yoghurts, a grapefruit, a lettuce, the crispbread and a jar of low-calorie tartare sauce – these would hardly keep body and soul together. Her fringe stuck damply to her forehead, the columns in the little red book swam before her eyes.

She set off again, passing a wall of stacked cat-food tins, '5p OFF!', and turning down the aisle which displayed Ivy Pearson's Miracle Menus. Then, just beyond Miracle Menus, she all at once came upon the answer to her problems. Shop-Kwik Slimline Suppers. 'Each portion is a complete slimmer's meal and displays the calorie content clearly on the label. Slimline Suppers do your calorie counting for you – so you're free to count the inches slipping away.' She might have inhibitions about feeding Keith out of packets, but this was different – besides, hadn't she, in a manner of speaking,

74

given up eating? Hardly bothering to check which was meat, fish or chicken, she piled packets into her trolley. When the trolley was full she felt light-headed, purged, as though she were suddenly freed from temptation.

She must have vented her relief audibly, for a seedy-looking man hovering by the next cabinet turned round and shot her a most peculiar stare. Embarrassed, she made a performance of searching for the fastest route to the check-out. And it was then, of course, that she saw it, the cabinet opposite. She was not safe, not free, the enemy had merely been regrouping its forces.

Fizz shifted in her seat with a groan, while Spike rose to replenish their glasses. On the monitor Tel Travers lurched fleetingly into frame, made a funny face at the camera, then vanished. A few moments later he reappeared with a further series of grotesque facial contortions, hips thrust forward, hands in lapels, and it dawned on Fizz slowly that he was giving them his James Cagney impersonation. Spike had assured her that he was a well-loved family entertainer, but for Fizz's part the more she saw of the man the more she was grateful she never watched television. Though, according to his agent, he had been let go from *Hot Property* over a contractual dispute, Fizz would scarcely been surprised to discover he'd been caught for stealing tights from the studio dressing rooms or exposing himself outside the ladies.

James Cagney had metamorphosed into Humphrey Bogart by the time Spike returned with the drinks.

He surveyed the monitor. 'Looks like our Tel's perked up a bit since lunch.'

'Of course he's perked up. Where do you think those two bottles of burgundy went?'

'He hit the mark spot-on with the last Mum. And he only fluffed his lines twice.'

'Nevertheless, he's beginning to slur. And all those ghastly double-entendres about nibbles and naughtiness!'

'They're part of his act, Lucrezia. They fit in well with my campaign theme.'

'They don't fit in well with Granny Garfunkel's morality guidelines. How many times have we been onto Coleby to get him to stick to the script? And you're telling me he's not pissed. Ohmigod, it's so—'

'Unprofessional, Lucrezia?' Spike downed a couple of chalk pills with a gulp of Stella Artois, 'Oh, I agree.'

Fizz sighed. 'I am only drinking this small glass of shampoo, Spike darling, to calm my nerves. We've been here – what is it? – an unbelievable ten hours already. And we've hardly found anyone who's half-way usable.'

'I thought a few of the Mums before lunch were pretty good.'

'Ohmigod.'

'Well, what was wrong with them? Too fat? Too thin?'

'No style.'

'Lucrezia, they're real people. Real people don't have style.'

'Ohmigod!'

'They're Mums, Lucrezia. You can't expect them to look like Paloma Picasso.' Spike gulped his beer, staring moodily at the scrawl on his paper napkin. He crossed out a few words. 'Well, what do you want us to do? Go again?'

'Ohmi*god*!'

'You're worried about Genghis?'

'I'm worried about me. If I have to spend another day in this car park I shall require a straight-jacket.'

'Yves St. Laurent? Or I gather Azzedine Alaia is doing a fetching line this season.'

Fizz resisted an impulse to violence. 'You seem to forget, Spike lovey, I have business to run. Heaven knows what cock-ups are occurring right now in the office, with The Donkey braying and eating thistles. She's probably let the Tancred Toiletries group steal our overhead projector again. In fact, to be on the safe side, I'd better phone—'

'Shush, Lucrezia!' Spike had lowered his pentel and was staring at the monitor. 'Looks like we've got another Mum at last.'

It was another of those clever tricks that supermarkets went in for, Maggie supposed – putting a whole cabinet of fancy cakes directly opposite the Slimmer's Cod with Bean Sprouts, making sure the packs were well and truly visible, the photos of chocolate flakes and butter icing and piped Chantilly cream. She tried not to look, as she might have tried not to stare at someone in the street behaving strangely. But her eyes were caught and held by the pack nearest her. 'Fudge,' it said, 'fudge, chocolate, whipped cream, nuts and Maraschino cherries.' She fought with her longing, she tried not to hear the little voice that murmured, 'You've been such a good girl, Maggie, choosing the Cod with Bean Sprouts. Doesn't a good girl deserve a teeny treat?'

She couldn't have hesitated more than a moment before tearing her glance away. But suddenly she could feel someone at her elbow, heard another voice join the voice in her head.

'Oooh! Naughty, naughty!'

The seedy man had sidled up and was leaning against the cabinet, leering suggestively. 'Who's a wicked girl then, thinking sinful thoughts?'

The best thing was to ignore him and hope he moved on. But he only edged closer, breathing out a blast of extra-strong mint.

'Dieting, are we, love? Trying to get a puncture in the old spare tyre?'

He was not prepossessing, with his pouchy yellow face and dyed bouffant hair. Yet there was something familiar about him as well, something about that loud tie and shiny mohair suit, something about the slimy moustache wriggling like a limbo dancer from under his beaky nose. Maggie racked her brains to think where she had seen him – the electrical shop in the High Street, the butcher's she'd stopped using because of all the smut about 'a nice bit of skirt'. Never mind, he was pestering her, and if he did not stop she would complain to the management.

'Excuse *me*!' she said.

To her horror, his response was to dive into her trolley and seize *Your Pocket Calorie Counter*. 'Ooooh, we are being strict with ourselves, aren't we love? Still, I bet we fancy a nibble now and then.'

She wondered if she should ram his ankles with the trolley or whether it would be better just to scream.

'Do you, love – fancy a sinful little nibble? *Go on, You Can Tell Tel!*'

'Golly gosh!' said Spike, seizing Fizz by the arm in his enthusiasm. 'Nice extra touch, that calorie counter. I'd say she'll do, wouldn't you, Lucrezia?'

Fizz stared at the monitor and saw a Tweetie Pie woman. Tweetie Pie women were frequently found as lapwarmers and knitting pattern models and were especially prevalent in the suburbs, although they could crop up anywhere – Fizz had even been at school with one, Andrea Jukes, who'd always been cast as Puck or Ariel in the summer play. Like their cartoon namesake, Tweetie Pie women had faces heavily overbalanced in favour of the upper features, large, bright eyes, often exaggeratedly lashed, and wide hamster cheeks, declining via a small pert nose into a rosebud mouth and negligible chin. Tweetie Pies were often characterized as sweet, vivacious and chirpy. They were the kind of girls young men aspiring to Ford Granadas and Rotary Club membership considered ideal wife material. This Potter's Park version was Tweetie Pie par excellence, albeit twenty years on and two stone overweight. She had the mousy King Charles II perm they all currently favoured, the simpering laugh, the self-consciously breathy 'ladylike' voice.

'Well?' said Spike, and Fizz was aware of his fingers still exerting enthusiastic pressure on her forearm. 'What d'you think?'

'Oh, I don't know.' Spike's fingers were long and thin, the sort that were always suggestive of sensitivity in romantic novels. Concert pianist's fingers, brain surgeon's fingers.

'Come on, Lucrezia. She has no warts or other obvious deformities, her powers of communication extend beyond grunts. In fact she's saying all the right things – anxious to diet, can't resist biscuits and chocolate, prepared to give Pandora a whirl.'

'She's too old,' Fizz said.

78

'I agree she's no teenager. But she's not exactly geriatric. What would you say – thirty-nine, forty?'

'Precisely. Too long in the tooth.'

'Like the two of us, you mean?'

Fizz snatched her arm from his grasp abruptly. 'Thanks a bunch!'

'I'm sorry. I assumed, since we both went up to Cambridge in the same year—'

'Do you mind, Spike. I'm thirty-seven.'

'Golly gosh, Lucrezia. My mistake.' He surveyed the screen, sipping his Stella Artois with concentration. 'I still think she's a possible. Nice smile, not unattractive. In fact she reminds me a little of my first wife.'

'Ohmigod!'

Such creative fingers, shame about the talent. Fizz adjusted her position so he would not touch her again.

PART TWO

We thought they were really sincere people, seriously concerned to improve the world. Then we discovered they didn't eat wholemeal brand.

Terence McLaughlin: *A Diet of Tripe*

Court report of meeting held 8.30 a.m., 10 May, at Gourmet House, Croydon, between Granny Garfunkel's Gourmet Gateaux (UK) Inc. and BBW&S.

Present for client:	**Present for agency:**
Mr. A. Khan	Ms F. St Clair
Mr E. Minns	Ms B. Donkin
Mr J. Garthwaite	
Mr J. Pocock	
Mr S. Taylor	

Agency gave a progress report on the Project Pandora 'Sin and Slim' commercial. Agency stated that ten housewives had been short-listed, all of whom had shown a willingness to adhere to a strict eight-week calorie-controlled regime and to participate in the second stage of filming. A videotape of the ten selected housewives was then shown.

Client expressed a concern that the majority of the short-listed women did not present a youthful, aspirational or glamorous image.

Agency reminded client of the strategic objective of the commercial, which was, in his own words, 'to turn a turkey into a swan'.

Client reiterated his concern that Project Pandora, as an innovatory product, should not be associated with down-market losers.

Agency reminded client that the drama of the woman's transformation after dieting with Pandora might be somewhat diminished if she were slim and glamorous from the start.

Client reiterated with force his concern that Granny Garfunkel, as a modern, health-conscious, family-image company, should not be portrayed in any context that was ugly or unappetising or which implied the company's products were consumed by weak-willed slobs.

Agency pointed out that such a substantial alteration to the Pandora brief would necessitate a reshoot.

Client disagreed that the brief had changed. Any reshoot must be undertaken at agency expense.

Agency agreed that the Project Pandora housewife should be attractive, well-groomed, no older than forty and no more than 28lbs overweight.

A compromise short-list was drawn up. Agency agreed to go to second stage filming with only three women, Mrs Angie Noakes, Mrs Sharon Batt and Mrs Maggie Hapgood.

I

Maggie hadn't expected limelight. But all the same it wasn't every day she went shopping and found herself in front of the TV cameras. Though it was no more than a tiny blip in the general pulse, it registered a sizable jolt in hers.

Perhaps she should have remembered those Christmas singsongs before Dad died. He'd begin, of course, as master of ceremonies, swaying slightly, clutching the pewter tankard he'd won in a darts tournament, roaring the first 'O–O–O' of 'Oklahoma', then cutting out, full-throttle, like a jumbo jet stalling on take-off. Then there'd come Uncle Mick, singing 'I Met Her In Garden Where Praties Grow' because he was Irish, and Auntie Babs, with her impersonation of Edith Piaf rendering 'Milord'. Then a hush would fall, and there would stand Joy, eight or nine by this time, demure in her patent pumps and turquoise satin party dress, carolling 'Scarlet Ribbons', word perfect, with the mid-Atlantic accent she'd learnt from Radio Luxembourg. And afterwards the grown-ups would stare mistily into their glasses. And then, in the burst of applause, Auntie Babs would shriek, 'What about the baby? Haven't you got a song, Peg, to follow your sister?' And even before Maggie's mind had found time to become utterly blank, Dad would say, pulling Joy to him, squeezing her neck beneath the ringlets, 'Oh, Peggy's the shy one, it's this little lassie who's the natural born performer.'

Perhaps it was this lack of star quality in Maggie. Or perhaps attention could never be doled out equally in case there were not enough to go round. At any rate, though word had spread of the filming at Shop-Kwik, her own involvement caused little stir.

Ivy Pearson said, 'How brave, dear – not minding being caught without your make-up.'

Debbie Salt said, 'I don't mean to be rude, Maggie, but Justin tells me you let him eat cake-mix, which surprised me considering we all know raw eggs are absolutely crawling with salmonella.' And Maggie, having foolishly confessed that it was only butter icing, was thinking, during the consequent lecture on the evils of cholesterol, that if – *big if* – she agreed to mind Justin for the next two hours she would have to starve him unless she could rustle up a nice healthy apple, when Debbie suddenly drew breath and announced, 'Anyway, commercials like that degrade and exploit women.'

Nicki said, 'Not now, Mum!' as she attempted to beat her own time on the stairs.

Keith didn't say anything, but came home from work preoccupied as usual and ate the remains of the steak in brown ale with his nose buried in *The Joy Of Birds*.

Recalling 'Scarlet Ribbons', Maggie didn't think it worth-while to mention her moment of glory to Mum.

Only Jackie at work was impressed. But then Jackie, a divorcee, was a professional dieter. 'A new man, a new diet!' she would cry, mixing gritty powders from packets or rushing to the toilet to test her urine, already planning the figure-hugging wardrobe that must, any day now, repay her iron-willed dedication to the new regime.

Jackie said, 'Come on, Mags girl, tell us about the gateau! It sounds like the answer to a slimmer's prayer.'

Ah yes, the gateau.

Maggie had carried it carefully into the kitchen, intending to try a slice for dessert after her Slimline Supper. But later, chopping apples for crumble, smelling the steak in brown ale reheating gently on Regulo 2, she couldn't help feeling peckish.

But that was allowed, wasn't it? Hadn't Tel Travers said so? Slimming without sacrifice, a miracle product. It was all right to feel tempted.

She stared at the white box, cryptically stamped 'Pandora'. She lifted the lid. She gazed for a moment at the velvet ripples of fudge icing, the cherries set like jewels in scollops of cream.

Nicki came thundering downstairs and into the kitchen in search of her trainers. She caught sight of the cake. 'Oh puke!' she said.

'You finish your homework before you go round to Kimberly's. And make sure you have some supper.'

'Yes Mum, 'bye Mum.'

'Do you hear me, young lady? I said, make sure you eat.'

Nicki pulled a face at the cake. 'Honestly, Mum, what are you trying to do – fatten up Dad and me for a ritual sacrifice?'

'This isn't for you, as it happens. The film people want me to eat it.'

Nicki shook her head. 'You know you can get help, Mum.'

'I don't think I'll need any, thanks, love. It looks delicious.'

'I mean, for your problem. Food's an addiction, same as booze or heroin. Kimberly saw a programme on it. You can go to a clinic and they give you treatment.'

Maggie fetched a fork and a long-bladed knife. The knife slid in, softly, satisfyingly, crinkling the fudge icing and leaving ripples of cream in its wake.

'Overeating's self-mutilation, Kimberly says.'

Maggie made the second cut. Layers of fudge and thick chocolate filling and dark, moist chocolatey sponge were revealed.

'Puke, Mum! I can feel the cellulite sprout, just watching.'

Maggie plunged in her fork, squashing chocolate in a rich smear across the plate. 'That's what you know, Miss Smarty Pants. Guess how many calories this is?'

When Nicki heard, her mouth dropped open. She stared at the cake, then at Maggie. 'Well, go on – aren't you going to try it?'

Maggie raised the fork to her mouth. She chewed, she swallowed. She licked her lips.

'Come on, Mum. What's it taste like?'

Like nothing. Like closing your teeth around cotton wool. Like a mirage, real enough and tantalizing to look at, gone when you tried to touch it.

But no, on second thoughts . . . Nothing didn't leave that

slimy coating on your tongue, or that sickly-sweet aftertaste with overtones of . . . could it be sump oil?

Maggie pushed the plate away and went to the sink for a glass of water. So there were no miracles and she must buckle down to green salads and Cod with Bean Sprouts. She might have known it, might, after all, have realized that there was only one road to self-improvement, with no detours around pain.

When she returned to the table Nicki had taken up her fork and was chewing thoughtfully. 'Aren't you being a bit fussy, Mum? I mean, considering it's got fewer calories than the average grapefruit.'

Maggie closed the cake-box. 'I don't care. It's going in the bin.'

'Oh, I wouldn't do that. I wouldn't be so drastic. You don't know, do you? – you might change your mind later.'

And Nicki was right, Maggie did change her mind. When she had consumed her Slimline Supper and her 15-calorie apple, when she had sat for three hours in front of the telly trying to ignore the plaintive rumblings of her stomach, she began to picture the Pandora cake as it had looked when she had first opened its box. After all, bean sprouts were bland, cod without salt or butter was bland. And anyway she hadn't truly been hungry then, not as she was now, crazily, fixatedly hungry.

But when she looked for the box it was no longer in the freezer. Perhaps Nicki had taken it out to the dustbin after all. Maggie did not speculate. She felt a thrill of wickedness, like a child who has just poured her cough mixture down the sink. The biscuit tin caught her eye. Her hand reached out, her mind emptied.

On Thursday evening, when the film company phoned, she told the girl politely that she wasn't interested.

Mr Barnes of Craft Kitchens DeLuxe had promised much, in his sincere suit and fulsome tie. Only now did Maggie seem to remember a certain shifty glister to his cuff-links as they had flashed expansively about the showroom, dazzling her with work schedules and delivery dates. But the fact was, no work could commence until Mr Barnes came personally to measure up, and this was the third morning she had waited in.

When the bell rang at last, she raced to answer it. But a young lady stood on the step, and an unfamiliar gentleman in glasses.

'Hi, Mrs Hapgood – Maggie,' the lady said, smiling. 'We're sorry we're an eentsy bit late.'

Maggie blinked.

The lady was tall and slim and tanned and dressed all in white. 'I've been so looking forward to meeting you,' she said.

The lady's dark hair was shiny smooth as though it had been varnished. Her white outfit, tailored jacket and jaunty knee shorts, hung upon her without a wrinkle, as if it were still on the rail in one of those Knightsbridge boutiques where the assistants eyed you like a creepy crawly. Her accessories were beige, even down to her briefcase And she was thin – not the ordinary sort of thin you'd achieve by eating Slimline Suppers, but a rarer, more exclusive sort that somehow, Maggie sensed, wouldn't involve doing without things.

'You've come to measure up?' Maggie asked, knowing already it was the wrong thing to say.

The lady's smile faltered, ever so slightly.

'Instead of Mr Barnes? For the new kitchen.'

The lady gave a shiver of her elegantly padded shoulders which managed to draw attention to her gold watch-bracelet, her diamond ear studs, and even to the limousine with its uniformed driver which now, at last, Maggie noticed parked beyond the front gate.

'BBW&S, Maggie lovey. I'm Fizz St Clair, senior management director on Granny Garfunkel – here's my card – and this is Spike Bentley, our copywriter.' She had a refined nasal drawl, like a razor blade scraping glass.

Maggie took the card. She shook the manicured hand, snagging her fingers on the buttresses of a gold dress ring.

She shook the hand of the spectacled gentleman too. She felt herself flush from her neck to her cheeks.

'You are expecting us, lovey. The PA from Slik Piks phoned last week to make the appointment.'

'Well, someone did phone, but I—'

'I've come all the way from London. We've been so excited since we saw your rushes.'

'The thing is, I—'

'Spike's been dying to take you through the script, haven't you, Spike darling?'

'You see, Mrs Sinclair—'

'Please, do call me Fizz.'

The smile was firmly in place again, flawlessly pencilled lips stretched wide over glossy teeth. She was not young after all, this Fizz lady – that was merely the illusion created by the page-boy hair and the little-girl shorts. Yet the fact that she was Maggie's age somehow rendered her perfection more of a reproof. If Maggie had stood out on the windy step her perm would have ravelled itself into a pot scourer (come to think of it, hadn't she meant to wash it this morning?). If Maggie had ventured outdoors in that white suit she would have attracted stains like a magnet. And if Maggie had dared wear those shorts – she stared at the tanned knees and thought of her own, pasty and dimpling beneath Nicki's cast-off track suit pants. She seemed unreal, this Fizz, like an illustration in one of Keith's bird books, the ideal specimen, drawn accurately in every detail, too perfect for nature.

Maggie began to babble foolishly about Mr Barnes. It was true his appointment had been for eleven and it was now gone twelve, but the showroom had sworn blind he was on his way, he wouldn't let her down, not the third time surely, he might arrive any second . . .

'Typical,' said Fizz St Clair . 'The British disease. We could learn a thing or two from the States, couldn't we? You can get anything fixed in Manhattan, how you want, when you want it.'

'Oh yes,' Maggie agreed, and felt more foolish than ever – Majorca was the extent of her foreign travel.

'Well then, may we come in?' Fizz St Clair breezed past her before she could answer, over the step and into the hall in a gust of expensive perfume, with the bespectacled man at her heels. At the lounge doorway she turned decisively, as if she already knew the house, was familiar with its layout from another incarnation. 'Oh,' she was exclaiming, almost before she had crossed the threshold, 'what a charming, characterful room!'

'It's a bit of a mess,' said Maggie, automatically – stupid again, for had she not tidied in expectation of Mr Barnes?

Yet messy was how the room seemed, all of a sudden, when she saw Fizz St Clair at the centre of it in her gleaming white suit. If Ivy's presence revealed the odd smear of dust, Fizz St Clair forced a pitiless inventory that noted down the greying shag pile, the chipped skirting, the self-assembly sideboard they'd bought before Nicki was born, always intending to replace as soon as cash flow allowed. As Fizz St Clair cast a cool eye over the Hapgoods' worldly possessions, compelling Maggie to see what she had made a pact with herself to avoid seeing, she wanted to excuse herself – 'Of course my husband and I have plans to redecorate.' But she could hardly add that the plans had been made four years ago, since then, as with the kitchen, she'd prevaricated, developed her phobia – well, you never knew what might crawl out of the woodwork when you began moving things around.

'Delightful, isn't it, Spike darling?' exclaimed Fizz St Clair. 'Of course we'd need to re-art-direct it a touch for shooting purposes – and maybe prop it out differently . . . But then, on second thoughts, if you're installing a new kitchen, perhaps we should shoot there.'

'Mrs Sinclair—' Maggie said.

'But then, we've so much to discuss. We're both dying to hear how your diet is going and what you thought of Pandora.'

'Mrs Sinclair, Fizz—'

She was glancing at the settee, Maggie noticed, brushing lingering Fluffy hairs from the cushion.

'Oh, pardon me. Please – take a seat, won't you.'

Stupid again. Once settled, they appeared so permanent,

the bespectacled man in Keith's armchair by the hi-fi, Fizz clicking the combination lock on her briefcase, spreading out her papers, elegantly crossing her legs. Suddenly she reminded Maggie of someone. But perhaps it was only Nicki's pal, Kimberly. Although she was not, after all, young, she had that same superior, youthful knowingness that left you wilting.

Maggie drew in breath, determined to set her straight, to tell her it was all a mistake, that the girl on the phone had simply got a crossed wire.

'I-I'll make some coffee,' she stuttered, fleeing to the kitchen.

While she was out there – juggling with the best cups, decanting instant into a pot and wishing she'd bought the kind that was supposed to deceive your guests you'd sewed up real ground coffee – the doorbell rang. Mr Barnes, at last, come to save her.

Ivy Pearson stood on the step, resplendent in a lime-green catsuit and gold and silver dangly earrings like metallic fried eggs.

'I came to see if you were all right, love,' she said, craning her neck to catch the view past Maggie, down the hall.

'I'm fine, Ivy, fine.'

'I noticed the car, you see . . .'

Yes, of course, Ivy. Burglars often pull jobs round here in a Jaguar XJS complete with chauffeur – shows what a nice neighbourhood it is. 'Very kind of you to worry, Ivy. Just some unexpected visitors. I would ask you in for a cup of coffee—'

'Well, only if you're making it, love,' she said, edging quickly over the doormat.

At the lounge door she paused, taking in Fizz St Clair and the bespectacled gentleman with a coy giggle. 'Ooooh, I do hope I'm not intruding. I'm Ivy, number fourteen. Just popping.'

When Maggie returned with the coffee, Ivy was regaling her visitors with details of her Florida holidays.

I've lost four pounds this week, to squeeze into my swim-suit. But then I'm an old hand at dieting. When I set my mind to it the weight drops off, just like that.'

'Gosh,' said the bespectacled man.

Fizz St Clair was smiling as if her face would crack.

'Oh yes, I've been trying to give Maggie a few tips. Well, she's a bit of a novice when it comes to calorie counting, aren't you, love?'

'Oh, I wouldn't say that.'

'But didn't you tell me yesterday after all your effort you'd actually put on—'

'Coffee, Ivy,' Maggie said, thrusting the cup at her with what she hoped was a crushing stare – though she might not be interested in appearing in the commercial, she still had her pride. 'I'm doing quite nicely, thank you very much.'

'Of course you are, Maggie lovey,' said Fizz St Clair soothingly. 'Now perhaps we'd better recce your kitchen so you can describe the look your designer intends to give it, when he finally shows up.'

'Oh, did he let you down again, love?' Ivy's fried eggs jingle-jangled, all sympathy. 'Well, they've got long waiting lists, Craft DeLuxe. We were glad we got our order in while they were only a small firm, just starting up. As a matter of fact, though we say it ourselves, it was really Alan and me that discovered them.'

'Gosh,' said the bespectacled man.

'Well, now here's an idea. If you want see a Craft DeLuxe in situ, you could pop to number fourteen.'

'We wouldn't trouble you,' said the bespectacled man.

'Its no trouble, dear. You could look round the house while you were at it. You might find it interesting – I mean, it's a similar layout, but Maggie and me see decor differently, don't we love?'

'Well, I'm not sure . . .' said the bespectacled man.

Maggie was speechless.

'It'll only take two ticks.' Ivy jumped to her feet with a skittish wiggle which offered a display of her negligible hips.

'That's what friends and neighbours are for, isn't it? Anything to be of help.'

Fizz St Clair put down her cup. Though she had transferred a crimson half moon to its rim, it was extraordinary how her lipstick remained vivid, as if it were topping itself up like everlasting ink. By contrast, Ivy's fuchsia pink was blotchy, beginning to leach into the downturns of her mouth.

Fizz St Clair drew back her perfect lips and trained their perfect smile upon Ivy. 'Thank you so much, lovey. We have enjoyed meeting you.'

'Oh,' said Ivy, harpooned by the smile, transfixed, mid-wiggle. 'The pleasure's mine, I'm sure.'

'And as for your kitchen, Maggie – we're not shooting for two months, which should give this DeLuxe outfit ample time to get its ducks in a row – right?'

'R-right,' Maggie said.

'Oh – right,' said Ivy, jangling the fried eggs, attempting to rally. 'As I say, my pleasure. In fact Maggie and me were only mentioning – well, it's only by chance we didn't meet before. I usually go to Shop-Kwik on a Tuesday, but I get carried away, working on one of my decorative collages. Otherwise we'd have met up, wouldn't we, in front of the cameras?'

'Oh, I don't think so, lovey,' said Fizz St Clair, still smiling. 'We have a very precise casting brief which excludes the mature age group. And now we must push the peanut forward, mustn't we, Maggie? We must pump the adrenalin, right? – get you up to speed for the terrific contribution I know you're going to make to our team.'

'Er – right,' said Maggie. 'Right, Fizz. Th-thanks.'

Maggie sat paralysed while Fizz St Clair took her through diet sheets and shooting schedules and a cartoon story board of the script. She knew she must find the moment to tell Fizz, to explain she was the shy one, not the natural born entertainer, to confess to her haunting by the Phantom Chocolate Digestive, to reveal what she had so rashly admitted to Ivy – that, since discovering the bathroom scales under Nicki's divan, she had been able to measure her achievement as a dedicated slimmer – a gain of three pounds. But the moment never presented itself, Fizz St Clair words gushed from her perfectly-painted lips like water from a geyser, without fluctuation in pressure. And besides, Maggie seemed beyond interrupting, a stranger in her own body, nodding her head when she meant to shake it. Even when Fizz at last put aside her papers, declaring a need to visit the toilet, Maggie could only mumble directions, nodding and smiling obligingly.

Maggie and the bespectacled man were left staring at each other in silence. Not that he'd said much before, anyway, not that he'd exactly had the chance. Maggie had scarcely looked at him, she realized – Fizz St Clair had that effect, soaking up everything around her like blotting paper, absorbing all the detail and colour into herself so that what was left seemed featureless by comparison. Now, examining the bespectacled man properly, Maggie saw with surprise that he was not as she'd made out from the corner of her eye, not at all the slick advertising executive she'd expected. Though he was thin, thinner even than Fizz St Clair, his was a worn-down, nervous thinness, as if life were whittling him. His face had a whittled look, too, all lines and anxious furrows. Though he was not scruffy precisely – his fingernails, she noticed, were scrupulously clean – yet there was a sense of make-do-and-mend, a thrift shop air about him. She would never have let Keith leave the house in that state – with an unironed shirt, and that button missing from the crumpled linen jacket. Even the spectacles had been roughly mended at one hinge by means of a paper clip. Nevertheless, as Maggie looked at that paper clip it comforted her. It seemed to bring him down to her level, suggested he too might flounder for words and forget names when he was introduced.

He smiled, and Maggie realized how rudely she was staring. 'I'm sorry, Mr . . .'

'Spike,' he said.

He had an odd, crooked smile, untidy and anxious like the rest of him. He reminded Maggie of the boys when they were in the throes of their A Levels, not so much Brian, who was more placid, but Neil, tousled and biro-stained, forgetting to chain up his bicycle or eat his cereal.

'Pardon me, Spike,' – she was aware she was flushing again – 'I should have offered you another drink.'

'Drink? Well, gosh yes, that would be brilliant.'

Maggie wondered whether to sneak some chocolate digestives onto the tray – but perhaps she'd much better nibble one quickly while she was out in the kitchen. 'I'll just put the kettle on.'

'Ah.' His face seemed to fall. 'Well, if you're talking coffee . . . it's a little close to lunchtime . . .' The anguished smile became apologetic.

'Oh. Oh, you mean . . .'

'Not if it's . . .'

'No, no. My fault. Sorry, I should have thought.'

There were some bottles in the sideboard, the Beaujolais she'd forgotten to open for Fluffy's wake and others left over from over from Christmas – Bailey's Irish Cream for Mum, a finger of the Malibu Brian and Stephanie had brought, some Shop-Kwik gin for the Pearsons.

Spike accepted a gin and tonic. 'Gosh,' he said, taking a big swallow, then another. 'Cheers, Maggie.' His hand shook, she had noticed as she had given him the glass – perhaps he was shy too, shyer than she was. This, like the paper clip, reassured her. It was as though, now Fizz St Clair was absent, they could come out from behind their party masks, kick off their shoes.

Fortified by her clandestine chocolate biscuit, snatched at last while she had been slicing lemon, Maggie felt brave suddenly, wondered if . . . but, paper clip or not, he still came from Fizz St Clair's designer-briefcase world. And besides, wasn't he firmly under her thumb, hadn't she patted his arm as one might a slow-witted child, and called him 'darling'?

'Spike, I—'

'Tell me, Maggie—?'

Maggie giggled nervously. Then she took deep breath. 'I can't do it. I can't do the commercial. I told the girl on the phone, and I've been trying all this time to tell

96

your Mrs Sinclair, but I've just never managed to get the words out.'

He laughed. 'Golly gosh, Maggie, I know the feeling.'

'Then you do see?'

'Oh gosh, yes. Talking to Fizz is like standing in the fast lane of the motorway trying to reason with an oncoming heavy goods vehicle.'

'But you see what I'm saying? – that I'm not interested. Well, I mean, that sounds rude, it's not what I do mean, it's not that the commercial's not interesting, it's just that I can't, I'm not . . .'

'Oh, I do see.'

She giggled gratefully.

'Though naturally I'm sorry.'

'I'm sorry too, for wasting your time.'

'It would have been fun working with you, Maggie.'

'Oh.' She wished she could stop this idiotic giggling, it reminded her of Nicki and Kimberly. 'Oh – well anyway – to be honest my diet isn't going too fantastically.'

'Then give it up, why don't you? I think you're OK, Maggie – very OK, in fact – just as you are.'

She was aware suddenly of his eyes behind the spectacles. 'That's what my husband says. But then he would, wouldn't he? I mean, men just say things to shut you up, don't they? Oh – I mean, I'm ever so sorry, I wasn't trying to imply . . .'

She was shuffling with embarrassment. The silence that ensued, though it could only have lasted a moment, seemed to stretch like double strength elastic. Maggie remembered Fizz St Clair, upstairs in the bathroom. She seemed to have been there a long time. Was she subjecting the decor to a detailed inspection, noting the cracked tile above the basin and the sliver speckles in the mirror?

'Do you think Mrs Sinclair is all right?' Maggie asked.

Spike smiled his quirky smile. 'Just powdering her nose,' he said.

'What do you think I should say when she comes back? I mean, so she realizes I can't do the commercial?'

'Difficult. Fizz attended some self awareness seminar in her youth where they taught her to discount "no" as an acceptable answer.'

'Then do you – I mean, Spike, could you—?'

'Tell her for you? Maggie, I had you down as a friend. Now I see you're dying to read of my mutilated remains being disinterred by some casual dog-walker.' Catching sight of her face, he laughed. 'Yes, of course. Just let me get her out of here and back to the office.'

'And meantime?'

'Oh, play along with her, it's much the easiest thing.' He glanced down at his empty glass with a sigh. 'We should be off anyway, it's long past lunchtime.'

Maggie was embarking on a lengthy speech of gratitude when footsteps creaked on the stairs. She and Spike sprang apart, moving to opposite ends of the room like guilty children.

Fizz St Clair was sniffing, dabbing at her nostrils with a tissue. If Maggie had sneezed or caught something in her eye she would never have retained three coats of mascara, yet none the less there was encouragement in this small imperfection. Fizz St Clair must have been sensitive about it, however, for when Spike (very sympathetically, Maggie thought) asked if her hay fever was troubling her she flashed him a blow-torch look. But it lasted only an instant. Soon both bars of the smile were switched on, she was gracious as ever, even accepting a gin and tonic when Maggie poured another for Spike, despite her only drinking champagne as a rule, and then never at lunchtime.

Fourteen white boxes of Pandora were brought in from the car, a two-week supply. Then at last they were on the step, with Spike mouthing 'Don't worry!' over Fizz St Clair's shoulder.

'It's been terrific to get such positive feedback from you, lovey,' said Fizz, smiling, smiling. 'Our client is one hundred per cent sold. You're definitely our front runner.'

Maggie wondered how you could be made to feel so small simply by someone being charming. She was closing the door when she realized who Fizz brought to mind.

Well, it was obvious, now she thought of it. Joy – who else?

'Tel Travers!' said Mum, as Maggie, on all fours, peered beneath her settee. 'You met Tel Travers, Peg, and you never uttered a word.'

Maggie rose painfully. Whatever mysterious agents had spirited away Mum's glasses, they had not stashed their booty in the lounge. Checking, as an afterthought, the bridge of Rene's nose, she transferred her search to the kitchenette.

'But you know I never missed that show of his, whajercallit – *Lost Property*?'

'*Hot Property*, Mum. You told me you couldn't abide it.'

'I told you he was one of my favourites. "You Can Say It To Tel." He has such a lovely, sincere smile.'

'You said he was slimy. You said he looked like one of those doorstep antique dealers who con pensioners out of Chippendale chairs.'

'You should know, Margaret, you met him. To think I had the Leprechaun going nineteen to the dozen about at toothpaste he uses and how he likes his eggs. And I could have got it straight from the horse's mouth. That would have put her in her place.'

Maggie paused in her search of the fridge to remove a glass of stout which had been lurking behind a bowl containing something indistinguishable and furry. The stout had been prudently covered with a saucer – curious how looking in someone else's fridge gave you a glimpse of the underside of their life, like reading some sordid private diary.

'What does poor Mrs O'Brien have to do with it?' she said, tipping the stout down the sink.

'One of her neighbours on the estate got herself filmed – and a relative, a second cousin. Of course, I could have said – a second cousin's hardly a daughter, is it? But here am, a prisoner to my legs, with nobody bothering except my little grandchild, popping in on her way home from school to make sure her for Nana's still in the land of the living.'

'So it was Nicki told you about Tel Travers?'

99

'She's a good girl, Nicola, always got time for her poor old Nan.'

Maggie was gratified by this confirmation of Nicki's finer feelings.

'She says I should get some wax earplugs. Or borrow her whatsit – her personal pop-music contraption. Well, I'll never hear the end of it from the Leprechaun otherwise. Not now her relative's been chosen.'

Maggie paused in her examination of the oven.

'Oh yes, the Leprechaun's cousin's had the film people visiting her, saying she's going to star in the advert, telling her she's God's gift.'

Maggie felt a pang. A moment ago she'd been pleased she had kept her encounter with Spike and Fizz St Clair to herself (only Ivy knew, and Ivy wouldn't tell since, if she interpreted yesterday's frosty glare correctly, numbers sixteen and fourteen were currently not speaking). But now she heard a razor blade voice say, 'You're our front runner.' Now she saw Spike smiling his anguished smile. 'It would have been fun working with you, Maggie.' The Leprechaun's second cousin had become God's gift by default. Suddenly Maggie wondered why she had turned it down, this small chance to make her mark, why she had said no automatically, without proper consideration.

'You wouldn't have wanted me to do it, would you, Mum, just so you could torment Mrs O'Brien?'

'Oh no, I'll tell her – my daughter isn't one to make an exhibition of herself.'

Ah, that was the catch, wasn't it? Say no and you let the side down, say yes and you were an exhibition. You just couldn't win, could you, if you were stick-in-the-mud Margaret? Now if it had been Joy, appearing on one of her often-promised visits, if it had been Joy who had chanced to walk into Shop-Kwik . . . Maggie sighed, concentrating her thoughts upon the missing glasses. Bread bin, tea caddy, biscuit tin . . . ?

Biscuit tin. Garibaldis, ginger nuts, a packet of milk chocolate Hobnobs, already open . . .

100

'Of course I won't tell her the real reason,' Rene was saying.

Maggie tried not to look at the chocolate Hobnobs. Yet she felt their pull, felt her will mastered, her fingers drawn inexorably towards the tin. 'What's that, Mum?'

'I won't repeat what a little birdie told me.'

If she acted with speed, turned her back, covered the movements of her hands with her body, she could cram a Hobnob into her mouth and crunch it down quickly without Mum ever seeing. Just one. Just one little chocolate Hobnob.

'You couldn't stick to your diet, could you, Peg?'

Maggie's hand froze with the Hobnob half way to her mouth.

'No will power. Just like your father. That's why they didn't choose you for the advert.'

No will power. Fat, stick-in-the-mud Margaret.

But they *had* chosen her! Spike and Fizz St Clair, they'd believed in her, hadn't thought she would be an exhibition. They'd seen her with different eyes, seen her potential, known she was capable of better things. Oh, supposing she'd said yes, that would have shown them – shown Mum, shown Nicki (that treacherous little bird), shown Joy, shown Keith . . .

She remembered last night, how he'd had it again, that look she dreaded. She'd been making rhubarb fool for the freezer and suddenly there he'd been in the doorway. She'd felt the falling sensation, the tooth-dream feeling; she'd thought, not now Keith, please, not the end of the world now, not while I'm stewing rhubarb and there's Bergerac starting on the box any second. She'd tipped the rhubarb into the Kenwood and switched the motor to full speed. And after a while, beneath its roar, she'd heard him creep back to the lounge. Armageddon postponed. Until tomorrow, or the day after.

But if she'd shown him how she could change . . . Too late, poor Mrs O'Brien's second cousin had seized her place on the life raft. And anyway – Mum, Nicki, Keith, weren't they the ones who really knew her? She lacked the strength to change. Here he was, powerless even over one chocolate biscuit.

Lifting the packet of Hobnobs from the tin, she carefully eased the stolen biscuit back inside the wrapper.

'Of course, the will power's on my side of the family,' Rene was saying. 'Now if you'd taken after your poor old Mum, more like your—'

Maggie was closing her ears resolutely when she observed that something had been dislodged by her removal of the Hobnobs – a battered leather pouch, wedged into the bottom of the tin.

Triumphantly, she lifted it out. 'Specs, Mum. That's where the fairies hid them. Probably they were taken a bit peckish in the middle of the night – perhaps you should talk to them about will power. And, by the way, since you and Nicki seem so interested, I'll have you know I'm starting a brand-new diet tomorrow.'

II

The Creative Department viewing room, a windowless box where the air conditioning did not penetrate, smelt of stale socks and beer exuded from after-lunch pores. On the monitor Mrs Angie Noakes, former Miss Teen Charm, Happy Haven Holiday Camps, simpered demurely in her pink polyester shell suit, batting her lashes and tossing her beauty contest curls. Fizz flicked the remote control.

'Ohmigod! Spike, will you stop scribbling! This is a five Michelin rosette crisis we have here.'

Power and responsibility had their downside, Fizz was reminded. When the going got tough the part-timers shrugged their shoulders and took the 6.15 home to their wives and children. But the true professional soldiered on, keeping her cool, pumping the adrenalin, motivating the troops. A lapwarmer who stayed until nine mis-typing charts might be rewarded with a bottle of shampoo, or even an invitation to lunch. But when Fizz worked till all hours, shouldering the burden of million dollar decisions – well, it was expected, wasn't it?

Of course it didn't help that when the pressure was on everything seemed to conspire against you. Never mind the politics (it wasn't merely a question of watching your back at Brooks Bellini, here they'd happily stab you in the front). It was the sheer incompetence of the people around you, so that, as if you weren't stretched sufficiently, you had to waste time covering their mistakes.

Take The lapwarmer, for instance.

She might persist that the cleaners were a day late with Fizz's Jasper Conran, but Fizz knew perfectly well the lazy little slug simply hadn't bothered to collect it. How was Fizz supposed to get up at some ungodly hour if she had no notion what to wear? And, as if that weren't enough, she had possessed the temerity, the creature, to raise her eyebrows when Fizz had claimed delay this morning due to a gynaecologist's appointment. But that was as nothing, compared with the flowers.

Fizz had noticed, as she was pouring coffee, that the enamel vase was missing and had fondly assumed it was being replenished with irises. But when The Lapwarmer reappeared – without knocking, of course, just as Fizz was exchanging this morning's fresh bottle of Perrier for the bottle in her draw – the vase contained an alien arrangement.

Fizz stared at the blooms. They had spiky purple heads like craft-shop pomander.

The Lapwarmer, without comment, set the vase on the table and began tweaking the arrangement.

Fizz coughed.

The Lapwarmer stood back to admire her endeavours. 'Actually, Fizz, I couldn't find any irises. I thought these would make a nice change.'

'Scarcely David Hockney, are they, lovey?'

'But don't you think they're rather unusual?'

'Very. They wouldn't look out of place bordering a plague pit. And,' Fizz paused, wrinkling her nose, 'I can smell something strange.'

The Lapwarmer wrinkled her nose too and sniffed obligingly. They both sniffed in concert for a moment.

'Garlic!' Fizz exclaimed.

'Actually, I said they were unusual.'

'Essence of Paris metro in midsummer. Ohmigod. Take them *away*.'

The Lapwarmer considered the flowers. She had the effrontery to smile. 'Actually Fizz, think positive. You won't have any trouble from vampires.'

'Get rid of them, lovey. Take a taxi to Moyses Stevens, get me some irises. And on your way out find Barbara Donkin. Tell her I need her in this office ASAP.'

'Actually, Barbara's not in today, Fizz.'

Fizz stared. Really, was there no limit to the creature's

ineptitude? 'Of course Barbara is in, lovey. There is a major crisis on Project Pandora which requires all hands to the pump.'

'Actually Fizz, she left a message. She's away on an important new business project for the Chairman.'

'Brooks doesn't have any important projects. There is nothing more important than Project Pandora.'

'Well, actually Fizz, I wouldn't know. Actually all I know is what she said in her message. Actually.'

How typical of The Donkey to disappear on some kinder-garten project just when Fizz needed her for leg-work. Didn't she realize that any association with Brooks was career death? Well, she would soon find out, Fizz vowed, should there be a cock-up on Pandora. Fizz would see it as no more than her duty to inform Stretch of The Donkey's cavalier attitude.

A pungent waft of garlic reminded Fizz that, distracted by this new drama, she had permitted The Lapwarmer to escape without removing the flowers. Fizz buzzed the intercom, but there was no reply. The fumes encroached stealthily, brushing her skin with fetid fingers, thickening the air to a miasma. In vain she sprayed Arpege and buzzed. Eventually, breathing, tasting, sweating garlic, she was obliged to swallow her dignity and go out to hunt for the creature.

A noise, Fizz observed, was emanating from Tancred Toiletries, a screeching of bag-carriers, a popping of corks. During her absence in suburbia, she remembered, the con-struction of Dick Saunders Blair's new office had finally been completed and now he must be holding a pre-lunch office-warming party. The Lapwarmer was disloyally chummy with Saunders Blair's minion, an Alice-band harpy of the same age and class. Perhaps Fizz had better drift by. Besides, it was important to discover whether Stretch had accepted an invitation.

Passing the blue filing cabinets, crossing into alien terri-tory, sauntering down the corridor, Fizz cast a casual glance through Saunders Blair's door. What she saw made her recoil in shock. Oh, it was not The Lapwarmer, although Fizz thought she made out a treacherous flash of lambswool amongst the crush of below-the-liners soaking up free shampoo. It was not Stretch – unlike several of her fellow directors, he had clearly found more pressing demands on his time. No, what brought Fizz up short was the view from the doorway, a view of panoramic dimensions, a vista of wall space and carpet that dwarfed the furniture, even the hulking repro desk. How had he done it, how had he blackmailed Stretch or bribed the architect? Dick Saunders Blair's office was larger than hers by a whole extra window, some forty or fifty square feet.

And so the day had continued. Wasn't it bad enough that Dean hadn't phoned, that her answering machine had been blank for three days – well, as good as blank, the only message being from Cissie, her old Cambridge friend, with an invitation to some dreary at-home? Wasn't it bad enough that she'd woken this morning to find her jaw-line sagging and her stomach bloated? And now this message to phone Mrs Angie Noakes, urgently.

Spike glanced up, innocently nibbling his pentel. How dare he scribble away at whatever it was – sushi or social scientists – fiddling while Granny Garfunkel burned.

'What are we going to *do*?'

'Personally, I shouldn't have said there was much I could do, under the circumstances. Or you either, Lucrezia.'

'But Mrs Angie Noakes is our front runner.'

'It's only six and a half weeks till the shoot.'

'Meaning?'

'Maybe it won't show.'

'Spike, the creature is already two months pregnant. She is hardly going to demonstrate dramatic weight loss through adherence to a calorie-controlled diet. Besides, can you imagine the newspaper headlines? "Gateau Girl in Pudding Club." "Miracle Cake Slimmer Confesses – I Had Bun in Oven." '

'Hmmmm.'

'Well – what?'

'I was just wondering – have you noticed it, Lucrezia? An overpowering smell of garlic?'

Fizz clenched her knuckles, resisting an impulse to scream. 'Spike, will you concentrate! We were already deeply enough in the poo when Genghis reduced our short list to three.'

'You agreed to it, Lucrezia.'

'Do you think I didn't outline the dangers – all the hidden variables, diet failures, holiday plans, illness, acts of God? Are you accusing me of not standing up to Genghis?'

'Golly gosh, no, Lucrezia.'

'If anyone can put Genghis back in his box it's me. But in this case I was obliged to accept the validity of his arguments. He has a point, vis-à-vis the whole company image of Granny Garfunkel.'

'Gosh, yes.'

'And anyway I had confidence in Mrs Angie Noakes.'

'You said she had fewer brain cells than Barbie. You said, as I recall, that anyone prepared to be seen dead in that candy-floss nylon shell suit deserved to be—'

'I said she was young, keen to diet, only a stone overweight, with a bubbly, attractive personality. And Genghis favoured her. How could she do this to me?'

'Outrageous behaviour, I agree, Lucrezia.'

'Doesn't she realize this is the most prestigious FMPG launch of the decade?'

'Appalling sense of priorities. But then, that's the problem, isn't it?'

'What do you mean?'

'With using housewives, Mums, real people. Real women do have babies.'

Fizz, to whom tears in the office were anathema, found her eyes inexplicably hot. Conscious that Spike's pentel was poised to resume the sushi, however, she drew herself up. 'We must be proactive. We must evaluate the situation, right?'

'Gosh yes. Right.'

'We must see where this leaves us.'

'Right.'

'And where it leaves us is with Sharon The Scrubber and Tweetie Pie. Where once we had ten possibilities, now we have two, right?'

'Wrong.'

'We have two possibilities – right? – neither of which—'

'Wrong, Lucrezia. We have one possibility.'

'I beg your pardon?'

'I told you, Maggie Hapgood isn't interested.'

'Bullshit.'

''Fraid not, Lucrezia.'

'Of course she's interested. Doesn't she realize—?'

'This is the most prestigious UK FMPG launch of the decade? I can't say, Lucrezia. All I know is, she told Slik Piks—'

'Bull-shit!'

'I did mention it when I saw she was on the short list.'

'Don't give me this crap, Spike.'

'Perhaps you weren't listening, Lucrezia. Although I do recall you saying it didn't matter as she was too old, had zero personality and stood as much chance of losing two stone as a pig stood of hang gliding. You said she was on the tape as back-up, to make the short list look good.'

'But that was when we had ten possibilities.'

'Well, now we have one, Sharon The Scrubber.'

Fizz closed her eyes tightly for a moment. 'Ohmigod! How I detest real people!'

When she opened her eyes, Spike was delving in the pockets of his battered linen jacket, producing a packet of chalk pills from the left and from the right a can of Special Brew. She watched him draw back the ring-pull, heard the scrape, the satisfying hiss of carbon dioxide. She wished she had thought to bring her Perrier bottle.

'I must say, you're taking this very calmly, Spike lovey.'

He was washing down chalk pills with great gulps of lager.

'I certainly shouldn't be sitting here coolly swilling beer in your situation.'

He lowered the can, wiping his mouth.

'I mean, we're talking megabucks here, right? We're talking big production sixty-second spots, we're talking OTS, TVRS, peak viewing time, saturation coverage, a campaign to blast the competition out of the air waves. And what have we got? What are we relying on to fill our sixty seconds? Sharon The Scrubber – and zero back-up.'

'I agree it doesn't look too promising, Lucrezia.'

'Not promising? This, my dear Spike, is not a mere cock-up. This is a twenty-two carat, gilt-edged, designer-label, certified catastrophe. And Stretch and I will want to know who's responsible. There'll be an investigation into this that will make the Spanish Inquisition look like a play-ground.'

'Gosh.'

'We'll want to know why Slik Piks put Tweetie Pie forward if she wasn't available.'

'Gosh.'

'We'll want to know who chose Slik Piks as the production company.'

'Gosh.'

'We'll want to know why the Creative Department recommended the script, why they allowed us to sell Granny Garfunkel a campaign using real housewives when it wasn't feasible.'

'Golly gosh.'

'You're on the line here, lovey.'

He downed another gulp of beef. 'Golly fucking gosh.'

Fizz stared at him. She watched, infuriated, as he took up his pentel. 'Jesus, Spike. Je-sus!'

He examined his pad, crossing out a word or two. Then he looked up at her with his lopsided lapwarmer's smile. 'Do you know, I have a dream, Lucrezia. I dream of walking out of my flat one day and never coming back. I dream of washing my hands of it all – the mortgages, the alimony, the palimony – giving up this decadent materialism, going on a spiritual quest. I've always quite fancied becoming a hermit. Or perhaps a Cistercian monk.'

Fizz leaned over. She snatched the pentel from his grasp. She hurled it with force at the wall.

He made no move to retrieve the pentel. Instead, draining the last drops of lager, he crushed the can with his brain surgeon's fingers and sat back, surveying her mildly.

She felt spent and defeated. Her head throbbed from the

109

garlic and she was certain her stomach, despite an overdose of water-retention pills, was even more distended than this morning – perhaps she was menopausal, this bloating merely the first symptom of irretrievable disintegration, the fibroid-swollen belly of age. She wished she had not worn these clinging Donna Karan leggings, she wished she could rush out to Covent Garden, buy other clothes and change. She felt a sharp craving for one of her restorative sessions in the executive ladies, but she dared not leave the viewing room in case Spike took the opportunity to vanish.

'What *are* we going to do?'

'I, for one, Lucrezia, am going to give the matter my very full consideration tomorrow morning. A siren call reminds me that the happy hour is now upon us and draws me inexorably towards The Lamb and Flag.'

'God, you're a flake, Spike. Why won't you take this seriously? Why won't you take *me* seriously?'

'Oh, but I do, Lucrezia. Oh golly gosh, yes. It worries me, all this *Sturm und Drang* and throwing of pentels. I shouldn't like to see you go down with a nasty case of executive burn-out, my goodness no.'

Fizz stared at him suspiciously, but the lopsided grin seemed amiable enough. She wondered . . . perhaps she had been playing too hard to get. It had occurred to her, when she had driven him home after the shoot and he had excused himself from inviting her in, that perhaps he and that over-endowed lapwarmer in TV Admin. were still an item – what was her name, Dottie, Tottie? – but she had since seen Dottie-Tottie in the Braganza, jiggling her DD cups at a producer. Not that it was of the slightest consequence, of course. How could Spike be any substitute for Dean? But then poor Dean was obviously up to his eyeballs not to have phoned her – didn't printers work until all hours? She was reminded that she had not had sex for nearly a fortnight. And it was good for you, a little low-commitment sex, made you look younger, delivered the best ever exercise for flagging stomach muscles. Besides, didn't she deserve consolation?

110

'OK, Spike darling, I'll join you for an aperitif. Then maybe we can work out a plan of action over dinner.'

'For chrissake! Why here?'

'I'm doing a thousand words on "Entertaining Clients". I was going to cover this next Thursday, but since you so kindly offered to treat me, Lucrezia, and *L'Entrée* are giving me grief over my expenses . . .'

'A trifle downmarket for *L'Entrée*, surely? And can you imagine bringing Art here?'

'It's good copy, Lucrezia. Besides, I'll lay you London to a house brick Genghis would love it.'

In the simulated gaslight of Nanny Manners' Nursery faces were flushed, convivial hands clapped shoulders, moist lips leered. A businessman whose girth did indeed recall Genghis was being taken to the Little Boys' Room by a uniformed red-head. His jowls shivered as, thrusting sausage fingers beneath her abbreviated hem, he was rewarded with a thwack from her cane. Fizz permitted herself a shudder. From the light's perimeter, above anaglypta dados, daguerrotyped Victorian infants primly echoed her distaste.

A bottle blonde in a pertly-starched cap and fishnets showed Spike and Fizz to their table. 'Hi, I'm Nanny Crisp. I'm here to see we all mind our Ps and Qs this evening.'

'Ohmigod,' said Fizz.

'Did I hear language, young lady? If you were a little gentleman, Nanny would have to be strict.' Unfurling their table napkins and thrusting Spike's into his collar, Nanny Crisp went in search of the wine list with a minatory clack of her stilettos.

At adjacent tables other nannies ministered to their charges, each carrying at her belt a suitable instrument of correction, a ruler, a hair brush, a high-heeled slipper. Fizz observed she was the only female diner tonight. She thought she had never seen so many biros in top pockets, such yardage of shiny grey polyester mix and drip-dry Bri-nylon – Nigels, Adrians and Kevins up from the provinces, salesmen and middle managers, purveyors of industrial chemicals and double glazing. Now, determined to shed convention, they yielded instinctively to another conformity, the pack urge of the football terrace. A howl went up as Art Khan's doppelganger was brought back from the boys' room and sent to stand in a corner, where he was enthusiastically pelted with bread rolls.

'Fish cakes,' Fizz read from the menu, 'Spam fritters, Prunes and Custard, Spotted Dick, Tapioca.' *Tapioca*?

'EAT UP – YOU'LL BE GLAD OF IT SOME DAY,' admonished an embroidered legend above the dado.

'No Dom Perignon,' said Spike, perusing the wine list. 'No Epernay at all, Lucrezia. You'll have to slum it with Reims.'

'BREAD AND BUTTER BEFORE CAKE,' scolded a second motto.

'Elbows off the table,' snapped Nanny Crisp, reappearing to take their order.

'What I can't believe,' said Fizz, when the decisions were over – fish cakes for Spike, roast chicken for herself – 'what I simply can't swallow is the arrogance of the creature.'

'It's only a spot of fun. Nostalgia for the Golden Age of Childhood, Lucrezia – the days when rules were rules, and eating was a moral imperative, not a fashion statement.'

'Oh, I don't mean that peroxided harpy with the ladder in her fishnets. I mean Tweetie Pie. What does she mean, she isn't interested? Who does she think she is, Meryl Streep?'

'She's just a nice, ordinary, unaffected Mum, Lucrezia.'

'God, you're as bad as Genghis. He says she's "genuine" – whatever that's supposed to mean.'

'For once I agree with him. She is genuine. She needs a Granny Garfunkel commercial like a hole in the head.'

'It's not *her* needs I'm concerned with, Spike darling. Perhaps Slik Piks got the signals wrong. Perhaps she was only wavering.'

'It wasn't just Slik Piks, she told me to.'

'Oh really?' Fizz eyed him over the rim of her champagne glass. 'She confided in you, did she, Spike darling? Behind my back?'

He appeared all at once preoccupied with the wrapper of a fresh packet of chalk pills. 'She seemed pretty adamant. Still,

I suppose you could go to Potter's Park, have another talk with her.'

Fizz succumbed to a small chill shiver. Nobody knew – no one should know – what these suburban trips cost her. The Golden Age of Childhood? It was all very well for Spike, from the almost-acceptable perspective of his Guildford rectory. But for her – oh, the shame of it, those dismal years adrift in the social limbo of the lower middle classes. Identikitland. She had only to drive down those streets with their rows of dwarf conifers and glassed-in porches for it all to be evoked, the pain, the humiliation, the furtiveness. 'Don't you tell the neighbours what goes on in this house,' Mother would caution, twitching the cross-over nets; and Fizz would find herself screaming 'But nothing goes on! Nothing ever goes on here!' Yet this nothingness was a taint in itself, this petty poverty of existence. Oh, it was so unfair. She'd always felt she was a changeling; as early as seven she'd fretted for a London postal number, pined for five star hotels on those caravan holidays in Dorset. And later at boarding school, watching, learning, she'd longed to be orphaned; she'd invented new parents, a mother who wore a hat to Speech Day, and didn't use air freshener words like 'toilet' or 'pardon', a father who was silver-haired and elegant, a barrister or a diplomat or an actor-knight. Of course there was no reinventing Mother on those once-a-year duty visits at Christmas, or Father, watching soccer in his woolly cardie. But she'd recreated herself. She'd expunged the taint, no trace of it marred her gleaming surfaces; she appeared now as impeccably provenanced as a Sotsass chair or a Philippe Starck vase. Yet, as she had stood in Tweetie Pie's bathroom, taking in the Artex ceiling, the avocado suite, the knitted fairy doll toilet roll tidy, the pain had flooded back. It was Fizz's view that the whole of Identikitland would be greatly improved by saturation bombing.

A roar issued from the next table, where one of the Nigels was being served Bedtime Story, the speciality of the house, a concoction, according to the menu, of whipped cream, fruit salad, Grand Marnier, Curacao, Grenadine and Cointreau, to be spoon-fed to the recipient by a nanny perched upon his knee. Rearranging her chicken, Fizz glanced across at Spike. So Tweetie Pie had confided in him, had she? Really, to stoop so low as to flirt with punters – the man was utterly lacking in style. And to think she, Fizz, had contemplated . . . An idea suddenly struck her. She replaced her knife and fork in the space on her plate she had apportioned for them. She smiled.

'Do you know, Spike darling, I think Tweetie Pie has the hots for you.'

Spike, extracting a bone from his fish cake, did not look up.

'Oh yes, I definitely detected a frisson. That's why she unburdened herself to you when she wouldn't to me . . . And, besides, it makes logical sense when you consider it – I'm not the right person to talk to these women. I'm too aspirational, they can't identify. Whereas a man's impartial, there's no threat, no competition – particularly a man who's attractive, yet empathic . . .'

'No, Lucrezia.'

'Come on, Spike darling. If you were to dazzle Tweetie Pie with your media glamour—'

'No.'

'There'd be a lunch in it if you succeed. Tante Claire, Le Gavroche.'

'Just drop it, why don't you.'

'Spike lovey, there's a lot riding on this. A monastery's fine, but the hours are lousy and the pay isn't terrific.'

Spike pushed the remains of the fish cake to the side of his plate. 'I've told you, Maggie Hapgood doesn't need us.'

'You're very protective of dear Tweetie Pie all of a sudden.'

'She's happy as she is. In fact, she probably has a much happier life than—' He broke off as Nanny Crisp click-clacked sharply to a halt beside their table.

'Tut tut!' said Nanny Crisp. 'This won't do, will it?' She stood, arms akimbo, inspecting their plates. Then 'Waste not, want not,' she said, fingering her hair brush.

Fizz stared at the creature, honing an appropriately cutting dismissal. Then, all of a sudden changing her mind, she

114

bestowed upon her a contrite smile. 'Calories,' she said. 'You know how it is.'

At once Nanny Crisp beamed with fellow feeling. 'That's OK, love. Have to watch it myself, getting into this sodding uniform every night. Sheer sodding torture, innit, being a sex object? But' – here she snapped back instantly into her nursery persona – 'what about the little gentleman? Who hasn't eaten his greens or his nice fish cakes?'

'Do you think, Nanny dear, he left them on purpose?'

'Testing, you mean? Just seeing what he could get away with?'

'Look—' said Spike, while Fizz delved in her handbag.

'Naughty boys don't get away with much around Nanny Crisp.'

'I say—' said Spike, while Fizz deftly slid a twenty-pound note beneath her napkin.

'And this one looks like a very naughty boy,' said Nanny Crisp, eyeing the napkin. 'Oh yes, a very naughty boy indeed.'

'Look – gosh—' said Spike.

'Not another word,' said Nanny Crisp, sweeping up the napkin. 'I want to see a nice clean plate when I come back in five minutes. Otherwise, it'll be six of the best.'

'Golly gosh,' said Spike, gazing after Nanny Crisp's well-muscled haunches. 'You don't suppose she really means it?'

At the next table the chaiiking swelled once more to a howl. The Bedtime Story Nigel, his polyester mix now liberally hatched and daubed with cream, was set upon by his fellow Nigels and debagged, while his nanny stood by, flexing her ruler.

'B-but—' protested Spike, 'I'm a restaurant critic, a mere onlooker.'

'It'll be great copy, Spike dear.'

'But what about my ulcer?'

'It's only a spot of fun, Spike darling. The Golden Age of Childhood. Now, where were we? Oh yes, we were discussing whether you should surrender your virtue for the sake of Project Pandora—'

'For heaven's sake, Lucrezia!'

'Of course, I could try to intercede with Nanny on your behalf. Though naturally there would be certain conditions . . . Spike? Spike, what the hell are you doing?'

He had torn the napkin from his throat and had thrust it into his lap, swiftly tipping after it the contents of his plate. Now he was groping beneath the table.

An instant later he was upright again, smiling his lopsided smile, calmly taking out a Gauloise.

Fizz stared at him. She glanced down. 'Ohmi*god*! Not my handbag! But for Christ's sake, it's Hermes!'

He was rolling the Gauloise in his concert-pianist's fingers.

'Ohmigod, Spike Bentley, you're going to owe me one for this. *You are going to owe me.*'

III

'You can't just go without lunch, Mags,' said Jackie.

'Better than feeding off the dead flesh of, like, innocent animals,' said Sheena, wrinkling her nose.

Jackie lifted the burger from its polystyrene container, examined it for a second, then, holding it with both hands, bit into it firmly till relish oozed out in a gory frill. 'Blimey,' she said, chewing, licking ketchup from her chin, as Sheena pedalled her chair backwards on protesting castors. 'Ooh blimey, ooooh yes!'

'It's, like, junk,' said Sheena, shielding her tupperware bowl of tofu and alfalfa. 'Like, poison.'

Jackie took a chip and dunked it in relish, lifting it slowly to her lips, tonguing its scarlet tip, closing her teeth upon it languorously. 'But it reaches the parts salad cannot reach.'

Jackie was fat, Maggie realized suddenly. Despite her constant dieting she was fatter than Maggie. Not that Maggie had failed to notice Jackie's generous dimensions – it was simply that years of friendship had discounted the need for labels. Had she been obliged to describe Jackie, she would have used the word 'big' – big gestures, big open-throated laugh creasing her several chins, big bold stripes on her clinging T-shirt, pink and orange like a day-glo bumble bee, so that the office buzzed when she was in it, vibrated with colour and warmth.

Indeed it was Jackie who made Magipost bearable. Mr Gupta was all right, plump little Mr Gupta in his mohair suit, overseeing them from his glassed-in cubby hole, where he was forever boisterously, incomprehensibly on the phone – he was decent enough when you asked for time off to wait in for the kitchen man, he twinkled at Jackie and called them all 'girls'. And the hours suited. But, oh, they were

117

long hours, punching names and addresses from advertising coupons into the computer – this week, 'Wonder Wok Offer'. The magazines might wax eloquent about modern woman's need to fulfil a multi-faceted role, but Maggie had loved being 'just a housewife', had enjoyed the freedom – the luxury, so it now seemed – of organizing her own day. Did fulfilment really consist in dragging on tights every morning and sitting cooped up like a battery chicken? Still, she had the time now there was only Nicki at home, and what with putting the children through college they needed the money. (True, Keith had said they'd manage, suggested she try for some qualifications, go in for teacher training or the Open University, but it seemed too much like school – and anyway, why was he so busy thinking up schemes to keep her occupied all of a sudden?) So here she was, Tuesday to Thursday, 'Unbelievable Oven Glove Offer' one week, 'Wonder Wok' the next, with only the thought of the lunch hour to keep her going. And the lunch hour was Jackie, chatting about men and the meaning of life as they sat at their desks, nibbling carefully prepared titbits, resting their eyes from the green dance of computer script, reminding themselves, for those sacred sixty minutes, that they were not mere extensions of the machine.

Except that today was different. Today Maggie was not eating lunch. She thought she had read somewhere that by starving yourself you could shrink the size of your digestive organs, and thus shrink your appetite. Drastic, perhaps, but after the failure of Slimline Suppers her problem demanded drastic measures. Jackie, nibbling celery and cottage cheese, would certainly be sympathetic. But Jackie had announced she was forsaking all diets. Her latest Mr Wrong, a long-distance trucker, had been found to have a long-distance Mrs Wrong, with three little Wrongs, and Jackie was going on a binge.

Maggie tried not to look at the hamburger, but she couldn't help breathing in the aroma of ketchup and onions like a dog snuffling up a scent. By ten, typing in Wok data, she had wished herself back with Unbelievable Oven Glove, had fought visions of stir-fried pork and steamed dumplings. Now, sipping machine coffee, black without sugar, she felt

118

dizzy, almost faint. Stealthily she eyed Jackie as she crammed her mouth with chips. Yes, Jackie was fat – there was no doubt about it.

Sheena, who dealt with Customer Complaints, was thin and thirtyish, and engaged to a yoga teacher at the Adult Education Centre. 'It's, like, you're not just disrespecting your own body, Jackie. You're disrespecting our whole, like, ecosystem and all living creatures.'

'Do us a favour,' said Jackie, taking another lingering bite from the burger.

'Seriously, if it wasn't for mass production and the poor countries growing cattle feed for the West, people all over the world wouldn't be, like, starving.'

'You sound like my old Mum, bless her soggy cabbage, telling me to think of the starving millions. Only it was supposed to get you to eat meat then.'

'And what about poor Mr Gupta? Think of his feelings. The cow's, like, sacred where he comes from.'

'Poor Mr Gupta sneaked off ten minutes ago to The Fox and Hounds, where he's ordering steak sandwiches with his pint of lager – I know, I've seen him.'

'It's not what I'm saying. All I'm saying is it's not just yourself you're, you know, killing.'

'Give us a break, girl. Here am I, for once in my life fancying a teeny little binge – and suddenly, single-handed, I'm responsible for Third World debt, the destruction of the rain forests, the poisoning of the ecosystem and the rape and pillage of the entire flipping planet.'

Jackie swallowed the remains of the burger defiantly. All the same, Maggie noticed, she chewed with less enthusiasm now, parcelling up the incriminating chip bag and the poly-styrene carton, quickly stowing them in the bin. Her second parcel she opened furtively, consuming the contents – a slice of Black Forest Gateau – with speed but without any obvious enjoyment, as if she were not tasting, not even thinking, but merely working to empty her plate.

Maggie felt sorry for the malice engendered by her hunger. The label 'fat' seemed to deplete Jackie, rendering her

119

high spirits joyless, her colour garish, her warmth the mere flush of bravado. Maggie took the label back. Nevertheless, struggling against her own deprivation, she could not help staring while Jackie wolfed the Black Forest Gateau.

Sheena was watching too, as she sipped delicate spoonfuls of live yoghurt. Jackie, aware of their eyes upon her, gulped down the last morsel of gateau, thrusting the paper plate into the waste bin on top of the burger wrappings. 'Look, it's only cake, girls. Nobody died for it, OK?'

'It's still poison,' said Sheena. 'Like it's refined. White flour, white sugar.'

Jackie stared for a second. Then she threw up her arms in mock surrender. 'OK, OK. I didn't enjoy it, I feel guilty. I'll bring in some nice healthy rabbit food tomorrow.'

A silence fell, in which the smell of the burger lingered like wickedness unexpiated. Sheena, taking aim with a non-aerosol canister of air freshener, fired a crusading salvo of eco-friendly Pine. Then she drifted to the cloakroom to fetch water for her pot plants, while Jackie collected coffee from the machine. Maggie sat where she was, trying not to think of stir-fried pork and Black Forest Gateau.

Lighting a cigarette, Jackie sat down opposite her. 'Flipping heck!' Though her head went back in a peal of laughter, there was a defensive note to it, Maggie observed from her new perspective. 'I mean, I can understand her' – Jackie jerked her cigarette towards Sheena's workspace – 'it takes them that way, veggies, they get fired with missionary zeal like Jehovah's Witnesses. But you're my mate, Mags. You still haven't said why you're on hunger strike all of a sudden.'

Maggie sighed. It occurred to her, unworthily, that, bingeing or dieting, Jackie had remained the same weight all the time she had known her, that her fat, her 'bigness', whatever you chose to call it, was not a temporary condition, but the result of some intractable disorder that might even be catching. Maggie reproached herself instantly for her treachery. Hadn't she been longing to talk to Jackie, ask her advice, accept her comradeship in adversity? She began to relate her failure with Slimline Suppers.

'. . . but it's not just that I need a proper meal afterwards, so I'm eating twice as much as when I started. It's . . .' She hesitated, wary even of uttering the words for fear of what they might invoke. 'It's – well, I've developed this uncontrollable craving for – chocolate biscuits.'

Jackie laughed. Her head went back, her chin wobbled, her throat swelled, and there was joy in her laughter once more, a great warm tide of it that swept Maggie up, enfolding her, restoring her to fellow-feeling.

'Join the club, girl!'

'But what can I do?'

'Starving yourself's no good. You need a regime, Mags, a programme. I'll bring in some of my slimming books tomorrow.'

Opposite Magipost, directly in Maggie's eyeline when she glanced up from her VDU past Jackie's right shoulder, was a giant advertisement hoarding. Currently selling Caribbean holidays – or rum, perhaps, or suntan lotion – it featured, against a background of palm trees, a girl in a one-piece swimsuit clinging-wet from the sea.

The girl's lips were parted to indicate happy abandonment, her limbs struck a carefree pose. Her eyes were trained upon the palm trees where, swinging in a hammock, a handsome young man in Bermudas returned her jaunty wave. She had clearly inherited Paradise, this girl in the swimsuit; and you had only to look at her – those slender arms, that concave stomach, those thighs innocent of cellulite – to see this was no more than she deserved.

But how had she managed it, Maggie wondered, her head still aching from Jackie's books. Had the Paradise girl begun every meal with papayas or grapefruit? Did she melt away calories by protein-induced ketosis or excrete them daily in fibre-rich stools? Did she trim her hips with muesli, flatten her stomach with diuretics or purge her whole body with weekend fasts sustained by camomile tea? How high were her brown fat stores, what were her Alpha/Beta Receptor ratios, her Fat Metabolizing Hormone

121

levels? Did she supplement her diet with bran pills, amino acids, thyroxine or Human Chorionic Gonadotrophin? Had she tried acupuncture, hydrotherapy, aromatherapy, meso-therapy, hypnotherapy, lymphatic drainage, liposuction, calisthenics or omnikinetic resistance? Did she know avocados weren't really slimming at all, but dangerous because of their fat content? Did she worry about free radicals? How did she feel about olive oil – was it a natural, healthy alternative to polyunsaturates, or was it cellulite-in-a-bottle, with fat-per-gram scores soaring right off the graph?

Above all, Maggie pondered, as Wonder Wok gave way to 'Pantastick Savings', how did she feel, the girl in the swimsuit? Had she found a 'new you', as promised? Had her self-worth increased, was she confident and creative? Was she ready to take on a new hobby/career/wardrobe/relationship /challenge? Or was she, behind her bright facade, thoroughly confused?

'Look,' said Jackie, now virtuously restored to cottage cheese and celery, 'it's simple really.'

Maggie chewed crispbread with peanut butter. 'But I thought potatoes were fattening. And pasta.'

'They used to be. Under the old rules. But now Rule Number One says protein's bad, fat's bad, fibre's good – so long as it's wholemeal, of course.'

'Ah.'

'Which brings me to Rule Number Two. White things are bad, brown things are good. Except for brown sugar, which is Rule Number Three – sugar is bad, and since most things contain sugar, from frozen peas to gravy granules, or salt, which, Rule Number Four, is also bad on account of hypertension, you'd much better avoid them, which is Rule Number Five, and go for Rule Number Six—'

'Which is?'

'When in doubt stick to lentils and salad.'

Maggie sighed. 'I don't really enjoy lentils or salad.'

'Rule Number Seven – you're on a diet, Mags, you're not supposed to enjoy it.'

'Listen,' said Sheena, wheeling up her chair and opening a pot of cauliflower paté, 'it's like, you know, simple.'

'Do us a favour,' said Jackie.

'Like you need to think holistically, love the universe around you. You've got to reject the speciesism which allows animalized protein, you've got to choose natural foods and reject commercial mass-production. It's like, you know, white flour is really, really bad, but wholemeal flour is—'

'Flipping heck, didn't I just say that?' said Jackie.

'But you're missing the, you know, spiritual dimension.'

'Maggie doesn't want to turn into a flipping maharishi. She just wants to get slim.'

'Slim is a sexist stereotype, Jackie. It isn't necessarily healthy.'

'I'll tell that to the doctor when he's nagging about my blood pressure.'

'You've got to be healthy in mind as well as body. Food that's produced by the suffering of your fellow creatures isn't just, like, physically polluting – it poisons your soul.'

'Give us a break,' said Jackie, casting aside her tub of cottage cheese. 'Look, Sheena girl, I've heard you whispering words of love to that manky tradescantia on the windowsill. And I bet you'll tell me your being so matey with it helps it grow. I'll bet you maintain it understands every word, that tradescantia—'

'That's not what I'm saying, Jackie. In a holistic universe—'

'In a holistic universe you can't have it both ways. You can't claim that tradescantia wouldn't scream blue murder if you pulled it up by the roots.'

'You're, like, missing the point, Jackie.'

'Oh, do us a favour! The point is, I wouldn't serve up my cat as an Irish stew either.'

'You're being illogical, Jackie.'

'Logic doesn't come into it. It's cultural prejudice. I don't eat cats, you don't eat tradescantias, Mr Gupta isn't supposed to eat steak sandwiches. But we've all got to eat something. Something somewhere's got to suffer and die – otherwise we do.'

'That's not what I'm saying,' said Sheena with a dismissive squeal of castors, swivelling her chair, turning her fervour upon Maggie. 'What I'm saying is you can't have, like, peace of mind if your body's, you know, full of poison. You've got to eat things that are pure and natural – fresh fruit, not sugar, margarine, not butter—'

'Margarine?' said Maggie tentatively. 'But I thought—'

'What I'm saying is, most diseases are man-made. The wrong food causes disease. If you were, like, an Eskimo or lived in the Caucasus or the Karakoram Mountains, you wouldn't have, like, heart attacks or cancer of the colon. If you, like, purify your system by eating pulses and raw vegetables—'

'What did I tell you, Mags,' said Jackie. 'It all comes down to lentils and salad.'

'What I'm saying to Maggie is with a whole-food vegan diet she could live, like, years longer.'

'Or even for ever,' said Jackie, laughing her throaty, fat-woman's laugh.

Maggie sighed. The crispbread and peanut butter had not proved satisfying, but the bathroom scales, announcing this morning that she had lost a mere two pounds, decreed she should remain hungry. From somewhere at the periphery of her consciousness the Phantom Chocolate Digestive beck-oned, daring her to invest its shade with tangible being.

'Tell you what, Mags,' said Jackie, retrieving her tub of cottage cheese from the bin and setting about its remains. 'I'll take you to Pound Shedders. There's a meeting this evening.'

'My mind just goes blank,' said the girl in the orange shell suit. 'I mean, I sort of go into a black-out. Like a serial killer.'

A hush had fallen upon the church hall, with its attentive rows of women perched on tubular stacking chairs. Maggie glanced about her, though she had received ample opportunity

124

to study her fellow Pound Shedders in the hour's weigh-in preceding the meeting. She had been conscious then of a sense, almost, of disappointment. What had she been expecting – a room full of women from 'Kiss Me Quick' postcards, crimson-faced caricatures of obesity from whom, by smug comparison, she could draw comfort? Alas, the crowd queuing to be weighed seemed no more freakish than the average line at the tills in Shop-Kwik – middle-aged women like herself with maybe a sneaky bulge or two concealed by their track suits, girls in their twenties, sturdy-thighed perhaps but hardly chronically overweight. Indeed, as she and Jackie paid their membership fees and joined the line, Maggie could not help noticing that Jackie seemed the heaviest person present.

Yet, as the line moved forward towards the weighing machines, a disconsolate succession of women peeled off in a second queue, holding out the backs of their right hands to a Counsellor, who stamped something on them in ink. Maggie had reached the scales herself before she saw what this was; the stamp left a purple imprint in the shape of an elephant.

'Jumbo indicates weight gain,' whispered Jackie. 'I often get one when I come regularly. Embarrassing's not in it – you get asked to share your midnight chockie-bar orgies with the group.'

The woman sitting next to Maggie on the other side from Jackie was a Jumbo, and so was the girl with the toddler two down. So was the girl in the orange shell suit, who was sharing now.

'It's as if I'm not in my body, as if I've gone sort of a long way off. And when I come back – I see the empty biscuit packet lying there. Like a corpse.'

That's me, thought Maggie, and immediately felt hungry.

The Counsellors, Marji and Sue, rocked on their heels sympathetically. Their clip-boards and navy blue blazers reminded Maggie of the holiday camps of her childhood.

'I look at what I've done and I feel ashamed. Guilty. Unworthy.'

125

'That's me,' whispered Maggie to Jackie, feeling hungrier still.

'I think – what's the point? Dieting's pointless. Life's pointless. I'm pointless. How am I supposed to go on when everything is totally, completely pointless?'

The orange Jumbo broke down in sobs. The toddler emitted a wail of commiseration, setting off a baby in the third row.

Marji stepped forward, raising her voice but maintaining her chirpy, happy-campers expression. 'Well done, Julie. Now, does anyone in the group have any advice to offer Julie, or any identification?'

'She should practise her Affirmations,' said someone in the front row.

'She should look at her Motivational Chart and re-evaluate her Responses,' said someone else.

'She should have faith in the Programme. Since coming regularly to Pound Shedders, I've found a new boyfriend, passed my driving test and now – how's this, girls – I'm only two pounds off my target!'

A tumult of applause greeted this last announcement. Maggie shifted in her seat. Her hunger was growing. On stage, behind the Counsellors, a collage clipped from magazines was propped on an easel. To the left, beneath a caption reading 'SETBACKS', were pictures of chocolate bars, ice cream, hot dogs and burgers. To the right were pictures of lettuce, tomatoes, green peppers, under the caption 'OPPORTUNITIES'. Try as she would, Maggie could not help her eyes being drawn to the left. Somewhere between a Mars bar and a Knickerbocker Glory, small yet still distinguishable, she seemed to make out an all-too-familiar image.

More Jumbos shared slips. Then, while Sue handed out diet sheets, Marji began Consciousness Raising. Maggie's stomach rumbled and though she tried to focus on the slogans – 'WHERE THERE'S A WILL THERE'S A WEIGHT-LOSS' and 'SHED POUNDS, NOT TEARS' – the picture of the chocolate digestive on the SETBACKS collage seemed to rivet her attention. It appeared to be growing, obliterating the Mars bar and the Knickerbocker Glory, acquiring depth, strength, a third dimension.

They clapped Marji, they clapped themselves. They joined hands and chanted: 'Every week, every day, together we'll shed pounds, the Pound Shedders' way.' They clapped themselves again, drowning out the screams of the toddler and the baby, and the meeting broke up.

Maggie felt dazed with hunger. Every thought that was not food-centred had been expunged from her mind. As chairs were stacked and the chattering crowd surged towards the door she found herself separated from Jackie, pushed up against a counter which sold literature and measuring spoons and other aids to following the Programme. Scarcely knowing why, except perhaps to dull her cravings, she bought a Pound Shedders Work Book and some kitchen scales, although the moment she had handed over her money she was telling herself she could manage quite adequately with the scales at home. Searching for Jackie, she began to add up what she had spent – £5 for the meeting, £2 new membership subscription, £8 for the book and the scales. Well, she had certainly shed pounds, one way or another.

Maggie was chewing her low-fat cheese and crispbread according to the instructions in the Pound Shedders Work Book, Page Five, Learning To Love Yourself, Section Seven, Love Yourself By Eating Everything Slowly.

'Do you know,' she said, swallowing with difficulty the glutinous paste into which the crispbread was transformed by the thirty-third chew, 'when I weighed myself this morning I'd only lost another pound.'

'Do us a favour,' said Jackie, inspecting her date and carrot salad grimly. 'I've put on two.'

'And I've got spots. Teenage acne at forty – would you credit it?'

'Your skin's, like, purging itself,' said Sheena, looking up brightly from a bowl of tempeh. 'It's, like, all the poison coming to the surface.'

'It's not having enough to eat,' said Jackie.

Maggie yawned. Her jaw ached, and she could barely summon the energy to chew another mouthful. 'I'm so lethargic. I feel as if my blood's been drained.'

'It's your system, you know, withdrawing from its addiction to toxins. Maybe your glands are blocked. Maybe you should try, like, an enema.'

'Give us a break!' said Jackie.

'And I feel so depressed. And scratchy. I'm snapping at Keith and I've had three major set-tos with Nicki this week.'

'Maybe you're making too much adrenalin. Maybe you've got stress in your acupuncture points—'

'Its hunger,' said Jackie. 'It's starvation, malnutrition, physical and psychological deprivation!'

'But that's what I'm saying, Jackie. It's, like, spiritual hunger—'

'Flipping heck!' said Jackie, disgustedly pushing aside her salad. 'Maybe we just need toning up. Exercise is supposed to be flipping spiritual. We could try Slimthetics. They've got classes every evening at the Leisure Centre.'

'And ONE and TWO and STRETCH and BEND, and twist to the SIDE, to the SIDE, and . . .'

And back – no, front – and left – and back, I mean front, now back, oops—
  'Margaret Cribbens, you're not concentrating!'
  'Please, Miss, I am, only—'
  'Left, girl, *left*! Can't you tell your left foot from your right?'
  'Please, Miss, I'm trying, only—'
  'Only *what*, for pity's sake?'
  'Only it's like my Dad says, I'm not a natural born performer, I've never been able to waggle my ears and wiggle my nose at the same time.'
  'Margaret Cribbens! Any more cheek and you'll find yourself outside the Head's study. Now *concentrate*. Follow the girl in front of you.'

128

The girl in front of Maggie was the thinnest girl she had ever seen (not that anyone in the Slimthetics class seemed particularly fat – as with Pound Shedders, poor Jackie was probably the heaviest). But the girl in front of Maggie was so thin that only her long blond hair distinguished her as female. No curves distended the shiny second skin of her sleeveless lycra cat suit, either at breast or buttock. No soft flesh moved on her arms, only tight, corded muscle. No sweat beaded her forehead as she pumped and jumped and stamped and high-kicked. Maggie's forehead, by contrast, was streaming, her mouth salty, her eyes blinded. She was aware that she was wheezing, could hear herself above the cruel beat of Nicki's favourite Madonna record, could hear Jackie too, somewhere to her left (or was it right?) puffing and groaning in her day-glo fuchsia cycle shorts and spluttering 'Flipping heck!'

Left, right, up, down. The rest of the class appeared to have no problem with it. Glance at the clock. Lord, only ten minutes gone, another thirty to suffer – oh, watch it! *Margaret Cribbens, watch what you're doing!*

Well, yes, she had been to blame, no need for an action replay, she freely admitted it. Jumping forward, she had hurtled into the girl in the lycra cat suit, who, with the rest of the class, had been jumping backward. Somehow their legs had become entangled, sending Maggie crashing down on her coccyx with Lycra Cat Suit on top of her, causing a domino effect on three others in front. Yes, it had been undignified and humiliating. But had she, apologizing, feeling Lycra Cat Suit's sharp angles in all her soft places, deserved that vengeful grind of a trainer upon her outstretched fingers.

Hobbling to the side, she observed that everyone else had picked themselves up and fallen instantly back into rhythm, lifting their knees, pumping their arms, Lycra Cat Suit too, lifting and pumping more determinedly than ever. Maggie watched the fixed eyes, the taut jaw muscles, a room full of women, each alone, though all moving in unison, each one isolated in her own fiercely competitive space. Maggie massaged her swollen fingers. I am guilty, I am unworthy.

A snuffling alerted her to Jackie, stranded on the mat beside her like a huge, shiny beetle.

'Don't you dare laugh, Jackie.'

'Flipping heck, Mags, I think I'm having a seizure. What do you say to sneaking off quietly while we're both in the land of the living?'

'But – I mean, won't we get told off, hauled up in front of the class?'

Jackie gave her a sideways look. 'Mags, we're grown-ups.'

Nevertheless, as they struggled down the steps of the Leisure Centre they were giggling like truanting fourth-formers.

'Fancy a coffee, Mags?'

Keith's supper was ready for him in the slow cooker, she wasn't expected for another hour. 'Decaffeinated, with skimmed milk and no sugar?'

Maggie had never noticed Luigi's Snack Bar and Ristorante, tucked away as it was in a side road near the station. But, from the greeting issued by the woman behind the counter, Jackie was obviously a regular.

'I do drop in occasionally,' she admitted. 'On my way home. Congenial atmosphere at this time of day. Not what you'd call ritzy – but nice and peaceful.'

Peaceful Luigi's certainly was. Apart from one old man reading an evening paper while forking baked beans into his mouth, the formica-topped tables were deserted. Perhaps the returning commuters, requiring fortification after their sardine-can ride from Waterloo, preferred the Station Arms. Or perhaps, thought Maggie, they were deterred by the pall of frying fat which enveloped you as you stepped through the door. The place seemed clean enough otherwise, for what was really no more than a workmen's caff, a greasy spoon, as Keith would have called it – the tables scrubbed, the cutlery gleaming, paper serviettes in a glass beside the condiments. Nevertheless, Maggie experienced a growing unease. The chalked-up menu caught her eye. 'Bacon, sausage and chips, Steak pie and chips, Spaghetti Bolognese and chips.' Dough-nuts sweated under glass beneath the counter, and eclairs and

130

cheesecake. An espresso machine spat cappuccino whose froth was surely not low-fat. After her days of self-denial, Luigi's seemed a den of iniquity to Maggie.

'Oh yes,' said Jackie, settling her bulk, smiling. 'It's off the beaten track, Luigi's. Makes you feel sort of incognito.'

'Of course,' said Maggie, trying to keep her eyes from the menu, 'we're just having coffee, aren't we? What's a – what does it say? La Dolce Vita?'

'Speciality of the house, Luigi's La Dolce Vita. Look, he's having one, the old boy over there.'

Maggie turned to see a tall glass being carried to the far table. She averted her glance hastily. 'Oh no! Whatever is it?'

'Maria!' called Jackie.

'Jackie, don't!'

Too late. The blowzy waitress swivelled her ample belly in their direction, displaying genial gold teeth.

'Maria, my friend wants you to tell her about La Dolce Vita.'

The teeth twinkle 'Isa ver ver nice. Isa mocha ice cream, chocolate ice cream, chocolate sauce, caramel sauce, banana, chop nuts anda whip cream. Isa ver good, Miss Jackie, yes?'

A premonition of disaster overwhelmed Maggie. 'You've tried it, Jackie?'

'Oh – once or twice. As a matter of fact – flipping heck, after all the calories I've just used up nearly giving myself a pulmonary embolism – well, I might go for a Dolce Vita right now, why not? I've earned it.'

The teeth gleamed. '*Due?*'

'Oh no,' said Maggie, hearing panic rising in her voice.

'Go on, Mags.' Think of the calories you burned flattening that snotty head prefect in the cat suit.'

'Oh, I mustn't,' said Maggie. Yet the memory of her humiliation somehow increased her yearning. Didn't the books say you could burn up 650 calories an hour by vigorous exercise? And besides if Jackie ordered one – could she bear to sit, watching her eat it? Wasn't she hungry herself, oh, so hungry? Hadn't she been ravenous for days?

'Go on, Mags girl. Be a devil.'

Well, it was only a pudding, wasn't it, nowhere near as bad as ordering spaghetti and chips? And anyway, hadn't Jackie said they'd earned it?

'Oh – all right then.' Just to utter the words, despite their wickedness, filled her with an overpowering sense of release.

The Dolce Vitas arrived in two fluted glasses, accompanied by special long spoons – what had Jackie said about the devil? They stared, Jackie and Maggie, for a moment, gazed as if overawed by the snow peaks of whipped cream, on which paper flags were planted, English and Italian, as well as Pompadour biscuits and a cocktail umbrella. They nibbled the biscuits, extracted the flags. Silently, they set to.

The silence held for some moments, punctuated only by little murmurs and sighs. Then Jackie uttered a demonic chuckle. 'Useless calories!'

'Refined sugar.'

'Instant hypoglycaemia.'

'Like, poison, as Sheena would say.'

'Do us a favour. Would you rather have lentils and salad?'

Maggie giggled, licking cream from her nose.

'Anyway, everything's bad for you nowadays, if you believe what they say on the telly – doctors, scientists, the government nagging about health statistics.'

'Mmmm,' said Maggie, delving for chocolate sauce and banana slices, thinking of Debbie Salt suddenly, and the hoo-ha about the healthy green apple. How had Maggie been supposed to know that apples were no longer healthy, that they were coated with layers of pesticide that wouldn't even wash off under the tap? And why had Justin needed to mention the wretched apple in the first place? She had thought long and hard about having him last Monday, but -- well, it wasn't his fault he buckled under the third degree, poor little lad. She had given him a cereal bar this time, sesame seeds, whole grains; that, at least, should earn Debbie's approval. Still, you couldn't count on anything now. Jackie was right, suddenly everything was poison.

'It gets to you in the end. You can't win, can you?'

'Mmmm,' agreed Maggie, spooning up caramel and ice cream. It was true, it did get to you. She remembered the carrot she had weighed last night. Fourteen calories, a nice slimming carrot. All the same, she'd found herself thinking those fourteen calories were still fourteen calories she'd be better off without. If she hoped the scales would show another pound gone by the morning, the carrot was only marginally less deadly than a chocolate digestive. Everything was poison, everything contained calories. But then you'd got to eat something, hadn't you?

'Still, you've got to eat something,' echoed Jackie, scraping the bottom of her glass with the long spoon.

'Oh yes, you've got to eat.'

'So you may as well eat what you flipping well like.'

They continued licking and scraping in silence. Maggie put down her spoon with a sigh. She felt – no, not replete, for she could easily have consumed a second Dolce Vita – but warmed, bathed in a soft glow of well-being, as if a nagging headache had been magicked away. She stretched her legs under the table. She smiled at Jackie. A renewed sense of their friendship came upon her, and with it a liberation, a shedding of inhibitions.

'What I don't understand – I mean, Jackie, you're so cynical about diets—'

'So why am I always on one? Well, it's obvious, isn't it?'

Maggie hesitated.

'I'm fat.'

'But you don't – I mean—'

'What you mean is, why don't I ever lose any weight with all this dieting? I suppose the binges don't help. But mainly it's my metabolism.'

'So it's sort of a medical problem?'

Jackie guffawed. 'Do us a favour. Talk to my doctor, he'll say it's a little difficulty in the moral fibre department. But really it's the dieting. Slimming makes you fat.'

Maggie stared.

'Don't look so horror-struck, girl. It won't happen to you

133

– you're a virgin, so far as slimming goes. And anyway, I'd be laughing if I had your figure – what's a stone or two between friends? But me, I've been dieting ever since I can remember. Even as a kid – my Mum didn't like having a fat daughter, bit of a let-down in front of the neighbours, like having tatty lino when everyone else has fitted Wilton, so she used to take me to doctors, snoop around like a KGB agent monitoring my carbohydrate intake (it was the old rules, then). Of course, I used to eat to spite her, raid the fridge, nick loose change for crisps, pinch extra puds at school dinner. But then, later, there were boys – and, well, you know how it is . . . It worked to start with. Believe it or not, I once got down to a size twelve. But then gradually – well, I'd lose a bit, pile on a bit, lose a bit, pile on a bit more, until I was fatter than when I started. It's your metabolism, you see. When you deprive it of food it goes to panic stations, thinks famine has set in like the Middle Ages, starts burning your surplus fat stores. But you can't fool it for ever. It's like the burglar alarm sounding off opposite me in the dead of night – sooner or later, your poor old metabolism thinks flipping heck, pulls up the duvet and carries on sleeping.'

Maggie felt treacherously relieved that she was not yet likely to contract Jackie's problem. All the same, though she nodded sympathetically, she couldn't help wondering . . . didn't this metabolism theory sound suspiciously like making excuses? 'But you haven't stopped dieting, Jackie.'

'Because I don't know any different. Because, Mags old love, I've no idea how normal people – thinnies – eat.' Jackie stared into her glass, twisting her spoon, making jagged patterns in the filmy residue of ice cream. 'And besides, where there's a diet, there's hope. It's not the fun you might think, donning the motley to excuse your existence. It's not fun being sneered at by spaghetti strands in clothes shops, or having people assume fatso equals dimbo. Like dear Sheena – "You're missing the point as usual, Jackie". I wanted to go to college, but you should have heard them at school – that fat slag Jackie Birtles, do us a favour? And then there's the men. Oh, it's always hunky-dory to start with. Take my ex. "Come here,

Jacko, you're a great big luscious handful." But then, when his eye starts wandering, it's another story. "What's the difference between a tub of lard and my missus? The tub of lard's quite tasty – ha, ha, ha!" '

Jackie's smile of bravado embarrassed Maggie. She wished she had not embarked on this conversation, with its insight into an alien world even a glimpse of which, she suddenly felt, might taint her. Hadn't God created fat people as a warning?

'No matter,' said Jackie. 'I've got my dreams. First sign Mr Wrong is about to be lured into my web, I reach for the diet books. Well, you never know, do you? Miracles can happen. Maybe, just as he's getting the gone-offs, sharpening his delivery of fat-lady gags, I'll wake up one morning a tiny frail wilting creature and he'll gather me into his arms and we'll drive off into the sunset in his company Lada. Well, there's no charge for dreaming, is there?' She paused, scraping the bottom of her glass thoughtfully. 'Funny, though. I saw her the other day, my ex's new old woman – and would you believe she made me look like a racing greyhound. Men! Would you credit it?'

'Men!' echoed Maggie.

'Not that you can complain, Mags old love – what with your gorgeous hunk. I'd pack in slimming tomorrow if I was happily married to Mr Perfect – considerate, sense of humour, totally devoted . . .'

Maggie flushed. Her Perfect isn't so perfect, she wanted suddenly to shout. His eyes have wandered too, oh yes, and a lot more besides. Then she caught sight of her empty Dolce Vita glass. An awareness came to her of what she had done, of how many calories she had just eaten. 'What's the difference between a tub of lard and my missus?' She bit her lip.

Jackie, too, pushed her class aside. 'Well, stuff what men think. Why shouldn't us girls have a treat when we want?'

Reassessing her calculation of the calories lost by exercise, Maggie remembered they had only endured ten minutes of

Slimthetics. Which meant, not a loss of 650, but 650 divided by . . .

'Why should we be victims of social pressure? Why should the thinnies always have the moral advantage?'

A mere 100 calories. And two ounces of ice cream alone . . .

'I mean, take Sheena, for instance. You'd think it wasn't just food she was on about, but the quest for the flipping Holy Grail.'

Maggie's waistband cut her flesh like cheese-wire. Her skin seemed to ooze and her teeth felt slimy.

' "It's not just yourself you're killing, Jackie." Once I was just a fat slag, now I'm ecological pollution. Give us a flipping break. Do you know, I read in the paper the other day that with all the beans veggies eat they pump out more toxic gas to destroy the ozone layer than CFCs.'

Maggie tried to match Jackie's laughter but her face had stiffened. Jackie, too, faltered before she had reached her crescendo. They stared silently, dismally, at the empty ice cream glasses.

'Trouble is, she gets to you, doesn't she, old Soya-bean Sheena.'

Maggie nodded.

'If you ask me it's no accident there's eating involved in Original Sin.'

Maggie looked away, fired with sudden anger against Jackie. How could Jackie do it – tempt her, corrupt her, bring her to this place where they would be anonymous like two seedy businessmen visiting a vice den? Now Maggie had squandered her hard work and suffering, now she would have to begin all over again. Perhaps she had been right in her suspicion that, never mind fancy theories about metabolic malfunction, Jackie's disease was catching.

But wait – Jackie hadn't tied her to the chair, had she? Jackie hadn't forced the caramel and chocolate and whipped cream down her throat. It was she, Maggie, who was weak, worthless, guilty. Small wonder she was unloved and unwanted. Close to tears, she stared at the Dolce Vita glasses. If only Maria would come and take them away.

As though reading her mind, Jackie transferred the glasses to an adjacent table. She cleared her throat. 'Talking of men,' she said brightly, 'did I tell you Mr Gupta pinched my bum while we were in the store room yesterday?'

But they scarcely had the enthusiasm even to speculate about Mr Gupta.

Maggie was weighing salad ingredients on her new Pound Shedders scales when Keith came into the kitchen. She could see in an instant he had The Look again. But then she should have guessed he was working up to it – the furrow between his brows had been deepening all week.

Strangely this time she found herself not so much frightened as angry. How could he do this to her when she was already so tired and tetchy, already living on her nerves? How could he do it when he knew she'd just had another set-to with Nicki (and what, come to that, was that little cow Kimberly thinking of, persuading her daughter to go in for weight training – it couldn't be healthy, could it, Charles Atlas muscles on a sixteen-year-old girl)? No, if he was setting the stage for the Big Confession he had chosen the wrong moment.

Nevertheless, he must be distracted. 'Do you know,' she said, 'there are only three calories in an ounce of fresh cucumber.'

'Maggie—'

'And only four calories in fresh raw mushrooms.'

'Mags, please—'

'Whereas fried mushrooms, as well as being very unhealthy, are fifty-nine calories an ounce.'

'Mags!' There was a crash as he brought his fist down suddenly upon the kitchen table. It seemed to startle them both, she jumping, shedding cucumber slices, he staring at his hand, withdrawing it slowly, as if he suspected it of taking on a life of its own.

'Sorry,' he said. 'But – look, love, when are you going to knock this on the head?'

'What?' she said, bending to retrieve the cucumber slices.

'This obsession of yours? You're driving yourself doolally.'

137

'It's not an obsession. We've all got to lose weight and eat a healthier diet. And, by the way, that was the last of the butter tonight – from now on you're having low-fat polyunsaturated margarine, so you don't get hardening of the arteries.'

Yet, despite her defiance, her hands were trembling as she peeled the clammy discs of cucumber from the vinyl. Keith never shouted or hit things. Her stomach lurched as she watched him pull out a chair and slump into it, pushing the hair back from his forehead.

'Mags, love, we've got to have a serious talk.'

She stared at the cucumber slices lying damply in her palm. She wanted to be sick. Didn't he realize she was doing this for him, starving herself, suffering, so he would love her again? Couldn't he just give her a little more time? A fortnight, even a week, and surely the pounds would begin to drop off, he'd see her changing. But perhaps it was too late. What did the agony aunties say? 'Infidelity may be a symptom of dissatisfaction with your relationship, rather than the cause. Perhaps it had always been too late. She must think of something, do something, she could not bear to stand here and watch his lips coldly forming the words that would destroy her. She must divert him, offer him a hostage.

'Mags, I've been thinking—'

'I've been thinking too, Keith. And I think – I've decided – I don't want the new kitchen after all.'

It had worked. He appeared to be staring at her, quite put off his stroke.

'I mean, I've waited in four times now for that Mr Barnes of theirs, so if they can't be bothered I can't be bothered either.'

He was still staring at her strangely. He seemed, she noticed incredulously, almost relieved. 'I thought you'd set your heart on it, love?'

'It was only Ivy looking down her nose that made me feel I couldn't manage. But now, well, I'd rather just keep things as they are.'

He pushed his hands through his hair again. He gave an odd little laugh. 'And to think – I've been looking at our finances, you see, and what with the cut-backs at work, redundancies, I – well, there won't be any bonuses this year, that's for sure. So I was trying to find a tactful way to ask you . . .'

Now it was Maggie's turn to stare.

'I was going to ask if you'd mind calling a halt with Craft DeLuxe. Just for a few months. Just till – well, till we see how things are.'

Maggie experienced an anticlimactic sinking. So she had surrendered her hostage needlessly.

'To be honest, love, I was expecting you to do your nut.'

She was, indeed, suddenly furious. Having let go of the kitchen she wanted it back now, the limed oak cupboards, the waste-disposal, the dishwasher, wanted them all with a passion they had not aroused in her before.

'I mean, you're sure you don't mind? I feel I've let you down. After all, it's important to you, isn't it? I know how you love cooking – or used to, anyway. Believe me, Mags, if things were different, I wouldn't ever ask it of you. I'd buy you six Craft DeLuxes, gold-plated, if it would help cheer you up.'

Her anger grew. So that was it, was it? The kitchen was just a sop, like everything else, like getting a kitten or his Open University suggestion, or that time he'd asked her if she'd like a break, a holiday away with a girl friend. Throw stupid fat old Margaret a toy to play with and she won't notice what's going on around her.

'I just want you to be happy, Mags, love.'

'*Do you?*' she said.

The venom in her voice seemed to astound them both, the force of four years' accumulated anger distilled into those two words. They stood for a moment bewildered, transfixed. She saw, now, that she had done it, kicked the rock that would cause the landslide, stumbled despite all her talismans and precautions, saw that, for the sake of one unguarded second she could not take back, they were falling, falling and nothing would stop them.

The phone began to ring. The sound split the silence, making them both jump. Keith's eyes left hers. He pushed back his chair and went out into the hall.

She stood alone in the kitchen, aware that she was shaking and that her hand was still closed upon the cucumber slices. She scraped the watery green mush into the bin.

No point in dieting. You could only diet if you had a future to look forward to. And while the end of the world might have been postponed, just for the moment, she could see now that this was only temporary. She might as well accept it. No more diet, no more Homes and Gardens kitchen, no more future. She might just as well give up.

Keith had reappeared in the doorway. She blinked at him, dazed.

'It's for you,' he said. 'The phone. A Mr Barclay – Bentley?'

140

IV

The paper clip still held his spectacles together. A second button was missing from the crumpled linen jacket. He seemed to Maggie, as at their first meeting, lost, worn down by the complexities of existence, certainly harmless. Yet, taking in his presence on her doorstep, she was struck by a sense of something unsuitable, of unspoken expectations and shifting ground rules. Why had she failed to give him an outright refusal on the phone?

Oh, she supposed it was flattering, the persistence of these advertising people – at least someone in the world felt she had something to offer. But why had she woken this morning with a fluttering stomach, why had she rushed out early, furtively almost, to Shop-Kwik and bought a fresh bottle of gin? Her decision had not altered, she had told him so, he had driven all the way from London for nothing.

Yet here he was, nevertheless, leaning against her porch, grinning his skew-whiff apologetic grin. She grinned back nervously.

'Gosh, Maggie, this is jolly generous, you know. Giving up time on your day off to help me out of a jam.'

'Spike, I'm not sure – I really don't think—'

'Worry not. It's as I said last night, I shan't try to persuade you or commit you to anything. I just have to go through the motions. You know what these Heavy Breathers in multi-national corporations are like – once you've been observed to shed blood they slacken the thumb screws, postpone the execution for another day.'

'You mean' – Maggie's image of multi-national Heavy Breathers was the more ominous for its being shadowy – 'you mean they could fire you?'

'If I listened to all the empty threats flying round in this business I'd be a gibbering wreck – well, more of one, anyway, than I am already.' The grin widened ruefully. 'No, what you and the Breathers have bestowed upon me is that blessing of all blessings, a chance to skive.'

It was, she thought, disarming, this frankness of his, this ready admission of his powerlessness where others might have blustered. She took him in afresh – a gangling man with floor-mop hair and a school-boy grin, a grown-up teenager who needed regular meals and his collar straightened and generally to be taken in hand. Yes, definitely harmless.

'You'd better come in.'

'Oh, and' – his eye went down to the parcels beside him on the step – 'I'm afraid Fizz insisted I brought you these. Your next fortnight's supply of Pandora.'

Maggie stared at the stacked white boxes secured with string, remembering that the previous parcels were still in the garage where she had stored them, finding no room in the freezer, yet too conscience-stricken to throw them away.

Spike, to her embarrassment, seemed to read her expression.

'I'm sorry – I mean, it's a very nice cake really—'

He was laughing. 'Bin them, my dear Maggie, set up a stall at your church bazaar, poison the starlings. I just need to tell Fizz I delivered them.'

Someone had disposed of the previous consignment of Pandora, she was pleased to observe when she carried Spike's parcels out to the garage – Keith probably, tidying his work-bench. When she returned to the lounge Spike was standing before the fireplace, sipping his gin and tonic.

'Gosh, Maggie, you know it's good to be in a real home for a change, somewhere comfortable, lived-in.'

She began her customary sorry-about-the-mess speech, but he overrode her.

'Nonsense. This is a proper room, not some interior designer's bid for a spread in Vogue. Clock on the mantelpiece, chairs you can sit in without counting your bones, horse brasses – I had an aunt who collected them, they used to

142

fascinate me as a child.' He paused wistfully, swallowing gin. 'Oh gosh yes, you get disgustingly nostalgic for it all when you're a refugee, living out of crates and boxes. But' – he seemed, at Maggie's look of concern to pull himself up, visibly to straighten his shoulders – 'that's another story. I couldn't help noticing your photographs. This is you, of course.'

Maggie followed his glance and saw with embarrassment that it rested on the leather-framed wedding photo, Keith in that sixties suit with too many buttons, and she in her empire line shift, striving to hide her bulge with her cascade bouquet.

She found herself giggling inanely. 'Oh, well, of course it's ever so dated.'

'You look lovely, Maggie. And – if I may say so – you've hardly changed.'

Though he was obviously being polite, she could not prevent herself from blushing. 'Oh, if only—'

'And are these your children?' He had moved to Brian and Neil in their cubs' uniforms, to four-year-old Nicola cuddling the late-lamented Fluffy.

'Yes, well they're a bit bigger now, I'm afraid. Brian's in computers – quite a whizz-kid, he can give you spots in front of your eyes going on about megabytes and whatnot. And Neil's off to Zaire to do VSO when he's finished his exams, although he does visit once in a blue moon to lecture us on acid rain and the evils of whaling. Of course, Nicki's still at home . . .'

She paused, aware that she was babbling, conscious that his expression was wistful again.

'Do you have children, Spike?'

'Four. Three boys and a girl. Amy's the youngest. She's five.' He replaced the photo of Nicki and the cat, turned away suddenly. 'But of course I don't see them very often.'

She had been stupid, clumsy. 'Oh, I'm sorry – I mean, not to watch them growing up – you must miss them very badly.'

'You could say that. But then it's inevitable when lawyers get involved. You've got to try to accept it.'

When he turned back the crooked smile was in place, more

143

skew-whiff than ever, a parody of itself. 'Anyway, I didn't come here to treat you to a diatribe on my mis-spent life. It's all your fault, Maggie. You shouldn't be so sympathetic.'

She felt the silly giggle rising in her throat and was grateful for his empty glass, glad to busy herself with spooning ice and slicing lemon. His vulnerability touched her, she felt she must deal carefully with him, not on her own account, but for fear of blundering further. The lines and creases of his face seemed like the scars of old wounds, imperfectly healed.

'I'm sorry, Spike, really and truly, about the commercial. You won't lose your job will you – seriously?'

He had flopped on the settee, was swallowing some tablets from a silver-paper roll he had extracted from his pocket. 'Oh golly gosh, no. Shame – I quite fancy a generous pay-off and early retirement.'

'But wouldn't you miss it – the glamour and that?'

He threw back his head in uproarious laughter. 'Oh my dear Maggie! Oh gosh, that's beezer!'

She watched, disconcerted, as he lit a cigarette, reclining amongst the settee cushions, extending his long, skinny legs. 'D'you know, when I was about two months into the business I went on my first photographic shoot – name photographer, big budget, the works. There we were, two clients, the agency art director, myself, the photographer and his two assistants, seven of us assembled in this vast studio in a forest of lighting umbrellas, with the assistants taking polaroids and testing flash guns, everybody in earnest discussion. And what were we discussing, what were we staring at, the seven of us, as if our lives depended on it? There on a podium in the middle of all this vastness was a plate of baked beans on toast. And there, bending over it, was a home economist with a paint brush, working away like Michelangelo in the Sistine Chapel, refining her brush strokes, sweating with concentration, painting tomato sauce onto those beans, each one individually. I remember thinking then, what if Martians suddenly landed? They'd get straight back in their saucers, file a report when they got home – "Intelligent life on earth? Forget it!" '

He paused, drew on his cigarette. 'But I suppose those Martians would have twigged – it wasn't beans we were gazing at, but money. We were looking at your mortgage and my mortgage and the unemployment statistics and the stock market and the IMF and the whole machinery of western capitalism. "Aha!" the Martians would have observed sagely, "here we see, in these beans, the concept of economic growth." Sell more beans, eat more beans, beat inflation, make a profit. And next year, sell more beans, eat more beans . . . and the next year and the next and so on, sell more, eat more, sell more, eat more, spinning on a wheel in faster and more frantic circles, clinging on for dear life in case the wheel stops suddenly, throwing us off, sending us all hurtling to destruction. Well, I fancy being thrown off, Maggie, I fancy letting go and whirling sideways into the outer darkness. I'm sick of eating beans just to keep the corporate digestion working. I'm tired, I've had enough.'

She gazed at him, puzzled. 'But what would you do? Would you find another job?'

'Once I was going to be The Great Novelist, England's answer to Joyce and Proust.'

'Well – there you are, you could write a best seller.'

From his laugh she was worried she had prodded another nerve but he recovered in an instant. 'Alas, there's no money in art, Maggie. Oh, if only I could learn to live simply. I have this great longing for small ordinary pleasures, a clean white room, a bed, a chair, a table, frugal meals. But then I remember the school fees, the tax man. Try telling the Inland Revenue money isn't everything. I only got into this baked beans lark in the first place for the money – well, I married young and went down from Cambridge in debt.' He sighed, swallowed more tablets. 'I've made all the wrong choices in my life. You don't know how I envy you all this . . .'

She followed the sweep of his hand uncertainly. Did he mean the room? Surely, once politeness was dispensed with, he could see the tired furniture, the battle-scarred wall paper, the stains on the carpet where poor Fluffy had tiddled. Or did he mean the empty routine of her days, the trips to

Shop-Kwik, the ironing, the hoovering, the neck-stiffening, brain-numbing hours at Magipost? To suggest that days of Wonder Wok and silent evenings in front of the telly offered more sustenance than the exotic delights of studios and famous photographers – well, it smacked of perversity, to say the least.

'That's why I'd never try to persuade you to do the commercial, Maggie. You don't need Granny Garfunkel's E-numbers and ersatz Maraschino cherries. You've got a real, rich Dundee cake of a life.'

She wanted to tell him that the fruit was full of stones, the almonds bitter, the whole mixture sour. Fired by that blind anger that seemed to keep rising in her nowadays, she wanted to disabuse him of his fantasy, to point out that you lost your children anyway, sooner or later, that length of service in marriage didn't guarantee security, that you could wake up one morning and find your dedication to shirt-ironing and underpants washing wasn't proof positive of caring but merely of your bone-headed refusal to recognize a con-trick when you saw one. She was distracted, however, by his sudden sharp intake of breath.

'Sorry,' he whispered, groping for his tablets. 'Only my ulcer reminding me I should have fed it breakfast.'

Her anger left her. Sitting there, his features crunched, his spectacles awry, he seemed so helpless. Helpless? Hopeless, more like. Just like Neil, agonizing for the world, yet never remembering clean socks without prompting. She felt an absurd impulse to put her arms around him.

He placed his knife and fork together. He scraped back his chair with a sigh. 'A tour de force, Maggie. Robust, playful, yet symphonic in scope.'

'It was only bangers and mash, Spike.'

'But what exquisite counterpoint of sausage and potato, what subtle resonance in the bass notes of the gravy.'

'Of course, if I'd known I was going to be put to the test by a famous restaurant critic—'

'My dear Maggie, you have no idea of the tortures I suffer.

146

Lambs' brains with Roquefort cheese and Kiwi fruit coulis, microsurgically quartered quails' eggs, chicken disguised as Swiss Roll. Whereas here you have the evidence of your culinary achievement, a feat even Michelin rosettes can seldom accomplish – observe, an empty plate!'

She laughed, refilling his wineglass – what a mercy she had remembered Fluffy's Beaujolais, still unopened in the sideboard. At his prompting, she poured herself a top-up too, though she was light-headed from the first glass, could feel a flush spreading over her cheeks. But then it was warm sitting here in the kitchen while a shower drenched the patio, cosy with the fug of cooking and Spike's fierce-smelling foreign tobacco, peaceful, shut away, safe and dry, listening to the splatter of rain and the drone of the Expelair.

His face was gentle in repose. A sensitive, sympathetic man, once you penetrated the barrage of words – too sensitive, perhaps, for his own good. She had asked him about his children as he had watched her stir gravy and cream potatoes, had listened as he'd talked of alimony demands and custody battles. Though he had gallantly avoided apportioning blame she could not but feel for him. If, God forbid, she and Keith ever parted, would she see only pound signs? Would she let a bunch of lawyers persuade her he was no longer a human being, would she deny the good years of friendship and trust, permit the children to call some stranger 'Daddy'? Poor Spike, though he was brave and resigned no wonder his grin was skewed with sadness.

Not that he was all talk; he could listen too, had drawn her out till she found herself telling him about Brian and Stephanie and the grandchild, and Nicki's weight-training, and Magipost and Jackie. She had made him laugh as she related the tribulations of her slimming, laugh so that he had taken off his spectacles to pinch the bridge of his nose. (He had nice eyes, she noticed, grey and surprisingly thickly lashed, but sad like the grin, despite his laughter.) Oh, there had been one or two little moments of embarrassment – when, for instance, she'd confessed that it wasn't only her slimming failure that had made her turn down the commercial.

147

'You see, Spike – it's mostly that I haven't the confidence.'

'Nonsense,' he had said 'You're not putting on an act like so many women I meet. That's real confidence, Maggie.'

She had blushed then, retreating into her wineglass. Yet now she wondered. She did feel confident, sitting here laughing with Spike, holding her own in the conversation despite his education and his eloquence, chattering away to him as openly as if he had been Jackie – or Keith, once upon a time. She felt giddy and light-hearted, quite her old self again, better than she'd felt for months.

She watched him stub out his papery foreign cigarette. He had long fingers, she noticed, artistic fingers, sensitive like the rest of him.

Tipping his empty plate into the sink, she fetched rhubarb crumble from the oven, crowning it with scoops of home-made coffee ice cream.

'Gosh, Maggie! Pudding?'

'Keep your hair on, Egon Ronay. It's only heated-up left-overs.'

She sat, sipping her wine, while he consumed the crumble, crunching its topping of oat flakes, scraping juice from the sides of the bowl. He replaced his spoon. He dabbed his lips with his paper serviette. He took off his glasses.

'Your heated-up left-overs, Maggie, are other people's gastronomic triumphs.'

Strange how eyes which usually hid behind glasses looked, without them, so very naked.

'You're daft, Spike Bentley.'

'And you, Maggie Hapgood, are a beautiful woman.'

Snatching up his dessert bowl, she turned to the sink.

'You know Granny Garfunkel's just an excuse, don't you?'

She twisted the taps, squirted washing-up liquid.

'You know why I really wanted to see you?'

'Spike Bentley, you've got enough flannel to make a nightdress—'

For such a thin, uncoordinated man he showed surprising speed and deftness of movement. It took her a second or two

148

to realize that she was now turned away from the sink and some seconds longer to register that not only was he kissing her but that she, arms around his shoulders, hips pressed hard against his bony pelvis, was responding. His mouth tasted of wine and ice cream and French tobacco. She was still holding the washing-up cloth, she noticed. It was dripping steadily down his back.

'Oh, Spike!'

'Oh, Maggie.'

'Oh goodness!'

'Gosh, you taste exquisite, Maggie.'

'Oh goodness, no, Spike!'

'Gosh, I could eat you, Maggie. Didn't you say I need feeding up?'

'Oh, goodness. Oh, no. Oh, Spike!'

The doorbell rang. She disentangled herself, staring at him wildly. 'Do you realize it's probably Ivy next door?'

'Number fourteen, just popping.'

'She could give MI5 lessons in surveillance.'

Casting aside the dish cloth, Maggie rushed into the hall. She paused for a moment, straightening her T-shirt, wiping her mouth with the back of her hand.

A small, dapper man with prominent shirt cuffs stood on the steps. 'Mr Barnes, Craft DeLuxe, Mrs Hapgood. Apologies for any delay or inconvenience. Would this be an opportune moment to measure up?'

Two dozen roses. Two dozen red roses, delivered first thing on Monday, in a cellophane bouquet tied with white ribbon. She couldn't remember when anyone had last sent her roses – except Keith, of course, when she'd been in hospital having Nicola. She couldn't remember when she'd last been kissed, properly kissed, either – except by Keith, of course. And that wasn't exactly recent.

Looking at the bouquet, she knew she should feel guilty. And yes, certainly she did. Hadn't she been having little spasms and twinges all weekend – picking the milk bottles off the step, taking margarine from the fridge, cleaning the bath,

149

thinking 'I let a strange man kiss me'? But then . . . it hadn't been anything really, all over apart from flustered goodbyes once Mr Barnes had started in with his tape measure (it hadn't seemed such a good idea, given the circumstances, to mention they were thinking of cancelling the order). It had been innocent really, a silly mistake. Spike saw that too – witness the card taped to the cellophane: 'Profuse apologies, S.' She was hardly his type when you thought of all the glamorous advertising women he could choose from. And he wasn't her type, either, come to that – too skinny, too brainy and complicated. It had been no more than a rush of blood to the head, no point in doing penance for it.

All the same, she knew she ought to throw away the flowers. Oh, if Ivy should ask, she supposed she could say they were from Keith. And she could tell Keith and Nicki . . . that Debbie Salt had brought them as a thank you present for baby-sitting Justin. (Not that this was very likely since Debbie's complaint about the healthy cereal bar – 'I don't want to be rude, Maggie, but you know that brand contains dried fruit, which means it's sixty per cent sugar, worse even than chocolate'. Still, Keith rarely saw the Salts from one week to the next – they were probably avoiding him on account of never having returned the hedge trimmer.) Of course it would mean telling Keith a lie, something she had not done in all her years of marriage. But then disposing of the bouquet would involve deceit too. She couldn't just throw it in the dustbin or even go to the public dump, she would have to drive to the other side of Potter's Park, reconnoitre for a deserted litter bin like a character in a spy film. If these were the complications arising from one innocent kiss, how did anyone summon the energy for full-blown adultery? But then adulterers grew skilled, she reminded herself grimly, they grew so practised and clever they could tell you bare-faced lies without blink-ing, they could make you believe that you were in the wrong, inventing suspicions, that what you'd seen through the shed window had been your imagination, that they really had been innocently watching redshanks that missing weekend.

She would brazen it out. What a waste, after all, to

150

throw away such beautiful roses. They would look perfect in that Scandinavian glass vase the children had given her for her thirtieth birthday. She would set the vase on top of the telly where she could look at it every so often and think to herself, 'I was kissed by another man, just for a split second a man who was not my husband found me desirable.'

She was arranging the roses, breathing in their scent as she lifted them one by one to snip their stems, when it occurred to her that perhaps she should phone Spike to thank him. Think of all the money he had spent, he would want to know the florist had delivered his order. And besides, wasn't it simple politeness?

Though she had long since thrown way the folder of diet sheets Fizz St Clair had given her, she seemed to recall a compliments slip attached to the latest consignment of gateaux. But Keith, alas, must have been to the garage before her – strange, she hadn't noticed the boxes out by the dustbins, he must have dropped them off at the dump when he had called in on Roger, his bird-watching crony. By the time she had extracted the number from directory enquiries she felt flustered and her hands were trembling so that she nearly misdialled.

At last a bored voice announced that she was through to Brooks, Bellini, Waldo and Stretch, then another, more jaded than the first, declared Spike Bentley was probably in a meeting. 'Name-please-and-what-is-it-in-connection-with?'

This was ridiculous, Maggie thought, as she mumbled 'Well, it's – er – personal' and was put on hold to the strains of a Country Fayre Cheese Slices jingle. Didn't he regularly rub shoulders with models and TV stars? Even this bored secretarial voice – wasn't its owner young and slim, a Fizz St Clair clone with perfect lipstick? Maggie Hapgood? She was probably far in the past now, her face a mere blur. He hadn't been wearing his spectacles, had he, when he'd kissed her?

The jingle sang:

Country Fayre, ooh you know that's nice
Twenty per cent less fat per slice
Choosy Mums choose Country Fayre
'Cause our cheese slices show you care.

By the third repetition Maggie's legs were trembling so badly she was forced to sit down, and when the singers suddenly vanished, mid-note, she was left speechless.

'Maggie?' said a voice. 'Gosh, Maggie, is it really you?'

'Spike, I—'

'I was terrified I'd offended you.'

'Spike, I just—'

'All the time that repulsive little gnome with the cuff links was prancing around, declaiming about drawer glides and magnetic door catches, I was desperate, I thought you'd never speak to me again.'

'Spike, I just wanted—'

'Oh, Maggie, you've no idea—'

'I just wanted to thank you for the roses.'

'Did they make you think of me a little?'

'They're lovely, Spike. And your apology—'

'Don't tell me it wasn't needed. I do apologize, Maggie, most abjectly and sincerely. My behaviour was appalling, one hundred per cent out of order. But I want you to know I don't regret it. God, I've been in torment all weekend, but now that you've phoned, now I know I'm forgiven – Maggie, will you have lunch with me? This week, Friday, your day off. Or even sooner if you can swing it.'

'Spike, I—'

'Oh, do let me feed you lunch in return for your exquisite bangers and mash. Le Caprice, Tante Claire, Langans—'

'Spike, I can't.'

'Well, Le Gavroche then, or the Connaught. Or perhaps you'd prefer something ethnic, Thai, Indonesian, Vietnamese, Caribbean. Or there's a terrific little place I know in Fulham that does pigs' trotters in oregano . . .'

'Spike, I'm married, remember.'

'One tiny lunch, one simple, innocent lunch I'll behave this

152

time, no touching or tasting. I'll just feast my eyes on you, Maggie, I'll just sit there and starve for your beauty—'

'Spike Bentley, you need your specs adjusted.'

'But you are beautiful, Maggie. God, you're delicious.'

'Spike, I'm fat and forty and about to be a grandmother into the bargain.'

'You're not nouvelle cuisine, that's true. You're not a spartan little portion tarted up with rosetted tomatoes. You're French country cooking, Maggie, generous, satisfying, succulent with rich juices, prodigal with flavour. You're carré d'agneau aux haricots, andouillettes, pot-au-feu, faisan a la choucroute—'

'Spike Bentley, you're taking the Michael.'

There was a pause. Then his voice returned, very low. 'I mean it, Maggie. I can still taste your mouth. I'm starving without you.'

'Oh Spike, I'm sorry.'

'I haven't eaten all weekend—'

'Spike, I just can't.'

'Well, if you won't have lunch with me, may I phone you?'

'I – it's not very practical—'

'Please. Grant me a few crumbs.'

'I mean – it isn't such a problem Mondays and Fridays, but Mr Gupta doesn't like personal calls in the office, and there's only the odd half hour morning and evening when Keith and Nicki aren't in—'

'Oh please, Maggie. Please. Have pity on my ulcer . . .'

Of course, it meant nothing that he hadn't phoned. True, he'd phoned every morning and evening for thirteen days, even twice last weekend though he wasn't supposed to; she'd had to pretend his first call was a wrong number. But this three-day silence – well, he was probably very busy at work.

She couldn't help wondering if she'd offended him, couldn't help running over that last phone call to see if there'd been something she'd missed. Of course it had been difficult, talking on a Sunday with Nicki upstairs revising and Keith out at Roger Entwhistle's but – who knew? – likely to walk in any minute. It would naturally leave you dissatisfied, that sort of conversation, with a sense of things unsaid. Still, Spike had seemed his usual self, he hadn't hinted at anything. They'd talked about black pudding, she remembered; he was writing some article about how it was becoming quite a rarity nowadays. And then he'd begun his usual nonsense – well, it was nonsense, wasn't it? All the same, it was lovely to listen to, made you feel more of a woman.

And then, on Monday, nothing. She'd taken her coffee to the phone to be ready at 9.15 – he'd always rung punctually, dead on the button. At first she'd just assumed he'd overslept or been unexpectedly called into one of those meetings of his. When, at ten, the doorbell had sounded – yes, she had to confess her stomach had turned to water for a moment. Even when she'd found it was only a delivery man with two more parcels of Pandora, she'd somehow expected a note slipped in amongst the boxes, had felt foolishly disappointed by the unsigned compliments slip. Still . . . he'd no doubt put in his 5.15 call as usual.

But he hadn't. Nor had he phoned on Tuesday or Wednesday, morning or evening. Oh, of course it didn't matter. What was she doing, lying to Keith about wrong numbers, telling Nicki she'd been chatting to Jackie? It had been a silly fantasy really, silly and dangerous. She'd only met Spike twice, it wasn't as if she even found him attractive – though there was something in that skew-whiff grin of his, something in his openness, his helplessness, the gentleness of his voice . . .

Perhaps if she hadn't said no so often, perhaps if she'd consented, just once, to meet him for lunch . . . Maybe he was sitting across a restaurant table with someone else even now, someone thin and sophisticated, Fizz St Clair or the jaded secretary. Maybe he was telling her about black pudding or pigs' trotters, comparing her with French country cooking . . .

Maggie stared at her own lunch, a sliced-bread cheese and tomato sandwich she had packed half-heartedly this morning, scarcely able to face the thought of food. Indeed, over the past two weeks, as this dangerous secret life of hers had set her stomach churning, her appetite seemed to have dwindled, until, in the last three days, it had vanished altogether. Even the Phantom Chocolate Digestive had apparently been exorcised. Now every so often a surge of acid burned her throat, as if her system, renouncing food, were quietly consuming itself. 'You've lost weight,' Jackie had remarked yesterday; and, stepping cautiously onto the scales this morning, she had discovered it was true – half a stone, in addition to the weight she had shed on her diet, a whole eleven pounds altogether. At least that was something, she supposed. At least it would be a piece of news to tell Spike when – if – he phoned.

But how could she sit here, thoughtlessly dwelling on her own unhappiness? Wasn't it obvious why he was silent? Something had happened to him – his ulcer, perhaps, or a car crash as he'd been setting off in quest of the perfect black pudding. Or perhaps one of his children was ill. And now he was in distress somewhere, wondering why she'd made no effort to get in touch, thinking her uncaring. It it was true when she'd finally plucked up courage to phone this morning the jaded voice had not indicated tragedy, merely announced that Spike Bentley was out of his office. But then the voice couldn't know the importance of Maggie's call, since she'd failed to leave her name.

Coming in through the front door, pausing only to shout up the stairs in case Nicki were home, Maggie seized the telephone and began dialling. Her heart was pounding and the receiver slithered in her palm.

At two, avoiding Jackie's questioning eye – hadn't she asked her three times why she was so quiet? – Maggie had pretended to visit the toilet and had rushed across the road to the public kiosk; but the jaded voice had declared Spike Bentley was out to lunch. At four he had been in a meeting. Now, at five fifteen, the phone rang and rang into an apparent void.

'Creative Department,' said a voice, just as Maggie was giving up. It was a male voice, young and slightly slurred, projected above giggles and squeals and all the general sound effects of a party.

155

'Who did you say? Can you speak up, love, there's mayhem in here. Spike? I'll see if he's around . . . Hold on, who's calling? Maggie Hopwood? Ah, sorry, Maggie, no sign . . . Well, if you've left messages, he'll probably call back tomorrow. Listen, got to go now before this oversexed bimbette on my knee gets her sticky little mitts where she oughtn't. Try tomorrow, love, OK?'

As she replaced the receiver, Maggie was seized by the conviction that she would never hear from Spike again.

At five thirty, Fizz St Clair was seated at her desk, studying the latest delivery of memos.

> *To: All Staff. From: Office Management. Subject: Poisonous Fungus.*
> *It has been brought to our attention that due to some staff extinguishing cigarettes and pouring drinks into the plants, we are currently experiencing a bright yellow mushroom type Fungus which is hazardous and can have a tendency to cause rashes and allergies by spawning tiny flies . . .*

'There you are, Fizz,' The Lapwarmer had screeched, thrusting this communication triumphantly across the table. 'Actually that's where the flies are coming from. Actually, it's nothing to do with the flowers.'

Fizz sighed. She could not bear to look at the sleek enamel vase; indeed, looking was unnecessary, for she could feel, not to say hear, the abominable presence. Tiny flies? These were hefty blue bottles, homing in greedily from all corners of the building, thudding against the window, buzzing, whining, dive-bombing her boisterously. And as for allergies and rashes – typhoid and cholera seemed a distinct probability, not to mention amoebic dysentery.

'Actually,' The Lapwarmer had said, gazing proprietorially at the shaggy screaming-orange blossoms, 'they're a rare sub-tropical species. More expensive than irises, actually.'

Actually, the creature had severely overstepped the mark. First, to claim there were no irises to be had (at the beginning

156

of June?) and then, having faithfully promised to remove the abomination before Fizz returned from her Pecan Paradise meeting, to forget, accidentally-on-purpose; to swan off to the Creative Department's drinks for No-Ads Brad's birthday without so much as a by-your-leave. Fizz had pencilled in ten minutes tomorrow morning with the Human Resources Director. She hoped this time he could be induced to comprehend the gravity of her problem, without obliging her to recall last year's Agency Sports Day, when she had stumbled upon him behind the club house, hunting for golf balls with that pimply youth from Dispatch.

Nevertheless, aside from the latest contretemps with The Lapwarmer, things were looking up. Of course a night with darling Dean always worked on her like a tonic, left her confident, invigorated, as though the act of penetration were a therapeutic injection, boosting her resistance with the serum of his youth. She had received several comments on her radiant appearance this morning, admittedly in the main from below-the-line people; but Stretch had also remarked upon it, sliding his snake's eyes over her Missoni mini-shift and agreeing without demur to her installing a fax in the Porsche (up yours, Dick Saunders Blair!). The age gap brought its tensions – the adjustments to the lighting, the strenuous holding-in of stomach muscles, the rushing to the bathroom the moment lovemaking was over to check one's fringe was still in place. Yet it was worth all that (and the other trifling peculiarities) when one could look in the mirror the next morning and know that what one saw was still desirable, that the face-lift fund might continue accruing interest for another day.

And then, the evening before, there'd been the private view at Camden Lock. Giorgio whatever-his-name-was, such an interesting artist – absurd to think of meeting him at Cissie and Rod's dreary at-home. Of course when she'd heard about his exhibition she'd said she simply couldn't bear to miss it. How intriguing – hadn't she virtually conceived the idea herself on that trip to Cannes with Spunky Dunkie, hadn't she said, as they were walking round the market at Grasse, 'Someone should put all this in an art gallery'? And now here

157

it was, the bistres and rose dorés of patés and salamis, the pale ellipses of cheeses already sweating under the arc lights, the boxes of mesclun and indigo-tinged curly endives, the lacquered scarlet and cadmium of sweet peppers. Of course, Giorgio had worked up the concept, extended it a little. The point was not simply to look, to marvel at the sheer range and diversity of cheeses and patés, to dwell upon the curve of an aubergine here, the purple spikes of an artichoke there, to wonder at such plenty and man's ability to harvest it. The point was to take in this splendour and then, over the month it was to remain exhibited, to observe its decay. 'What we are making,' Giorgio had said, 'is a statement of alienation, we are exploring the parameters of man's relationship with organic matter in a technology-based society which is negatively aspected towards man's own existence as a degradable organic form.' Of course, if one had not the time to visit the exhibition in its various stages, to observe for oneself acidic oranges and pinks break out in the cheeses, to chart the hatching period of maggots or inhale with a connoisseur's interest the burgeoning odours and gases, a set of photographs, available in a limited edition, would document the complete experience – Fizz wondered whether they might not prove the answer to the naked walls of her spare bathroom.

However, it was not so much his artefacts that truly spurred her interest in Giorgio as his usefulness as a guest at the select little dinner party she had decided to give for Stretch. There would be undeniable cachet in offering up an avant garde artist for Stretch's delectation – Dick Saunders Blair's cronies were all investment brokers and ex-guards officers, good on the Dow Jones index or gun-dog training, but without the slightest instinct for style. She would get caterers in, order something suitably post-nouvelle – red mullet in a mango coulis with sun-dried tomato bread, or plovers' eggs in aspic with geranium petals and baby sweet corn, followed by a kumquat sorbet and with scallops in filo pastry for hors d'oeuvres. The wives would have to be invited, alas, vulgar Mavis Stretch with her architectural hair and that harpy of Giorgio's, who had dogged his elbow at the private view, insisting on nodding and smiling all through his conversation with Fizz, though she was plainly way out of her intellectual depth. And for Fizz's own partner to balance the place-settings – well, Dean would hardly do, poor love, limited as he was in the conversation department (though amply endowed in others). Spike, perhaps? Maybe he could be persuaded to comb his hair and send his Versace suit to the cleaners . . .

Curse these blue bottles! Two squatted on her pad, suggestively kindling their legs. She flicked them way with the memo on Douglas Pilkington's early retirement. 'After years of unwavering commitment to United Breweries, etc., etc . . .' Poor Douglas. But not before time, as she'd frequently emphasized to Stretch. Shame about the wheelchair-bound wife and the three sets of school fees, but advertising was a young person's business, one simply couldn't afford to have balding, sweaty Douglas with his hernia and his Burton's suit representing the agency in what was now, after all, a designer market, with the key product discriminator being the style statement made by the pack. She would point this out to The Donkey when she finally emerged from her Nielsen presentation; as in the lager market, so in life.

Mind you, The Donkey had been suitably docile since Fizz had taken her aside and given her that discreet warning about associating with Brooks. Stick with the winners, she'd said. Of course, the poor Donkey undoubtedly couldn't recognize a winner when she saw one – only this morning Fizz had been obliged to draw attention to the prominent ladder in her tights. Still, she had been biddable enough, compiling those punishment presentation charts without a murmur, unprotestingly accepting the late-night crises that seemed always to coincide with her Scottish dancing clash.

But then, times were tough – even The Donkey must see that. Running costs were up, budgets and profitability down. Aside from Douglas Pilkington there had been some blood-letting of the sort not dignified by memos – juniors, middle ranks. She herself had been obliged to sacrifice a taxi-hailer, although Saunders Blair, mind you, had been forced to yield up three. Yes, if there were satisfaction to be derived

159

from the memo about Douglas, it came not simply from its appropriateness, but from the comforting sense that the Angel of Death had once more passed over. For she was aware that she, herself, was sailing awkwardly close to the wind.

Oh, she could busk all right – busking was her forte, witness her today, reassuring Genghis, giving glowing reports of the progress on Pandora. And at least she had back-up now, at least she had persuaded Genghis to entertain Mrs Kelly Slack as a substitute for Pudding Club Angie, had managed, after days of wheedling and cajoling, to convince him that Kelly's speech impediment was not a problem, since they could always use an actress to dub the voice, with no one any the wiser. But Genghis still wanted Tweetie Pie. God alone knew what he saw in the woman – maybe she reminded him of his mother – but his blank piranha eyes acquired a fishy glitter whenever she appeared on the screen. Fizz could only console herself that the matter was in hand – Tweetie Pie was still accepting, and therefore presumably consuming, her fortnightly supply of Pandora. For the rest, only time would tell.

Confidence, positive thinking, that was what was required, Fizz reminded herself, brushing a blue bottle from her forearm. Fear and doubt were for losers.

Pouring a top-up from her Perrier bottle, she considered No-Ads Brad's birthday drinks. Although not directly invited, she might find it worthwhile to drift down to the Creative Department, keeping aloof, as her status demanded, yet releasing, to selected ears, her coup in acquiring the fax for her car phone. It would also be provident to check the gathering for the presence of Stretch; an informal conversation indicating the success of her meeting with Art would not come amiss, and she could float the idea of the dinner party. Besides, she could scarcely leave Stretch for Dick Saunders Blair to monopolize; God knew what poison, even at this moment, he might be pouring into Stretch's ear.

The warbling of the telephone caused her a spasm of irritation. Curse The Lapwarmer and her dilettante attitude to gainful employment. After some moments, when the warbling failed to desist, she lifted the receiver and composed

160

her lips to reproduce the Hon. Son's mangled patrician vowels.

'Fizz St Clair's office. Can I help you?'

'C-could I speak to her please?'

'Actually, I'm afraid she's in a meeting.'

'Oh. Well – could I leave a message? Could you tell her it's Mrs Hapgood, from Potter's Park—'

Fizz narrowly avoided slopping Perrier. 'Hold on a moment, caller. Actually, I've just seen Fizz go into her office. Hold, please, while I put you through.' She paused, hand over receiver, emptying her face, rearranging it into an expression of empathy and charm. 'Maggie, lovey, hi! Great to hear you.'

'I'm sorry to bother you, Mrs Sinclair, only I've been trying to call Mr Bentley—'

'Your voice is a little indistinct, lovey. Poor you, have you come down with a cold?'

'It's – just hay fever. I was trying to call Spike – Mr Bentley – but I couldn't get through. I just wanted to say—'

'Yes, lovey?'

'I just wanted to say I've changed my mind. I should like to take part in the commercial. If it's not too late.'

When Fizz replaced the receiver she remained undismayed by the sight of an exceptionally large blue bottle drowning untidily in her Perrier. Fetching a clean glass, she poured herself a celebratory measure. Darling Spike. He had certainly earned his dinner invitation, let alone lunch at Le Gavroche.

PART THREE

'Food, in a hungry country, is power.'

Michael Buerk: *Africa: Deadline for the Dark Continent*

Granny Garfunkel Gourmet Gateaux (UK) Inc.: Creative Guidelines.

Part VII: Film Production.

Section 9: Video Vampires.

It is at all times to be remembered that the product is the *hero* of the commercial. Any elements which *distract* from the product's central role will be viewed as *video vampires* and may render the film liable to rejection by G.G.G.G.
Particular care should be taken in the following areas:

1) Set/Location/Props i) Interiors should be stylish and aspirational without being grandiose or ostentatious. Whenever possible a kitchen environment should be utilized to convey associations of home baking.
ii) Elaborate table-cloths or willow-patterned plates *have no place* in a Granny Garfunkel commercial. All table dressing must be subdued and a plain white china plate must be used as specified in Section 6.

2) Product Enjoyment Shots While these shots are key to conveying appetite appeal, the actress/housewife should be directed to communicate her enjoyment in a way which does not *detract* from the viewer's appreciation of the product's texture, ingredients and overall aesthetic. Lip-smacking,

165

murmuring, excessive smiling or other overt projections of personality are to be discouraged by the director. (For Slicing Technique, Portion Size and Crumb Control, see Section 5.)

3) Role of Housewife/ Presenter.
While a human element is necessary for viewer identification, this must at all times remain *subsidiary* to the product.

i) *wardrobe*: should be aspirational, yet uncluttered and recessive. Strong colours, 'high fashion' styles and, needless to say, sleeveless or low-cut tops must be *avoided*.

ii) *Accessories*: should be kept to a *minimum*. Jangling bracelets and coloured nail varnish can distract the viewer's focus.

iii) *Performance*: The housewife/ actress provides the context for the product and all aspects of her performance should be geared towards this role (see Product Enjoyment Shots, above). The desired viewer take-out is that she is a channel through which a direct experience of product attributes and benefits may be conveyed, a *reflection* of the product rather than a personality in her own right.

Any commercial failing to observe these guidelines will be judged by Granny Garfunkel's Gourmet Gateaux (UK) Inc. to be *wholly unacceptable* for on-air transmission.

I

Four weeks to the shoot, 13 lbs to lose.

Oh, Maggie Hapgood, another fine mess you've gotten yourself into.

She hadn't told anyone about the commercial yet, apart from Jackie and the kitchen man – not Keith, not Nicki or Mum. At least Mum had stopped going on about it (the Leprechaun's cousin Angie had apparently dropped out for some reason). And Maggie had meant to tell Keith when she'd come clean about the kitchen, but – well, it had sounded fishy, hadn't it? 'The bad news is we'll lose our deposit if we don't go ahead. But here's the good news. Our Craft DeLuxe kitchen will make the perfect backdrop for this film I just happen to be appearing in . . .'

Anyway, she didn't want to think about it. She felt sick at the very idea of TV cameras. Besides, she had other things on her mind.

She wanted to confess to Jackie. She'd nearly spilled it out yesterday, in the cloakroom at Magipost.

'Hi there, movie star!' Jackie had carolled, bursting out of the cubicle, wriggling into the mirror space beside her.

Maggie had made a face into the glass. She was worried about her hair. Now that her double chin was receding and even those hateful cheeks of hers were beginning to fine down ('Chubby-chops!' Joy would taunt, pinching them scarlet when Mum wasn't watching) – well, did this frizzy perm really suit? Didn't it look out of balance somehow, shapeless and frumpy?

'Oh don't, Jackie,' she'd said.

'You go for it, girl. Flipping heck, what's wrong with excitement and glamour? You're not likely to OD on it round here. Speaking of which – excitement and glamour, that is – listen here till I tell you, while Sheena isn't about to earwig – I'm starting a new diet tomorrow. And you know that means only *one thing*.'

'A new Mr Wrong?'

'Promise not to breathe a word. Ganesh – Mr Gupta – he's asked me out. For dinner and dancing!'

Maggie had stared at Jackie's reflection, shimmying and wriggling, and at her own, squeezed alongside it, giving out echoing tremors of delight, and she'd wanted to tell suddenly. She'd wanted to pour it all out in the confessional of this dank little room, look straight into the mirror, see herself forming the words. 'I have a Mr Wrong too. Me, Chubby-chops, Frizzy-mop, stodgy old Margaret. I have a man who says I'm beautiful. He telephones every day (apart from the week he was suddenly sent to Huddersfield and almost went crazy, poor chap, not being near a phone at any of the times that were safe to call me). He sends me flowers. He tells me I'm Chocolate Marquise, Tiramisu, ripe Ogen melon. He's probably, let's be frank, a little bit barmy. But I don't want to hurt him. So, in three days' time, when everyone thinks I'm safely at home doing my chores, I'm sneaking up to London and we're going to have lunch.'

Keith had been so good over the kitchen, swallowing her story about the contract (it wasn't really a story, it did say in the small print you could lose your deposit, but she'd omitted to mention she'd never actually told Mr Barnes they'd wanted to cancel the order). She'd had to steel herself to break it to him over his favourite supper of toad-in-the-hole and sticky toffee pudding; but, after looking dumbfounded for a moment, he'd simply shrugged his shoulders. 'Well, I did promise it you, Mags. I suppose it'll add to the value of the house if we ever need to sell it.'

She had paused then, in the act of ladling walnut sauce onto his pudding, had stared at him suspiciously. Why should they

need to sell the house? But he had continued to be so reasonable, agreeing to throw himself, nights and weekends, into
the work of demolition, so that Craft DeLuxe could install
the new units in the space of a mere three weeks (it was
amazing how Mr Barnes had been galvanized by the mention
of the commercial, swearing he would pull out all the stops
to achieve the impossible – 'You have my solemn promise,
dear lady.')

Keith had been reasonable too about consuming Miracle
Menus, heated in Jackie's borrowed microwave in the
temporary kitchen set up in Neil's room. 'I'll just keep
thinking of all the toad and sticky toffee you'll cook when it's
finished, love – that'll keep me going.'

Yes, he'd been the soul of reason over the whole business,
so that her suspicion niggled, so that she found herself gazing
into the skip at the kerb, eyeing the grey-white molars and
incisors of extracted cupboard doors with a small shiver. What
had he meant about selling the house? And why had he been
so reluctant to commit himself over the kitchen? But
there she was, being daft again, wasn't she? These weren't
prognostications she was staring at, but battered old doors,
cheap planks of chip-board with broken hinges, not even of
interest to skip scavenger.

Bringing Keith tea, she stood for a moment, watching
as he wrenched wood and nails from plaster, hunching his
shoulders, grunting, his T-shirt dark at the armpits, his forehead sticky.

'You're very good, love,' she said.

'Well, a spot of hard labour takes your mind off things,
doesn't it?'

What things? Her distrust returned. Oh yes, something lay
behind this saintly act of Keith's. His guilty conscience, no
doubt. She must weigh that in the balance whenever her own
guilt oppressed her.

She felt guilty about Nicki, too. Was it the act of a caring
mother to curse under her breath because her illicit phone calls
were cut short by her daughter returning early to concentrate
on her revision? She should be relieved that Nicki was taking

169

her exams seriously at last and even seemed to be seeing less of Kimberly. Poor little mite, she was beginning to look peaky from the strain of studying, wearing heavy jumpers although the temperature was up in the seventies and spending hours huddled in her room. And she was getting skinny – Keith had noticed too.

'Nicki love,' Maggie called, still standing by the telephone table as Nicki slouched past her towards the stairs. 'Nicki sweetheart, come and have something to eat.'

'Not hungry.'

'But you can't work on an empty stomach. Let me micro-wave you one of those nice packets of lamb stew.'

'Mum, I've already told you, I don't eat meat any more, OK?'

'Cod in parsley sauce, then? Or vegetable lasagne?'

'Puke and megapuke!'

'Come on, love, you've got to eat something.'

Nicki paused on the landing, staring down at Maggie, who had followed her half way up the stairs. 'Why should I?' she said. 'You don't.'

The howl of the CD player rose up to drown Maggie's knocking. She pushed open Nicki's door.

'Nicki, I'm not eating because I'm on a diet.'

'Oh wow, Mum! And here's me thinking you were going in for Mastermind with calories as your special subject. I'm really, really pleased you set me straight.'

'We'll have a bit less cheek, young lady, if you don't mind.'

'Yes Mum, no Mum, is that all, Mum? Can I get on with my revision?'

'Not until you've eaten some supper.'

'Look, I've told you, I'm not hungry, I don't want nothing—'

'Anything.'

'N-O-T-H-I-N-G, nothing, geddit? I'm on a diet too, as it happens. I just don't bore for Europe on the subject.'

'Oh, Nicki love – don't be daft.'

170

'What's daft about it? Why is it daft for me to diet and not daft for you?'

'Because I'm fat and forty – you were the one who pointed it out, remember? And you're a teenager and still growing.'

'So I don't want to grow any more, OK?'

'But look at you – you're all skin and bone. Has that precious Kimberly been getting at you again?'

Nicki sniffed. 'Who gives a puke about stuffing Kimberly Butcher? She's not so stuffing perfect anyway, she's got huge flobbery tits like bags of frog spawn.'

'Nicki! I thought you and Kimberly were supposed to be best mates.'

'Oh puke!' Seizing the nearest textbook from the pile on the unmade bed beside her, Nicki began ostentatiously to study the Asexual Reproduction of the Amoeba.

Maggie surveyed her helplessly for a moment. Then she waded through the debris to the CD player and turned down the volume.

'It's these exams, isn't it, love? But you mustn't worry. You've got to have confidence in yourself. Dad and I believe in you, we know you'll pass with flying colours and go on to college like your brothers—'

Nicki closed her book with a snap.

'Only you've got to keep up your strength, sweetheart, you've got to—'

Nicki hurled the Asexual Reproduction of the Amoeba at the dressing table, sending the lamp crashing, scattering lipsticks and dirty Kleenex, shattering a bottle of cologne.

'Mum, will you piss off! Go and measure a carrot or weigh a lettuce leaf, but just fuck off out of my hair!'

Maggie swallowed her shocked reproof. She stared at Nicola, her lovely, bright-eyed little girl, now sallow and hunched, the corner of her mouth snagged by a cold sore, her hair unwashed. She stared at the mess, which seemed, like some organism, to be growing, spilling out of drawers, bulging from the wardrobe, swamping the bed, as if Nicki, huddled in its midst, were feeding it with her distress. The

171

smell, too, had grown, had acquired vegetable overtones with a sickly hint of decay.

Maggie sighed. She could hear the spilled cologne drip-dripping steadily onto a pile of CDs. She righted the lamp and mopped up the cologne with the dirty tissues. Then, collecting the broken glass carefully, she carried it across the landing to the makeshift kitchen.

Muesli. Nicki till ate that, she had caught her in her nightie spooning down a bowlful the other evening. Maggie fetched the packet of Alpen from the food store in Neil's wardrobe, added skimmed milk and sliced a banana into the bowl for extra nourishment.

Nicki was where she had left her, hunched in her cramped little island on the bed, making no pretence at study, listlessly twirling a strand at the sleeve of her jumper. She greeted the muesli with a half-hearted sneer.

'You're sick, Mum, you're obsessed.'

'I'm not leaving till you've eaten it.'

'Banana? Honestly, Mum, with all those diet books you've read – don't you know by now banana's a real killer.'

Maggie took the bowl over to the dressing table. Carefully she scooped out the banana slices, depositing them in a dirty Kleenex.

'There you are, Miss Fussyboots. Now let me see you take a spoonful.'

'Banana. I mean, I ask you – you're a real amateur, Mum. At least when I diet I do it properly.'

'Let's have no more talk about dieting, young lady. Just eat your muesli.'

Nicki's eyes burned defiantly for an instant. Then, rather to Maggie's surprise, she plunged the spoon into the bowl and, piling it high, spilling milk and oat flakes, rammed it brutally into her mouth.

'Satisfied, Mum?' she asked thickly, through a dribble of milk. 'Now will you get off my case?'

'Only if you promise to stop this silly dieting?'

'So it's called, do as I say, not as I do?'

'Listen here, young lady—'

'I mean at least there's some point in my dieting. But you, at your age? Honestly, Mum, it's embarrassing—'

'Nicki—'

'I mean, I'm young, I've got a right to be slim while I'm still fanciable. But you – really, Mum, can't you see it's a joke?'

Poor Nicki. At least she had eaten the muesli; she'd even removed the empty bowl from her room, perhaps by way of apology, leaving it beside Neil's hand basin for washing up.

Rummaging furtively in the wardrobe, trying on lunch out-fits while Keith was at work in the kitchen, Maggie reminded herself that when she'd been sixteen, twenty had seemed over the hill. Her life wasn't over yet, not by a long way, although something inside her had been dead for a while. But now that something was painfully, gloriously coming alive; the fear, the guilt, the confusion, the racing pulse were no more than the tingles of its resurrection.

She examined her new body proudly. Yes, she had thirteen more pounds to lose, but already there was infinite pleasure in discovering waistbands baggy and skirts voluminous. There was a purity, she thought, in this melting away of flesh, so that she felt not just slimmer, but cleaner, as though purged by some chastening astringent. The hunger pangs had returned, of course; but now she relished them for the added virtue they lent to her self-denial, now she would even summon up thoughts of food for the euphoria induced by each victory over temptation. The Phantom Chocolate Digestive had returned too, although in a new guise; no longer silky sweet, its siren call was raw with unthinkable horror, its seduction the lure of the cliff edge or the tube train compelling you onto the live rail in its wake.

There was a dress in the depths of the wardrobe, she recalled, a slinky pink shift of knitted cotton, which, caught rear view on its only outing, had spitefully revealed to the Entwhistles' bathroom mirror every shaming sag and bag. But now, if she hoisted up her bra straps and held in her stomach . . . She could wear the gold high-heeled sling-backs she'd bought last year for the Polar Foods function, and the

173

belt that matched and, with a gold chain or two and her charm bracelet, she'd look every bit smart enough for the poshest restaurant. Shame about her hair. She wished she'd plucked up courage, dipped into her rainy day money and made an appointment with Hair 'N Now in the High Street, dared a complete re-style, something more youthful, a bob perhaps, like Fizz St Clair's. Now she'd need to work some miracle with heated rollers.

But still . . . Gazing at the mirror, she self-consciously struck a model girl pose, hand on hip, pelvis jutting. Past it? Not this new Maggie with her neat waist and taut jaw-line. She was no longer a failure, useless, unworthy. And the proof was that in seventeen hours she would sweep into one of Princess Diana's favourite restaurants, and there would be Spike, rising to greet her.

'Spike, darling,' screeched the girl in the baggy silk shirt, 'kiss, kiss!'

'It's been an age,' drawled the girl in the floppy linen dress and plimsolls. 'Haven't seen you since Cannes, Spike – Zak's party, wasn't it?'

Nothing was ever the way you dreamt it. Even teetering out to the car in her heels, Maggie had felt shifty, conscious of Ivy's inquisitorial stare behind number fourteen's Jardinair curtains, interpreting underhand intent from her very un-latching of the front gate. And then, in the train – sitting stiff as a doll for fear of dirtying her dress or disarraying her carefully curled hair – the wretchedness, as if she had suffered some irrevocable loss, as if she had left behind some part of herself for ever. Her stomach swam, her knees wobbled, her feet were already beginning to hurt. But that was as nothing to the ordeal of the restaurant.

How was it waiters could always tell you didn't fit in? They had kept her hovering by the desk for so long while they checked Spike's reservation she was almost afraid they would ask her to leave. And then, the condescension in the curled lip, the scornful 'Bella signora', as she had been led to the empty table – 'Signor Bentley is no arrive yet.'

174

Of course, in her nervousness she had tripped down some stairs, engaged in an unseemly tussle over who should pull out her chair, instantly lost her freshly unfurled serviette, to have it returned to her, not with discretion, but with an ostentatious flourish and cries of 'Eh, signora!' which seemed designed to focus the attention of everyone in the restaurant. She wished she had not been those fatal few minutes early, wished she had idled up and down the street. She made a pretence of examining the menu, only to find it was in Italian and she could not understand one word.

Even when Spike had arrived, proof positive that she was not here under false pretences, she had not felt comforted. She had built up an image in her mind's eye – Spike, sitting at her kitchen table, his face naked without his spectacles, the overwrought schoolboy. But here, in this alien place, his haphazard air seemed to carry authority, a confidence that set the scornful waiter fawning. Even the paper clip seemed a badge of assurance. She felt, despite the skew-whiff grin, that she was gazing up at a stranger.

Then, before they had scarcely exchanged a word, those girls had swooped. Disregarding the waiter who was shepherding them to their table, they had pounced upon Spike, planting kisses, throwing their arms around him, shrieking across Maggie as though she were not there. Yet she was not to be offered the comfort of total invisibility; while Silk Shirt chattered, Linen Dress and Plimsolls was considering her sideways, assessing her and dismissing her in one brief glance.

Maggie struggled not to blush. She did not blame Plimsolls, she could see her contempt was justified. She studied the pair as they chatted to Spike, noted their tans and the cool understatement of their floppy outfits, noted their manes of hair, curly, not as hers was, but kinked like strands of untwined rope. She saw her own stiff coiffure and Christmas tree jewellery and tarty gold sling-backs as Plimsolls saw them. She was overdressed and middle-aged and downright common. No wonder Spike had made no attempt to introduce her.

She focused her gaze upon the table-cloth. She became

dimly aware that the girls had finally taken their departure, and that Spike was touching her hand.

'I – I can't stay,' she said.

He raised his eyebrows.

'Well, don't you see it's daft?' She fumbled for an appropriate explanation. 'I mean, Spike, I'm on a diet. Here's you wasting money on an expensive restaurant when I can't eat the food.'

Spike grinned. He twined her fingers with his. 'Gosh, Maggie, what's food got to do with it?'

'So there it is. Tanya can take William and Jake to Oman with this unmitigated nerd she's married, and my solicitor says I can't do a thing.'

Poor Spike. Here she'd been, worrying about her hair, when he had real burdens. She imagined how she would have felt, had anyone tried to take her boys away. Suddenly there came into her mind Keith's remark about selling the house. She pushed the thought from her, reached for her wineglass. 'Tanya – that's your first wife?'

'Second. Melanie and I split before there were any children. She said I'd changed, sold out. She ran off with the plumber to a commune in Wiltshire. Sometimes I wish . . . Maggie, I've wasted my life. Everything held such promise, I could have written The Great Novel once, I know I had it in me. But now – a snappy slogan for blackheads is about my limit. Some mornings I wake to the screams of my brain cells dying.'

She watched him as he gulped down tablets with a draught of white wine.

'Spike, I wish I could say something helpful.'

'But you do help. Gosh, bless you, you listen. Most of the women I know are happy to prattle about who's jumping on who or the latest trend in designer watch straps – but try mentioning anything real and their eyes glaze over as if someone's just shot valium into their veins.'

Maggie secretly hoped he was referring to Plimsolls. She felt more comfortable now. The waiters, the assessing eyes, all had receded until they drifted, the two of them, cast off in an agreeable haze. Food had not presented a problem. Spike had ordered for her – melon and carpaccio (she was glad he had not told her it was raw meat till afterwards). But in any case the portions were tiny – 'Thanks for the snack,' Keith would have said, 'now where's the meal?' – and the waiter seemed too absorbed in his own ritual dance with the pepper mill to care whether they ate. Still, she must remember that wine contained calories too, and somehow they were already well into their second bottle.

Spike was smiling now, clinking his glass with hers. 'I'm so glad you decided to do the commercial.'

The thought sobered her at once. Of course he would expect her to discuss the advert. She was relieved the waiter chose this moment to sing his hymn to the sweet trolley, for the sudden lurch of her stomach precluded any treacherous longings for profiteroles or chocolate mousse.

'But I'm not an actress, supposing I dry up in front of the cameras. And anyway – I mean, I'm not the right image.'

'You're a human face amongst Martians, Maggie. And gosh, you've got beautiful breasts.'

'But, seriously—'

'Seriously, I can think of only one improvement.'

Her heart sank.

'You could take off your bra so I could see your nipples beneath that pink thing. I bet they're hard and full like ripening gooseberries.'

'Spike Bentley, you're a pervert.'

'But you could save me, Maggie. You could save me from myself.'

'You're daft, d'you know that? One dumpling short of a hot-pot.'

'I'm serious, Maggie. You could beam me down from Mars, rehabilitate me, redeem me. Oh, Maggie, let's start now. Let's skip the coffee, find a hotel—'

'Oh, Spike—'

'Lets make wild, primitive love, Maggie.'

'Spike, I—'

'And afterwards let's send out for something wicked –

177

cream horns. Or doughnuts. Let's get sugar between our toes, Maggie, and jam all over the sheets.'

'But we've just had lunch, Spike. And anyway—'

'And anyway you're a respectable married woman.' Sighing, he lifted her fingers and touched them with his lips.

Though he showed no impatience, only a melancholy resignation, she still cringed inwardly at the clumsiness of her response. After all, he had been kind to her, had treated her with courtesy, as if he were blind to her hair and her sling-backs and her ineptitude with serviettes. But now her primness seemed of a piece with these other defects. It was not enough to lose weight, she saw; that was merely the beginning.

Three weeks to the shoot, 9 lbs to lose.

The root perm, the highlights and the cut had taken over four hours and nibbled quite a hole in Maggie's rainy day money. Perhaps that was why, examining the result in the stylist's mirror, she had expected something different; yes, different hair, but something more – a different face, a different person?

Mum said, 'For what they charged you, Peg, you'd think at least they'd have brushed it.'

Ivy said, popping again (curiosity about progress on the kitchen having triumphed), 'You should have asked for Howard. I always insist on Howard or make another appointment.'

Nicki said, 'Honestly, Mum! And by the way, are those my leggings you're wearing?'

Of course Keith wouldn't say anything, Maggie reflected bitterly. He would just shovel down his duck à l'orange and bury his nose in *The Dictionary of British Birds* as usual. Perhaps, on the whole, that was a blessing. All the same, as she heard his key, then his trudge upon the stairs, she felt the beginnings of anger prickle behind her eyes.

178

In the doorway of Neil's room, however, his steps paused. 'Blimey,' he said.

She turned from the microwave with the packet of Duck à L'Orange in her hand. She stared at him. He stared back.

'I'll never say a word against wife-swapping again. Someone's just swapped my missus for a luscious blonde.'

Maggie was caught for an instant off balance. 'Look, if you're going to be sarky—'

'Sarky? Honest love, I—'

Oh she saw what he was about. He was trying to get round her with is Mr Reasonable act. Well, she was geared up for anger, she would not be cheated of it now. 'If you can't say something nice, don't say anything at all.'

'Mags, love—'

'I mean, I know you don't care. I know it wouldn't make any difference to you if I wore a black plastic bin liner over my head—'

'Mags, I'm trying—'

'Well, I don't give a stuff, do you hear? It's my hair and if I want to wear it in dreadlocks and dye it sky-blue-pink then I bloody well will. And if you don't like it, that's your problem, you'll just bloody well have to lump it—'

'For Pete's sake, Mags!' Putting his hands on her shoulders, he shook her gently. 'I'm trying to tell you I think the new barnet's terrific. Straight up. You look a million dollars, a real glamour queen, years younger—'

'Oh, so you think I was looking old before?'

'Younger than ever is what I mean, love. In fact, I'm even coming round to this slimming business, what with the barnet and these sexy skin-tight pants of yours – whajercallem, leggings? You've always been a knockout, Mags. Now you're a real dazzler.'

She stared at him. In another life she'd have scrounged for such compliments. Now they left her deflated, as if he'd outmanoeuvred her, denied her some real satisfaction.

179

'C'mon glamour-puss,' he said, sliding his arms round her waist. 'Give us a kiss.'

'Don't!' she said, fending him off with the packet of duck à l'orange. 'I didn't spend hours under half a ton of curlers so you could mess it all up.'

She was a little disappointed Spike did not comment on her hair. But then he'd received another letter from Tanya's solicitor. And, anyway, hadn't he just now told her she was beautiful, focusing such sad eyes upon her that she'd been obliged to gaze down at her plate.

She'd been determined to get things right this time. Taking the early train, she'd braved the Knightsbridge shops with their snooty assistants. She'd done her research beforehand of course, bought the right magazines, not the ones with knitting patterns and barbie recipes, but the glossy sort that assumed you squeezed a high–octane career in between parties and trips to Mustique and Gstaad. Now, in carriers in the cloakroom, cosseted in tissue, were a cream linen suit, a white lycra shift, and a floppy cotton jacket, stylishly belted. The raw silk shorts suit she wore, with the olive silk shirt, tan pumps, new handbag and earrings. It had gobbled a fair chunk of her rainy day money, this transformation, so that, arriving at the restaurant a careful ten minutes late, she had still felt nervous – should she have picked smaller earrings, different shoes, another colour? But, glimpsing her reflection in a distant mirror, she'd been pulled up short, scarcely recognizing herself. Mightn't she, in a good light, be taken for ten years younger?

Spike's soulful gaze seemed to confirm it.

'Gosh, Maggie,' he said. 'I feel earthed, talking to you. Oh, let's escape from all this' – this gesture dismissed with one sweep the restaurant's chandeliers and mirrors – 'let's do something real. Let's take a train to Brighton, make love under the pier. Let's eat saveloys and pickled onions and cod and chips from the paper. Oh sweetheart, I want to taste chip fat on your lips, I want to bury my face in your breasts and drink in salt and vinegar and ozone . . .'

★ ★ ★

Two weeks to the shoot, 5 lbs to lose.

Maggie extracted the small bowl from the back of Mum's refrigerator and lifted the saucer that covered it. 'Yuk!' she said, wrinkling her nose.

'Did I ask you to go ferreting in the fridge, Peg? My Petrolager won't be in there.'

'Who knows what the fairies get up to.' Averting her gaze, Maggie scraped the contents of the bowl into the pedal bin. 'What was it, anyway, when it was alive?'

'Only half a kipper left over from my tea.'

'About ten years ago, by the niff to it. Honestly, Mum, why don't you just throw things away?'

'Because I can remember the war, Peg, and rationing.'

'Oh, Mum.'

'And before that, when ordinary folk were lucky to get meat once a week. Do you know, when they called up the young lads to fight the Germans, half of them were unfit through malnutrition?'

'For goodness sake.'

'You youngsters don't know you're born nowadays.'

'Don't tell me. With half a second-hand kipper and a little ingenuity you'd have knocked up a nourishing meal for six.'

'That's right, you mock your poor old Mum. In the olden days the elderly got respect. They reckoned you got wiser as you got older, you didn't so much age as mature.'

'Oh yeah? Like cheddar?'

'Now everybody's got to keep pretending they're teenagers. Look at you – what do you call that, a skirt or a pelmet?'

Maggie, in spite of herself, found her fingers plucking at her hem. 'For goodness sake, Mum!'

'All this bleaching your hair and going on silly diets.'

'Have you been talking to Nicki again?'

'Mind you, she's as bad. I said to her yesterday, Nicki, if you carry on like this I won't have to open the door, I'll just move the draught excluder and you'll slip in through the gap.'

'Nicki's fine. She only went off her food worrying about her CSEs.' Indeed, now the exams were over Nicki was eating

181

at least one good meal a day – Maggie stood over her to make sure of it. Last night, after her glass of vegetable juice and her tuna and cheese pizza she had even volunteered to consume a bowl of ice cream. Watching her gobble it, right to the last spoonful, Maggie consoled herself that the hunger-strike, like the weight-training, had been no more than a passing phase.

'Now, Mum, let's concentrate on these fairies.' Maggie struggled from the stool, where she had perched to scan the top shelves. 'Honestly, though, I think they've defeated me for once.'

'There were two bottles, Peg. Both almost full.'

'The fairies must have used them and forgotten.'

'Since yesterday? I'd hardly use two bottles of laxative and not know about it. Do have some sense.'

'I'd trust the Leprechaun with the crown jewels—'

'Well, somebody's had them.'

'Must have been those burglars.'

Rene's eyes fixed her for a moment, glittering balefully. 'If that's your attitude, thank goodness I've got two daughters. At least Joy doesn't think her poor Mum's soft in the head.'

'So how's Joy going to find your Petrolager from Los Angeles? Telepathy?'

'She won't need telepathy when she comes home to see her poor old Mum.'

Maggie drew in breath. 'You never said Joy was coming on a visit.'

'You never asked, did you?'

'When's she arriving?'

'Yes, dear, I think she's thriving.'

'Mum! Did she give you a date?'

'No, she's not in a state, she just said she might need a bit of space from Duane.'

'When, Mum, when? And what does she mean, a bit of space?'

'Don't ask me, I'm only a senile pensioner. How would I understand all this fancy modern jargon? I'm pig-ignorant, me. Though I knew enough at your age not to go round as mutton dressed as scrag end—'

'Mum! Really, it's not fair. You wouldn't go on at Joy this way.'

'Joy's different.'

'You're right there. She's older than me. And look at those snaps from California – matador pants, boob-tubes, bikinis.'

Mum's pink cheeks spread sweetly. 'But Joy can take it, dear. You've always been the homely one, Margaret.'

'We'll see about that,' thought Maggie in the beauty clinic, as her body was pummelled, her eyebrows were tweaked and her pores galvanized by electric currents. A further chunk of her rainy day money had been swallowed, but now the mirror revealed a flawless mask of foundation and lipstick as impervious as Fizz St Clair's.

'Gosh, Maggie,' said Spike, 'when I talk to you I feel I could write again. Let's sneak away for the weekend. Let's find a little cottage deep in the country. Oh sweetheart, let's make love on the flagstones amongst the mud and the dog hairs and wake in the morning to the smell of bacon frying . . .'

One week to the shoot, 5 lbs still to lose.

'Hullo! Mr Barnes? Hullo? Hul-lo!' Maggie struggled to keep her voice from sounding shrill.

At the other end of the line there were distant mutterings as if from a dialogue elsewhere. Eventually, with a thump and a clatter – the sincere cuff-links, perhaps, colliding with the receiver – Mr Barnes returned unctuously. 'A thousand apologies, dear lady.'

'Mr Barnes, it's taken four days to get you on the phone.'

'Story of my life, dear lady. Busy-busy.'

'Your workmen have vanished off the face of the earth. And there's still the doors and worktops to be fitted and the appliances to be plumbed in, not to mention redecorating the whole kitchen.'

'Ah well, you know how it is. Absenteeism, sickness, you just can't rely on people nowadays, can you? Let's see . . . with a fair wind and Venus in conjunction with Saturn, I can

183

probably get you someone back on site – how would this be?
– Tuesday week?'

'Mr Barnes, the film people are coming next Friday.'

'Dear lady, much as I'd love to, I can't work miracles.'

'But you said you would. You said you'd pull out all
the stops to get me a Country Style Craft DeLuxe kitchen
complete with dishwasher, waste-disposal and built-in
microwave. You guaranteed it. By next Friday.'

'Dear lady, I'm not a paid-up member of the Magic Circle—'

'You gave me your absolute, solemn promise.'

'Ah, well. That's it, then, isn't it? You were only on a
promise, nothing definite, dear lady.'

Slumped on the third rung of the step-ladder, Maggie contemplated the skeleton of her dream kitchen Catching sight
of the Craft DeLuxe brochure, glossy amongst the builders'
debris, she seized it and hurled it at the bones of a leaded-glass
wall unit. Several of the bones, disarticulated by the impact,
promptly clattered to the floor. Maggie let out a howl and
burst into tears.

Keith appeared in the kitchen doorway, followed by
Nicki.

'Mags, love,' said Keith, 'I know Craft DeLuxe are a bunch
of cowboys, but it's not the end of the world.'

'You don't understand.'

'Honestly, Mum, you don't need a new kitchen just to
weigh up cottage cheese.'

'You don't understand.'

'I mean, I can't say I relish that packet muck, Mags, but
we'll cope for a couple more weeks.'

Maggie rose up from the ladder, her eyes streaming. 'You
just don't understand, either of you. It's got nothing to do with
food, this kitchen. It's got nothing to do with toad-in-the-hole
and sticky toffee pudding and whether or not you've gone off
bananas. It's to do with me, do you hear? It's to do with me
having TV cameras and Tel Travers and important people
from the advertising agency coming round here next Friday to
film an advert in my brand new Craft DeLuxe Country Style.

184

It's to do with me, Maggie Hapgood, getting a bit more from life than the Order of the Oven Glove, Third Class!'

Silence fell.

'Pardon, Mags love? I'm not sure I'm following you.'

'She said something about an advert, Dad. You don't mean that slimming ad, Mum? The one with the cake?'

'Why do you think I've had my hair done and bought new clothes? Why do you think I've been starving myself for weeks?'

'But you don't eat the cake, Mum, you just dump it in the garage.'

'That's none of your business. I'm being filmed for Granny Garfunkel with Tel Travers next Friday. It's bad enough that I'm five pounds over my target and the weight simply won't shift. But I said the kitchen would be finished. And now I've let them all down.' She meant Spike, of course. A further silence followed, in which she fumbled wretchedly for a tissue.

'Oh, Mum,' said Nicki. 'How could you?'

'Nicki!' said Keith.

'Well, honestly, it's embarrassing, Dad.'

'Nicki, I'm warning you—'

'I mean, I don't know where to put myself as it is, with her dolled up like some old rock star trying to make a come-back—'

'Nicola, go to your room!'

'But how am I going to show my face if my mates switch on the telly and find my mother sandwiched between Yukko Washes Whiter and Puke-o Kills All Known Germs?'

'*Nicola!*'

'Ok, Dad.' Nicki slouched to the door, sighing. 'But honestly, I could die.'

Maggie waited until Nicki's feet could be heard dragging upon the stairs, then she rounded on Keith. 'Go on, now it's your turn. Well, spit it out. "You're the homely one, Mags. You should know your place, which is definitely shackled to your non-existent Country Style kitchen sink." '

'Shush, Mags.'

'I've been shushing for twenty-two years and look where it's got me.'

185

'Mags!'

'Everyone has a right to one moment of glory. I've got a right to make an exhibition of myself if I want to, and if you and Nicki don't like it – well, hard bloody Cheddar!'

'Mags, for Pete's sake – I agree.'

Maggie paused to stare at him.

'What I'm trying to say, if you'd bloody well let me squeeze a word in for a change, is – if you want to do this advert, go ahead, do it. If it makes you happy, if it gets what's eating you out of your system, then it's a good idea. It's just come as a bit of a surprise, that's all.'

Maggie surveyed him suspiciously. 'Because I'm not a natural born performer?'

'Look, you're my girl, I'm sure you'll have them rocking in the aisles. I'm just surprised because when you mentioned being filmed in Shop-Kwik you said you weren't interested.'

'You mean you heard? You mean you were actually listening?'

'So I assumed – well, I'm surprised you never told me you'd changed your mind.'

'It doesn't say in the marriage service you have to mention it if you sneeze.'

'As a matter of fact, I'm relieved. What with all the sexy new gear and you plastering your face with gunge every night like something out of The Mummy's Shroud—'

'Are you referring to my wheat-germ face pack and my avocado eye pads?'

'What with that, and the secrecy and the phone calls, well – I was beginning to wonder . . .'

Maggie stiffened.

'But if all this titivating is in aid of the advert, that explains it, doesn't it?'

Maggie found his eyes suddenly full upon hers. She looked away, searching for refuge. 'So, Keith Hapgood, that's fine, isn't it? You've given me your gracious permission to appear in the commercial. But what about my kitchen? I'm standing here in a heap of rubble and you say its not the end of the world.'

186

'Be reasonable, love—'

'You're supposed to be the DIY expert.'

'Oh, come on! If Craft DeLuxe had even delivered all the units—'

'There won't be a commercial if I don't have a kitchen.'

'So, I'm supposed to work miracles?'

'You sound like Mr Busy-busy Barnes. You couldn't honestly give a toss, could you? Pat the little wifey on the head, tell her of course you don't mind her making a pathetic attempt to do something with her life. But don't so much as lift a finger to help her—'

'That's downright unfair.'

'Of course if it was Joy it would be different.'

'What on earth does your sister have to do with it?'

Oh, he had that innocent look, hadn't he, down to perfection. Maggie paused, wishing she had not been carried away. However, though Mum was vague about the dates, he would find out sooner or later. 'If you must know, she's coming on a visit.'

His face remained infuriatingly neutral. 'That'll be nice.'

'Oh, nice is the word. Very apt, very eloquent.'

'What am I supposed to say?'

'Think about it, Keith Hapgood. You just think. And in the meantime, since you're complaining about my beauty routine – The Mummy's Shroud, did I hear you call it? – you can move your things into Neil's room. Or on second thoughts, since Neil's room is now the kitchen, you'd better make up a bed on the settee.'

'Mags, for pity's sake!'

'It seems the ideal solution. You don't like my wheat-germ face mask and I don't like your snoring. In fact, I really can't think why we've bothered to go on sharing a bed these last four years, can you?'

An expression crossed Keith's face that Maggie had never seen before.

'Fine, Maggie. I move my stuff downstairs. I agree with you, it's the ideal solution.'

★   ★   ★

187

'No problem, 'said Spike. 'We get the Art Director involved, send some set builders round a couple of days in advance – and bingo, a Vogue Interiors fitted kitchen, complete with Sabatier knives, Le Creuset pans, and the obligatory fern, dressed to camera left. No one, sweetheart, will ever notice the difference.'

She squeezed his hand. It was good of him to be so understanding, despite having so much on his mind, what with William and Jake, and Amy's mother now, threatening a revision of visiting rights if he didn't up his maintenance payments. But then that was Spike's nature, the artist in him, sensitive and sympathetic. You couldn't imagine him making wife-swapping jokes, or snoring in front of the telly.

He refilled her glass. 'Maggie, let's run away, why don't we? Let's find a Greek island and live on pitta bread and olives. Or perhaps we could fish. I'll write during the day, and you'll be my inspiration, and in the evening we'll row out with our nets. Oh, sweetie, I want to make love to you under the stars, far out to sea, I want to ravish you amongst the brine and the fish scales . . .'

Three days to the shoot, 4 lbs to lose.

Maggie peered into the Magipost cloakroom mirror. She twisted her body. She pummelled the flesh at her hips and belly.

'Posing again, are we?' said Jackie. 'Flipping heck, we'll have to move this mirror into the office soon if we want to see you.'

'Leave it out,' said Maggie, sighing.

'So what's the problem? You look like one of those magazine make-overs. And I'll bet you didn't get that tan between downpours on the patio.'

'I did treat myself to a couple of sun-bed sessions.'

'Whereas look at yours truly. Three weeks on the new diet, and I'm like the python that swallowed the elephant. My metabolism isn't just on strike, Mags, it's handed in its notice.'

Maggie sighed more deeply. 'I think I've caught it.'

'You what?'

'Metabolic burn-out.'

'Give us a break!'

'But, Jackie, I just can't lose these last four pounds. I've tried starvation, exercise, diuretic tablets. I suppose there's always liposuction or plastic surgery, but it's a bit late for that.'

'Slim is slim, girl. What's four pounds between friends?'

'But I'm supposed to lose two stone. Apparently, in the advert they can call it nearly two stone and it'll add up to the same. But still – I mean, I know Spike says it won't affect what he calls the "end take-out"—'

'Spike?' said Jackie. 'Who's this Spike, all of a sudden?'

'Oh, just someone from the advertising agency.'

Jackie was staring, her lipstick poised half way to her mouth. This was the moment, Maggie realized, for her confession, her triumphant announcement to the mirror. Yet now it was upon her she felt curiously shamefaced.

'It isn't anything. Just a few lunches, the odd kiss in a taxi. Oh, well, and last time he drove me part of the way home and we had a bit of a snog in a lay-by. It's innocent really. But quite romantic, if you know what I mean.'

Maggie waited for the giggles of camaraderie, but they did not come. Instead, Jackie's mouth, stretched wide to receive the lipstick, seemed to freeze in a rictus of disapproval.

Maggie was nettle. 'So what's wrong with it? You've got Mr Gupta. Why shouldn't I have some excitement in my life?'

'But what about Keith?'

'Well, what about him?'

'I don't think I'd want to risk Mr Perfect for a snog in a lay-by.'

Maggie's eyes flashed. 'I wish you wouldn't keep calling Keith that.'

'Well, he is, isn't he? – if saying any geezer's perfect doesn't involve a built-in contradiction.'

'Keith may act the innocent, but it's the innocent ones that need watching.'

189

'Come off it, Mags. So what's he done then? Forgotten to take his bird books back to the library? Or run off for a dirty weekend with the lesser crested grebe?'

Maggie stared into the basin, where a tongue of green soap blocked the drain. 'He did have a dirty weekend, if you must know.'

'Keith? Give us a break.'

'Four years ago.' The sharp green of the soap blurred and receded. 'He had an affair four years ago. With my own sister.'

Maggie only dimly heard Jackie's whistle of disbelief. The words she had crushed down for so long burst out angrily, like wasps from a jar. 'I tell you, I saw them, Jackie. Joy was over for Mum's seventieth. Keith went to the shed to get more charcoal for the barbecue and I saw Joy follow him. When they didn't come out – well, Joy was pretty merry, I thought she might be under the weather or something. So I went to the window and looked in. And there they were. In a clinch.'

'But, Mags, one drunken kiss—'

'It wasn't just one kiss. Joy was going to Sheffield that weekend to see an old boyfriend and, yes, Keith was off on one of his jaunts – not grebes, as a matter of fact, redshanks. Redshanks at Filey Brigg. He set out on Friday night, supposedly with his mate Roger. But on Saturday I saw Roger Entwhistle in the High Street. He was on crutches, Jackie, with his leg in plaster.'

'So what did Keith say? Did you confront him with it?'

'He said they were meeting Roger's brother, so when Roger dropped out he still drove up to Filey as planned.'

'Well . . . there you are, then.'

'Except that we've known the Entwhistles for twelve years, without one mention of any brother.'

Maggie heard Jackie expel air between her teeth. 'Men! Flipping heck!'

'So after that I never said anything, I just tried to carry on as normal. I couldn't let him touch me, of course, but apart from that – I suppose I hoped if I ignored it then it might go away.

But it never has. It's always there, the suspicion, the fear he's going to blurt it all out any minute . . .'

Maggie's anger was spent. Extracting the soap from the drain, she squeezed the slimy mass with concentration. 'You see, it was Joy he went out with in the first place. He only noticed me after she took a shine to Martin Brewer and his Lotus Elan. And I know he still thinks about her. Otherwise why won't he talk to me any more? These days even getting a smile out of him is like pulling teeth.'

'Oh, Mags.' She felt Jackie's fingers kneading her shoulder. 'Still, look on the bright side, girl. Joy's a continent away. And didn't you tell me she's remarried?'

'Joy changes husbands like the Pearsons trade in Ford Granadas. Mum says she's coming home. And when I told Keith' – here the soap became a distant splotch once more – 'when I told Keith he picked a row and moved out of our bedroom.'

'Men!' sighed Jackie. 'Give us a break!'

Maggie heaved in breath and held it. The ball of soap returned to focus. Her nails were growing at last, she noticed, thanks to the Vitamin B supplement she'd been taking every morning. She must phone Hair 'N' Now for a manicure appointment.

She threw the soap into the waste bin. She squared up to the mirror. 'That's right, Jackie. So if I fancy a snog in a lay-by, I'm entitled.'

II

Sometimes Fizz woke in the night with fear sitting on her chest. It squatted like a black buddha, tightening its thighs about her ribs, squeezing the air from her lungs, so that she rose up sweating and gasping.

At that instant all the elements of fear, the big fears and the spidery whispering fears and those still unnamed, coalesced into a single definite terror; she was going to die of a heart attack, alone and unloved in a tacky hotel bedroom.

But this was not room 406. Though the chairs were the same and the melamine wardrobe and the coloured-by-numbers print, she could see now in the half light that these objects were reversed, a photographic negative flipped over. Nor was she alone. She could hear snoring, smell aftershave and an alien ketchupy reek. She peered at the lump in the sheet.

'Spike?' she essayed.

Even before the lump had groaned and rolled over, revealing a flabby arm and hirsute folds of beer gut, she knew her hopes had been misplaced.

Of course, everyone misbehaved on shoots. What else was there to do, cooped up for four nights in some suburban Dewdrop Inn amongst the nuaga-hide and the musak? You sought consolation from the bar, and after a few drinks or a line or two of fast white, well, if there was a chance of easing the pain with some low-commitment sex you took it. But naturally there were limits. LCS with your own kind was perfectly acceptable, an agency colleague, the producer, the director – LCS with the director might be perceived as conferring a certain status. Though actors were dubious unless extremely famous the first assistant might serve at a pinch, particularly if, as on the Pandora shoot, he was young and hard-muscled. But this? Though the head was buried beneath the pillow, the

192

Saturday-night-up-the-disco aftershave suggested the clapper loader or even the grip.

Fizz gave an involuntary shudder. She could not think how she had been brought to this error of taste. Yes, she had consumed the odd glass of shampoo, but she could hold her drink, unlike others she could mention. Searching her memory of last night, she recalled a row with the barman over his claim that the bubbly had run dry; she remembered a nosebleed and falling down some stairs in the ladies – yet no explanation suggested itself for this disaster. One thing was certain, however, without alerting the lump by her movements, she must dress and escape. For chrissake let her handbag be there – let it not be like that time in LA when she'd had to rouse night security for her room key.

Outside, in the corridor, possessed of her bag (although her French knickers were missing and her bra was unaccountably damp), she was struck by the injustice of her situation. Why did these things have to happen to her? All her life she'd tried harder than others, struggled to come up to expectations, fought to be perfect; and all her life she'd been on her own. She remembered her friend Cissie fainting at some Cambridge party. She'd probably only had one sherry over the eight, Cissie had never been a drinker; but there had been Rod, her fiancé then, cradling her in his arms, stroking her forehead, doggily devoted. And Fizz had thought, 'Why does she deserve this and not me? No one has ever been concerned for me, no one ever will be.' Now, as she stood in this night-lit, static-prickly corridor waiting for the lift, it seemed her prophecy had come true.

Perhaps she should have married, but who had there been, who'd come halfway up to standard? And even the substandard men had treated her badly, had used her, then dumped her, slinking back home to their wives. She couldn't remember when last someone had said they loved her. She couldn't remember when anyone, out of simple affection, had put their arms around her. And yet she'd worked so hard at being what men wanted, never clinging, never making

193

demands, taking her own sexual pleasure with a sophisticated coolness that matched theirs – you wouldn't catch Fizz St Clair making cow eyes the morning after, she'd be as casual as take-it-or-leave-it.

Oh yes, she'd worked, worked, striven for perfection, but what price the house, the car, the platinum Amex, without the man to complete the picture? Your womanhood was in question if you couldn't lay claim to a partner, it was like admitting you were menopausal, forget mere emotional considerations, you needed a man to compete. Yet where did Fizz stand, for all her endeavours? Dean had cancelled at a mere four hours' notice before their last date. And Spike? A tear trickled slowly down here nose as she descended in the lift. She had been making real progress there. Now the crew would be bound to gossip, it might easily get back to him, this aberration. It was wretchedly unfair. But then it was of a piece with everything else – take the dinner party, for instance.

It scarcely helped that Fizz's cleaning lady had chosen that week to give in her notice. Of course the creature was thick as bricks and going through the change into the bargain, recounting her hot flushes in such threatening detail that Fizz took care to communicate only by note. All the same, you would think after two years she might have come to some understanding of Fizz's art direction, observed that the black marble ash tray was always placed at dead centre of the Morozzi table and that the Kuramata chairs were angled with the table just so. A simple matter, not hard to grasp, yet this was the third note in as many weeks Fizz had been obliged to pen on the subject. By rights, surely, it was she, Fizz, who should have taken umbrage. Nevertheless, the creature's display of temperament was a nuisance. Fizz had looked forward to conducting Stretch and Giorgio on a guided tour, modestly demurring to their admiration. Now the Morozzi table was filmed with dust and the Kuramata chairs cried out for polish.

Yet this was as nothing to Giorgio's wife, phoning to cancel at the very last minute on some feeble excuse. Really, when

194

one had held out to Stretch an of-the-moment artist, Cissie and Rod were scarcely an adequate substitution. Fizz could see the disdain in Mavis Stretch's glance as she had priced Cissie's ethnic frock and sandals. She could foretell with appalling certainty that Rod, who had once freelanced for the *Guardian*, would collar Stretch after his third glass of wine and favour him with his speech on the evils of selling white sliced bread to the masses.

No one made much headway with the food, although it conveyed the definitive style statement, served with due ceremony by the caterers on Fizz's matt black styrene plates. Scrambled eggs with cherries, breast of guinea fowl poached in zucchini water with a Kiwano fruit coulis, rosewater sorbet flavoured with Salepi root – later when, out of curiosity, she sampled the left-overs she could see no reason for her guests' reluctance. True, the guinea fowl brought to mind a cork bath mat, but this was mere detail when you observed how the vibrant green of the coulis coordinated perfectly with the table linen. True, there was overmuch mastic in the sorbet if you valued your fillings. But what was this, compared with the cachet of mentioning you had dined out last night on the root of a rare Mediterranean orchid? Fizz despaired. She supposed you could hardly expect Rod and Cissie to under-stand nuances of presentation. But, really, she had anticipated more of Stretch.

And then there was Spike's inexplicable failure to realize he was expected to sing for his supper. Though guzzling, between chalk pills, large quantities of her Cloudy Bay Sauvignon Blanc, he had scarcely uttered a word. The only occasion on which he had shown the slightest animation was during the white sliced bread argument, when he had evinced a perverse tendency to side with Rod. Surely, if he chose to be reckless with his own career, he might at least consider hers. Besides, was he not grateful for an evening of elegance and civilization after his suburban wallowings? – she'd seen his expenses, all those lunch-time 'script conferences' in the cause of duty. Of course, he had done sterling work with Tweetie Pie. Indeed, though he had earned Le Gavroche, it had occurred to Fizz, contemplating this evening's arrangements, that the chance presented itself to bestow a more generous reward. Yet, though she flashed vivacious smiles down the table, permitted the strap of her St Laurent slip dress to fall waywardly from her shoulder, he remained fixed on his wineglass. When the Stretches at last rose, cueing Cissie and Rod to murmur about baby sitters, she feared he would follow. It was with relief that she watched him lurch towards the stairs.

Dispensing hostessly goodbyes, she returned to the drawing room and waited. She waited ten minutes, twenty. The guest bathroom was empty. She paused, befuddled. He could scarcely have made his escape. She moved unsteadily towards her bedroom.

And there he was. Of course. She had misread his signals, failed to see the frustration in his lugubrious silence, the longing for the others to be gone. There he was, stretched out on her futon, waiting, as she had waited for him. Well to be more precise, he was fast asleep, but then she had been uncharacteristically slow on the uptake. Poor Spike. He was still fully dressed, even down to his Oxfords. Contemplating him as he lay, foetal, cheek pillowed on his hand, glasses askew, she felt curiously touched.

She would surprise him. When he opened his eyes he would find her bending over him, spectacularly naked. Slipping out of the St Laurent, she tiptoed to the mirror, viewing her stomach critically in profile, checking her eyeliner for smudges.

'Spi-ike!' she called softly, hunkering down beside him. 'Spi-ike, I'm here.'

No response.

Carefully, she removed his glasses. His hair stirred in the steady current of his breathing.

Bending forward, she let her breasts sway close to his cheek. She brushed his parted lips with her left nipple. 'Wake up, Spike darling. Lucrezia is waiting.'

His lips moved, he muttered something that sounded to Fizz like 'rice pudding'.

She pressed her nipple into his mouth and felt his tongue rise

196

to meet it. Then all at once his lips were retracted, he turned his head away. 'Rice pudding,' he said, distinctly. 'Rice pudding with golden syrup.'

'Spike darling, it's Lucrezia.'

'I don't want spinach, I want rice pudding.'

'Spike, for chrissake!'

'I want my pudding. Robert had seconds.'

'Spike, will you snap out of it!'

He rolled over suddenly, burying his face in the futon. 'It's not fair, not fair!'

Though she pummelled his ribs, he seemed to have lapsed into a profound stupor. Perhaps a little fast white would revive him. She fetched the packet from her jewel box, cut four lines and, rolling a fifty-pound note, snorted two herself. Then she brought the remaining lines, laid out neatly on her hand mirror, over to the futon.

A dead weight, he took some heaving and tugging before he eventually lay face up. She showed him the mirror, she coaxed him, she slapped his cheeks. Licking her index finger, she ran it over the mirror's surface.

'Open wide, Spike darling. Lovely rice pudding.' She lifted his upper lip, massaging his gum with her finger. 'One for Mummy, one for Daddy . . .'

After a while his eyelids flickered. At last, with a sigh, he was gazing up at her blearily.

'That's it, lovey. One for the tax man. And the bank manager . . .'

His groans reassured her. She set to work quickly, removing his shoes and socks, unbuttoning his trousers and hauling them down to his knees. She tugged at his boxer shorts. He sighed. Applying like ointment a judicious slab of fast white, she was rewarded with a discernible stirring.

'That's it lovey. One for poor little Johnny Thomas.'

He sighed again. She flung herself astride him, lowering her head.

Fizz had always considered herself an expert in the arcane uses of lips and tongue. She'd even read a book on the subject, comparing the speed and precision of the South

American bordello with the subtler, symphonic patterns of the geisha. Yet no joyful burgeoning rewarded her erudition, no further stirrings, beyond the regular whistling of his breathing, acknowledged her provocative rhythms, her teasing arabesques.

Of course he was embarrassed, poor love. That was why, when she'd woken sore-headed the next morning, he'd already taken his departure. That was why in this last week he'd seemed so evasive, running off from meetings, seldom answering his phone. He had his stud's reputation to live up to, the usual masculine fear of losing face. He'd let her down – Fizz St Clair, of all people. Still, she would prove she could be generous, leave him hanging for a couple of days but then indicate she was prepared to make an exception. After all, though the dinner party had been less than satisfactory, they had made a beginning. He had declared his objectives, she had initialled them, action standards had been set. If his performance indicators could be brought up to scratch, well – when she took a rounded view, though Spike was scarcely high-status, he was available. Though he might lack Dean's pectorals, he undoubtedly also lacked Dean's wearing little foibles. Altogether, there were advantages to their becoming an item: if she thought positive, if she played down his lavatory cleaner commercials and emphasized his novel and his column for *L'Entrée*, she might even present him as quite a catch. And as for Spike – the benefits were obvious. Wouldn't he welcome intelligent conversation after the mindless succession of lapwarmers, wouldn't he be grateful for the cachet conferred by a high-powered woman who could re-art-direct his suits and his career?

All Fizz need offer was a demonstration of forgiveness, and here was the ideal opportunity: three days shooting Mums in Identikitland. She had merely to lure Spike away from the group at the bar, suggest drinks in her room. Last night had seemed so promising. If only Coleby Whiteside and his producer had acknowledged their duty, had not left her to nursemaid Tel Travers for the third night running; if only she had noticed Spike, slipping off early to scribble his freelance. She had half-resolved to make her own discreet exit, to knock on his door. But then someone had bought her another champagne cocktail. And, after that . . . Fizz winced as she struggled with the plastic card that served as her room key. It did not bear thinking about. She would not think of it, and then perhaps it would go away.

It had not gone away when Fizz awoke three hours later to the shrilling of her alarm call. It lurked like a dot on her mind's horizon, growing as she staggered to the bathroom, taking shape as she reached for the codeine bottle, looming behind her eyeballs, hammering for attention, manifesting glimpses of itself in flashes of despair. She whimpered. It was the clothes she recalled principally, as she had scrabbled in the dark, disentangling them from her own; grubby levis, a sweaty T-shirt, a trainer nestling under a chair beside her handbag – that Fizz St Clair should end up in bed with a man who wore *trainers*, ohmigod!

She clung to the basin, swaying, gulping back saliva. After a while, raising her head, she saw someone else's face in the mirror: puffy cheeks, bloodshot eyes, broken veins. She struggled to the fridge, whose stocks seemed disappointingly low. No shampoo, gin or vodka, only orangeade, two cans of lager and a bottle of Fernet Branca. Of course, she did not normally drink at seven in the morning, but today was an exception. She selected a lager and, as an afterthought, topped it up with the Fernet Branca.

Later, when she had showered and washed her hair and flossed her teeth, her confidence returned. Think positive, everyone made drunken mistakes once in a while. If she could not remember climbing into bed with The Lump, the chances were he was equally oblivious. She would brazen things out with her usual cool detachment.

Besides, today she would need all her reserves of professionalism. The previous two Mums, Sharon the Scrubber and K-k-kelly, had been predictably uninspiring and, as if that

199

weren't enough, there was the problem of Spike's so-called celebrity, Tel Travers. His projection was down, his performance stilted, his hand trembled visibly whenever he had to offer the Pandora pack to camera, and he'd fluffed his lines so badly they'd been obliged to tape prompt cards all over the set. But today there must be no hiccups, today Tel must be word perfect: this was their last day of shooting, and Tweetie Pie was scheduled.

Sometimes Fizz wondered if she did her job too well, enthusing Genghis, inspiring his confidence. Once you managed to hammer an idea into his brain he was so hard to deflect. Take Monday's phone call – she'd just happened to mention promotional material and PR opportunities, just thrown thoughts out, casually, as it were – and now he'd acquired an idée fixe about having a Granny Garfunkel Slimmer of the Year, someone who not only launched the TV campaign but appeared in point-of-sale photographs, gave newspaper interviews, probably, for all Fizz knew, opened fetes. Of course you had only to watch Genghis raising his dorsal spines at the sight of Tweetie Pie's video to guess who he'd already cast in this role.

Fizz worked before the mirror, shading out blotches, brushing in colour, willing her palsied hand to draw lips and eyes with its customary precision. If Tweetie Pie performed she would be one step closer to Deputy Managing Director. And as for Spike – there was always tonight's end-of-picture party.

All the same, she wished she had examined The Lump more closely. It was one thing not to know the name of last night's bedfellow, quite another, when avoiding action was required, not to know his face.

Well before Fizz's cab drew up outside number sixteen, Spellthorne Avenue began to manifest signs of Slik Piks' occupation. First loomed the charabanc used to transport the unit to the location (an indignity Fizz had learnt to avoid by being, each morning, a judicious hour late). After the charabanc was parked Coleby Whiteside's Range Rover, and

200

next to that the Mustang driven by his producer, Flash Rees. Opposite, at the evens kerb, was the winnebago that served as star dressing-room to Tel Travers, then the van carrying the generator for the lights, then the catering van, which, to the bemused fascination of a gaggle of bystanders, was by now dispensing stewed coffee and bacon sarnies.

Averting her eyes from the queue of bejeaned, betrainered figures at the coffee urn, Fizz followed an uncoiled intestine of cable up the front path, where Jed, the hard-muscled first assistant, was being berated by a crone in a lime green cat suit – number fourteen, 'just popping' to make her views known on the noise, litter, lack of parking space and general inconvenience to the neighbourhood. In the hall the cables snaked across polythene sheeting already slimy with cigarette ash and spilt coffee. In what Tweetie Pie had proudly designated her 'lounge', a refrigerated cabinet had displaced the draylon and, at a trestle table, a home economist was already making incisions in a specimen Pandora, dissecting it into scientifically calibrated slices that would demonstrate optimum product aesthetics and crumb control in the close-ups.

Determinedly ignoring two more T-shirted beer guts which sucked themselves in to permit her progress, Fizz picked her way down the hall, following the cable towards the centre of light and activity. Here, in what had once been Tweetie Pie's kitchen, a controlled disorder prevailed. Along the window wall a bank of units – leaded glass cupboards, dishwasher, sink and double drainer – was ranged like a showroom display. The wall had been papered, an Austrian blind had been erected, the floor had been laid with quarry tiles to one third the width of the room. Within this demarcation line, arranging copper pans on the pristine work surface, was a solitary props man. Beyond it, pressed against bare plaster walls, tangled in a jumble of hanging wires and cables and camera boxes, was the camera itself and the rest of the crew. Technicians laid tracks or adjusted spots from ladders, the lighting camera-man brandished his meter, the continuity girl clattered at a precarious typewriter; hunched over the camera, the bearded bulk of Coleby Whites gloomily conferred with

201

the operator; a gofer squeezed through the press of limbs and machinery with steaming styrofoam cups on a tray.

Surveying these two worlds, the one peaceful, clean, idyllic, the other fervid and sweaty, oppressive with swearing, hammering and cigarette smoke, Fizz was irresistibly reminded of some medieval Last Judgement. Racked by her hangover, she seemed to see Hieronymus Bosch eyes squint at her inimically, hear crooked mouths snigger. The props man, the sparks up that ladder – any one of them could have been The Lump. Gales of laughter drifting from the hallway made her flesh crawl. There was no sign of Spike. She needed more codeine or, better still, a medicinal inhalation of fast white powder.

Climbing the stairs to the bathroom, she found her escape cut off by Flash Rees, the producer. 'Hi there, Fizz baby. Seen the set, like it? Seen Mum dressed in her outfit? My, you're looking gorgeous this morning, if I may say so!'

Flash was a small man fighting a fierce rearguard action against middle age. Had direct eye contact with Flash ever been desirable, it was rendered arduous by the distracting lavatory brush sprouts of his recent hair transplant, which even now held Fizz in appalled fascination. She tore her eyes away, examining with distaste his sporty batik shirt and his etiolated legs in their Bermudas.

'Someone looking after you, fetched you coffee and a bacon butty? Oh, and – keep schtum, we're talking special people, read me? – I've got some shampoo in my boot if you fancy a quick reviver.'

Fizz stared at him suspiciously. What did he remember about last night? Why should she need reviving?

Flash was burnishing his palms with an optimistic vigour that never failed to suggest some rash over-promise or a nifty piece of creative accounting. 'Got to keep the Boss Lady happy. She's the one who's going to give us the client's OK, help us make those difficult decisions.'

Fizz's suspicion shifted. 'So there's a problem.'

'Oh, no problem, Fizz baby. Just – poor old Tel's a bit down this morning, won't come out of his winnebago.'

'The production company takes responsibility for the artists, Flash.'

'But the agency cast him, baby. Anyway, Coleby thought a little feminine charm might get his mojo working. Our Tel's taken quite a shine to you over these last two days, hasn't he? And who can blame him – you're a very desirable woman.'

Fizz's skin itched beneath her Versace silk shirt. She wanted suddenly, overwhelmingly, to lie down. God, how was it other people always sloughed off their responsibilities, loaded them upon her?

'Thanks, Fizz, great stuff! Oh, and afterwards could you run your eye over our Mum, give us wardrobe approval. Wow, have I told you, by the way, how gorgeous you're looking this morning?'

'Yes, Flash.'

'Must have been that sauna you had last night.'

Fizz's mouth, already parched, turned to sandpaper. 'Sauna?'

'When we all went to bed you were going off to test out the sauna and jacuzzi with that guy at the bar, the one from the Happy Pizza conference.'

So that was why her bra had been wet. Fizz's head cleared. Admittedly LCS with an off-duty pizza vendor couldn't be considered stylish, but at least he was an outsider, someone who, with luck, would have packed his bags by the time they returned to the hotel. 'Oh,' she said, smiling, 'I took a rain check on the sauna and tucked myself up with a book.'

Tel Travers glanced up as Fizz entered the winnebago and she could see his brain, like a damaged clockwork toy, churn sluggishly into action, struggling for a cheery greeting, a cheeky chappie innuendo. But, though the cogs whirred, they failed to make some vital connection and he subsided after a few creaks and clicks.

She surveyed him as he sat slumped over his coffee cup, cigarette burning down to nicotined fingers. Though made up for camera and wardrobed in his snappy mohair suit, he seemed insubstantial, his skin papery, the flesh shrinking from his collar. It was as if, beneath the panstick, Tel Travers, Entertainer, had shrivelled back into Terry Smith, travelling salesman – not the sparky youth to whom the talent contest had given the lucky break, but his ageing counterpart, too long on the road and hanging on desperately for his pension.

The fingers that held the cigarette, at last registering pain, wavered towards the ash tray. 'Sorry, petal. Be right as ninepence in a couple of shake. Just . . . just lost it for a second.'

No one called Fizz St Clair 'petal'. She decided to be brisk. 'Tel lovey, we're professionals here, right? We've got to push the peanut forward, and you're our key player.'

'Right, Mizz Fizz. Be up and at 'em in a tick. Tel's a trouper, twenty five years on the boards. Just need . . . a bit of a breather.'

Fizz watched as he struggled to lift his cup, abandoning the effort, despite employing both hands, before the rim was halfway to his lips. Lowering the cup, he stared, unseeing, at the lake of brown liquid spreading over the fold-away table. 'Thing is, my bottle's gone. Oh, only temporarily, of course . . .' He raised his eyes, fixed her with a mournful yellow gaze, at once confiding and imploring. 'You're a woman, Mizz Fizz, I can tell you this, you'll understand – though it's hush, ever so hush, got to keep it out of the tabloids. I've been in this clinic, you see. My agent thought – well, after that bit of bother that lost me *Hot Property* . . .'

Fizz bristled. It went without saying there was no room for 'bother' on Granny Garfunkel's agenda.

'Oh, not really trouble as such, more sort of . . . personal problems.'

'Ah, yes?'

'Nervous exhaustion, they call it.'

'Do they?' said Fizz.

'Clinic only discharged me four days ago. And it knocks your confidence, you see'. . .'

Fizz averted her gaze from the pleading yellow eyes. Having spent three evenings watching Tel gnaw his thumbnails as

204

he lingered over a lukewarm diet coke, she had little doubt as to the cure for his nervous exhaustion. It would be risky, of course – there was always the danger of over-medication. And it was irritating, too – hadn't she taken her minicab on that tedious diversion to serve her own personal need? Nevertheless, the camera must turn over, decisions must be made.

Removing the carefully-wrapped parcel from her bag, she tore it open and set its contents on the table. 'If you've lost your bottle, Tel lovey, we'll have to find it again, won't we?'

The yellow eyes glittered thirstily for an instant, Fizz swore they did. Then, all of a sudden, he was pushing his chair back, pressing his whole body into retreat.

'Oh no, petal. Tel mustn't touch that.'

'Just a small therapeutic snifter.'

'Oh no, pet. I've been detoxed, dried out, you see. Poison to me, that stuff is now. I'm twenty-five days clean and sober.'

There was a pathetic pride in these last words which increased Fizz's irritation. The creature was preposterous, who did he think he was kidding? She might drink a little too much herself sometimes – last night was an unfortunate example – but she had only to look at Tel Travers to see he was a hopeless alcoholic. Really, what difference did one vodka more or less make to an alcoholic? There were careers riding on this shoot, her own not least among them. And besides, time was passing, the meter was ticking away. She had Tweetie Pie's wardrobe to check, phone calls to make, and she had not found Spike yet, had not set eyes on him since her arrival.

'Fine,' she said, picking up the bottle as if to restore it to her handbag. 'Then I'll see you on the set, Tel lovey. Twenty minutes, right?'

'I er – well, yes, pet, I . . .'

The bottle held him, in spite of himself, she was pleased to see. His pupils contracted as she swayed it gently by the neck, as though the movement were mesmeric.

She smiled. 'Think positive, Tel. Granny Garfunkel's

signed you for a terrific deal here, generous buy-out, rock-solid contract. Shame to give the lawyers a present. And, as you say, the tabloids are such vultures . . .'

Better, on second thoughts, not to leave him the whole bottle. Better to hold his interest with a double or a treble. Going to the sink, she found a glass. When she returned she saw that two large tears were carving channels in the panstick.

She placed the glass beside his coffee cup. 'See you in twenty, Tel,' she said.

'Definitely not,' said Fizz. 'Sorry, lovey, but I can't approve it.'

So that was where Spike had vanished to – Tweetie Pie's bedroom. They'd been alone together, with no sign of Wardrobe or Make-up, and there'd been a furtive scuffling when Fizz had made her entrance. Really, the poor boy was a glutton for punishment. The game was already won. Tweetie Pie, you could tell at a glance, was star-struck, camera crazy, well and truly hooked.

In truth, Fizz would scarcely have recognized the creature as the wilting matron the camera had ambushed in Shop-Kwik. Of course there was the weight loss (still three pounds off target, however – no brownie points there). And there was the crimping – Sharon the Scrubber, K-k-kelly, they'd all been spurred on that annual pilgrimage to Unisex Hair Trends by the prospect of their names up in lights. But this one had outdone her rivals, by far.

Fizz considered the blond streaks, the Bahamian tan, the crisp white shorts suit, chain store imitation of a design now relegated to the depths of her own wardrobe. Sad, really. Money had been expended, an effort, undeniably, had been made. But – once a suburban housewife . . . Why did these women not realize style was a basic you couldn't purchase? It irked Fizz, the money squandered shooting these nobodies, the time expended turning them into sixty-second celebrities, women who didn't know caviare from cornflakes, who had made nothing of their lives. It irked her to see Tweetie Pie now, directing that misty-eyed glance at poor Spike, as if she expected him to condone her self-deception.

'No, I can't approve it,' Fizz repeated. 'I'm afraid we need a serious rethink here.'

'A rethink?' Tweetie Pie stared stupidly, her mouth agape.

'Gosh,' said Spike, 'what's the problem?'

'Everything's the problem.'

'But the outfit's fine, surely, Lucrezia? White's good on camera. And Siggy's been quite restrained with the make-up for once.'

Fizz had caught it, the helpless little glance Tweetie Pie had shot in his direction. She had noted, too, his alacrity in leaping to her defence. How typically male, always to over-egg the pudding. But then, poor boy, perhaps he had been brainwashed by his forays into Identikitland, had forgotten where his true interests lay.

'Guidelines, lovey,' she reminded him.

'Ah. Golly gosh, yes.'

'Guidelines?' ventured Tweetie Pie.

'No high-fashion outfits. I'm afraid that includes Jasper Conran rip-offs.'

'I bought it specially. And it's not a rip-off, it's—'

'We've got to be professional here, haven't we, Maggie? Where's Wardrobe, for chrissake? And we need Siggy to fix the hair.'

'The hair?' echoed Tweetie Pie.

'OK, we have a before and after situation, but the punters need to recognize you, right? We're talking synergy, lovey.'

'I'm not sure—'

'And besides, there's the credibility issue. Pandora may be a miracle product, but it won't turn you blonde overnight.'

Fizz sent Spike to find Wardrobe and Make-up while she began a search of Tweetie Pie's rails. When he returned with Siggy and Daz she was holding up a pink knitted dress by its hanger.

'Mmmm,' she said thoughtfully. 'Now that's more the image.'

'Oh, but—' objected Tweetie Pie.

207

'Nice and clinging. Good for demonstrating the weight loss. What does everyone think?'

"But I don't—' objected Tweetie Pie.

'What accessories do you reckon? These gold sling-backs look spot on to me. Everyone in agreement? Let's put it in the budgie's cage and see if it gets a nibble. Great, we're making real progress here.'

Out on the landing, wheeling Spike firmly beyond the range of further beseeching glances, Fizz permitted herself a sigh. Tweetie Pie had looked dangerously tearful, despite being reassured that she was their key player. God, Tel Travers had been burden enough, without some Mum deciding to play the prima donna.

'Gee, thanks for your support, Spike,' she said.

He withdrew his arm from her grip. 'Did you need to be quite so hard on her, Lucrezia?'

'Guidelines are guidelines. Remember Genghis.'

'But all the same—'

Retrieving his arm, she patted it gently. 'Look, sweetie, I know you've toiled in the kitchen, just for me, and I'm grateful. But the soufflé's risen, OK, no need to overcook it. Just keep remembering who pays the lunch bills.'

It was hot as Maggie stood waiting on her mark under the lights – no, not just hot, but stifling, sweltering, as she imagined the Sahara might be. Though, in the shadows beyond the eye of the camera, a press of bodies seethed, she felt she was alone, as if she were truly in the desert, lost in this searing waste of light. Nausea surged in her stomach, yet her parched throat refused to swallow.

Of course it was too late now, too late to back out. Perhaps if she had managed even an hour's sleep, perhaps if Nicki and Keith had been halfway cooperative . . . Given Spike's warning that the shoot could go into overtime, well into the evening, it had seemed only sensible to suggest Nicki stayed at Kimberly's, considering how she'd virtually lived there in the past. But no, suddenly Nicki would rather a park bench than the Butchers', it had taken all evening and the bribe of new trainers before she had agreed to go round to her Nan's. Keith, too, had been grudging about spending the evening with the Entwhistles. And when the crew had roused the household – indeed, the entire street – at six this morning, a fragile truce had given way to sulks. Nicki had flounced out, refusing breakfast. Keith had left early for the office without so much as wishing her luck.

And then there was Spike. They'd agreed it would be difficult, made themselves rules – no touching in public, no lingering glances. Though this had compounded her nervousness, it had buoyed her too with the usual excitement, the thrill of conspiracy. She'd felt Spike at least was supporting her, willing her to do her best. But then had come the episode with Fizz St Clair. It wasn't that she'd expected him to make a stand, exactly – she'd supposed Fizz was only doing her job, and he must do his. But afterwards he'd seemed to be avoiding her, and when at last she'd managed to speak to him his eyes had vanished shiftily behind his spectacles.

'But, Spike, I've tried so hard to change.'

'What's that old song that gets everyone's Auntie Doris going? "Stay As Sweet As You Are", Maggie darling.'

Maggie, who up till now had rather liked Nat King Cole, had not been reassured, but he'd merely switched the subject, hardly seeming to care how she felt.

Humiliated was how she felt, if anyone was interested, humiliated and ridiculous, standing here in the tarty pink dress with her hair rinsed mouse brown and rollered into frumpy curls. Job or no, who did Fizz St Clair think she was? 'Wrong time of the month, ducks,' Siggy had said, easing Maggie's head over the basin. And certainly when you examined Fizz closely you could see the ruched skin beneath the eyes, the cracks in the paint. Oh, she wasn't so very glamorous, Ms Fizz St Clair, once you took away the designer shirt and the lipstick. But she was powerful, she was in control. The last of Maggie's rainy day money had been gobbled by that Jasper Conran outfit, she had preserved it with polythene and tissue paper on a wooden hanger, had checked it in the wardrobe every morning like a delicate plant under nurture. It had seemed the very symbol of her apotheosis, of the new adventurous Maggie who swept, assured, into restaurants. But now she was common-or-garden Margaret again, and Spike was someone she did not know.

She blinked, afraid she would splotch Siggy's make-up. Oh, the endless waiting. They had waited once while the director, vetoing an artistically positioned chicken brick, had considered in its place a series of objects, an egg rack, an old-fashioned coffee grinder, a fern, before returning at last, full circle, to the chicken. They had waited again for Tel Travers, but now he was in position, dancing on his mark like an athlete before the starting gun, making faces, exchanging quips with the crew. Now they were waiting . . . for what? A man up a ladder was readjusting a light, the director was conferring with someone, Tel Travers was doing an impersonation – was it James Cagney or Robert Mitchum? Maggie's feet were beginning to swell in the hated sling-backs.

She tried to think of her lines. She was supposed to talk spontaneously, in her own words, but Spike had told her not to worry about that – the time constraints of a sixty-second commercial and the legal caveats would mean she'd need to be scripted. He'd rehearsed her carefully, as he'd promised. Tel Travers would say, 'So, Maggie, have you given up your naughty little nibbles? You can tell Tel.' And she would say . . . she would say . . . Maggie's legs turned to jelly. Her mind was a blank.

A small man edged past the camera and crossed the line of quarry tiles into Maggie's desert. Earlier the provider of chicken bricks and coffee grinders, he now carried a large white dinner plate and on it a gateau.

Maggie flinched guiltily. 'Of course it doesn't matter that you don't actually like the product,' Spike had said. 'All the same, better not to mention it.'

'But what about the eating shots?'

'Worry not, sweetheart. They'll let you spit it into a bucket.'

All the same, she did worry. It struck her, now that it

was too late, that she had been dishonest. Only last night, remembering the garage, she had rushed out to check for incriminating evidence, had blessed the empty space on Keith's work-bench where the final consignment of white boxes had stood. Now she eyed the gateau shiftily as the small man, to shouted instructions, moved its plate left-a-bit, back-a-bit on the work surface beside her. When he paused for the camera to reflect upon these manoeuvres, she half expected him to fix her with an accusing glance.

Instead, his eyes twinkled. 'Luverly grub, innit?'

Maggie looked reluctantly to where the fudge icing rippled, the cherries glowed in their scollops of cream. A single neat slice had been cut, exposing rich seams of sponge and filling. 'Oh – er, yes, delicious,' she said.

The small man gave a wheezing chuckle. 'Bet you fancy getting your teeth into that.'

'Yes – yes of course,' Maggie said.

The small man, chuckling, doubled up in the grip of a smoker's cough. 'You'll need a dentist if you do!'

'Pardon?' said Maggie, as he continued to splutter.

He righted himself at last with a chest-tearing wheeze. 'The icing's plaster, the sponge is foam rubber, the cream's shaving foam – oh, and the cherries, I believe, is made of plastic. Real thing's useless for filming, see. Melts under the lights.'

'My goodness,' said Maggie.

'We're stuck with it for the close-ups, of course, but we go with this for the master. Ah, hold on, excuse us a sec, lady.' He cupped his hand to his ear, listening. Then he whipped from his pocket a yellow duster. 'Hang about, got to catch up on the housework.'

Maggie watched as, breathing fiercely on the cherries, he buffed each in turn with his duster. 'There you go, lady,' he said, twinkling. 'Don't eat it all at once.'

Somehow the fraudulence of the cake made Maggie's own fraud seem less reprehensible. None of this was real, after all – the Austrian blind didn't run, the dishwasher didn't wash, the kitchen unit doors didn't open. (She remembered Keith's

211

face draining of hope when she had explained this. 'So it's a pretend kitchen, is it? Well, that fits, around here.') No, this wasn't real, it was only acting. She wished she'd gone in for drama at school – that sheep in the nativity play had proved the extent of her theatrical experience. She groped once again for her lines and was relieved to feel words coming. 'Yes, Tel, I've lost nearly two stone with delicious Slimmers Supreme as part of my calorie-controlled diet . . .' Nothing awful could happen, no one actually died of stage fright, it was only a figure of speech.

The young man called Jed, whose job seemed to be shouting at everyone, was shouting again. 'Quiet, boys and girls! We're going to turn over. Let's go for a take straight away.'

It took Maggie a second or two before the force of this hit home. Her mind emptied, her legs began to tremble.

'OK, Slate One, Take One. Sound running. Camera turning over. Action!'

Maggie wished she had something to support her. She wished she could see Spike, but now the faces behind the camera were a shadowy blur, now she could only see Tel Travers. His mouth was opening and closing very slowly as if he were under water, and waves of extra-strong mint rolled ponderously towards hers. Her mouth began to open too. She felt immensely heavy, as if she were labouring against a flow tide. Words fell from her lips, then sank like boulders to some unfathomable depth.

'Cut!' yelled Jed. 'Save the red. Mark it. Print it?'

Maggie stood, reeling, waiting for someone to say something, to point out all the things she had done wrong.

A voice from the camera muttered. 'NG. We're getting flare from those cherries.'

The small man appeared at her elbow with an aerosol canister, which he trained upon the gateau.

Jed was inspecting his watch. 'OK, break for lunch, boys and girls. Back on the hour.'

'Dead quiet, everyone, *please*! Slate Seven, Take Fifteen. Turn over. *Action*!'

'Yes, Tel. I've lost nearly two stone with delicious Slimmers Supreme . . .'

'*Cut!*'

For the fifteenth time Maggie spat gratefully into Spike's promised bucket. 'Lift the fork, give the product a lingering look, insert it between your lips on the word "Supreme" and chew with discreet appreciation.' Lift, look, insert, chew, spit – she felt like a machine. Perhaps this, at last, would be *the* take. But there was always something. If she didn't forget her words, then the morsel of gateau looked wrong or fell off the fork, or the angle of her head was askew or there was something mysteriously referred to as 'a hair in the gate'. She knew it was her fault. She wished Coleby, the director, would deliver some comment on her performance, but all he ever said was 'higher', 'to the left', 'raise the fork a gnat's more slowly, love', as if she were no longer quite human.

'NG for sound,' announced a voice from the camera. 'Plane going over.'

She felt it was her fault too that the wind had changed, setting Spellthorne Avenue on the main flight path to Heathrow. She wished she could see Spike. She'd glimpsed him earlier, watching from the doorway, but now he'd vanished. She had not spoken to him since they'd started shooting. At lunch, eaten in the coach down the road, the arrangement of seats and tables had split the company into fours, isolating Spike with Fizz, Coleby and Flash, while she had ended up three tables away with Jed, the lighting man and Tel Travers. Picking at her goulash – quite passable, considering, although she was only allowed a spoonful, while everyone else, despite vociferous complaints, was wolfing second helpings – she sensed these groupings had not come about by chance. Even when, leaving on the hour to return to the set, she had glanced down the coach, vainly hoping to catch Spike's eye, Fizz had held him engrossed in conversation. Later, when Maggie had spotted him in the group of watchers behind the camera, Fizz had always been there; Fizz whispering in his ear, Fizz laughing, Fizz leaning a proprietorial arm on his shoulder. Maggie remembered their first visit – months, it seemed years, ago – how Fizz had patted his knee then and called him darling. Helpless, fettered by microphone wires, penned by the camera in her make-believe kitchen, Maggie tried to ignore the tight little knot in her throat that threatened to choke her.

'*Right*! Let's go again quickly before Concorde comes over. And *quiet* when the red's up, OK everybody.'

Siggy rushed in to retouch Maggie's make-up. The small man clasped her fingers around the handle of yet another fork with its burden of gateau. Lift, look, insert, chew, spit.

'Right, now when I say *quiet*, I mean fucking QUIET. Slate Seven, Take Sixteen. Sound running, turn over. Action!'

'Yes, Tel, I've lost nearly two stone with—'

From the hall came the sound of altercation. 'I'm asking,' said a familiar voice, 'who broke the urn in the front garden?'

'*Cut*!' screamed Jed, elbowing his way to the kitchen door. 'Listen, I asked for Q-U-I-E-T, absolute, complete silence. What are you out there, fucking brain-dead or something?'

'Don't you use language to me, matey,' snarled the familiar voice. 'Don't you address me like a piece of dirt in my own home!'

There was a thud, the sound effects of a scuffle. Those nearest the doorway surged into the hall. Grunts followed, then placatory noises, then Jed's voice, rather breathless. 'OK, take it easy, squire. Just a little misunderstanding.'

The crowd around the doorway parted to reveal Keith, his tie crooked, his jacket hanging from one shoulder.

Maggie stared at him, mortified. She was aware of silence all about her, then of someone beginning to snigger.

'Mags, love—' he began.

'How could you? Keith Hapgood, how could you?'

His dazed look vanished. He whirled from the doorway. She heard his footsteps thunder down the hall, heard the letter box rattle as, abortively, he slammed the front door against its wedge of electric cable.

The silence held an instant longer before bright, embarrassed chatter broke out. Maggie realized she was still gripping the fork, which had long since shed its burden. The small man appeared and eased it gently from her grasp. Siggy touched her arm. 'Glass of water, duckie?' Jed emerged from the crowd, massaging his shoulder. 'Sorry, Maggie love, didn't realize it was your old man . . .' Everybody now seemed to be talking at once. Maggie stood mute. In the doorway, Ms Fizz St Clair was half-turned towards someone, her head thrown back, laughing. Maggie knew, without needing to see, that the someone was Spike.

III

Fizz sat on Tweetie Pie's patio, sipping champagne from a styrofoam cup. Though the day had delivered its predictable quota of ennui, the Dom Perignon had worked its charm, casting last night's little slip-up into oblivion and inducing a renewed sense of assurance, of life being once again firmly under control.

A few more takes and they would be onto the product shots. Tel Travers, his day's shooting mercifully completed, had already been despatched to sleep off the effects of his relaxation therapy, and Tweetie Pie was labouring over her final close-ups – a backward glance through the French windows at the video monitor showed simultaneous playback of her mouthing, 'Now I can sin *and* slim.'

Fizz tilted her Ray Bans, extended her bare legs to the evening sun. She had phoned both Stretch and Genghis with glowing descriptions of Slik Piks' progress. She had called The Lapwarmer to check the political status quo at the office and had been gratified to find everything calm, with no reports of sinister activity in the Saunders Blair camp. She had called The Donkey regularly, of course – no harm, now it had gone six thirty, in calling again to ensure the creature hadn't seized the chance to skive off early. But, for the moment, her vodophone idle, Fizz was content to survey the garish profusion of hardy annuals in Tweetie Pie's back garden. Briefly considering the trampled lawn and the half-eaten sandwich lurking in a nearby tub of begonias, tokens of four o'clock's statutory tea break, she glanced across at Spike, where, beside her at the sunshaded patio table, he scribbled his freelance – Chinese, he'd said, though whether Chop Suey or Cultural Revolutionary she couldn't immediately recall.

He was grateful to her, she could see, particularly in view of that unwarranted intrusion by the irate husband, throwing his weight about, threatening to punch poor Jed, who was, after all, only attempting to do his job. Heaven knew what predicament Spike might have faced if Fizz hadn't extricated him from Tweetie Pie's advances. But now, as long as he kept a low profile, he was safe. At the current rate of shooting they would probably wrap at eight thirty. Then he could escape with Fizz in Flash's Mustang, avoiding lingering goodbyes, the past few weeks already consigned to reminiscence, already the stuff of after-dinner stories inspiring the comradely laughter of those who have endured and come through.

Reaching across for the champagne bottle, Fizz permitted her hand to rest lightly on his knee, so that he looked up, nibbling his pentel and favouring her with his distracted, lapwarmers' smile. Oh yes, he was grateful. Taking measure of his gratitude she felt in the pit of her stomach a pleasurable lightness. She contemplated the end of picture party and the backless, body-revealing Ralph Lauren suede shift she would wear.

The crew was packing up. Maggie could hear them below her bedroom window shouting and whistling as they loaded their van. She knew she should make a start on tidying the house: both toilets were blocked, the lounge looked like a furniture saleroom, chewing gum had been trodden into all the downstairs carpets – and there was Keith's precious urn of geraniums, of course. Strange, he'd never been violent, not in twenty-two years. She wondered what had got into him. Yet didn't she feel it too, now that her part in the filming was over, a sense of violation, of uncaring eyes disregarding her treasured possessions? Flash had promised to pay for any damage, everyone had been very polite, but all the same this house had been just another location – today Potter's Park, tomorrow Spain or Venice. Yes, she knew how Keith felt. She knew he was probably blaming her for letting these strangers chip his paintwork and stub out their cigarettes in Brian's athletics trophies. And yes, she was guilty, this, like

217

everything else, was all her fault. Yet somehow her guilt only served to increase her anger. Why had he not gone straight round to the Entwhistles'? He'd no business barging in, ruining the take, ruining her big day, showing her up in front of everyone.

But had she needed Keith to show her up? A shudder convulsed her as she recalled her performance in front of the camera. 'Fabulous', 'marvellous', they'd all said as they'd made their goodbyes, but she knew from their false smiles they were disappointed, secretly shaking their heads or, worse still, laughing. Maggie's big day, her chance to make something of herself? Jane Fonda and Cher need not be frightened.

So, of course, she couldn't blame Spike, could she, not entirely? Although it had come as a shock when, hunting for him during the packing up, she'd been told the agency people had already gone, had driven off to their hotel. She should have understood, she should have seen that it, too, was make-believe, their friendship, flirtation, affair – what had it been exactly? – she should have known it would be struck like the set the moment shooting was over. But then she was an outsider, not speaking the jargon, not knowing what a dolly was or that a 'gnat's' meant a gnat's whisker – even Siggy and Daz, though they had been kind, had conversed over her head for the most part, absorbed in the gossip of an alien glittery world. How she must have embarrassed Spike with her ineptitude and her lack of sophistication. Keith hadn't helped, thrashing around in the proverbial china shop – had he heard something, was he suspicious? And then, of course, there was Fizz.

All the same, Spike had seemed such a gentleman. Maggie had never imagined he'd leave without so much as a goodbye. Rising heavily, she went over to the wash basin, where, in the mirror, her old face confronted her. Siggy had said the mousy rinse would wash out, but she couldn't wash out common-or-garden Margaret, mouse to the bone.

Out in the street an engine started, she heard the front door slam, the van rev away from the kerb. No more restaurants, no more fingers twined over crisply laundered tablecloths, no more reverential waiters abetting stolen intimacies with coffee and liqueurs. Back to real life now, Magipost, and Mum's shopping, and Keith, making up the settee with sheets and blankets, dreaming of Joy's visit.

Maggie crawled back to the bed. She knew she should change out of the pink dress, splash cold water on her face, began clearing up, but her body felt heavy, as if her legs might buckle under its weight. She crept beneath the duvet, pulling it over her head.

A soft knocking brought her upright in an instant. Spike stood in the doorway, grinning his skew-whiff grin. She was so taken aback that his arms were around her, his mouth on hers, before she had properly registered his presence. She struggled for breath.

'Gosh, Maggie, you're delicious, I've been so hungry for you – my ulcer's been giving me gyp all day.'

She caught his hand where it had moved purposefully up her thigh.

'What's the matter, sweetheart? Is that husband of yours due back any minute?'

'Spike, I—'

'You didn't think I'd gone? I made myself scarce until the crew was out of the way. Nice place, your garden shed, reminds me of my childhood – so evocative, the smell of creosote.'

She was smiling despite herself.

'That's better, sweetie. You should be dancing on the table and popping champagne corks to celebrate your triumph.'

'Spike, not you too?'

'You were wonderful, magnificent.'

'Spike Bentley, you weren't even watching.'

'I could see it on playback. You were your usual beautiful self, Maggie. Sweet, modest, sincere.'

'Please, I know what I was like.'

He caught her gently by the chin, tilting her face towards him. 'Post-shoot blues. Everyone feels flat when it's over. But, gosh, when you see yourself on screen you'll be surprised, I promise.'

She looked up at him, probing the eyes beyond the spectacles, wanting to believe him. When his mouth descended upon hers she forgot, for a moment, to resist.

'But what about Fizz?'

'Fizz?' He seemed genuinely puzzled. 'You mean that business over the wardrobe? Oh golly gosh yes, I'm sorry. But you looked delicious in the end, you know you're scrumptious in this pink thing. In fact, I bet if you took off your bra your nipples would stand out like—'

'Ripening gooseberries? Spike Bentley, for heaven's sake!'

The grin acquired a self-deprecatory twist. 'You know there's no arguing with Fizz, it's like standing in the path of a panzer division. Give me credit, sweetheart, I did try – but when all's said and done, she's the one who signs my expenses.'

'I thought you didn't care about your job?'

'Gosh, I don't.'

'What about your Greek island?'

'Golly gosh yes, I'm making plans. But you need money for plans, you need money, alas, just to keep breathing. Still, one day, Maggie, one day . . .' Removing his glasses, he placed them carefully on the bedside table. 'Oh, Maggie, succulent, delectable Maggie, say I'm forgiven. Say I'm forgiven so I can ravish you right here on this duvet. And afterwards, let's raid your larder, let's eat peanut butter and chocolate spread and condensed milk straight from the tin . . .'

She was laughing as he lowered his weight upon her, working with that deftness that always surprised her, unfastening her bra, worming his hands beneath the despised pink dress. She fought to remember her rules, hard won between dashboard and gear lever during their tussle in the lay-by. Breasts were permitted, but below the waist was a no-go area. Yet, as his fingers stole into her pants, her thighs parted treacherously, she heard herself moaning as her own hand, seemingly endowed with independent volition, began to unbutton his fly.

She opened her eyes and glimpsed over his shoulder the familiar view from a new perspective, the little boudoir chair, the kidney dressing table, the mirror. Still dangling from the mirror frame was an assortment of Keith's ties.

'Oh, no, Spike—'

'Oh please, Maggie.'

What did Keith care? He had relinquished this view, given up his place in the bed; he would throw away twenty-two years, should Joy only beckon. There was a striped tie, blue and red, and a paisley, and that kipper painted with the naked lady, Nicki's idea of a joke last Christmas. Maggie had meant to take the paisley to the cleaners.

'No, Spike. Not here.'

He rolled off her and they lay for a moment, she with her dress hitched up to her armpits, he with his trousers around his ankles, undignified, vulnerable, she thought, the two of them, like sea creatures out of their shells.

'Back at the hotel, then?'

'Oh, Spike, I can't.'

'There's a party.'

'I ought to clear up.'

Reluctantly she met his eyes, naked eyes with their thick lashes.

'Oh Maggie, have pity . . .'

What did Keith care? He only cared about his blessed geraniums.

'Djerwannerknow what I like?' said Tel Travers, threatening to slop wine on Fizz's Ralph Lauren. 'Djerwannerknow what really turns Tel on?'

Beside the indoor pool, beneath plastic palm trees, the crew were letting their hair down with warm Muscadet and piped Bert Kampfert. They had sampled the Hawaiian buffet – ubiquitous pineapple chunks and curry powder. Chairs had been pushed back, between patio tables a couple or two were already dancing. Flash had sworn Spike had taken a lift with Coleby, Coleby had seen him board the charabanc. Glancing about her, weather eye open for pizza salesmen, Fizz suddenly froze.

Djerwannerknow, Mizz Fizz? Djerwan ol' Tel to tell you?'

221

She could scarcely believe what she was seeing. After all she had done for Spike, after the effort she'd put in to save him – surely he realized how unprofessional this was, burdening Flash's budget with an uninvited guest, favouring one Mum above the others. What if Sharon and K-k-kelly discovered they had been omitted from the celebrations? And couldn't he see what a fool he looked, flaunting this woman on his arm – this simpering woman with her dated stilettos and her brassy frock more suited to a knees-up at The Pig and Whistle? Couldn't he see how this error of style and judgement would appear to everyone, not least to her, Fizz?

Of course she had probably persuaded him into it, Tweetie Pie, the little wifey, clinging like a burr as they all did, Spunky Dunkie's wife and the others, with their valium and their migraines and their PhDs in emotional blackmail. Now that the heavy husband had stormed out it was probably any port in a typhoon. And here was poor Spike, with his helpless look and his convenient hotel bedroom. However, Tweetie Pie would need to rethink; it was not for nothing Fizz had donned her Ralph Lauren.

'You're an unnerstandin' woman, Mizz Fizz. Very unnerstandin' woman.'

Fizz was distracted by the yeasty exhalation that moistened the bare skin of her shoulder.

'Likes a nibble, does Tel. Really fancies a naughty little nibble.'

'For chrissake, Tel, the shoot's over. Cut, print, check the gate.'

Tel Travers' dank moustache, hovering unsteadily near Fizz's right bicep, descended suddenly. Before she could stop him he had taken the soft inner skin between his teeth and administered a sharp, wet nip.

She jumped up, toppling several glasses, staring incredulously at the purple tooth marks.

'Tha's Tel's thing, you see. Ol' Tel likes to nibble the pretty girlies.'

★ ★ ★

'So Tel Travers is drunk, Lucrezia? We're all drunk. This is supposed to be a party, remember.'

At the centre of the pool, around a raft thatched to resemble a tropical hut, other hotel guests dog-paddled or floated, bellies up like poisoned fish, pallid and glimmering in the unnaturally blue water. A solitary enthusiast, ploughing a vigorous crawl at the perimeter, churned up a wake of chlorine that threatened Fizz's suede.

'Don't be a flake, Spike. Try to grasp what I'm saying.'

'Gosh, I'm doing my level best—'

'Our so-called celebrity is a pervert, right? That's probably the real reason he lost his game shoes. And here we have a swimming pool, near-naked women. We risk the whole Pandora campaign if he runs amok.'

'Lucrezia, he's fast asleep, face down in his Tropicana Trifle.'

The girls frolicking on the shallow side of the raft seemed, on closer inspection, disquietingly familiar. Weren't they part of the Happy Pizza contingent? Fizz endeavoured to close her mind to such thoughts as the swimmer's return progress forced a further retreat from its spray.

'Frankly,' Spike was saying, 'I don't see why you dragged me away from the table.'

'You could hardly expect me to go into detail in front of the general public.'

'Maggie isn't the general public.'

'And that's another thing. I'll book Le Gavroche the moment we're back. I don't need proof you got into her knickers, OK?'

The swimmer, snorting and blowing, began to heave himself from the pool.

'Maggie and I—' Spike was saying.

'Forget Tweetie Pie. Me, Fizz – I'm the one in need of protection.'

'Anyway, I didn't catch – are you saying Tel hit you?'

'Not *hit*, Spike, no. Don't make me repeat it, it's too, too gross.'

The swimmer sat at the pool's edge, rubbing chlorine from his eyes. Water trickled over his belly, pleating its hairy

223

folds. With his overflowing gut and bald dome he looked like a mangy sealion, Fizz thought distractedly.

'If it's physical violence you want, ask Jed. He's good at thumping people.'

'Spike, darling, I'm asking you.'

As she stroked Spike's lapel she was aware that the sealion's eyes bulged intently in her direction.

'Oh darling, you know why. Doesn't what happened after my dinner party . . . ?'

Though she had looked away rapidly, she had been too late. The sealion's whiskers were bristling, his chops broadening to emit a gleeful bark.

'Spike, please—'

'Gosh, isn't that guy waving at us?'

'Please, let's go to the bar. Or up to my room.'

'Yes, he is. That bloke at the shallow end. I'd say he was waving at you, Lucrezia.'

Maggie shifted uneasily as she watched them together, Fizz gesticulating, Spike, shoulders hunched, sipping his wine.

A moment ago she had been dizzy, spinning from the welcome they'd given her. 'Hey, over here. Maggie!' 'Come on, you old sinner and slimmer!' 'Try this glass of plonk as part of your calorie-controlled diet.' Siggy had kissed her on both cheeks, her friend the props man had leapt up to offer his seat, even Coleby had flashed her a grin from the recesses of his beard.

She wondered how she had ever felt an outsider. It was true they were all a little merry, but then she, too, was flushed with the gin Spike had poured her – he had finished the bottle while she had searched Nicki's wardrobe for a party dress unscathed by the scissors. Spike had been right, she'd suffered no more than post-shoot blues. Now she saw that she had triumphed. It was all a triumph – the film, her weight loss, her blond streaks restored, her sitting here beside Spike in Nicki's long-sleeved crushed velvet, free at last, doing what she wanted to do. Ah yes, that was *the* triumph.

But then Fizz St Clair had appeared, freezing the laughter

224

with her glacial smile, carrying Spike off for this urgent meeting.

'Hey, Maggie duckie, sup up! You're well behind the rest of us.'

Maggie forced a grin. By what right did Fizz St Clair hold herself superior? There had been wine stains down the front of that suedette dress, two clownish horns of scarlet tweaking those perfect lips. Margaret might have been intimidated, but not triumphant Maggie, with her own expert lip gloss vivid and true. She had earned her presence at these victory celebrations. Nevertheless, she felt the weight of guilt descend. Spike was in trouble, and it was all her fault.

Yet, when she dared glance back at the pool, Fizz had vanished and Spike was weaving a path to the table.

'Golly, gosh. There's no holding Fizz when she's been powdering her nose.'

'But – I mean, was she angry? What about your job?'

'Stuff the job!' Pouring more wine, he lifted the glass to the table in general before clinking it with hers. 'To Greek islands! Oh sweetheart, give us a kiss.'

'Here, in front of everyone?'

'Dance with me then.'

'But this isn't dance music.'

'Sweetie, who cares.'

And it was true, nobody seemed to mind as he pulled her to her feet, propelling her into the shade of the plastic palm trees. Nobody raised an eyebrow that he held her so close, his pelvis crushed against hers. And when his lips descended, filling her mouth with the sour-sweet taste of wine, did anyone bother to notice? Flash was entwined with his blonde PA, Jed clutched two girls in bikinis Maggie had never seen before. Even Coleby was dancing – with Siggy, she was surprised to observe.

In this world anything was permitted. And she was part of it now. She had rocketed upwards, far above a universe of twitching nets and teenage back-row-of-the-cinema demarcations. What was fidelity but a con-trick, a way to keep staid Margaret in her place? In Fizz St Clair's world no one grew fat

225

and grey, settling like dust before the television, surrendering light and air to sons and daughters. Everyone had a lover – it was expected, the appropriate accessory, like a Hermes bag or a Jasper Conran label. When your body was taut and tanned and youthful it was natural to make use of it. Only the fat clung to old-fashioned words like adultery as, fearfully, they clung to their clothes.

All the same, coming up for air, Maggie remembered the empty gin bottle, standing on the sideboard for Keith to find.

'Oh Maggie,' said Spike, pressing her closer, 'let's slip away to my room.'

'Spike, I—'

'Don't put me on rations. Don't promise me steak and serve me salad.'

'Spike, I'm not sure . . .'

But what was there not to be sure about? There was Flash's PA, seated astride him now, her blouse conspicuously unbuttoned. There was Daz, casting off her Doc Martens and her baggy black robes, stripping unashamedly for a swim. There was Jed, muscular in his boxer shorts, chasing the two squealing girls between the tables. And there was Tel Travers, roused from his slumber, staggering after the girls as they raced Jed to the pool.

'My goodness,' said Maggie, as a chorus of shrieks rose up, 'Tel Travers has jumped in with all his clothes on.'

'Gosh, so he has.'

'I hope he won't drown. Oh look, he seems to be trying to save himself by clutching hold of that girl.'

'I wouldn't have disturbed you, miss,' said the night security man doubtfully. 'Only the others in your party – Mr Rees and Mr Whiteside, is it? – they insisted you were the one to phone.'

Typical. Nobody had cared what had happened to Fizz, nobody had bothered to look for her after her hasty departure from the pool – until there was a disaster, of course. Still, almost anything was preferable to spending the evening imprisoned in room 406, unable even to creep down to the bar for fear of the pizza vendor lying in wait behind a pillar. Here, at least, in this unfrequented corridor behind reception, she was safe.

The night security man busied himself with his key ring. 'I've tried a couple of times to escort the gentleman to his room. But – well, there's a problem.' He pushed the door cautiously, almost immediately slamming it again. 'Oh lor!'

A typical specimen of suburban manhood, this night security man, despite the 'Who Dares Wins' moustache, Fizz observed. A poodle in rottweiler's clothing, happy to share a seamy joke in the pub, yet shaken to his foundations by the thought of 'ladies present'.

'Let's cut the crap,' she declared.

'I did try him with a dressing gown, miss, after he stripped off his wet clobber.'

'He won't have any fixtures and fittings I haven't seen before.'

The night security man flushed to the roots of his hair. 'Well, if you're certain – better nip in quickly in case he makes a dash for it.'

The office was small, little more than a cupboard, with a desk wedged in one corner and banks of security monitors offering monochrome views of all parts of the building. The sight of so many television screens had clearly struck Tel Travers as a challenge. Casting off the towelling robe for greater freedom of movement, he had set himself the task of out-performing them, muttering, waving his scrawny arms, shaking his withered shanks in a soft-shoe shuffle.

Fizz and the night security man surveyed the naked figure, he with austerity, she with a weary distaste. On the upper row, third from the left, the monitor trained on the pool seemed to disclose an only-too-recognizable couple swaying in each other's arms, before Daz, in sudden close-up, obliterated them. Breasts glistening and precarious in her sodden bra, she appeared to be attempting a belly dance, egged on by Jed.

The night security man sucked in his moustache with a hurumph of disapproval that comprehended Daz, Tel

Travers, and even Fizz herself. 'Your friends certainly get into the party spirit, don't they, miss?'

'You know how it is – everyone likes to wind down once the movie's in the can.'

'Ah, films, is it?' A ray of understanding lit his features. 'Oh, well – now you say so . . .' He surveyed Tel's shrivelled nakedness all at once with a benevolence bordering on enthusiasm. 'Funny, I thought I'd seen him somewhere before. Isn't he in that telly show – what is it?' He began to click his fingers. '*Hot Line, Hot Air, Hot Seat* . . . ? No, don't tell me.'

'So you see, Mr—'

'Bert, miss, call me Bert.'

'Well, Bert, you can see how imperative it is we avoid any kind of a scandal situation. At least he doesn't appear to have done much damage in the pool.'

'Those two girls seemed quite happy, miss, after you'd had your little chat with them.'

Fizz crackled the envelope containing what remained of her emergency float. 'And we're certainly grateful to you, Bert, for dealing with our little problem so discreetly.'

Bert watched as the notes were counted out onto the racing paper that lay open on his desk. He stared, beaming, at the puny, gibbering figure of Tel Travers as if its presence in his office conferred positive honour Tel, his unconscious registering this heightened audience response like a surge in voltage, snapped out of the soft-shoe shuffle, thrusting his pelvis forward, squaring up pugnaciously to the monitors. 'Derry ra'! You derry ra'!'

'What's he saying?'

'I think you'll find it's his James Cagney impersonation.'

Bert's moustache shivered with enlightenment. 'Got it! Dick Danvers, isn't it? You can stick with Dick . . . No . . . No, hold on, it's coming, I'm going to get it any minute.'

'Meanwhile, perhaps you can think of a way to keep him in that robe long enough to frogmarch him to his room.'

Deflated, Bert considered the naked figure. 'We could always wait till he passes out.'

'Why not assist the process with a swift uppercut to his jaw?'

'Oh, I couldn't do that, miss. Not with him being such a celebrity. I was thinking, maybe he'd give me his autograph, you know, like, for the wife and kiddies . . .'

Fizz sighed. On the third upper monitor from the left she could once more pick out the familiar couple. She thought of the hours she had spent walled up in 406. As the minutes had passed, her incredulity had mounted. Weren't she and Spike, after the dinner party, practically an item? Her instructions, though hasty, had been quite specific: he was to follow her to her room. Yet here he was, still flaunting himself with this vulgar woman. It was – there was no other word for it – an insult.

She glared at the monitor. Then, all at once, her expression lightened. She considered Tel Travers, who had switched from Cagney to Humphrey Bogart.

'Hang on, Bert. I have an idea.'

'Oh, Maggie,' said Spike. 'Don't be like the others. Don't chew me up and spit me out. Not like all the others.'

Reception was not only clear of pizza vendors but completely deserted, Fizz was relieved to observe. The night receptionist too was unfamiliar – a sleepy youth had replaced the steely-eyed ex-sergeant-major of the previous night's shift.

'So sorry to trouble you,' said Fizz, fluttering her lashes, 'but I've just done the stupidest thing. Would you believe, I've locked my key in my room.'

The youth smothered a yawn as she recited her name and room number, drifting somnambulistically down the line of pigeon-holes without consulting his computer.

'How kind,' said Fizz, scooping up the key and sliding a note into its place. 'And, I wonder, could Room Service rustle up a bottle of vodka? I'll sign for it here, and take it upstairs myself.'

★   ★   ★

'Oh, Maggie, don't show me the menu, then tell me the kitchen's closed. You know how much I love you.'

'Spike, I think I'm tiddly. What did you say?'

Fizz could have wished the service lift were faster, as Tel Travers, trussed in his towelling robe, nuzzled her left ear. But still, the bribe had worked.

'Nearly there,' she said, fending him off with the blunt end of the bottle. 'Now, Tel, just remember, right? You can have vodka and all the nibbles you like – once we get to my room.'

'Nearly there,' said Spike, fumbling with the key to room 412. 'Oh sweetheart, we've snacked on canapés, we've filled up on the soup, we've made do with the paté and the fish course, but, oh golly gosh, this is the moment I've been famished for.'

The key's sudden connection with the lock precipitated them untidily through the door.

'At last, sweet Maggie, the entrée!'

They staggered, blinked, aware, before it came into focus, of the alien presence in the room. A naked figure was sprawled on the bed, waving a bottle.

'Anyone fancy a li'l nibble. Go on, y'can tel ol' Tel.'

The house was in darkness as Maggie's minicab deposited her at the front gate. At least Keith had not waited up. Tipping out her handbag in despair of her key, grovelling in spilt earth and crushed geranium blossoms, she began to see an advantage to their recent sleeping arrangements. If she took off her shoes she could steal upstairs without needing to face him.

She was negotiating the telephone table when the light was snapped on. She started, shedding a shoe. 'I left you a note, didn't I?'

'For Pete's sake, it's three in the morning.'

He was still wearing his business suit, she noticed, though his chin was murky with stubble and his eyes red-rimmed.

Had he been sitting in the dark all this time drawing up a list of reproaches? Well, thanks to Tel Travers she had done nothing to be reproached for – worse luck.

'Mags, are you tipsy?'

'What if I am? Can't I have a little fun for once in my life without you trying to ruin it?'

That took the wind out of him, she was pleased to observe. He glanced away, shuffling his feet.

'Look, love, I'm sorry about this afternoon. I was in a bit of a state, I rushed home without thinking—'

'*You* were in a state? Oh my, if that isn't typical!'

'Mags, love, please. There's something I need to tell you.'

She let drop her other shoe. Not now. Not at three in the morning, not when her tights were torn, her head swimming, not in a house knee-deep in dirty paper cups and with two blocked toilets. What was this – tit for tat for the empty gin bottle?

'Love, I realize it's late, but there's never going to be a good time for this . . .'

'You're dead right, Keith Hapgood. And since I know what it is, don't bother to say it. Just what do you expect, sympathy? Poor Keith, he can't help it? Well, I don't want to listen, do you hear, not now, not ever. Only, while you're so busy destroying our lives, just think for a second – what about the boys and poor little Nicki? Oh, you can let me down, Keith Hapgood, I'm used to it, I don't care any longer. But what are they going to think of you, your poor wretched kids?'

He had recoiled as if she had slapped him. She saw with shock that his eyes had filled with tears. She put out her hand, took a step towards him. But this was mere force of habit, she reminded herself. What right had he to play upon her emotions, acting as if he were the injured party? Joy, Joy, that was all he thought about, even at three in the morning.

Her own tears came halfway up the stairs. She staggered on, not looking back, stumbling along the landing, flinging herself through the bedroom door and across the unmade bed.

Later, raising her eyes from the duvet, she saw, in the

glimmering dawn, her right arm stretching away towards the pillow, bearing the hand, fingers crooked, palm upwards, distant, foreign, like some curious flower. She inspected this bloom with a detached fascination, slowly rotating the slim stem of the wrist to display the scarlet petals of the nails, noting with surprise a certain perfection.

Grief, guilt, fear? Change was painful, after all, splitting and sloughing off the hindering shell, inching slowly upwards to the light. But Spike loved her. Here was something she could cling to.

IV

Now, when it no longer mattered, the kitchen fitters had reappeared. Maggie could scarcely hear her own voice above the hammering, let alone Spike's, painfully distant at the other end of the line.

'. . . good news, sweetie, and bad news . . .'

'Pardon!' Maggie screamed, clutching fast to the receiver.

'Bad news about lunch on Friday, I'm afraid.'

A sick uncertainty assailed her. Parted from Spike, she found the reality of her new life dwindling. They played games with reality, these advertising people. Perhaps for some reason, comprehensible in his world, though not in hers, Spike too was playing with her.

'It's Lucrezia – I mean Fizz – again. She's fixed up yet another lunchtime meeting. She's got me working late as well, not to mention going up and down between here and Dean Street like a demented yoyo – recut this, re-record that, give it your personal attention, Spike. She seems to think she owns me. Unfortunately, I require her signature on some heavy expenses I'm currently finessing through the system—'

'It doesn't matter,' Maggie said weakly.

'Golly, gosh, sweetie, it matters to me. I tell you, I'm – good grief, what's that?'

A tooth-jarring screech now emanated from the kitchen.

'Sweetheart, are you all right?'

'It's just the machine to cut the quarry tiles. Listen, I'd better go. They'll be wanting more tea any minute.'

'Maggie, hold on! I haven't told you the good news.'

The whine of a drill rose up to counterpoint the screech.

'Sweetie, are you there? The good news is, Genghis loves the rough cut.'

233

'Pardon?'

'Our esteemed client, the main man, the Heaviest Breather. He adores the commercial. Oh, he wants six million alterations, of course, and about three million more pack shots. But basically – and this is unheard of – he thinks it's pretty jolly beezer. Or rather, he thinks you're beezer, Maggie my sweet. And it's given him this brainstorm. Golly gosh, it's the only time I've felt like clapping an arm round his flabby shoulder – he wants to make you Granny Garfunkel Supreme Slimmer.'

'Pardon?'

'*Supreme Slimmer!*'

The tile cutter and the drill abruptly ceased their duet. Receiving the full force of Spike's words, Maggie reeled, her ears ringing.

'It means slimmer of the year, really. But Genghis thought the play on the product name would give greater pack registration.'

'Goodness, what does it involve?'

'You'll be a sort of symbol for Granny Garfunkel's Slimmers Supreme. A living embodiment of company virtues. Genghis is a bit vague at the moment, the concept's in its early stages, but he's got one firm plan. He wants to give a party to celebrate the first airing of the commercial. At this knees-up you'll be invited to meet the senior members of the sales force, maybe even the press.'

'Oh Spike, I don't know—'

'But don't you see, sweetie, aren't you grasping what this means?'

'I'm not sure – well, the press and everything—'

'Maggie, when did we last see each other?'

'Oh, I—'

'Not since that infernal cock-up after the shoot, not for sixteen and a half days. And when are we ever going to see each other, given your family breathing down your neck and Lucrezia trying to turn me into a workaholic? But now we've a legitimate excuse. There'll be photo calls for posters and press ads, PR briefings. This isn't a one-off like the shoot, this is ongoing.'

'Oh Spike—'

'Oh, Maggie. No more jam tomorrow, we'll be able to wallow in it at last.'

'When is this party?'

'Two long weeks away. But, gosh, sweetheart, we'll have apricot and damson and raspberry conserve, we'll have runny honey drizzling from crumpets slithering with butter, we'll smear Cornish cream with dollops of sticky red strawberry, clotted with fruit . . .'

Though the drill was wailing again, and the tile cutter, keening a piercing treble above the base rhythm of the hammer, Maggie scarcely heard. Granny Garfunkel Supreme Slimmer. Photo calls, press adverts, posters. While the thought turned her stomach to water, yet she could see – this was no trick of the light, no gauzy deception of filters, but something definite at last. She was no longer just Joy's baby sister or Keith's wife or the kids' Mum or even the woman Spike loved. She had a future, a value, a career.

She was Granny Garfunkel Supreme Slimmer, yet see if her family cared. All the same, what Spike had said was true. They seemed to be watching her suspiciously.

Keith, for instance. Though, mercifully, he had not dared to refer to their confrontation on the night of the shoot, since then he had worn a wary, closed-down look, slinking silently out of the house each morning and avoiding her on his return. Yet twice, rushing home to phone Spike, she'd found him already back from the office, offering the bogus excuse that he'd been let off early – although he'd muttered this so shiftily that perhaps he was merely up to some devious trick of his own.

The kitchen was completed at last. There it was with its sterile worktops, its virgin oven and unblemished hob, a shrine to order and efficiency, to state-of-the-art convenience living. Last Sunday morning, Maggie had glimpsed Keith sitting at the brand-new breakfast bar, gazing about him like someone waiting for service in a station buffet. Roast beef, Yorkshire pudding, sprouts, gravy and roast potatoes? He'd got another think coming, she told herself, ploughing on up the stairs. When she remembered the Sunday dinners she had cooked, all the roast potatoes alone – four per person, twenty a meal in the days when the boys were home . . . Fifty-two times twenty, times twenty-two . . . Near enough twenty-three thousand roast potatoes during her married life, fat spitting, scorching her wrists, searing her eyes with heat and fumes as she edged the dish from the oven. And for what? Get your Keith better trained, Ivy had said. He was used to Miracle Menus now. As step two of his training, he could learn to operate the microwave. And if he didn't like it – then he could try his luck with Joy's cooking.

He had not attempted a further announcement of Armageddon. Perhaps, skulking in the garage over his work-bench, he was pondering what Maggie had said. In any case, she was grateful for this stay of execution. Mum could offer no up-to-date news of Joy's arrival, but every extra hour, extra week was a gift, bringing closer the moment when Maggie could counter his betrayal with lofty contempt. So what, Keith Hapgood? I'm a TV celebrity now. And I've a lover who loves me.

Sometimes she wished, oh, how she wished he could see where he was pushing her. Sometimes she almost hoped his suspicions would harden into a challenge. Watching him trail his nightly burden of blankets into the lounge, she remembered his face, unravelled by sleep, his teddy bear look. He was a worn teddy now, she thought uncomfortably, his plush threadbare, his stuffing sagging.

Still, he had only himself to blame. He'd hardly miss her when she was gone – apart from her roast potatoes, of course, her thirty-five thousand odd Brussels sprouts, her eleven thousand Yorkshires.

Nicki, too, now the summer term was over, haunted the house like a rebarbative ghost, lurking in her room, sullenly absent, yet shaking Maggie's days with the disco-beat thud of her presence. She had taken to locking her door, even on the rare occasions she went out, Maggie discovered.

236

One morning, Maggie came upon her as she was turning the key.

'Hoping to barge in, were you, Mum?'

Maggie was taken aback by this hostile stance. 'I – I just thought I'd pop you some clean sheets.'

'So you can pinch a bit more of my gear while you're at it? No thanks. And now – I gotta go.'

Yet, though she had pocketed the key, she remained braced defensively in the doorway, as if it were Maggie who was expected to take her departure. She was not putting on weight, Maggie saw, despite the pizza. Her face was drawn, her head seemed oversized for her body, giving her the look of a greeting card waif. Perhaps a visit to the doctor was called for.

'Mum, gotta go, OK?'

'Oh, Nicki love—'

'Mu–um!'

'I just thought – well, I haven't seen you for ages.'

'You saw me yesterday.'

'But not for a chat. You know, like we used to – how you're feeling, what you're up to.'

'Can we save the third degree till later. Like I said, I'm in a rush.'

Maggie sighed. Of course getting Nicki to the surgery would be an achievement. Better to wait maybe, see how she progressed over the next couple of weeks.

'The fresh air'll do you good. Are you off to meet Kimberly?'

'Jesus, Mum!'

'Nicki!'

'Well, are you dense or what? How many times do I have to tell you, I can't be bothered with pukey Kimberly Butcher?'

Maggie stared at her daughter. Nicki's huge eyes glittered, angry bubbles of saliva trembled on her lips.

'But you and Kimberly were such mates.'

'Yeah, well.' The wild eyes brimmed suddenly, the chin shrivelled. 'If you must know, Old Mother Butcher decided I wasn't good enough for her precious Kimmie-wimmie.'

237

'Of all the nerve!' Anger propelled Maggie across the landing, protective arms outstretched.

'Get off!' screamed Nicki.

'Nicki, love.'

'Get off of me, do you hear!'

Through the sweater, Nicki's bones felt brittle and weightless, dry twigs like poor old Fluffy. 'But, Nicki darling—'

'You just want to weasel round me, so you can nosey poke in my room. Well, I'm not a kid any more, I'm entitled to my privacy. So just get off my case. Get away from me, will you?'

Growth was pain, Maggie reminded herself as she pedalled her exercise machine, pain was growth. Soon she would feel the spurts of fire that preceded the endorphin rush, soon Neil's bedroom wallpaper would blur as white heat tightened her chest and swelled her veins, threatening explosion.

She was going to be Granny Garfunkel Supreme Slimmer. BBW&S had phoned to confirm it – not Fizz St Clair, thank goodness, but Barbara someone, a nice young lady with a friendly North Country accent. Maggie was going to be Supreme Slimmer, and beside this all else receded.

Ivy, since her confrontation with Slik Piks, was, in any case, not speaking, and Maggie would not be baby sitting for Debbie Salt, not after last Monday and the incident involving the glass of water. It had been water from a bottle she had given Justin, of course, not tap water with its threatening nitrate levels. Apparently, however, any old bottle would not do. 'I mean, I don't want to be rude, Maggie, but you must have heard – some mineral waters are worse than tap water for contamination with bacteria, not to mention the sodium content, which, as you know, is really, really dangerous for your blood pressure.' Maggie's blood pressure had certainly soared (it hadn't helped that a voice inside her was beginning to assent to Debbie's nutritional concerns). Still, though she would miss poor little Justin, it was as well Debbie understood she was no longer available to be taken for granted.

Mr Gupta, too. Apart from the days she had missed

recently because of the shoot and the kitchen men, hadn't she always been a reliable worker? Yet here he was, questioning her demand for more leave. 'We're highly delighted you're a movie queen, love. But the business can't just hang about, can it, till you decide to drop in?' Afterwards, when she thought of the firmness of purpose with which she had handed in her notice, she was shaken by this unfamiliar assertiveness, this new strength of character. She thought fretfully of her wage packet too from time to time, and of how she would miss it. But that was all she would miss about Magipost – apart from Jackie. Yet Jackie, too, had changed, acquiring as the boss's girlfriend a self-contained air, restraining her expansiveness with a straight-jacket of discretion.

Yes, Maggie was grateful for this paring away of extraneous detail. At last she was free to dedicate herself to her new life. Though she had achieved and exceeded her target loss of two stone, she had not discontinued her diet. (Here was a conundrum, how did you stop? True, by carrying on you might lose too much, but if you gave up wouldn't you be bound to gain weight?) Now, however, the title of Supreme Slimmer conferred authority, the permission to pursue and refine her regime, to take up any slack when, as was inevitable, her weight-loss slowed, to strive for new feats of self-denial. Then there were the work-outs, the facials, the manicures, the sun-bed, the hair appointments, the aromatherapy massage once a week, not to mention the trips to town for essential additions to her wardrobe. Soon she was wondering how she had ever found time for distractions.

The question of funding still niggled. Seeing the exercise machine in a sale, she had (admittedly without telling Keith) slipped it onto their joint Visa. For the moment the card must bear her other costs too. Barbara had promised to sort out her expenses from the shoot, she would pay everything off sooner or later. She was an athlete in training, grooming herself for the big event; the money, like the time, was an investment, a small down-payment on the future.

Pedalling her exercise machine, Maggie felt the lift,

the surge of conquering energy. Soon, body subdued, will triumphant, she would reach the end of the long climb and preside over the view from the summit. Then, drenched in redemptive sweat, she would begin coasting. She coasted through streets where heads turned and a whisper went up, 'Isn't that the Granny Garfunkel Slimmer?' She coasted through restaurants where head waiters bowed, she free-wheeled past children with autograph books, she once even steered, thump, bump, down a staircase and found herself on the set of a chat show.

Sometimes she would feel her tyres gliding, slow-motion, over silver sand. A villa would appear against a vivid back-ground of sea, a typewriter would clatter on a terrace. Spike would look up and wave, and she would wave back. Lithe, slim and eternally youthful, she would wave in happy abandon-ment like the Paradise girl in the suntan oil poster.

The more Fizz dwelt upon it, the more the insult rankled.

Even the unexpected phone call from Dean had failed to diminish it. As she squeezed herself into her Janet Reger basque, she burned with injustice. She considered the props laid out on the futon, the long black gloves, the feathered Chloe evening dress, the spare suspender belt and stockings. Recently Dean had begun grumbling about the time their rituals took – as if she, Fizz, had chosen this performance. Uncoiling the two belts, the silver chain mail, the Chanel gilt and leather thong, she bound her knuckles in an angry knot. This was how men used her. While she spread herself unstintingly, they treated this abundance like a free buffet at some third-rate function.

She had put herself out for Spike, risked her status. If the Tel Travers incident had not been enough, if the ribbing he'd received on the charabanc trip home had not inflicted sufficient humiliation, the return to London should certainly have worked its civilizing influence by now. But no, he continued to goggle lubriciously at the footage of Tweetie Pie. Whenever Fizz dangled Le Gavroche – pressure of work had obliged her to shift the invitation to dinner –

he always managed, on some feeble pretext, to slither off the hook.

Of course, Genghis was largely to blame. By this time Tweetie Pie's reality should have been dissipated, carved up piecemeal by the editor's scalpel, reduced to mere feet per second, rendered cloying and bland by endless repetition, as ubiquitous and unvarying as fast food. But here was Genghis waxing enthusiastic over this absurd Supreme Slimmer concept; and now Tweetie Pie had been reconstituted as a living presence, a three-dimensional individual who would be feted at parties and garner applause at presentations. Now Fizz would be obliged to perpetuate the pretence that this nobody was somebody, while Spike continued to wallow in his *nostalie de la boue*.

Still, Genghis was pleased, oh yes indeed, highly delighted. And herein lay the paradox, Fizz saw. With the successful launch of Pandora she could not fail to ingratiate herself with Stretch. She needed Tweetie Pie, the creature would ensure her elevation to Deputy Managing Director. This dependence did not temper Fizz's loathing; rather, it exacerbated her sense that Spike's behaviour was part of a conspiracy, a planned and deliberate attempt to belittle her.

She cut two lines of coke, opened the Dom Perignon she had chilled in readiness for Dean. She appealed to her mirror for consolation. Here was whip-thin Fizz St Clair, provocatively armoured in the paraphernalia of fetish, black lace basque, patent thigh boots, investing even these clichés with her own unwavering chic.

Yet suddenly she discerned a withered look to the cantilevered cleavage, saw cellulite shuddering above stocking tops, tired pouches where boning displaced sagging flesh. Was this what Dean saw, what they all saw – this worn tart in tart's clothing?

She reached hastily for the champagne bottle. A second glass calmed her, a third reassured her that this unkindness had been no more than the mirror's caprice. The fourth and fifth glasses bestowed upon her the Deputy Managing Directorship. Ah, there would be changes then. Spike would be

241

brought to heel, Dean could be dispensed with. In the office too tremors would be felt. She had only to think positive, she had only to concentrate her will to achieve whatever she wanted. They would all of them shape up or ship out. Oh yes, they would find there was a price to be paid for slighting Fizz St Clair.

The Lapwarmer would be amongst the first to experience the rigours of the new regime. Fizz was scarcely surprised to observe the continued absence of irises from the sleek enamel vase. The plant, however, was another matter, squatting on her windowsill in its plastic container, stunted, insignificant, yet unpleasantly obtrusive.

'Drosera rotundifolia,' said The Lapwarmer, feigning a knowledgeable air when challenged.

'Dross,' said Fizz.

'You were complaining about the flies.'

'That was weeks ago.'

'Actually, you've been complaining for weeks. So I was talking to my friend Dinah – she works for Sebastian de Courcy, *the* garden design people – and she recommended this.'

A single sickly flower stem wavered from a circle of fleshy leaves like crimson-fringed carpet beaters. Fizz curled her lip.

The Lapwarmer produced a matchbox from her pocket. 'No, actually, just watch.'

'Lovey, this isn't kindergarten—'

'Watch! Just watch a minute.'

Before she could be prevented, The Lapwarmer had approached the plant and was shaking the matchbox vigorously. Onto one of the carpet beaters the plump corpse of a blue bottle was disgorged.

'Ohmigod!'

The carpet beater had become a tongue, quivering with pleasure, curling itself languorously around the sweetmeat. There were some moments of dalliance, as though the purity of this initial sensation, like the first September oyster, the first sip of a Premier Grand Cru claret, might with due care be infinitely protracted. Then the tongue became a jaw, snapping shut, interlocking its crimson filaments like teeth.

'It prefers live ones really. Those leaf things are sticky, according to Dinah, so when the fly lands it gets trapped, and then, as it starts to struggle—'

'Gross!' exclaimed Fizz, whirling away from the window.

'Actually, Fizz, it's eco-chic.'

'Get it out of here!'

'You know, nature's way. Like getting the greenfly to eat the ladybirds on your roses—'

'Get it out right now. And get me irises.'

'Cut flowers aren't really the thing any more. Not environmentally friendly.'

'Get me irises, OK. Irises! *Irises!*'

A couple of taxi-hailers had been drawn to the doorway by this interchange, so that Fizz became aware that she was screaming. She fixed the taxi-hailers with a glance that clipped their impudent sniggers and sent them scurrying back to the playpen. The lapwarmer, however, appeared unabashed.

'Actually, Fizz, I'm surprised, really I am. Dinah thought a carnivorous plant sounded just your sort of thing.'

The memo had been lurking beneath a cautionary note from the Finance Director, forecasting further cut-backs in client spending, warning of a deficient bottom line and urging directors to moderate their expenses. It was not until Fizz had filed this communication in the bin under N/A that the second sheet of paper caught her attention.

'We are pleased to welcome Sandra Belcher to BBW&S. Sandra joins us from Feldman, Troop, Harrington and Bechstein as Management Director on Country Fayre plc, and is appointed, with immediate effect, to the board.'

Fizz reached for the phone. No one had consulted her on this appointment, despite her own status as a board director. She was amazed at Stretch, failing to call upon his most powerful ally, omitting to seek her advice and endorsement. Had he done so, she would have told him there was no need for this impulsive hiring – particularly when economy was the watchword. Country Fayre was chicken-feed, Fizz could easily have taken it over. Besides, the Brooks Bellini board had no requirement for a second woman. Gulping a generous measure from her Perrier bottle, she had lifted the receiver when she remembered that, as of today, Stretch was on leave, enjoying the rustic pleasures of his eight-bedroomed, double-garaged Provençal cottage.

Research, however, calmed her. Although sources at Feldman Troop had not been forthcoming with useful dirt on the superfluous Sandra Belcher, an after-hours check on the Country Fayre suite had revealed she had taken up residence in Adrian Melrose's modest office, where no alteration had been made to the G-Plan and tired tweed sofa units. A plodder, no doubt, like The Donkey, conscientious, but utterly devoid of charisma. Besides, could one take anybody seriously with a name like Sandra Belcher?

In fact Fizz had quite edited the business from her mind when, several days later, as she was perusing a memo from The Donkey (requesting two weeks' holiday, would you believe, just nicely to coincide with the launch of Pandora) she became distantly aware of a figure in the doorway.

She delayed glancing up, scrawling across the memo an uncompromising 'no'.

The woman in the doorway wore a pink Karl Lagerfeld suit – or was it Versace? Yet, despite the designer suit, she had a pared-down look, neat court shoes, minimal jewellery and make-up, a look carefully sanitized of personal quirks, disagreeably redolent of efficiency, the look of a corporate tax lawyer or an accountant. More disagreeable still, she was slim – slimmer than Fizz. Observing her, Fizz felt her own body grow heavy with its comparative superfluity of flesh.

'Hi,' said the woman, advancing confidently.

Fizz struggled with the unaccustomed sense of being at a disadvantage. Relatively slim was never enough: the only true security lay in slimmest. The face behind the shiny-bright smile was convincingly youthful, too – thirty-one, thirty-three? Fizz resolved instantly upon a regime of total starvation.

'Great to meet you at last. I'm Sandi. Sandi Belcher.'

She pronounced it 'Bell-shay'. Fizz sought comfort from this pathetic affectation.

'I've been dying to meet up with the other female director – my partner in crime. I've come by several times to introduce myself.'

'You know how it is.' Fizz waved her Perrier glass airily. 'Things are heavy at the moment. A multi-million dollar launch on Granny Garfunkel. And that's just for openers.'

'I did try at start of play. But your secretary suggested that wasn't very hopeful.'

Damn The Lapwarmer. Where was loyalty? 'If one swims and works out, there's always the difficulty, isn't there, of beating the crowd to the showers?'

'Don't tell me. That's why I have a personal trainer specified in my contract.'

Fizz, seeking fortification from her glass, narrowly avoided choking.

'Oh dear. You OK? D'you know, I could use some Perrier too. Mind if I help myself?'

Before Fizz could protest she had reached across the table for the bottle. Fizz drew it back just in time. 'Glasses. I'll buzz.'

'But aren't those clean glasses? On that tray on the shelf?'

'It's – this bottle's flat.'

'You're drinking it. I don't want to be a problem.'

For an instant it seemed they might engage in an unseemly tussle for the Perrier bottle. Of course, if The Lapwarmer had provided the second virgin litre this morning as instructed, this absurdity might have been avoided. 'I'll buzz,' said Fizz firmly.

The Lapwarmer, appearing with fresh supplies, had not the grace to look contrite. Rather, there was something chilling in the way she said, ' If this one's flat, I'd better dispose of it, hadn't I?', so that Fizz was obliged to surrender not only the bottle but also the precious dregs in her glass. It was almost as if the creature *knew*. Fizz, who had been contemplating the hard lesson in obedience her secretary was soon to receive, found her satisfaction soured.

Miss Goody Two-Shoes, meanwhile, had pulled up a chair and had made herself at home, legs neatly crossed, hands demurely folded. 'Everyone here's been so friendly and helpful, getting me up to speed.'

'Still, you're bound to find Yellow Fats quite a challenge.'

'Country Fayre? I'm told there are meatier assignments coming my way, things I can properly get my teeth into.'

'Really?' said Fizz.

'And my office isn't sorted yet, of course.'

'I thought you were in Adrian's.'

'Those tweed sofas? I'm just camping there for the duration.'

'Really? Where—?'

'But at least – oh, I have to admit it, I'm thrilled – my car was delivered this morning.'

Fizz soothed herself with the vision of her Porsche Targa, gleaming, sleek as a bullet, in her personal parking space. What would Miss Two-Shoes merit as an incomer? A Lotus, perhaps, or one of those Japanese imitations.

'A Mercedes 500 SL. Signal red, metallic paint, black hide upholstery, position memory, heated seats. Plus all the usual extras. And a phone, natch.'

'No fax for the phone?' asked Fizz, attempting to rally.

'Great idea I'll get that nice Paul in finance to fix it.'

A silence fell, during which Fizz contemplated the precise detail of Miss Two-Shoes, her cybernetic smile, her preternatural slimness. Recalling that her glass contained no stronger comfort than virgin Perrier, she fought an impulse to hurl the insipid bubbles into that brightly smiling face.

Miss Two-Shoes, oblivious, was smoothing her Karl Lagerfeld skirt, replacing her own glass, neat and tidy, on the tray. 'We must we do some lunch, chew the fat, we two women. I'll get my secretary to liaise with yours. And now, terrific to meet you, but I must shoot. I'm doing lunch at Rules with Jim.'

'Jim?' said Fizz.

For the first time the smile wavered. A look of puzzlement replaced it. 'Our Chairman.'

So far had Brooks succumbed to Stretch's depredations that Fizz had ceased to think of him having a Christian name, as if it had been nibbled away with the rest. Miss Two-Shoes had much to learn, despite her thirty-two inch hips and her Mercedes. As she charted this learning curve, Fizz found her own smile returning. 'Enjoy,' she said.

Crouched over a lavatory seat in the executive ladies, Fizz cursed The Lapwarmer and Dick Saunders Blair's minion, whose prattle at the washbasins was interminably delaying her mid-morning inhalation. Worse still, they had been gossiping about her behind her back – she could tell by the way their laughter had died the moment she had entered. Laughing at her, Fizz, these below-the-line nobodies! They would find themselves laughing all the way to Renta Temp when she was Deputy Managing Director.

Nevertheless, she was aware she had not handled this morning's encounter with The Donkey with her customary diplomacy and charm. She had lost her temper, she would admit. But then the whole business had been preposterous. 'I'm sorry, Fizz, but I have to take my holiday next week. You see, I'm getting married.' The Workhouse Donkey, she of the billiard-table legs and centipede brow – who'd want to wake to that problem skin glowering from the pillow every morning? And, to top everything, when Fizz had gently suggested that a responsible person would hardly plan a wedding date which clashed with the launch of Pandora, what had the creature announced? Only that she was pregnant. Yes, Fizz remembered screaming about lost opportunities and ingratitude and unprofessionalism. But really, the whole thing was obscene. She relied upon The Donkey for leg-work and now she would constantly be taking time off for hospital appointments and antenatal classes, not to mention months of paid maternity leave, and Fizz would be obliged to train up some bag-carrier to replace her – if there was one available, given the rate at which Brooks Bellini was letting people go. What puzzled Fizz most was how The Donkey had managed to ensnare a man in the limited time left available by evenings of punishment

247

flow charts and statistical analysis. And what kind of man? Some pimply youth from Scottish Dancing?

All the same, when Fizz had looked closer she had seen the ring to prove it – a budget-store bauble dwarfed by the stumpy, hang-nailed finger. Fizz remembered the days, mercifully long gone, when she had travelled to work by tube – the women with their rings then, lumpy women, frumpy women, obese women with hairy legs and clashing skirts and sweaters, but all with their badges to say, 'Somebody chose me.' The pregnant women, too, with their sensible shoes and support hose, complacently thrusting out pomegranate bellies, 'I got there, I beat the biological clock.' Women with all the style of a bag of washing, yet somebody had chosen them, some man had picked them out as special.

Fizz's eyes stung as she crouched bedside the lavatory bowl with her credit card at the ready. Nobody had chosen her, nobody thought she was special. Even Dean preferred talking dirty over the phone these days. But then what of Dean, trussed with her Chanel thong, naked buttocks framed by black lace suspenders, tattooed deltoids stretching the fabric of her feathered Chloe or rippling coyly above the beading of her Dolce e Gabbana? She disliked being a dominatrix: she never knew how hard to wield the chain mail belt and anyway it was tiring. What was she to Dean but an extension of his perversity? Her twenty-three-year-old art-nouveau-bronze toyboy, chatting her up so assiduously at that production company party – it hadn't been her he'd desired, merely her spangled Katharine Hamnett.

At least Spike had never asked to borrow her lipstick or evinced the slightest longing to be tied up. The more she considered him, the more she could see his lack of taste was outweighed by other qualities. She thought of his sensitive brain-surgeon's fingers. Ohmigod, how she deserved sensitive treatment right now. Hadn't she a right to some support, some attention?

Spike had come round. After weeks of evasion, he had at last agreed upon dinner, though not at Le Gavroche. 'Jolly generous of you, Lucrezia, but there's this beezer new place *L'Entrée* is desperate for me to cover.'

Midas boasted canopied steps and a doorman cockaded and caped *au cocher*, so that Fizz was reminded of the entrance to a casino. Within, too, discreetly thick carpets and ubiquitous Edwardian plush declared a stifling respectability, as if disguising an altogether more raffish purpose, much as air freshener suggests the smell it covers. The concentration in the dining room was palpable: eyes were intent on plates; as poker-faced waiters dealt napkins and menus, lips were gnawed, brows were corrugated with the gravity of decision. No music played, no laughter sounded, only a muted murmur and the chink of jewellery.

'Gosh,' said Spike, his tone respectful of the gaming-house hush, 'you'll adore this, Lucrezia.'

Fizz recoiled from the menu. 'We've just had a memo ordering us to cut back on expenses.'

'But this is a once-in-a-lifetime experience.'

'Too right. You can't afford ever to eat out again.'

'Come, come, Lucrezia, it's not like you to be stingy. Besides, think – what does the name Midas suggest?'

Fizz considered the table setting, viewing with new comprehension the brocaded napkins, the gilded china, the glittering bands circling the rims of glasses.

'*Cuisine d'orée*. The last word in added value. It gives new meaning to conspicuous consumption.'

Fizz, returning to the blurb on the first page of the menu, read: 'All our dishes contain the ultimate ingredient, 24-carat beaten gold.' More followed, a potted history of the metal's symbolic significance, as well as a run-down on its magical and curative properties, from its use as a nostrum against the King's Evil to its valued place in the Chinese pharmacopoeia.

'Gold as a health food?'

'Take the guilt out of gilt? Well, why not? Gosh, where's your imagination, Lucrezia? If soya beans prolong life, if polyunsaturates promise immortality, why not gold? Think of the alchemists. In their book, turning their old tin cans

249

into ingots was only one step away from distilling the Elixir of Life.'

Fizz glanced about the dining room, at the dark-suited men and bejewelled women, eyes downcast, gilded knives and forks working purposefully at gold-encrusted plates. 'So that's what I tell the Finance Director? We came here in quest of the Elixir of Life.'

'Tush, Lucrezia. We came here because you have the style to appreciate it.'

'You mean, *L'Entrée* won't cough up.'

'A philistine, my editor, obsessed with mundanities like profit and loss. Gosh, where's my reputation as a restaurant writer if I haven't been to Midas? So once again I'm obliged to distrain upon the generosity of my friends.' Here, inclining his head, he favoured her with his crooked, consciously winning smile. 'I must say, Lucrezia, you've always proved a brick when it comes to supporting the cause of art.'

Distrust the smile as she might, his acknowledgement of their friendship warmed her. Yes, he had been reflecting, at last, and had come to understand on which side his Melba toast was buttered. A Kir Imperiale, in which glittering flakes swirled like a toy snow storm, served to mollify her further. After two more Kirs and a restorative trip to the gilt and marble ladies, her spirits burgeoned. In the candle-light gold winked from every least-expected surface, drifting in finger bowls, or burnishing bread crusts like Christmas wrapping: in Spike's fettuccine, fairy dust shimmered, on her own plate, asparagus (vinaigrette on account of her dairy allergy) flaunted gleaming tips as if they had been plunged into molten metal; when the waiter advanced with his gilded pepper mill she half anticipated it, too, would dispense a shower of tinsel.

It was true, she thought, surveying the effect through her champagne glass, observing flashes of brightness explode into hair thread cascades, like golden rain amongst the bubbles – who else could Spike have brought here? Who else would appreciate the exquisite decadence of the occasion, the rare combination of sophistication and vulgarity, an understanding of which marked out *conoscenti*? Certainly not Tweetie Pie.

Not that new bimbo in Art Buying he'd recently been spotted nosing around either. Oh, Spike liked his fantasies, but reality must obtrude sooner or later.

Taking up her knife and fork, she carefully prised the gold leaf from an asparagus tip and transported it to her mouth. To her surprise, it proved completely tasteless. She continued to divest the asparagus of its gilding until she had denuded every spear; then, bored by the predictability of what remained, she pushed aside her plate.

Next came a poussin with gleaming breastplate and greaves and, for Spike, a glittering trout. Another bottle of Dom Perignon appeared. Fizz felt well-being steal over her, as if the week's vexations were indeed, like the King's Evil, being magicked away. As with the asparagus, her interest in the chicken had faded once she had divested it of its golden armour. But then gold was the perfect food, she reflected. It offered no challenge of flavour or texture, it required minimal chewing, it contained no calories. Glancing across at Spike, she gave a sigh of satisfaction. Now there was only the evening's business to be concluded.

'I'll get the bill, OK, and we'll have liqueurs at my place.'

Spike's face rearranged itself into the charmingly abject smile. 'Gosh, Lucrezia, I'd love to. Alas, I have to rush home and write my piece.'

'Just an eentsy armagnac.'

'Sounds beezer. But my deadline beckons.'

Fizz felt panic rising in a great hot blast that threatened to stifle her. 'Please. Just for half an hour.'

His answer was a further helpless shrug. He had replaced his napkin on the table, so that she feared he might leave.

'You said you were my friend.'

'Gosh, so I am, Lucrezia—'

'Then why have you turned against me?'

'Look, I have a deadline—'

'You're like everyone else at Brooks Bellini, trying to stab me in the back.'

'Lucrezia, please.'

251

'Do you know, I caught two bag-carriers talking about me in the corridor today. Bag-carriers, I ask you!'

'Calm down, Lucrezia.'

'And I know Dick Saunders Blair's been firing off poison faxes to Stretch in Provence.'

'Lucrezia! I am not against you. It's just that I have a thousand words to write by 10 a.m. tomorrow. And in any case—'

'Yes?'

'Well – gosh, I value our working partnership, I wouldn't want to complicate it.'

'That didn't bother you before.'

This pulled him up, she noticed. He paused with a palmful of chalk pills halfway to his mouth. 'Before?'

'My dinner party, remember.'

His adam's apple bobbed as he gulped down the pills. 'Ah yes. I've been meaning to apologize about that.'

'It wasn't a star performance, if that's what's bothering you. But I'm prepared to put it down to first-night nerves.'

He was staring, no doubt taken aback by her generosity. She reached for his knee with hers beneath the table. 'Oh yes, I'm prepared to work at our relationship, darling, to give it every chance. You may not realize it, but this is as big for me as it is for you. That's why you've got to come home with me tonight.'

'Lucrezia – Fizz—'

Suddenly she did not care for his expression, or the way his knee remained so persistently elusive. 'What are you saying to me, Spike? Do you deny you slept with me?'

'Not if sleep's the operative word.'

'Do you deny climbing into my bed?'

'No, but—'

'But what? This is Fizz you're talking to, not some sleazy one-night stand.'

'Golly gosh, no. But look, you know how it is. We've all done it, haven't we?'

'Done what, Spike?'

'Got over-tired, gone on an Awayday to Amnesialand. It

was a stimulating evening, I felt this sudden need to do some lateral thinking. Gosh, I'm not proud of it, the moment I woke up and realized where I was I took myself off. My apologies couldn't be more profuse. It was just one of those things.'

Now it was her turn to stare. She lowered her glass. 'I'm an Amnesia Awayday, is that what you're telling me?'

'Hush, Lucrezia.'

'I will not hush!'

'Please, don't shout.'

'I am not shouting!'

'Please, Fizz—'

His eyeline had altered. She became aware of a dark bulk lowering at her elbow and, glancing up, observed the maitre d'.

'Madam, I must ask you to moderate your voice. Our other guests are complaining.'

He wore the look, she thought, of some minor council official, or a parking warden writing out a ticket, bloated with his own dignity and rectitude. She felt suddenly all about her an icy silence and, looking round the dining room, saw forks stilled, heads raised, other eyes echoing this sanctimony, bovine jaws ceasing to chew, owls puffed out with righteous disapproval.

She reached for her glass. The discovery that it was empty further inflamed her. 'How dare you use that tone with me. Go away and find me another bottle of shampoo.'

Spike was swallowing chalk pills. 'Fizz, I think we'd better leave.'

'Pay no attention. These people are devoid of style.'

'You shouldn't drive, I'll get you a taxi.'

'I don't want a taxi, I've just ordered more Dom Perignon.'

'Forget it. Let's just go.'

Oh, she saw his game now, she saw why he was pretending embarrassment. 'We're not going anywhere, Spike lovey. We're staying right here till we get to the bottom of this.'

'Please, Fizz—'

'We're staying here till we find out why you're throwing away our relationship.'

253

'If you won't leave, I'd better.'

'It's that tacky woman, right?'

'I'm going, Fizz.'

'You're dumping our relationship for tacky Tweetie Pie.'

'Leave Maggie out of this. You're over-refreshed.'

'You're the one who's over-refreshed, dumping me for Tweetie Pie, passing me over for a woman who says 'toilet', a woman with Artex ceilings and an inglenook fireplace, a woman whose highest ambition is undoubtedly a lounge extension with a cocktail bar and everything fully fitted in double-glazed, button punched, avocado PVC—'

He had pushed back his chair. The maitre d' loomed, bearing the bill and a portentous expression.

'I'm leaving, Fizz.'

'Fine. Go.'

'You'd better come too. Your nose is bleeding.'

'Go. Who gives a shit!'

He turned and began to walk away. She tried to ignore the tinny surge that filled her mouth, subduing her voice to a gargle. 'Nobody's leaving till I say so. Nobody walks out on Fizz St Clair!'

'Fizz, it's Cissie. I just called to see how you were.'

'Fine. Brilliant. Never better.'

This was not strictly true. Fizz's nasal passages were raw, her mouth tasted as if someone had dumped a truckload of manure on her tongue, her eyes were assailed with lurid flashes and, in decanting the day's supply of vodka into her Perrier bottle, her hand had shaken so badly that quantities of the precious liquid had been lost. The first glass had made her heave, the subsequent two were proving tardy with their medicine.

'It's just that I never know what to say when you phone in such a state.'

Fizz did not recall having phoned Cissie, not for some weeks, and certainly not in a state. Images of last night were hazy, brief clips from a movie too painful to see. Perhaps a phone call had featured somewhere. All the same, Fizz felt a

254

powerful sense of being wrongly accused. No doubt envy of her high-profile lifestyle impelled Cissie to criticism, fostered these crude attempts to catch her off balance.

'Rod says the next time the phone goes at two in the morning I shouldn't answer it. But I worry about you being so unhappy.'

Fizz's sense of injustice grew. Christ, how she loathed the solidarity of couples, the way they dispensed crusts like charity but, when hunger struck, never scrupled to point out that you were excluded from the table. She thought of Mother and Father all at once, sitting in the sun lounge in their woolly cardies, poring over the pools coupon, backs turned, heads together, communing over away wins and full score draws, sealed in that two's-company knitting-pattern world of theirs, to which there was no entry, never had been, for a third, the outsider. She remembered what Father had said after she'd phoned in despair over the debacle with Spunky Dunkie, 'I don't want you ever calling like that again. It only upsets your mother.'

Fizz's eyes were seared for a moment. 'Cissie, I said, I'm fine. Now, if you don't mind – the major deal of your day may be watching the socks go round in the machine, but I have work to do. Someone has to keep the country's economy ticking over.'

Slamming down the receiver afforded her no relief. Some-times she wondered whether there were a mark on her forehead she herself could not see, the mark of The Beast, branding her from birth as an outcast, doomed to watch others revelling in a happiness from which she was excluded. More likely, it was the malign operation of fate, of a game in which, however she coaxed the dice, however high she threw, her counter always landed on the longest and slipperiest snake. She thought of last night and Spike's atrocious behaviour. She thought of Tweetie Pie, who had occasioned it. She pondered the rules which awarded all the ladders to mediocrities like Tweetie Pie. She loathed Tweetie Pie with a passion.

In this loathing, as she stoked its fire, was comfort, warm-ing the chill space within her, so that soon other fuel crackled

255

in its flames: her cleaning lady for giving notice, and the man in the blue BMW who had cut her up this morning, and every taxi driver who had presumed to call her 'love', and politicians for extolling family values, and Christmas, and Mother's Day, and Mothercare, and Minty-Caroline-Ffiona and their horsy, disdainful parents, all consumed by a glorious, soaring, seething conflagration.

A flush spread to her cheeks as the vodka at last took hold. Think positive. Tweetie Pie was expedient. Everything would improve once she was Deputy MD.

She turned her attention to the morning's mail. Another memo from The Finance Director about expenses, a further instalment of The Plague of the Mushroom-Type Fungus. She came upon the third sheet of paper absently, unprepared.

'We are pleased to announce a new Senior Management appointment. Effective from today, Sandi Belcher will assume the post of . . .'

It took Fizz some time to read the document through to the end, and several readings before she could digest it. Only then, reaching dazedly for the phone, did she recall that Stretch was still in Provence. She stared at the signature underwriting Miss Two-Shoes' appointment as Deputy Managing Director. She read 'James Brooks', first with disbelief, then with an upheaval in her stomach.

PART FOUR

'We owe our children their birthright – to grow up unafraid of their appetites and proud of their bodies.'

Susie Orbach: *The Guardian*

*Telephone conversation, 22 August, between Mr Art
Khan, Managing Director, Granny Garfunkel Gour-
met Gateaux (UK) Inc. and Ms Fizz St Clair, Senior
Account Director, BBW&S Advertising.*

ST CLAIR: . . . So you're agreed the commercial is ninety-
nine point nine per cent there?

KHAN: We're all finally fishing in the same ball park, kid.

ST CLAIR: Wow, Art! It's going to be some party on the
twenty-fourth.

KHAN: You got Maggie Hapgood all lined up?

ST CLAIR: And Tel Travers, of course.

KHAN: It's the broad that's gonna get us day-after recall,
shift those boxes.

ST CLAIR: We're all agreed she's the perfect spokesperson for
Granny Garfunkel – wholesome yet provocative,
aspirational yet reassuring—

KHAN: She's got normalcy, humancy – she's got goddam
realistictivity, right?

ST CLAIR: Right on, Art. And – wait till you get this.
Beat this for a PR opportunity to throw into
the mix—

KHAN: Pitch it to me, little lady.

ST CLAIR: Maggie's going to be a grandmother in
December. How's that for realistictivity? A real-
live granny representing Granny Garfunkel . . .

I

'It's simple,' Spike had said. 'You're booked into the Lanchester for the night of the twenty-fourth. But you tell your family you're needed for a photo call on the twenty-third, and I tell the office I've succumbed to bubonic plague. Then we book for that night as well.'

'Isn't the Lanchester very pricey?'

'I'll wangle a job number from Barbara Donkin. With the dough Lucrezia's lavishing on this bunfight, she'll never notice a few extra bubbles in the yeast.'

Maggie had frowned into the receiver. 'But won't it get you into trouble?'

'Sweetheart, it's standard practice. Most people's expenses read like the Brothers Grimm. And anyway, we've both given our all for Granny Garfunkel, so it's more or less kosher.'

'Well . . . if you're sure . . .'

'Of course, I'd much rather treat you myself. In fact I was planning to. But the blasted lawyers slapped another maintenance increase on me yesterday morning.'

'Oh, darling. Is that for poor little Amy again?'

'Tarquin, my youngest son. You know – his mother's refused access from birth.'

'Poor Spike. I'm so sorry.'

'Let's not think about it. Let's just think of being together. I'll book the room in my name, of course. And oh, toothsome Maggie, we'll have two nights and a whole day to devour each other.'

As her taxi joined the snail's trail of traffic down Conduit Street towards Berkeley Square, Maggie's pulse fluttered. The women, expensively aloof in their dark glasses, the shop windows evoking the scent of hand-stitched leather and personalized colognes, the picture galleries, in whose carpeted hush she imagined gold-nibbed pens confiding outrageous figures to impervious cheque books – the sight of it all left her queasy with excitement. The very size of the buildings uplifted her, suggesting prodigality of opportunity, life conceived on a loftier scale.

She was amazed by how effortlessly she could now lie. Keith and Nicki had seemed to accept her story without question, nodding half-heartedly to her instructions about the Miracle Menus in the freezer and her request that they should video the commercial. She would phone home each evening, of course, and in a crisis messages could be left at the Lanchester's reception. After these weeks of conspiracy, the ease with which she had won her freedom had seemed almost an anti-climax.

Yet here she was, her taxi nosing out of Berkeley Square into quiet Mayfair streets. Here she was, freshly made-up and coiffured, sleek in her white Jasper Conran, mysteriously aloof behind her own dark glasses, keeping a four o'clock assignation with her lover at the Lanchester Hotel.

She was glad it was to be like this, despite the delays and frustrations. If she were to take this step, break her marriage vows, give herself to Spike, it should not be done lightly – not sordidly in some lay-by or drunkenly in that plastic suburban hotel. Even Spike's flat, from his description of its cramped spaces and makeshift arrangements, had seemed to lack due ceremony for such a gesture. But here was her taxi gliding into the forecourt of the Lanchester – newly built, she observed, without the traditional grandeur of the Ritz or the Dorchester, but imposing, nevertheless; already, through plate glass, she could glimpse marble, palms, chandeliers, all the trappings of honeymoon extravagance.

She fumbled hastily in her purse as the doorman lifted her new pig-skin-look suitcase from the cab. She drew herself up, straightening her dark glasses. Then she swept after her luggage, as if she had been making such entrances all her life.

★　★　★

262

No mere room, but a suite.

Clutching Spike's hand in the lift, she had regressed for an instant, struggling with that inclination to giggle. But now, making her tour, she was the sophisticate again, noting the four-poster and the jacuzzi, taking in every furbelow and chintzy swag, yet knowing better than to appear over-impressed.

Spike was watching her eagerly, she saw. 'Everything to modom's satisfaction?'

Suddenly she remembered the hotel in Penzance. The Bridal Suite, they'd called it, though it had only been a double bedroom, really. But even an en suite bathroom had been a novelty in those days and anyway, living with their parents, she and Keith had never been in sole command of so much space. She recalled how, still shedding confetti, they'd bounced on the bed, pressed all the light switches and the TV buttons, sprayed each other with the shower attachment, hooting and whooping. She pushed the memory away. 'It looks nice and clean and comfortable, thanks.'

The skew-whiff grin seemed oddly crestfallen. 'Come here, sweetie. Don't I deserve a kiss?'

He was waiting, she realized, for her to remove the aloof dark glasses. She pushed them to her crown while he pocketed his spectacles, then they kissed, rather formally, for some moments.

Replacing his spectacles, he held her at arm's length. 'Maggie, you seem different today.'

'Four weeks and you've forgotten what I look like.'

'Good Lord, it's not that. I can't count how many times I've seen you since the shoot, backwards, forwards, long shot, close-up, freeze frame, there, but not there. Oh, sweetheart, can you imagine the torture?'

'Perhaps it's my eye make-up. I'm trying a new look.'

'Gosh, very startling.'

'And my stylist's added more highlights and lifted my perm.'

'Well, anyway . . . you're here, we're here. At long last!'

They kissed again. This time when they drew apart an

awkward silence ensued. 'I think,' she said, 'I'll make a start on my unpacking.'

It was the luxury of their surroundings that made them nervous and overawed: soon the excitement would return. Indeed, there was Spike now on the lounge phone, ordering smoked salmon sandwiches and champagne.

Lifting out the treasured contents of the pig-skin-look suitcase, Maggie transferred each garment carefully to a smooth wooden hanger. Spike, crossing to the bathroom to unburden his holdall, paused to grin. 'Hope you've brought that pink frock.'

'You're joking!'

'But it's how I imagine you. The quintessential Maggie.'

'It's gone where it should have gone years ago – to Oxfam. You wait and see, you won't miss it.'

Oh yes, she thought, slotting hangers into the closet, here was a trousseau, crisp, mint-new, still smelling of fabric dressing – the trousseau she had missed out on. It had inflicted a terminal blow upon the ailing Visa card, but she would rather not think about that just at the moment. Better to admire the David Fielden halter-neck purchased specially for the party – a rush of blood to the head, but how could she regret it, seeing its fluid lines miraculously unscathed by the suitcase, stroking its sensuous black chiffon folds? Beside it hung the beige Nicole Farhi sarong suit for dinner this evening, then the linen two-piece for tomorrow's lunch. After that came the ultimate indulgence, the crepe de chine negligée and nightgown, evocation of some nineteen-forties' film. There were slippers trimmed with marabou to match the negligée, and two pairs of shoes, the tan pumps, the futuristic Stephane Kélian heels, making a proud line at the bottom of the wardrobe, virgin leather, not yet scuffed, not even creased to the foot. No maid who peered inside this closet would find occasion to sniff.

The dressing gown was Maggie's guilty secret, her threadbare blue candlewick robe, relic of breakfast-making and hoovering and late-night dustbin visits. She had packed it in a last minute panic, imagining make-up and bath oil smearing the romantic crepe de chine. Now it straggled like a vagrant across the quilted bed cover. Quickly she thrust it into a drawer.

This was it, there was no going back. The smoked salmon sandwiches had been eaten – well, Spike had consumed them, for she, who had in any case foresworn bread, could not have brought herself to swallow a morsel. The ice bucket containing the second bottle of champagne had been carried through to the bedroom. The 'Do Not Disturb' sign had been placed on the outer door.

In the bathroom, where she had retreated to check her lipstick, Maggie stared hard into the mirror. Why did this remind her of the swimming lesson where Yvonne Simms and Karen Pickles had dared her to jump off the top board?

The glass shelf beneath the cabinet caught her eye, with its sparse display of Spike's possessions, the bottle of Collis Browne and spare rolls of stomach tablets, the soap-mottled sponge bag, the battered brush darkly matted with hair. They shocked her, these objects, not just with their shabbiness but with their intimacy, their suggestion of unfamiliar secretions and smells. She wished she had more practice at this. She wished the champagne would begin working.

Determinedly, she fixed upon her own image. Her cheeks were flawlessly powdered, her cleavage and neck scented with Opium, her diaphragm in place. Did not the peach crepe de chine lend her the predatory air of a Davis or a Crawford? She experimented, lowering heavy lids, tilting her jaw. She was slim, a svelte eight stone eight, and that was what counted. He would not notice her stretch marks or the scar from Nicki's Caesarean.

She blotted her lipstick, treated her artistically tousled hair to a final salvo of hair spray. Then she drew in one last deep breath.

Somehow she had not expected his nakedness, or that this would so disconcert her, reminding her that she had only

265

ever seen one other man naked in her life. She paused, blushing.

The bed creaked softly as he rose, padding towards her across the carpet. 'Sweetheart, wouldn't you be more comfortable without that nightie?'

Perhaps she had assumed he would undress her, perhaps she had seen herself performing a slow and provocative strip (although that would have taken careful rehearsal). Now she could do no better than to tug the garment over her head, struggling to avoid damaging contact with her lipstick.

'Gosh, let me feast on you, Maggie, let me drink you in.'

The silence forced her to look up and take him in too. Of course, she had always known he was skinny, with his jagged elbows and gangling legs. That boyish lack of coordination – hadn't it been part of his attraction? But now, without clothes – the bony shanks, the concave chest, the pale skin stretched over visible ribs – it seemed almost indecent, this uncompromising display of veins and tendons and skeletal structure, exaggerating the fleshiness of his cock and balls by comparison, like a magnified section in an anatomical drawing.

Repressing the memory of Keith's love handles, she forced herself to continue looking. He was cultivated and witty, he knew about wine and the correct way to eat artichokes. She had just not expected him to be so skinny.

He was also blinking at her, she realized. 'You've lost weight, Maggie.'

'I'm the Granny Garfunkel Slimmer, remember.'

'But – since the commercial—'

'Another six pounds. Isn't it fantastic?'

'Gosh, fantastic, yes.'

His hesitation puzzled her. 'It's all down to you really, darling. You wrote the script.'

'Golly, gosh, so I did.'

The quirky grin reappeared. With deliberation he removed his spectacles. 'Never mind. You're a banquet, sweetheart, whether it's andouillettes or spare ribs.'

★　★　★

266

Maggie showered and applied fresh layers of make-up while Spike, riffling through the Good Food Guide, phoned about dinner. She was almost glad dinner had become an issue. It gave them something to talk about – other than The Problem.

'Gosh,' he'd said, 'I'm sorry.'

'It's me, isn't it?'

'Good grief, no. I don't usually have this trouble. Let's rest, shall we, for a minute?'

So they had rested and tried again. They had tried without the condom, tried different positions, tried yet more champagne. They had heaved and sweated and groaned till their bodies felt raw from grinding together. They had decided that the origin of the difficulty was an energy deficiency, easily rectified by dinner.

Spike's original plan, that they should dine in their suite, seemed out of the question for obvious reasons. The Lanchester's restaurant, 'international cuisine, passable if you can forgive lobster claws with everything', was, by this hour, fully booked. There was the T-Bone Grill, of course, but from this Spike recoiled in fastidious horror.

'Burgers, Maggie? Fried Chicken? Coleslaw?'

'Doesn't T-Bone mean steak?'

'And a chef who thinks "bleu" is the French for naughty movies.'

There had been an asperity in his voice which had driven her back to the bathroom. Now, wielding her mascara brush, she felt the familiar guilt. Though he had denied it was her fault, she could not help searching the mirror. Was it her lack of sophistication that had put him off? Was it the age rings the bathroom's unsparing fluorescent light etched into her neck? Was it her stretch marks or her hamster cheeks or the taste of her new lipstick? Or was it some unseen blemish, a flaw so fundamental that neither hair tint, nor exercise, nor even plastic surgery could repair it?

When she brought herself to emerge she could hear him in the lounge, still telephoning restaurants.

'Not till nine thirty? Good grief, all I want is a table for two . . . Not even behind a pillar or on the main drag to the gents?'

Though she had lost heart for the Nicole Farhi sarong suit, she changed and tidied her hair. After a while she became conscious of a profound silence.

He was slumped beside the telephone.

'Oh Spike, I'm so sorry.'

'It's not your fault.'

'But if it's something I'm doing—'

'You? Why you? Christ, what's going on in this city tonight? Times are hard, they tell us, even Michelin rosettes are touting for business—' He broke off, burying his head in his hand. 'I don't usually have this trouble.'

He was the schoolboy again, knee grazed, cap mislaid. She reached instinctively to stroke his hair. 'It'll be all right, Spike.'

'It will, won't it?'

She laid her cheek against his, he sought for her hand, squeezing her fingers. 'If I can't get us in somewhere decent, I'll try my B list. There's an interesting place in Shepherds Bush that does an excellent Doctor Fish Gumbo . . .'

'I'm sure it'll be all right.'

'Or, look, if you can stand the T-Bone Grill, I can stand it. I'll bring an extra supply of chalk pills.'

'Spike, it'll be fine,' she said.

It would be fine, she was certain of it. The T-Bone Grill, though not the debut she had dreamed of for the Nicole Farhi sarong suit, provided space, neutral territory, the noise and distraction of other people. They had left The Problem upstairs in their suite and during their absence it had been cleared away, along with Spike's cigarette stubs and the champagne glasses. Now clean sheets welcomed them, and freshly plumped pillows.

This time there was no pause for ceremony, this time they tore at each other with all the old fervour, recklessly attacking buttons and zips. They had reached Spike's shorts and Maggie's bra when he suddenly doubled up.

268

'My goodness, darling, what is it?'

'Aaaargh!'

'Should I phone for a doctor?'

'My ulcer.'

'Oh, goodness—'

'Said – the T-Bone – would be – disaster.'

'But your told me your entrecote was just the way you like it.'

'Maybe – the coleslaw.'

'You didn't have coleslaw.'

'The jacket potato then.' He was crouched, grey in the face, arms cradling his abdomen. 'That's – it. Jacket potato – poisoning.'

'Oh, heavens! What should I do?'

'Collis Browne – in bathroom. Or – in extremis – neat gin.'

'Table for one, madam?'

Maggie accepted mutely this unfeeling emphasis on her solitary state.

Waking, disorientated and stiff, it had taken her a moment to remember. She was sleeping on the lounge settee because Spike had jacket potato poisoning. She had risen unsteadily, waiting for the blood to return to her legs. The Collis Browne and the mini-bar's entire stock of gin miniatures had done their work well. Better not to disturb him, better to dress in the bathroom, then creep out and take breakfast downstairs.

Ordering orange juice, grapefruit and black coffee, determinedly rejecting croissants, she glanced about her. A table of grey-suited men, voluble on added-value marketing environments over scrambled eggs. Three American matrons, kitted out in battle fatigues for a day's sight-seeing, writing postcards as they consumed English muffins. A middle-aged couple silently chomping cereal. Married, of course. She remembered the games she and Keith had played amongst the Toby jugs and plastic wisteria in that dining room in Penzance. Spot the ones having a dirty weekend – they talk to each other over the toast and porridge. Spot the ones heading for a divorce. Spot the honeymoon couple – well, that's us,

269

isn't it? Handsome Keith with his blue, blue eyes and his dimpled chin and his long blond Scott Walker hair. She'd been so proud to come down with him, hand in hand, every morning; she'd wanted to shake the rustling newspapers, set the sleepy tea-drinkers aquiver, she'd wanted to sing out above the tinkle of spoons and the tick of the cuckoo clock, 'He's mine now, all mine!'

She felt a homesick ache for her shabby kitchen, fragrant with toast and frying bacon, for that quiet half hour before the certainty of chaos, the tumbled satchels and football kit, the yawning and squabbling.

Were Keith and Nicki missing her, even a little? She'd been surprised to receive no answer to her phone calls. Yes, it had been late the second time she'd called; it had taken a while to soothe Spike to sleep, and perhaps they, too, were sleeping. Even so, they'd been expecting her to ring.

Perhaps they had both turned over in their beds and decided not to bother. After all, it was gone now, wasn't it, this vision of home she ached for, consigned to the skip along with the old kitchen units and the rickety formica table. She tried to imagine limed oak and leaded glass and Keith and Nicki perched on high stools at the marbleized breakfast bar, but the picture eluded her. Her eyes burned, and the Lanchester's Colonial-style Coffee Shop receded.

Spike was up and dressed when she returned, already seated at the writing desk in a flurry of paper.

'Gosh, heaps better, thanks. And you, my poor sweetheart – no need to have taken yourself off to the sofa. But, look, I must apologize – there's this rush job I simply must get on a bike this morning.'

'Oh.'

'Five hundred words on a Professor of Archaeology. Shouldn't take long, only there's a lot of tiresome detail about skulls and Neanderthal dental arcades, and I seem to have lost half my notes.'

'Oh. I see.'

'Finished by lunchtime, of course. And, sweetie, I won't let you down this time, I'll get us in somewhere special – Cibo, L'Arlequin, Alastair Little.'

'Oh. Yes. Of course.'

'Meanwhile, forgive me. Still, I'm sure you've got your own plans.'

Maggie remembered a time when she had enjoyed window shopping. But that was before her diet, before she'd grown used to buying things. Now that the ailing Visa card rendered her a spectator once more, there seemed little pleasure in it. Every window displayed newer styles, more daringly modish accessories than her own wardrobe could boast, so that she felt a sudden panic. Fashion was a race, in which even the keenest merely struggled to keep up. Left behind on the pavement, she could only peer at their progress, growing, in last month's linen two-piece, older and frumpier by the minute.

Still, it was good to be out in the fresh air, away from the Lanchester Hotel, whose dense carpets and overstuffed settees now oppressed her, as if Suite 213 were a prison. At twelve, too, she could register for her own room, the room Barbara Donkin had booked. She could move her clothes and spend the afternoon preparing herself for the party, casting the last twenty-four hours from her mind, concentrating on her debut as the Granny Garfunkel Slimmer. Spike would not object; he would be relieved to be alone with his skulls and dental arcades. And later, at the party, they need not speak, or even see each other except at a distance.

Before joining the queue at reception she used a pay phone to call home, chancing that Nicki might be in. If Nicki were, the howl of the CD player had clearly rendered her deaf.

The girl at the reception desk wore impervious lipstick reminiscent of Fizz St Clair. 'I'm sorry, modom, we do not appear to have your booking.'

'The name's Hapgood. H-A-P—'

'Thank you, modom, I can spell.'

Maggie sensed that people were beginning to stare. With effort, she lowered her voice. 'Please. The room was booked for Brooks, Bellini, Waldo and Stretch. By a Miss Donkin.'

271

Impatiently, the scarlet talons stabbed the keyboard. 'We have no registration in your name, modom.'

'But—'

'If you wish to stay in the hotel and can offer proof of identity and details regarding method of payment, please complete this registration form and I will check if we have a vacancy. Now, if you don't mind . . .'

The other receptionist was engaged with a party of German tourists. Maggie edged along the counter in pursuit of Scarlet Talons. 'Excuse me—'

The bright nails scoured a registration form, before thrusting it back at the guest who had proffered it, a thin blond woman. 'No, that won't do. You've missed these sections here.'

'Excuse me, please,' said Maggie.

'Bottom of the class again,' said the blond woman. 'Silly me!'

In order not to respond to the woman's nervous giggle, Scarlet Talons was at last compelled to notice Maggie. 'Modom, I am occupied.'

'Blimey, you can tell she's been to charm school,' said the blond woman, as they watched her flounce away.

Maggie accepted this overture sheepishly for, despite her panic, she was aware that her fellow-sufferer might merit the receptionist's disdain. That poorly-cut white trouser suit, those tarty black patent heels, the blond crop itself, brassy with home peroxide – some people had no idea how they betrayed themselves. Then she caught the woman's smile and was instantly ashamed. She gave a sigh of fellow-feeling. 'Yeah. Wonder who her tutor was – Adolf Hitler?'

The woman was younger than Maggie, probably in her mid-thirties, despite the crow's feet puckering her fierce orange mask. Maggie received a nagging sense that her smile was somehow familiar. Her new friend threw her a wink as Scarlet Talons reappeared to check her handiwork. 'Ten out of ten this time? Then perhaps you could attend to this poor lady.'

'Modom, I have told you—'

Maggie struggled with a resurgence of panic. 'Could you see if there are any messages for me?'

'If you're not a guest at the hotel—'

'Could you try Suite 213?'

The pencilled brows made an exasperated arch. 'Really, modom, if you already have a room number—'

Maggie sighed. It had been difficult enough yesterday, trying to explain why Mrs Spike Bentley expected to receive messages under an alias. Now the embarrassment of it defeated her. Nevertheless, Barbara Donkin might have left some word that had been redirected. Keith or Nicki might have phoned. 'Please,' she begged. 'Just look.'

It was with the utmost satisfaction that Scarlet Talons returned to announce there were positively no messages for Hapgood. As Maggie dithered, helpless and flustered, she saw the blond woman yielding up her suitcase to a bellboy. It struck her again, this puzzling sense that they had met. Only as the lift doors were closing upon the white trouser suit and the perilous heels did Maggie at last remember: oh, she must have been ill to have lost so much weight, her cheery face was haggard, which was surely why Maggie had failed to place her – apart from the extraordinary coincidence, of course. For wasn't she also from Potter's Park, didn't she work in the dry cleaners in Station Close, the one opposite Luigi's?

'Worry not, sweetheart.'

Maggie could not help worrying. A hasty telephone call to Brooks Bellini had revealed that Barbara Donkin was on holiday, away for three weeks. Reluctantly asking to be transferred to Fizz St Clair, dreading the indignity of explaining about the missing reservation, Maggie had been almost relieved to hear that Fizz was out of the office. Nevertheless, people would surely be hunting for the Granny Garfunkel Slimmer by now, wondering whether she had forgotten this was her big day.

'Sounds like a typical Brooks Bellini cock-up,' Spike had said. 'But you've got the invitation – you know you're supposed to be in the Regency Room at 6.30 for live transmission of the commercial at 7.02. And you don't need Barbara's reservation. We're booked into the suite for two nights, remember.'

Maggie had smiled wanly.

'Listen, I wrote the script, as you so kindly keep reminding me. So cheer up, sweetie. I'll get you to this bunfight in good order.'

Maggie had tried her best to look cheerful. It was gallant of Spike, since he too must wish for escape. Lunch at Alastair Little's had been notable for its silences, with even the topics of Tarquin's maintenance and little Amy's school fees failing to provide more than desultory interchanges. Once, after a particularly protracted pause in which they had both focused intently upon their plates, she had heard him sigh. 'I thought you'd be the one to save me, Maggie. But perhaps I'm not meant to be saved.' She, not knowing how to respond, had been grateful for the opportune arrival of a second bottle of wine. Oh, the relief when he had called for the bill.

Even so, it was four o'clock by the time their taxi had deposited them at the Lanchester. Maggie, thinking of her preparations – face pack, hair-washing, an hour, at least, for make-up – seized the excuse to take refuge in the bathroom. She wondered again whether people were searching for her. In all her anticipation of today she had imagined herself calm, poised, radiant. She must not fret about Spike and how she had failed him. She was Granny Garfunkel Supreme Slimmer, she must project success. For was she not successful? She had lost an incredible two stone and three pounds, three whole pounds beneath her target (indeed, the misery of the last twenty-four hours might have whittled away a further pound or two as a bonus). She would do as the beauty books advised, she would confront herself in the mirror and utter loving affirmations.

Slowly she let fall her robe.

Perhaps it was the mirror. Perhaps it was the cruel fluorescent light. Instead of the Paradise girl, glorying in her firm young flesh, a hollow-eyed stranger peered from the glass.

And yet, not a total stranger. Maggie would admit she had occasionally glimpsed this woman, though piecemeal and from the corner of an eye, a fold here, a tuck there, fragmentary visions easily dispelled by the rosy after-glow of exercise and self-denial. But now, in this cold blue light, the fragments had assembled themselves into a stark, uncompromising whole that refused to be banished or glossed over.

Oh, she was thin, this woman in the mirror, there was no denying it. She was gaunt, emaciated even, with bones in all manner of unexpected places, tiny bones corrugating her cleavage, giant bones jutting, ungainly at her hips. Yet, though her flesh had retreated, her skin had obstinately refused to follow. Like a thrift shop garment regretting a more prosperous owner, it hung in limp pleats from her belly, it drooped, crumpled, about her midriff, beneath the empty pockets of her breasts.

Compelling herself to look, Maggie remembered the blancmange woman. Surely this was an improvement. Yet there had been a harmony in that soft moulding of skin to flesh, a fullness, a completeness. This thin woman with the empty fat woman's breasts had a haggard air as if, when her adipose tissue had shrivelled away, something deeper had withered to the bone, shrinking her very essence.

No parroted affirmations could conjure love for this vision. Small wonder poor Spike had failed to become aroused. Yet this was the prize Maggie had sought, this was the ideal to be acclaimed, to be honoured with the accolade of Granny Garfunkel Slimmer. She slumped down miserably on the bathroom stool.

Nevertheless, time was slipping away, she must run her bath, plaster on her kiwi-fruit face mask, ease this sagging carcass into the David Fielden black silk chiffon.

The thought of the dress encouraged her suddenly. It was a coveted size ten. That was what people would see – an expensive dress, bright lipstick, blond streaks, an ideal size ten figure. Who cared what imperfections you hid, it was what was on show that counted.

Maggie had wiped off the face mask and had just finished washing her hair when a knock on the outer door brought her

275

suddenly to attention. Yet, when she rushed into the lounge, expecting some message from Brooks Bellini, she found it had only been Room Service, delivering beer for Spike.

He paused, can tilted to glass, and she was all at once conscious of the sight she must present – greasy face, wet hair, bedraggled candlewick robe.

He continued to stare. Oh well, no matter, the time was past for romantic crepe de chine.

'Gosh, Maggie, you look luscious.'

It was her turn to gape.

'Yes, you do. Positively delectable.'

'Spike, I haven't got any make-up on.'

'I know. Exquisite.'

'And I'm in my grotty dressing gown.'

'Gosh, yes. Superb.'

'Spike Bentley! What have they been putting in that beer?'

He placed the glass and the can carefully on the coffee table. 'Oh sweetheart, you're pink-frock Maggie again, my Maggie, the Maggie who took me into her kitchen and fed me bangers and mash.'

'Spike, don't be ridiculous.'

He came towards her.

'Spike, not now!'

'Sweetie, please.'

'But I've got my hair to set. I've got my nail varnish to do.'

'Oh, please, Maggie, after this dearth, this famine—'

'I've got my eyebrows to pluck, my elbows to defoliate.'

'Please, sweetheart. Bangers with plenty of mash and gravy. Oh, please, now . . .'

They lay in the sunken bath, he on top, she beneath, like sardines in a can. At last he shifted his weight, levering himself up on his bony elbows. 'There you are, it's all right. Didn't I say it would be all right, sweetie?'

Maggie eased her left shoulder where it was crushed against the bath plug. Yes, it was all right, there was nothing wrong with her, she had finally been initiated, could officially lay claim to a lover. Lying very still, not opening her eyes, she

276

could feel sodden candlewick, clammy against her buttocks. She brought herself to consider the bruising between her legs. It came to her with relief that she had not removed her diaphragm.

'Gosh, yes, we'll reach our Greek island yet, sweetie.'

So this was it, this was what it amounted to, this per-functory clash of bone upon bone, this jarring of shins and elbows, this wrenching and straining of desiccated muscles. She sought not to remember Keith's sweet skin, how softly his tongue had explored her, how snugly, thigh to thigh, curve to curve, her body had fitted with his.

Floundering in the shower curtain, Spike hauled himself upright. 'Oh yes, we'll laze all day in the sun, won't we, drinking retsina and nibbling feta cheese.'

Yet already his voice sounded distant, echoing hollowly in the cold tiled space, like water swirling away down the drain.

'Oh goodness, whatever will they think?'

'Maggie, sweetie, you've got a full six minutes before the commercial's on air. And look, there's the sign, "Regency Room". We just follow that arrow to the left.'

At the double doors of the Regency Room two waitresses stood, one with a silver tray of champagne, the other with a tray of gateau. Dutifully accepting a slice, Maggie found her hands were trembling, so that she could scarcely lift the small china plate.

The Regency Room wore the forbidding air of a large space, inadequately peopled. The blaze of chandeliers added to this sense of exposure, for heavy crimson drapes had been drawn against the daylight, as though some daunting ritual required the room to be hermetically sealed. Shrinking from the glare, Maggie paused, braced herself to be set upon, questioned, scolded for her lateness. Not a head turned, not a rustle greeted her entrance. The stiffly-suited congregation was focused, in a rapt and obedient circle, upon someone making a speech.

Maggie and Spike sidled to the circumference. Peering

between grey worsted shoulders, Maggie saw a giant photograph propped on an easel, The Granny Garfunkel Slimmers Supreme pack, looming, oversized, like a graven image. Beside it, in front of the velvet curtains, a white-damasked altar bore offerings of gateau, while a banner proclaimed as holy writ the campaign slogan. The sermon emanated from a man directly beneath the banner, an enormous man, whose neck swelled in angry folds above his collar, whose blubber strained the seams of his shiny lightweight suit – he looked, Maggie thought, like a huge, over-heated sausage, about to burst under the grill.

His eyes bulged with the force of his oratory. Maggie caught the words 'megabucks' and 'cosmic breakthrough'. The circle was clearly well drilled to these utterances. Shoulders were squared, neck muscles clenched, champagne glasses held rigidly to attention. Maggie noticed Fizz St Clair in a fondant pink two-piece, and next to her Tel Travers, giving a plausible rendering of awed concentration, though he swayed a little. Then, to her amazement, she saw another familiar figure, hanging back awkwardly so as at first to be concealed behind Fizz St Clair; the lady from the Station Close dry cleaners, dressed in gold lamé with matching sandals and clutching a massive, cellophane-wrapped bouquet. Was it for her, Maggie wondered, this impressive floral tribute, had the dry cleaning lady somehow been drafted in to make the presentation? Had they been vexed that Maggie's absence had delayed the ceremony? She fancied Fizz St Clair had spotted her and was scowling.

The rusty transatlantic voice, like an over-taxed lawnmower, was hacking its final swathe. 'And so, you guys, A is for action, B is for breakthrough, C is for opportunity, right? Now we've gotten up a goddam head of steam, let's let it roll!'

A brief silence occurred in which the speaker straddled his bulk like a Sumo wrestler to withstand the onslaught of applause. Then, as the clapping came, and Maggie sought to compose her litany of contrition, his glance, moving around the circle, rested upon her suddenly. He stared. He swelled.

The angry bulges at his neck appeared to migrate, purpling his brow, ballooning his cheeks. He seemed, to Maggie's horror, to be heaving in breath for an enraged bellow, when the room was plunged into merciful darkness.

Five television monitors sprang simultaneously to life. Five labradors, appreciatively wolfing bowls of Meaty Doggi-Chunx appeared on screen at various vantage points, compelling the gathering to a second awed hush. The first commercial in the break. Maggie's heart thundered, her palms were damp.

The Doggi-Chunx can appeared, a title flashed, the screen was for a split second blank. Then, there it was, no mistaking it, the exterior of the Potter's Park Shop-Kwik, and Tel Travers, moustache twitching perkily as the camera moved in for an establishing close-up. Maggie bit her lip. Here it came, her moment of glory, her debut as a celebrity before those millions of unseen eyes in millions of lounges across the nation. Oh, if the commercial were a success, if everyone adored it, wouldn't Fizz and the fat man forgive her for being late?

Tel Travers had his fingers to his lips, was stealing up behind a plump figure caught unawares at the freezer cabinet. The figure swung round into startled close-up. A title appeared at the bottom of the picture.

Maggie stared numbly. The face blinking in shock from the screen was the face of the lady from the Station Close dry cleaners. The title read: 'Granny Garfunkel Supreme Slimmer, Mrs Sharon Batt.'

As Maggie continued to stare she was distantly conscious of a fondant pink figure at Spike's elbow, of a mouth like a gash spitting words in his ear.

'For Chrissake get rid of her, you flake! Get her out of Art's sight this instant, before you lose us the whole fucking Granny Garfunkel business.'

Maggie was packing, snatching clothes from the cupboard and cramming them haphazardly into the pig-skin-look suitcase, her hands working without thought, swiftly, automatically, with the impartiality of a machine.

'Gosh, sweetie, I'm sorry. I'm afraid that's Genghis for you. It just can't be helped.'

Maggie paused in the act of squashing the crepe de chine into a ball. She stared at Spike, at the gangling, helpless figure, at the evasive, apologetic grin. She felt, as she had felt on the shoot, a sense of shifting foundations, of reality, like Play-doh, being endlessly and ingeniously remodelled. She remembered how, during the pink-dress episode, his eyes had vanished behind his glasses.

'You knew, didn't you?'

'For God's sake, Maggie. I wasn't in the office yesterday, remember.'

'But you're not surprised?'

He was fumbling for his stomach tablets. 'Look, Genghis is legendary for chopping and changing at the last minute. It's outrageous but, gosh, it happens constantly in this business. You learn to take the knocks, go with the flow.'

Maggie crossed to the bathroom. 'I haven't,' she said.

When she returned, juggling bottles and jars, he was hovering by the bed. 'Gosh, you don't have to leave. It's early yet, perhaps we could still find somewhere for dinner . . .'

He made no move to stop her, however, as she tipped the jars into the suitcase. She let them rest where they fell, face cream and foundation mingling with linen and crepe de chine.

'Maggie, I know you're disappointed, but you can't blame me.'

Looking up, she saw the skew-whiff grin, defenceless, boyishly appealing. She did not blame him. She understood that in his world nothing was constant, no decision, no commitment – oh yes, you went with the flow, as he put it, you were swept along despite yourself until that was all you knew. And she was not disappointed. She was angry, mortified, ashamed, but not disappointed. What she felt most, she realized, was relief.

She thrust the candlewick robe into the bulging suitcase. As she was struggling with the lid a precipitate hammering began upon the outer door.

280

She hesitated, Spike twitched. The hammering persisted. When at last Spike went to answer it, a fondant pink figure burst in.

'A suite, Spike lovey? I'm thrilled you didn't feel obliged to stint yourself when you hijacked my job number, weaseled your sordid little piece of canoodling onto my bill!'

Maggie stared. If it were not for the fondant pink suit, she might almost have failed to recognize the figure in the doorway. The hair was dishevelled, the bloodshot eyes glittered through a blur of mascara, the mouth was a smear. As the lips drew back, exposing scarlet-blotched teeth, Maggie wondered if what flashed there were not a glint of madness. Then, above the reek of Arpege, a pungent exhalation rose to her nostrils. The swaying figure in the rumpled pink suit was merry, Maggie realized with shock – no, merry would not do, drunk was the word for it.

The barbed glare caught Maggie. She bent to her suitcase, throwing her weight upon its lid.

'Leaving, are we, lovey? That'll be good news to poor Art. The scales fell from his eyes the moment he caught the word "grandmother". For chrissake, we're talking an innovative company with a young aspirational image. There's no room for geriatric losers in the world of Granny Garfunkel.'

The locks of the suitcase connected at last. Maggie pulled on a jacket to cover the silk chiffon.

'Gosh, Maggie, don't go. An urgency had entered Spike's voice. Fizz uttered a cackle. 'Oh golly gosh, worn a bit thin, has it, the beezer romantic idyll? Spike's always had a short attention span, haven't you, lovey? Adores shaking the tree, gets bored with the fruit. And you're a bit on the ripe side for his usual tastes. In fact, he wouldn't have bothered if I hadn't suggested it would help with the commercial.'

'Maggie, I—'

'But then you know Spike. He's anybody's for a free lunch.'

'Maggie, it wasn't like that. Not once I got to know you.'

Maggie forced herself to look at him. She took him in carefully in every detail, the floor-mop hair, the flapping

281

jacket, the paper clip jutting from the wing of his glasses, the pathetic, exculpatory grin.

'Oh Maggie, you know I meant all that stuff about our Greek island.'

Maggie heaved her suitcase from the bed. 'Spike, I'm just as bad. It's time I stopped kidding myself I enjoy feta cheese.'

'Jesus, Fizz! Why did you have to do that?'

Observing a bottle of Dom Perignon on the coffee table, Fizz poured herself a glass. She enjoyed the feeling of being out of control, the sense that the fuse was lit, the flame tearing irrevocably towards the flash-point of destruction. In the morning would come the shame, the dismal flashes of recall. For now there was only freedom, an exhilarating consciousness of power.

It was true that Tweetie Pie's exit had not occurred as scripted. Indeed, as the creature had carried her cheap suitcase to the door, there had been an obstinacy in the way she had held up her head, not looking at Fizz, not acknowledging Fizz's victory, that had momentarily blighted its triumph. But here was Spike, cravenly gobbling chalk pills. Fizz was not dismayed by the anger in his voice. She had him trussed like a supermarket chicken. He might protest, but he was, as ever, a wimp.

'No point in Tweetie Pie having her moment of glory if I had nothing to gain from it, right? The TV department screamed blue murder about cutting together a new film in twenty-four hours, but they managed. You'd have been involved, of course. But you were laid low with your mystery virus, and not answering on your home number.'

'I mean, why did you have to burst in here? Why did you have to speak to Maggie like that?'

'Oh, for chrissake!'

'She's a decent person.'

'And you're the world expert on decency, right? What is it with you, Spike? What is this obsession with the primitive and unreconstructed? Still searching for the Golden Age of

282

Childhood, are we, the lost world of lumpy custard and rice pudding?'

'Whatever it is, I seem doomed not to find it.'

'Well, it's reality time now, lovey. We're discussing the little matter of my job number, remember. We're talking fraud, right? We're talking Spike Bentley with his sensitive creative fingers caught in the company till?'

He had turned away from her, shoulders hunched, fists thrust into the pockets of the shabby jacket.

'Honestly, lovey, did you think no one would twig? Or did you tell yourself, Lucrezia will fix it like she usually does? Oh, I know I betrayed her, but there's nothing Lucrezia likes better than a spot of ritual humiliation. Is that what you thought?'

He made no answer.

'Or were you perhaps planning to pay the money back out of your piggy bank? Come on, lovey, you must have given some thought to the consequences.'

He turned. Indistinctly, she saw the quirky, infuriating smile. 'Gosh, I'm not sure I cared.'

'The time to start caring is now. You're in deepest shit, in case you hadn't noticed.'

She paused to let her words take effect. She was conscious, as she stooped for more champagne, that she staggered a little, that the wine, disobligingly missing the glass, had drenched the skirt of her pink Cerruti. No matter, she was in command, his silence was no more than a bluff, the schoolboy sulks that presaged surrender.

'Of course, I could save you. Though you'd have to sell me. Still, here we have a luxury suite, all paid for on expenses, a four-poster, a jacuzzi. I guess if your strategy is proactive and your presentation thrusting, I might find your pitch sufficiently compelling . . .' She smiled, downing the dregs in her glass. 'We could use more shampoo. Be a doll and call Room Service, will you?'

As she began unbuttoning the Cerruti jacket, she was aware that he had gathered himself up. It took her an instant to realize he was shambling in the wrong direction. 'Lovey, the phone's on the desk.'

283

He was making for the door, she observed with astonish-
ment. 'Spike, we're talking your job here.'

'Golly gosh.'

'You screw me, or you're on the scrap heap, right?'

'Wrong, I'm afraid.'

Of course he was still bluffing, spinning out the inevitable
male face-saving charade. Nevertheless, she was seized with
panic. Cutting off his retreat, she grabbed his arm, clinging
to his sleeve. 'I don't mean just Brooks Bellini. I have clout,
I have contacts I'll see you're never employed in advertising
again.'

'I've been thinking of retiring, as it happens.'

'Ohmigod, not that hair shirt bullshit.'

'Since no one else will redeem me, perhaps I'd better work
on it myself.'

'Brother Spike? You can get pretty tired of Green Chartreuse
after the first six glasses.'

'I'm going to finish my novel.'

'Oh sure! The Pulitzer prize winner from the writer
who brought you the slogan: "Is your toilet flushed with
success?" '

He attempted to free his arm. She tightened her grip. 'And
what about your great career as a restaurant critic? What
happens, lovey, when there are no more expenses to fiddle?'

'I'm packing that in, too.'

Now she knew he was bluffing. 'How I Saw The Light
And Learned To Buy My Own Lunch – Foodie Makes Shock-
Horror Confession.'

'It's no fun any more. Now it's not what you eat, but what
you don't eat – as if we d all come down with some communal
eating disorder. There's famine in Africa, go down the Tube
and you'll find people begging. But, those of us who have
plenty, are we grateful? Golly gosh, no. We agonize over
every mouthful as if it were poison. Give me old-fashioned,
honest-to-goodness gourmandising. There's a decadence in
all this neurotic self-denial I just can't stomach.'

'Spike Bentley decrying decadence? My, that's rich.'

'At least I can see it'll take more to save me than giving

up white flour or eating sprouted lentils. At least I'll admit I'm a moral and spiritual bankrupt. But then that's scarcely surprising, is it? I've had twenty years' exposure to the likes of Genghis and Granny Garfunkel. Small wonder I'm a typical product of our bankrupt system.'

'Oh sure, when your corns hurt, or your ulcer plays up, easy peasy, just blame the system. May I ask, lovey, since we're talking bankruptcy here, in your new career as an anchorite what do you intend to use for money?'

His arm shifted in her grasp. 'Money's not important.'

'Oh–mi–god! Now I certainly have heard it all!' The laughter brought tears to her eyes. She shook, she rocked, she spluttered. 'Jesus, Spike, you're a flake!'

Yet, when he re-emerged into hazy vision, she made out in his face an unfamiliar fixity of expression. Of the taking smile there was no trace.

'I'm leaving now, Fizz.'

She dug her nails into his arm. Carefully, purposefully, he untwined her fingers. With a howl of rage, she hacked at his shins, bent to sink her teeth into his wrist. He wrenched his arm away, so that she fell sprawling to the carpet. She clawed herself up, reaching out to grab his ankle.

'Screw me, Spike, or you'll regret it.'

A violent jerk of his foot sent her sprawling again. She clambered to her knees, ripping off her jacket, tearing at her bra.

'Screw me, Spike. Look, haven't I got great breasts? Everyone says I have the breasts of a twenty-year-old—'

She heard the door handle turn. 'What's wrong with you, you bastard, why won't you screw me?'

'You're like Art's gateau, Fizz. You'd go straight through, with nil nutritional contribution.'

II

'And wait till I tell you – Sheena's only gone and got herself the push.'

Through a greasy little window, the early morning sun poured undimmed across Jackie's kitchen table, glinting in rings of tea and orange juice, brightening the butter to a waxy yellow where it oozed from its tin-foil wrap. How strange, Maggie thought, that the sun went on shining, how unfeeling this impartial, optimistic brightness.

'Yeah, some old bag wrote from Leeds to complain about the steak knives – remember, Mags, "Sharp Blades At Keen Prices"? So what does our Sheena do but write back saying the poor bitch shouldn't be sending off for steak knives in the first place, that she should be, like, renouncing the cruelty of speciesism, and learning to co-create with the, like, universe. Flipping heck, was there a stink!'

A small lake had formed at the base of the orange juice carton. Absently Maggie drew a river with her finger nail, adding tributaries.

'And then, what about Ganesh expanding into the restaurant business – did I tell you he's bought Luigi's?'

Two of the tributaries flowed together, forming a second lake.

'You haven't heard a word, have you, girl?'

Maggie looked up reluctantly. 'Another curry house. That'll be nice.'

'Do us a favour! Ganesh says what Potter's Park needs is an Olde English Tea Shoppe – you know, like there used to be before all the burger joints and pizza parlours took over. And here's one for your ears only. Guess who'll be managing it?'

Maggie stared blankly.

'Moi, yours truly. I'll be leaving Magipost in a few weeks too.'

'That's nice.'

'Don't drop dead with enthusiasm.'

Maggie hung her head. Jackie had taken her in last night without question, had made her cups of tea, listened to her for hours, moved piles of ironing and magazines to extend the rickety zed-bed, rummaged in cupboards for clean sheets. 'Oh Jackie, I'm sorry.'

'That's OK. Just eat the nice crispbread your kind Auntie Jacko dug out of the back of the cupboard.'

'I really am sorry . . .'

'Oh, well – don't walk over any drain covers, girl, you're liable to fall through the slits.'

When Maggie looked up from the orange juice lake she observed her hostess had helped herself to a second chocolate croissant, which she was even now larding with honey and butter. Though it pained Maggie to watch, she could not tear her eyes away, as if drawn to some perversion. 'What happened to your diet, Jackie.'

'If you must know, I've packed it in. Ganesh says he likes his women big, and for once I believe him. Fat women are a status symbol where he comes from. Starvation's a fact of life out there, they don't play around with it. Plump is prosperous, shows you can afford to eat. All Ganesh's goddesses are on the big side – big rounded bellies, huge mother-earth breasts.' Jackie's tongue explored her lips, rescuing croissant flake. 'Funny thing is, I haven't put on that much since I've been eating what I fancy. I may even have lost a pound or two. And the doctor says my blood pressure's down, would you believe?'

Forcing herself to look, Maggie was obliged to admit that Jackie, indeed, had not grown fatter. Rather, stretching out her legs, folding her arms comfortably over the soft mounds that swelled her T-shirt, she seemed, for all her generosity of scale, well-knit, fittingly proportioned.

Carefully Maggie winnowed the envy from her voice. 'I'm really pleased everything's working out with Ganesh.'

'Yeah, well don't get too carried away. Ye Olde Tea Shoppe is a sort of consolation prize. For him having a fourteen-year-old fiancée in Calcutta.'

'Oh, Jackie—'

Surprisingly, Jackie threw back her head in a guffaw. 'Nothing's perfect, is it, girl?' With one last luxuriant, unperturbed stretch she rose and began stacking dirty plates. 'The way I look at it, you can go on wanting more, more, more. But if that stops you seeing what you've got, it's crazy, isn't it? You may as well make the best of what's dished out to you.'

'All the same—'

'Like I said, nothing's perfect. And who the heck wants nothing?'

Maggie returned to the orange juice rivers. When she glanced up Jackie was adding crockery to the house-of-cards pile in the sink.

'Jacko, I couldn't stay a couple more nights, could I?'

'Come on, Mags—'

'Just till I find somewhere else.'

Deftly fielding a skittering plate, Jackie turned to survey her. 'Look, girl, it's not that I don't want you. But something tells me you're not cut out for the glamour of my bachelor girl existence. And anyway, you've got to go home sometime.'

Maggie sighed. She longed fiercely, indeed, for the comforts of Spellthorne Avenue, for chairs uncluttered by stray tights or take-away cartons, for her own accommodating bed.

'I haven't got a home.'

'Do us a favour, girl.'

'Keith doesn't want me. And I don't deserve him.'

'Look, whatever you've done, whatever he's done, your Keith's always struck me as a genuine sort of bloke. Mags, you've been married all those years.'

Ten o'clock. Keith would be at work by now and Nicki out, with any luck, or at least shut in her room. The car was there, of course, but Keith usually walked to the station. No twitching nets at number fourteen – that, at least, was a mercy.

288

Maggie unlocked the door and dragged her suitcase over the threshold. Then, like a burglar caught breaking and entering, she froze. A shadow loomed in the kitchen doorway.

Letting go the suitcase, she walked unsteadily down the hall. The figure did not step forward to greet her.

'Where the hell have you been?'

The words, which should have been shouted, carried more force from their restraint.

'Keith, I know I wasn't in the commercial, but I can explain—'

'I didn't watch the commercial.'

'I can explain. I tried several times to phone you—'

'You wouldn't have got me. I wasn't home.'

'The client changed his mind. It was all a misunderstanding.'

'I'll say. Some woman from the advert place – Fuzz, Fizz? – phones Tuesday afternoon to tell you your trip's been cancelled. When I say you've already left she informs me you're not due till Wednesday. Then the hotel says they've never heard of a Mrs Hapgood. So I'll repeat, Maggie – where have you been?'

Though he had still not raised his voice, his tone frightened her. 'Keith, if we're going to have a row, shouldn't we make sure Nicki's out of earshot?'

'Nicola isn't here.' Again she was alarmed by the finality in his voice, by the bleak, grey set of his face. 'Anyway what do you care? You'd rather be off with your fancy man than bother about our daughter.'

The injustice of it fired her. 'That's rich, coming from you, Keith Hapgood! I suppose butter wouldn't melt in your mouth, would it? I suppose you could turn tap water into Spanish plonk, you're such a bloody saint!'

She had jolted him, she saw. Attack was indeed the best method of defence. She moved in blindly, pressing her advantage, hurling the pent-up recriminations of four years. She felt no fear of consequences as the accusations poured out of her, the embrace in the garden shed, the bogus bird-watching trip, the daily treacheries of thought and longing;

she was conscious only of freedom, at last, and of a perverse triumph.

When she had finished she stood quivering, heaving in breath. Yet his shoulders did not droop, his eyes failed to darken with shame-faced recognition. Instead, his mouth tightened. 'So that's why there's been no pleasing you, that's why our sex life sank like the Titanic.'

'Are you denying it, Keith Hapgood?'

'And I thought it was the boys leaving home, or maybe the change of life.'

'Are you denying what I saw with my own eyes?'

'For pity's sake, Maggie!'

'You kissed Joy. At Mum's barbecue. I saw it.'

'Do you think I volunteered? When your sister's stotious, nothing in trousers is safe.'

'Oh, yes? Then what about Filey Brigg? What about Roger Entwhistle's non-existent brother?'

'Roger has a brother, Kevin, who lives near Filey.'

'And I'm Napoleon.'

His fist came down on the breakfast bar, toppling the cruet pots, spilling a silvery trail of salt. 'Flaming hell, Maggie! You live in your own little world, don't you? You've even met Kevin Entwhistle. Remember Roger's fortieth? Kevin was the one you cornered about old Fluffy's incontinence problem, the moment you twigged he was a vet.'

Maggie watched the salt pot roll slowly off the breakfast bar, fall to the quarry tiles and smash. A chill stole over her. 'Nobody said he was Roger's brother.'

'You only hear what you want to hear.'

'But you've always loved Joy.'

'Give me strength!'

'You loved her before me.'

'I took her out once. She sniffed at my bike and insisted on going to some club up West where you needed a mortgage to buy a Bacardi and coke. The only compensation was, I met her baby sister.'

'But Mum says—'

'Oh, pardon me. Of course what your mother says is gospel.'

Maggie glanced at the salt cellar. White crystals spilled like fine ash from its shards.

'But you stopped being there, you stopped talking to me.'

'Correction, Maggie. You stopped talking to me.'

'But – but I—'

'Heck, you've got a weird sense of humour. Lust after Joy? It's taken all my strength in the last twenty-two years to be pleasant to the ruddy woman.'

'You never said.'

'Because she's your sister. Because, although she's a grasping, self-centred, neurotic nymphomaniac, you and your mother, through some warped vision peculiar to the both of you, seem to think the sun shines out of her proverbial.'

Maggie stared at the grey face, at the bleak eyes surveying her with angry disbelief. No trace of her triumph remained, only the chill, sinking to the pit of her stomach. She glanced down at the broken salt pot. Too late for that redemptive pinch, flung over the left shoulder. Though she still searched Keith's face, almost hoping to find marks of deceit, she knew, too late, that this was futile. No countercharm existed to reverse what she had done, unmake the fact of her faithlessness, take back what she now saw had been merely a pointless gesture of revenge.

Keith swept his palm across the breakfast bar, spraying a shower of salt. 'For Pete's sake! Perhaps it's hereditary, this tunnel vision of yours. Perhaps that's why our daughter's in such a mess.'

Maggie stiffened. 'Nicki? Oh, Keith is there something wrong?'

'What the hell do you care?'

'Has there been an accident? Oh God! Keith, please – why did you wait to tell me?'

'It's waited till now, hasn't it? Till you could be bothered to turn up.'

'Please, how could you be so cruel?'

291

'You're not the one to talk of cruelty. Where were you while I was round the police station half the night?'

'Police?'

'Nicola was picked up for shoplifting, Wednesday afternoon, in Shop-Kwik.'

Maggie sank onto a stool. 'Oh, my God. But – they made a mistake, didn't they? Of course it was a mistake.'

'She nicked a box of frozen eclairs, an economy pack of Mars bars and two packets of biscuits. The stuff was found on her.'

Maggie buried her face in her hands. 'But – why?'

'She just fancied them, apparently. She's been at it for some time. Her room's a regular Aladdin's cave.'

'Oh Keith, I can't believe – where is she now? Oh Lord, is she in jail?'

'Hospital.'

'But—'

'She collapsed, so when I brought her home I got the doctor to her. He says she's three stone underweight. Anorexia nervosa. The slimmer's disease, they call it.'

Maggie stared.

'He said she was like a famine victim. If she doesn't start eating properly her life will be in danger.'

'But she was eating. All those pizzas—'

'She sicks them up again. Like the chocolate she pinches.'

'Oh, Nicki. Oh, my poor little girl.' Maggie pushed aside the stool. 'Which hospital, Keith? Please, drive me there now.'

'No visitors, they said.'

'But I'm her mother!'

'No family, particularly. Families can be part of the problem apparently. I was asked if anybody else in the household was slimming.'

Maggie took the burden of his words. She slumped down, once again, at the breakfast bar.

'In fact, do you know how it started? With that cake the advert people sent you. It seems Nicki and that Kimberly girl egged each other on to lose weight. When you didn't want the cake, they half-inched it. They thought if they could live on that and nothing else they'd get thinner faster.'

Maggie clutched her arms across her chest, rocking on the stool.

'Kimberly's mother cottoned to what was going on and put a stop to the friendship. It's a pity, isn't it, we weren't as observant?'

Maggie rocked to and fro, her arms folded tightly. Though she could sense him standing over her, he made no move to touch or console her.

'I tried to see she ate. I was going to take her to the doctor. Only . . .'

'Only you had other things on your mind, didn't you, Maggie? Now maybe you'll tell me where you've been for the last two days. I hope, whoever lover boy is, he was worth it.'

Maggie almost wanted to laugh. Yet the absence of pleasure scarcely constituted an excuse. She restricted herself to the bald facts, feeling his stillness as she spoke. When she had finished she raised her glance, vainly hoping her honesty might have earned some concession. His eyes, however, offered nothing. For a seemingly interminable while they continued to survey her as though she were unfamiliar.

'I see.'

He glanced down at his fists. He opened them, flexing and knotting his fingers as though to crush some invisible object. Then slowly he closed his fists again. His shoulders sagged. He lowered his head towards the surface of the breakfast bar until his brow was resting on his hands.

Maggie could not tell how long they remained, he slumped and still, she playing her fingers over the marbleized laminate, tracing with concentration its map of simulated veins. She wished he would rise up, shout, smash things. The silence seemed to stretch before them, swallowing up the future like a life sentence. She would have liked to go to him, to put her arms around him. The impossibility of soothing his pain, this pain she had inflicted, seemed to declare the distance between them in unsparing terms.

293

Climbing stiffly from her stool she fetched the dustpan and brush, kneeling like a penitent to the broken salt cellar. She wondered what was supposed to happen next, whether she was required to go upstairs and begin packing. Or perhaps he would simply rouse himself, collect his briefcase and depart for the office. It was ten thirty, she noticed. Perhaps, in view of Nicki, Polar Foods had given him compassionate leave.

She rose painfully from the quarry tiles, brushing salt from her knees. She tipped the pottery fragments into the bin. The clatter made him stir at last. He sat up slowly.

'Keith—' She could not think what to say or how to say it. Instead she asked, 'Is it all right – I mean, about work? Should you phone them?'

'What work?' he said.

She stared.

'I was made redundant a month ago.'

'Oh, Keith.'

'Part of the cut-backs. I picked up my P45 last Friday.'

Maggie thought of the Visa card bill, and of how she had failed to tell him there was no more money coming in from Magipost. 'Oh, love, why didn't you say?'

He laughed. He laughed so that his stool vibrated against the quarry tiles with a sour little screech. 'Give me strength! I did try.'

'But—'

'I even tried when I first saw it coming, when the restructuring was announced. But you wouldn't listen, would you? You insisted we went ahead with this undertaker's parlour of a kitchen.'

'But—'

'And then, when it happened, you didn't want to know. You were too busy being a film star. Oh yes, you were far too grand for a poor pathetic husband who couldn't bring home the bacon.'

'But—'

'What did you say? "I don't mind you destroying my life, Keith Hapgood, but just think how your kids will see you." Since then, I've kept my head down. Even since Monday I've

294

made myself scarce, gone up the Job Centre, sat in the library, made the rounds. Well, I didn't fancy any more lectures. I don't need your help to work out I'm a failure, thanks very much.'

Maggie stared, silenced for a moment. 'But I thought – I thought you were trying to tell me . . .'

Now he too stared, incredulous. 'You thought what? For pity's sake, woman! You and your bloody sister. If you've got to be jealous, at least pick somebody who's halfway worth it.' His face crumpled suddenly. 'You were my princess, Mags. You were more than good enough for me. Why weren't you good enough for you.'

Maggie moved, then, to take him in her arms, skirting the breakfast bar, reaching out to him. He shook her off so violently that his stool was sent crashing.

'Just – don't! Right this minute, I don't trust myself.'

She reeled from the blow he had not delivered as if it had struck her full in the face. She accepted the pain numbly. It seemed inevitable, the climax to an onslaught in which she had taken wallop after wallop until her head spun groggily and everything around her was shifting, splitting, crashing, raining in upon her, buffeting her with the force of its disintegration, while the quarry tiles slid from beneath her buckling legs. She took the blows willingly. After all, it was her fault, this falling apart of everything that had once seemed solid. She began to cry, silently, hopelessly, where she stood.

Dimly, she was aware of the doorbell. She ignored it. A second peal came. Whoever it was, Ivy or a door-to-door salesman, would soon go away. But the hand on the bell, refusing to be discouraged, set up a continuous, agitated clarion.

Keith thumped the wall. 'Flaming hell!'

Maggie groped towards the noise, smearing tears and mascara. On the step stood Arnie Salt in a crumpled sweatshirt. 'Maggie, could you take Justin for a couple of hours?'

Maggie blinked in bewilderment. 'It's – it's not a good time at the moment.'

Arnie seemed not hear. 'Debbie's in labour. She's five

295

weeks premature. Please. Just till Debbie's mother gets here from Manchester.'

A small figure was thrust over the step, a tiny damp hand slid into Maggie's. Arnie was running down the path, was through the gate before she thought to call after him, 'but what on earth can I give Justin to eat?'

'Slimming's what I'm good at. I'd rather be dead than over-weight. Anyway, if I die, who cares?'

Maggie would never get used to it, though she had heard every detail by now. She had heard about the laxative purges, the compulsions, the binges. She had heard her own daughter describe the technicalities of vomiting – you swallowed ice cream last, to help things come up easily, tomato juice first, as a marker, so you could see you'd got rid of everything – she had heard Nicki explain it with the coolness of a snooker player recounting a 147 break. Though Shop-Kwik, in view of the doctor's report, had decided not to prosecute, that worry had in any case grown trivial beside this greater threat: this was what Maggie could not get used to, this single-minded denial of life. It fired her with unreasoning anger. Yet, as she glanced across at her daughter, at the frail figure in the bagging dressing gown, the brittle Guy Fawkes doll with its ragged mouth and stringy hair, she felt her own limbs prickle. It was not just the waste of it, the pathos of this blank-faced child, all defiant angles, yet floundering too, trapped like a butterfly in a killing bottle. There was something in the over-large, mirror-bright eyes, a reflection that Maggie did not wish to see. Hers was an uncomfortable anger; the discomfort worked upon her, so that her anger grew.

'Nicki, how can you say such a thing? You know how much we love you.'

'Please, Mrs Hapgood.' The counsellor sat facing them, but between them, like a referee. A woman of indeterminate age with feathery hair, she had the plump dishevelled look of a baby owl. Her voice was indeterminate too, soft, impartial, like her owl's eyes behind the saucer rims.

Nicki stared ahead, not looking at Maggie. 'She doesn't love me. She's only saying it because she's my mother.'

'Nicki, how could you?'

'Please, Mrs Hapgood, let Nicola tell us how she's feeling.'

Maggie groped wretchedly for the box of Kleenex. Nicki was silent.

'What makes you think your mother doesn't love you, Nicola?'

A further silence.

Maggie blew her nose. 'She can't say, because it isn't true, she knows I love her—'

'There you are,' said Nicki. 'What's the point? She isn't interested.'

The owl's eyes declined upon Maggie in gentle but unmistakable reproof.

'I'm sorry,' Maggie said.

'Go on, Nicola.'

Another interminable silence. Maggie shifted in her chair.

'Well, that's it, isn't it?' said Nicki suddenly. 'She's not interested. Other people's mothers shout at them, tear them off a strip. But she can't be bothered. She doesn't even get on at me to tidy my room.'

'But that's because I don't want to nag you, like Mum nagged me—'

'Please, Mrs Hapgood, I know this is difficult . . .'

Maggie screwed the Kleenex into a ball and pressed it to her lips.

'She doesn't care what you do as long as you pass your exams and make her look good, like Brian and Neil. That's all she cares about anyway, my brothers. When Brian left home four years ago she started to lose interest, and when Neil went that was the end of it. She'd got me hanging about, and I was holding her back or something. I think I was a mistake and she blamed Dad for it. Anyway, she got the gone-offs with him, good and proper, poor old Dad. And it was' – Nicki too reached suddenly for the Kleenex – 'it was all because of me . . .'

Maggie opened her mouth, but then gagged herself hastily

with the balled-up tissues. Tears streamed mutely down her cheeks.

Snuffling, too, came from the chair beside her. 'I understand why she can't love me. I'm not clever like Brian and Neil. I'm not pretty. I'm not good at anything. But I don't think she ever wanted me. She never wanted a daughter. I was just a disappointment from the moment I was born . . .'

Maggie could not see the owl now for tears. In place of her anger came a wrenching perplexity, a confusion of anguish and guilt. She could not comprehend how she had failed so signally to communicate with her daughter, how things she had tried to do for the best could have proved so misguided.

As she reached for the tissues her hand collided with Nicki's. Her daughter abruptly drew away. 'I mean, you can tell she didn't care from the pukey name they christened me. Nicola? Honestly!'

Maggie's restraint broke. 'But I don't understand, Nicola's a beautiful name.'

'Oh yes, Mum. You try it. You see what it's like going through life with everyone calling you Wet Knickers.'

Maggie could scarcely remember what the fairies were supposed to have hidden – the door keys, Mum's arthritis tablets? At least it would not be laxatives this time. Besides, it hardly mattered. She was only here so that Rene could read out the latest missive from Joy. Numbly, Maggie busied herself with the fridge, retrieving a leathery slab of corned beef, a half-eaten cress sandwich from the butter compartment and, hatched in a teacup, a blue-green luminous egg-shaped object, like some space creature's spore.

'. . . mental cruelty, she says. "Mommy, he wouldn't let me socialize, though I told him, Duane, these guys are business contacts. He took away my plastic, though he knows you got to dress nice around here to make any kind of impression. He had me followed, he tried to keep me a prisoner in my own home . . ." '

The space egg, bonded by age and propinquity to the cup, offered strong resistance to being scraped into the bin. It might once have been a canned tomato, Maggie thought, or perhaps a lemon.

'. . . she says she's paying the attorneys a fortune. She says she's on tablets for her nerves.'

'Does she say when she's coming home?'

'She doesn't mention it, Peg. Oh, poor Joy, my poor baby girl. Do you think I should fly out to her?'

'Mum, we're a bit strapped for cash—'

'Well, yes, it would be a dash, but then why shouldn't I dash to my daughter's side at a time like this? She'd want her Mum to take care of her. My poor baby, she has such bad luck.'

'Four husbands, bad luck?'

It was amazing, Maggie thought, how Rene's hearing could recover miraculously. The pink cheeks stiffened, instantly alert. 'Of course you've never had any compassion for your sister, have you, Peg?'

Maggie hurled the teacup, contents and all, into the bin. 'Compassion? What I want to know is, how come Joy's above criticism? How come anything that happens to her is just bad luck, let's give her all our sympathy. Whereas, when my daughter's sick and my husband – when my whole life falls in around my ears, it's all my fault.'

A puzzled look furrowed the pink cheeks. 'I've never said it was your fault, dear, if you mean about poor little Nicki.'

'Of course not, Mum.'

'Come on, Peg, when have I said?'

'You don't have to, do you?' Maggie paused, wondering why she was shouting. 'Anyway, you're right. It is my fault, everything. And I'm sorry about Joy. I know how much you love her. I just wish you had a bit to spare for me occasionally, that's all.'

Suddenly exhausted beyond endurance, she turned away, making slowly for the lounge, groping for the settee and slumping into it, burying her face in her hands.

Distantly, she heard the thunk of the walking stick, and a rustle as piles of *Sporting Life* were shifted. Springs sagged as Rene eased herself down beside her. Papery fingers touched Maggie's knee.

299

'Peg, that's not fair. I'm your mother, I gave birth to you.'

Maggie did not move her hands from her face. 'But you prefer Joy.'

'You're both my baby girls. It's only that your sister needs me more, dear. Your life's always run smoothly. But poor Joy – even when you were little she was the one forever getting into scrapes.'

'Dull old Peg. And glamorous Joy, always up to something exciting.'

'Come on, love, you said it yourself. Joy may have big ideas but the world hasn't been kind to her – all those men letting her down, all those jobs that never suit. But you've always known what you wanted, haven't you, dear? You've made a real go of your life.'

Maggie glanced up. 'You've got to be joking.'

'You've got everything Joy would envy – settled home, loving husband, three beautiful kids.'

'Not any more I haven't.'

'But you'll cope with this Nicki business. You've always been a coper. Your sister still needs a bit of help from her poor old Mum.'

'And I don't?'

A regretful smile creased the pink cheeks. 'Think about it, Peg, when did you last tell me anything without me having to squeeze it out of you like toothpaste? You won't talk about your money troubles. You didn't even want to tell me about my poor little granddaughter. When did you ever want my advice?'

'Mum, for goodness sake.'

'It's not that I blame you, mind. You're very good to me, cleaning up and taking me shopping for my bits and bobs. But I know I'm a nuisance, a silly aggravating old woman.'

'Mum, please.'

'It's being so useless, you see. Once upon a time the elderly still had a part to play. But now old age is just a nasty disease no one wants to catch. So you sit around vegetating with your own thoughts, and after a while you slip into it – your hip goes, your legs go, you pick up funny habits, you become the useless doddering old biddy everyone keeps saying you are.'

'Oh, Mum.'

'You do everything for your kids, feed them, wipe their bottoms. And suddenly you're the child and they're the mother. They tidy you up and tick you off about the state of your fridge, then they go off, back to their lives.'

Maggie glanced down at the hand on her knee, a transparent hand despite its heavy dusting of freckles, blue veins knotted perilously close to the surface, rings wedged between crepe paper folds. It did, indeed, seem infinitely aged, this hand, far older than the pinkly powdered cheeks. Yet, like a weathered tree, it seemed resilient too, clinging firmly if crookedly to life. Maggie took it in hers and squeezed it. 'I'm sorry, Mum, I'm sorry.'

The hand squeezed back. 'And I'm sorry, too, dear.'

'I don't tell you things in case they worry you. But – oh, it's not just Nicki, things are so bad between me and Keith. I will tell you, I just can't bring myself to talk about it at the moment . . .'

The hand patted hers. 'You're a good daughter to me. Perhaps I should remember to tell you that. It's just not my way. It's not what we were brought up to, my generation.'

Maggie sighed deeply. 'Don't worry, Mum. It seems to me it doesn't matter what you do – you can't ever get it right, if you're a mother.'

An arm slid stiffly around Maggie's shoulders and, as she rearranged her body to respond, noses collided, mouths hovered awkwardly with the hit and miss of disuse. Then a cheek settled against hers, a dry cheek, furry like a peach, fusty with the smell of face powder mingled with carbolic soap and with the sweet female scent Maggie recalled from long-distant mornings, snuggling into the double bed in the space her father had vacated.

After a while Maggie shifted gently, turning to her mother. 'Mum, why did you call me Margaret?'

'What a funny question, dear.'

'But why? Why choose Margaret?'

301

'We never did. It was your Dad, drunk as usual, when he went to register your birth. You were supposed to be called Marguerite.'

Food was still the enemy. Though Maggie had promised, for Nicki's sake, to abandon her diet, she still could not view a potato or a slice of bread without recoiling. To cram these calories into her mouth, to imagine them flowing through her system, clotting, coagulating into fatty deposits, seemed brutish and perverse, a deliberate act of self-mutilation. Yet there were the cravings too, stronger, more pervasive than ever, grotesque longings for food she had never cared for previously, waffles gluey with Maple syrup, bowls of sugar puffs with extra sugar, Mars bar ice creams. The Phantom Chocolate Digestive had returned, no longer troubling with stealth, but flaunting itself like a street-corner flasher; at night it stole into the lonely bedroom, lurking, palpable, in the darkness, and if, as seemed seldom, she slept, it reared up luridly in her dreams. It was as though, after that first potato, that first slip, there was no recourse but to slide into an orgy of debasement. Maggie's heart went out to Nicki, still struggling with the hospital regime.

As if detecting her hostility, food found cunning ways of striking back. Perhaps it was the expensive sterility of her new kitchen, perhaps the unfamiliar oven or the unexpected locations of saucepans and trainers once automatically to hand. Pastry declined to be rolled out, egg custards curdled, vegetables, disregarded for the merest instant, mischievously boiled dry. Or perhaps it was lack of love that soured every-thing, perhaps it was this unforgiving silence that conjured lumps in the gravy, no matter how Maggie, wilting over the steaming saucepan, stirred and whisked.

Keith had lost his appetite too – the first time she had ever known it. The spartan menus decreed by their straitened circumstances scarcely helped. Whoever had called it the breadline was mistaken, Maggie thought – streaky bacon, belly pork, forcemeat balls, gammon joints stretched by judicious carving, then chopped for quiche or carbonara.

302

And sausages, of course. You could extract three meals from a large pack of Shop-Kwik economy sausages. Maggie was reminded of the early days of their marriage. Then, they would have laughed, cracked feeble jokes about sprouting curly tails. Now, trapped in the house together, yet meeting only at meals, they faced their plates of penance pig stonily, forking up what they could manage, then rising separately to decant the rest into the bin.

Tonight it was sausages again, sausage casserole with lumpy gravey. Maggie, remembering her duty to Nicki, tried her best but was defeated after three mouthfuls. As she lowered her fork, she heard Keith replace his. Glancing up he met her eyes. Though it had been for the briefest of moments, and then only by accident, it was the first time he had looked at her for two weeks.

'Keith, what are we going to do?'

'About me being on the dole? About your Visa bill?'

'About our marriage.'

He gazed at the mess on his plate.

Maggie felt the tears forming and running down her nose. She watched them plop into her food, making transparent pools in the coagulating gravy. 'Oh Keith, I'm so sorry I hurt you.'

He pushed his plate aside wearily 'Don't start that again. There were two of us, remember. I should have done something, picked you up and shaken you, made you tell me what was the matter. I should have seen what was happening to Nicki. We should have talked.'

Though he still would not look up, the length of this speech encouraged her. 'We used to, didn't we? We used to talk nineteen to the dozen.'

'We used to trust each other. But now that's down the drain, well and truly, isn't it? I don't think we'll ever get that back.'

He rose, picking up his plate. The crash it made in the sink sounded like a full stop.

'Do you want a divorce?'

He stood with his back to her, running the tap. She

thought, beneath the gush of water, she could hear him sigh.

'Let's – let's not decide anything final till we've got Nicki sorted.'

In Brooks Bellini's reception the redecoration was already under way. The grey and post-modern blue were being replaced by stark white with just a dash of yellow. Fried egg colours, thought Fizz, stomach heaving, as she searched for her reflection in the plate glass doors.

No Porsche keys to toss casually to Fred at his makeshift desk – today she had been compelled to arrive by taxi. Indeed, soon there might be no more tossing of keys. She had tried to explain to those officious cops: it was the camber of the road that had forced her to smash into the traffic island and, as for her turning the crystals green, the effect of two teeny glasses of shampoo must have been accelerated by the trauma of discovering that Dick Saunders Blair had been appointed MD. As to the further charge of using abusive language, she had merely protested at being treated like a common criminal, with no respect for her intellect or status. Small wonder she had been forced to take three days off sick.

She would have remained in bed today had she not been summoned to lunch by Brooks. In addition to the shock of the accident, she was suffering from depression, cystitis and four volcanic pimples on her chin (imagine, Fizz St Clair with zits!). She had emphasized her feeble state while on the phone to The Lapwarmer, hinting at whiplash, and explaining that a hospital appointment would considerably delay her arrival (she had naturally avoided any reference to her night in the cells). Still, ever since the news about Stretch's early retirement, she had been trying to work her way onto Brooks' lunch list, and now he had taken the initiative himself – his minion had even phoned her on her sick bed to check her attendance, so it must be important. She tried to ignore her quavering stomach. Though the posts of MD and Deputy MD were taken, Brooks would probably want to discuss some other promotion.

304

A gaggle of bag-carriers and lapwarmers taking early lunches tumbled out of the lift. No one greeted her. Even Fred's salute had seemed half-hearted. Was this a bad sign? Alone in the lift, she scrutinized herself in its mirrored panel. Despite the crisp lines of her new Sonia Rykiel, all she could see were her shaming pimples.

If Brooks had been intending to impart bad news he would scarcely have invited Fizz to his club. Nor would he be treating her to this tedious peroration on his aims for the company now he had been so propitiously restored to its helm. Pushing aside her mushrooms on toast, Fizz stifled a yawn.

A gravy-browning pall hung over the Mountjoy, with its ancient gravy drapes and sticky gravy-skin leather. Gravy spots freckled the hands of doddering waiters. A gravy aroma seeped from the carpet, the stale odour of men, institutionalized together, gleefully retreating from the civilization of women. Fizz sipped her Pouilly-Fumé (she had lacked the strength to maintain a display of abstinence, or the nerve to insist on shampoo). Brooks would not come round to the point of this lunch till the coffee and port – that was the way gentlemen did things. Meanwhile he was content to listen to his own plummy utterances. He had required a chart at presentations, she recalled, merely to say 'Good Morning' succinctly.

'. . . so, in short we've got to tighten our belts, shed weight, present a leaner, hungrier profile . . .'

Brooks had certainly not grown any leaner since he had ingested Stretch. Fizz watched his meaty fingers working dexterously at his platter of oysters. His cheeks swelled as he chomped, from his over-red lips ran a dribble of juices. He was a plump, sleek chalk-stripe spider, who, with stealth and patience, had consumed all his partners. As he squirted lemon juice on an oyster, Fizz thought she saw it flinch.

'. . . oh yes, we need new blood, young chaps with keen appetites. We've got to stop living on our fat and toughen up, put on some muscle . . .'

Fizz could scarcely bear to watch as the claret was decanted.

305

Brooks, having performed the usual rituals, waved the waiter away to let the sediment settle, disregarding the fact that her glass was dry. She wished she'd thrown caution aside, used her illness as a pretext for a vodka and tonic. She did, indeed, feel ill, shaky and sweaty and slimy-skinned. When, at last, the wine was poured, she made an attempt to stir herself. It was time she injected some pro-Fizz propaganda into this one-sided conversation.

'Jim, I agree things are sticky. But look at how Granny Garfunkel's bucking the trend. Billings are up, and we're getting positive readings on the launch of Slimmers Supreme.'

Brooks paused from demolishing his Lamb Chops Reform. 'Ah,' he said.

'Chicago couldn't be more delighted. Art's talking of doubling the budget next fiscal.'

Putting down his knife and fork, Brooks wiped his lips. With an air of irritation, as if noting her failure to observe due form, he reached into his breast pocket. 'I gather you've been out of the office for the last two days.'

Fizz stared at the folded page of newsprint he thrust towards her 'I – I've been off sick.'

She unfolded the paper. 'HOT PROPERTY STAR ON SEX CHARGE', the headline screamed. 'TV's Tel Nobbled For Naughty Nibbles.' Fizz stared at the grainy photograph of Tel Travers. It grinned back with a mocking display of canines and incisors.

'Ohmigod! Art Khan won't like this. But don't worry, Jim, I can handle it. I'll skip the coffee, get right on back to the office. I can handle it, just give me this afternoon, I know I can defuse the situation.'

Brooks had returned to his chops. 'It's already been handled,' he said.

'But I—'

'Naturally we've had to withdraw the commercial. However, Sandi's done a remarkable job of damage limitation.'

'Sandi? Sandra Belcher? But Granny Garfunkel's my account.'

Brooks broke off from gnawing the last shreds from

306

a bone. 'Ah, that's one of the reasons we needed this little chat.'

Fizz stared.

'Bright girl, Sandi, one of the new breed I was talking about, lean and hungry, lots of potential.'

'I've put seven years of my life into Granny Garfunkel.'

'Quite so. One can go stale on an account.'

'The client won't wear this, you know. Art and I have a special relationship.'

'Art Khan's received a new posting. Promotion from Chicago Area Supremo, Gateaux and Cookies, Malaysia.'

Fizz glanced about the dining room, at its old-school-tie patrons and moribund waiters. Doubtless he had asked her here in the hope she would be inhibited from making a scene. Well, he need not have worried, she was sick, exhausted, with all the fight knocked out of her. She needed a drink. Without waiting on ceremony, she seized the decanter. The wine imparted a glimmer of hope.

'You can't make me carry the can for Tel Travers. The Creative Department cast him.'

'I gather, however, that the copywriter responsible has left the agency.' Brooks gave the lamb bone a final crunch before discarding it. 'There are other issues, too. Time keeping, complaints about your expenses. I'm afraid the company sees no alternative but to let you go.'

PART FIVE

'Better is a mess of pottage with love, than a fat ox with evil will.'

Matthew's Bible: Proverbs, 17.

Report, 10 March, on research conducted by Consuma-
probe Ltd for BBW&S on behalf of Granny Garfunkel
Gourmet Gateaux (UK) Inc.

Subject: Granny Garfunkel Slimmers Supreme

Summary

Diagnostic research was conducted into the product's failure
to achieve its targets. Three areas were investigated: 1)
Advertising 2) The Product 3) The Product Concept. As will
be shown, the ten-week break in advertising, occasioned by
the search for a new celebrity presenter, cannot be judged the
sole reason for the failure of Slimmers Supreme. Other factors
contributed, not least the product concept itself.

(100 respondents were recruited, all housewives expressing
an interest in slimming, social classification C1,C2,D. The
sample was split into ten groups. Full details will be found in
Appendix A.)

1) Advertising
Three commercials were tested, 'Mrs Sharon Batt', 'Mrs
Lisa Joiner' (featuring the new presenter) and an alternative
campaign, 'Cartoon Calorie'.
   All three commercials failed to achieve credibility. Respondents found the campaign using housewife testimony
uninspired and 'samey'. The women in the commercials were
not felt to be 'real'. A typical verbatim response was 'they're
paid to say that by the manufacturers'. 'Cartoon Calorie',
however, also scored low on conviction. 'Stupid.' 'Just another
advert, talking down to us.' (*See Charts 1–16*).

311

2) The Product

The gateau itself failed to excite respondents. Verbatims ranged from 'a bit bland' and 'not very nice' to 'tastes like old socks' and 'just like the glue my husband uses for his model planes.'

Anxiety was also expressed as to the artificial and chemical nature of the low-calorie ingredients (*Charts 17–25*).

3) Product Concept

It seems the current discouraging economic climate plays its part here. When money is short, specialist slimming products are perceived as a luxury, even a self-indulgence. Respondents, with their spending power under pressure, prefer to concentrate on the basics. 'I'm happy if the family's healthy and getting enough to eat.'

However, the problem appears to go deeper. Most respondents rejected the idea 'Now you can sin *and* slim'. On the one hand, they seemed to feel 'if you're not suffering, you're not dieting properly.' On the other, they offered comments such as 'if it's not real chocolate, it's not real sin, is it?', 'when I sin I like to go for it' and 'if it's not wicked, what's the point?'

There were even some respondents who expressed the view that it was acceptable to eat whatever you liked, provided you did not over-eat, that there were too many prohibitions about food nowadays, and that in taking up faddy diets they were perhaps only giving in to social pressures. However, it must be stressed that these respondents were a tiny minority and their views were usually firmly rejected by other respondents in their group (*Charts 25–32*).

I

The Pearsons had moved out of number fourteen. This had transpired through the most extraordinary circumstance. The man who had come to mend the microwave had been stabbed to death in Ivy's kitchen. He had only stepped out to get a part from his van when his assailant – 'a jealous love rival', the local paper alleged – had followed him back into the house, transforming Ivy's perfect kitchen into the scene of a murder inquiry.

'I ask you, it's the third time I've waited in. And what's the betting they charge me for the call-out?'

However, the inconvenience was as nothing to the thought of the taint, the substances inimical to hygiene lurking invisibly in cracks and crevices, immune to any amount of bleaching and scrubbing. Even when the detectives and fingerprint experts had finally gone, Ivy could not bring herself to set foot there. The temple, once profaned, could never be reconsecrated. The house had been put on the market, and the Pearsons had moved in with Alan's sister in Kingston.

Since then, as the recession had taken hold, house sales had dropped off and prices had plummeted. Thus Ivy, on visits to check her empty property, still occasionally popped.

Now her cup and saucer rattled with indignation. 'We put our all into that house. Alan's sister doesn't even have a microwave, let alone satellite TV and under-floor heating. Still' – here, looking askance at the chaos of Maggie's kitchen, she curled her lip ever so slightly – 'I suppose we can't all have the same priorities, can we, dear?'

Maggie followed Ivy's stare, taking in, unashamed, the clutter that obscured the simulated marble, the flour bags, the greasy tins and bowls, the spoons drizzling trails of egg

313

and chocolate, the smears of whipped cream and butter icing. This was evidence of labour, and Maggie's priority was survival. Where she had once, she saw, had plenty, now she was learning to be grateful for every morsel.

It was Jackie who had suggested she use her talent for cooking. As well as helping out part-time at the Station Close Tea Shoppe, she provided fresh scones and cakes. Though the work of ten kept her on her feet well into the night, with what Keith brought home from his casual painting and decorating, they could just scrape by. His redundancy money had paid off her Visa bill and their small mortgage, so that at least they were not in debt, would not, for the time being, need to sell up like the Pearsons. They were not living grandly, but they were managing, and there was hope on the horizon – after all those letters of application, Keith had been summoned for an interview at last. It was only bookkeeping, would not pay as well as Polar Foods but, with jobs so scarce, they couldn't be fussy, not when Keith was a grand old man of forty-three and most companies only hired whiz-kids under thirty.

There were other morsels, too. Nicki, though it had been a long, slow haul, had reached eight stone, fingers crossed for continued improvement, and was back at school, studying for her A Levels. Mum had received a definite date for her hip operation. Joy had never made her promised trip home, but had written from Florida, where she was going into the health farm business with someone called Kurt – 'Oh, Mommy, he really is Mr Wonderful, I just know this time I'm going to be lucky.' Neil had come home for three whole weeks before flying to Zaire for his VSO. And, on Christmas Eve, Brian and Stephanie's baby had arrived, an 8lb 3oz baby girl. Amanda, Maggie's grandchild was called: a pretty name, meaning 'to be loved', no problems there (though, Maggie reminded herself, you never could predict for certain).

Yes, there was plenty to be grateful for, she thought, sipping her tea, half-listening to Ivy while mentally checking the day's order – a batch of fruit scones and two more

314

sponge cakes to come, besides those already in the oven. The new kitchen had proved an investment after all, and even the enemy was held at bay, its power blunted by this propinquity, this immunity conferred by daily contact. She had lost her innocence, she would never again take food on trust. Yet she was proud of the compliments bestowed upon her walnut cake and her death-by-chocolate gateau. She could lick a wooden spoon without wincing, she could tidy the cake-mix bowl for the washer-upper. She was not any longer thin, but neither was she obese; comfortable, she supposed the word was. Of the past, only her blond streaks remained, since Keith liked them (Nicki renewed them for her now, using a home kit involving a plastic bag with holes which made Maggie's head look like a sprouting potato). The rest was carefully buried. Only sometimes, leafing through a recipe book, was she reminded of Spike or, once, reading in a magazine about the scarcity of black pudding.

In October a parcel for Mrs Maggie Hapgood had been delivered from Harrods. It had proved to contain a chocolate cake – oh, not any old chocolate cake, but a masterpiece of the patissier's art, a blooming chocolate flower unfurling a rich rosette of petals above a thickly frosted stem. With the cake had come a letter. 'Sweets to the sweet, dear Maggie, with all my apologies. You were the only decent thing to happen to me for years, and I failed to deserve you. I still long to be saved, to live the simple life, finish the great novel, but I don't seem to know how. Whenever I think I've found the answer, the question changes . . .'

There had been more in this vein before the signature had sloped across the page, as angular and excruciated as its writer. The letter had been penned, not from a Greek island, Maggie observed, but from an advertising agency in Soho.

Maggie had disposed of this missive immediately, of course. The cake had seemed too splendid to waste. She had parcelled it up and taken it next door to little Justin. He was allowed to eat what he liked now, since Debbie's panic visit to the clinic over an American scare concerning pesticide contamination of mother's milk: a new doctor, discounting her

315

anxiety for the baby, had insisted on examining Justin, and had diagnosed him as malnourished and in imminent danger of rickets.

A fragrant summons wafted from the oven. Maggie rose, lifting out the sponge cakes, setting them on racks to cool. The crash of the cat flap announced the new kitten, a ginger tom, who, scrutinizing Ivy for a moment, flung himself into her lap, where, after an untidy landing, he commenced joyfully to make puddings with her lilac velour. Though Maggie retrieved the kitten, Ivy was already fluttering from her stool, brushing away hairs, checking her track suit for damage. Maggie followed her down the hall. Ivy had shrunk, she thought suddenly; she seemed to totter on the brave high heels, beneath the impressive edifice of hair her face appeared tiny, overshadowed.

For some nights now, Fizz had suffered a dream that her teeth were falling out. Perhaps it was caused by Maxine, the glue sniffer, snoring, or by Katya, the junkie, screaming and grunting in her sleep.

Fizz had explained to all the counsellors that she really should not be here, that this ridiculous incarceration was a mistake. She had never intended to take an overdose, it had only been stupid Cissie, misinterpreting her phone call, exaggerating as usual. If Fizz had 'abused' (as they put it) alcohol and cocaine, she had merely done what anyone would have done, given the sheer stress of her existence. Everyone in the advertising business did fast white and, as for the drinking, well, she drank Dom Perignon, not meths, you couldn't label her an alcoholic.

Of course, nobody listened. But then nobody in this wretched treatment centre possessed an atom of intelligence or style. Look at them all now, sitting in a circle in the day room, in 'group', as they called it. Yesterday, Kit, the most obnoxious counsellor of the bunch, had asked her to explain to the group why Fizz's view of life was so superior. She had explained, very eloquently and cogently, she thought. Yet all she'd received was hostility. More accusations of arrogance and grandiosity had been flung about, together with the usual clap-trap about 'denial' and 'getting real' and 'getting in touch with your feelings'.

Sue, an alcoholic, was getting in touch this very minute. Here she was, podgy and pallid, drivelling on 'It's, like, I feel like I'm feeling, it's like I'm suddenly feeling all these feelings . . .' Look at them, bedraggled and pimply and out of shape, pathetic girls and uncouth boys, in their uniform of jeans, sweaters and trainers. Fizz had been pressed into the uniform too on her arrival, when her suitcase had been searched and she had been informed all sexually provocative clothing was forbidden. Now she sat here as drab and frumpy as the rest. She could see the plot, of course, the attempt to drag her down to their level: Katya, who had given her to understand that alkies were very low class, that heroin addicts were the aristocrats of addiction; Sue, who kept on and on about her brilliant career (she'd been a lapwarmer, for chrissake); Dave, who imagined he was really somebody because he played the guitar for a second-rate band; Cyril, an unemployed office cleaner. Why should she care what these people thought, why should she listen to their criticism?

They mocked her, too, for being older than they were. Maxine had called her Grandma the other day, Cyril had shouted that she was a stuck-up old rat-bag. Thirty-seven wasn't old ('get real, Fizz,' she could hear Kit screaming, 'up-front it, you're forty-two.') She was still young and attractive, she could still get laid, inside she was no more than eighteen or nineteen.

Yet, increasingly, she felt – no, not just old, but aged. Increasingly, beneath this barrage of insults, her very identity was fading. Sometimes she would glance down at her feet in their clothing-cupboard trainers and wonder whose they were. And the worst of it was, her body was changing; her breasts, pendulous and painful, overflowed her bra, her thighs were broad as hams; every morning it became more arduous to button her fly over her belly.

It was the food they made her eat here, three stodgy meals a day, rice salad, potatoes, leaden wholemeal pastry: She had

317

tried to fast, even though they were always watching, but after a while, fighting her need for one life-giving vodka, just one line of white powder, she had been obliged to give in. Food dulled the pain, that itching, crawling discomfort, that sense that you'd cease to belong in your own skin.

'Your shifting your feelings,' Kit yelled. 'You're just switching addictions.'

Now, as if a dam had burst, her appetite rose up and overwhelmed her. She sneaked other people's leavings, stole sweets from lockers, one day in desperation she had dub up a turnip from the garden and consumed it raw. Yet, though what ate lacked taste or texture and failed to soothe her, though she was repelled by these cravings, she could not stop.

As Fizz lay listening to Maxine snoring and Katya muttering, the pains came once more, the clawing, wrenching, over-mastering hunger. She rose, tiptoed out of the dormitory and felt her way downstairs. In the darkened kitchen the fridge purred with promise. Searching the drawers, she found a carving steel to break the padlock.

Working systematically and with speed, not thinking, scarcely looking, she consumed what came to hand, rice salad, bottled beetroot, butter, raw eggs and bacon, mayonnaise, milk, left-over trifle, pastry dough, tomatoes, half a lemon, a packet of lard . . . She ate with the hunger of forty-two years till the fridge was empty. Then she broke the padlock on the freezer and, scrabbling amongst the ice, burning her fingers, searing her lips and throat, she gulped down bullet peas, cracked sausages with her molars, split her front caps on the mortuary flesh of chicken.

It was curious, Maggie thought, her courtship of this stranger, her husband, his wooing of her, as if they were teenagers again. Of course this was different in many ways, a tentative affair, prone to set-backs and failures of courage. They were restrained, as if by a death whose period of

318

mourning was still not over. Yet it was there, she could feel it, a quickening of anticipation. Once it had been like standing in the sea and waiting for the waves to hit you, dashing you down, bearing you up again, breathless and squealing; now the tide was calmer, the motion gentler, but there was still the buoyancy, the exhilaration, the shock to the senses.

Little Tom had taken to crawling under the divan just before bedtime and refusing to come out – a favourite trick once of Fluffy, who had liked nothing better than to chase phantom mice over sleeping bodies or settle on the pillow to scratch her fleas. Tonight they had tried all the usual ploys with Tom. They had drummed playful fingers and dangled the catnip mouse and snaked Keith's shoe lace invitingly until, at last, defeated by the mildly-intrigued but detached stare from beneath the divan, they had collapsed side by side, giggling.

'Daft cat,' said Keith. 'Good job there's not some documentary camera filming us, they'd think we were round the twist.'

'Well, there's not,' Maggie said.

'No, there isn't, is there?' He turned his head towards her, smiling, then focusing upon her a look she felt like a tremor. 'So how's about giving your old Pooh-bear a kiss?'

Later, when they had removed what remained of their clothing and climbed into bed, they lay together, he with his arm enfolding her, she, with her head in the crook of his shoulder, listening to the steady thud of his heart beneath his warm, cushioned flesh. She reached up to kiss his nipple and he squeezed her gently. 'I've missed you, Mags,' he said.

The kitchen was sweet with baking, the little cat rubbed against Maggie's legs. Through the steamy window, she could glimpse yellow stars of forsythia, and the Pearsons' cherry tree shedding a pink drift of confetti.

She drew in breath and felt her breasts rise, her rib cage swell, her stomach muscles stretch so that, as she expelled air

319

in a sigh, her body seemed to be unfolding, as though some space within her were all at once being filled. She stood with her hands on her hips, conscious of the weight of her breasts and the curve of her belly – Comfortable that was the word for it exactly, that was how she felt.